RICHELLE MEAD

razOr
bill

An Imprint of Penguin Group (USA) Inc.

Bloodlines

RAZORBILL

Published by the Penguin Group
Penguin Young Readers Group
345 Hudson Street, New York, New York 10014, U.S.A.
Penguin Group (USA) Inc., 375 Hudson Street, New York, New York 10014, U.S.A.
Penguin Group (Canada), 90 Eglinton Avenue East, Suite 700,
Toronto, Ontario, Canada M4P 2Y3 (a division of Pearson Penguin Canada Inc.)
Penguin Books Ltd, 80 Strand, London WC2R 0RL, England
Penguin Ireland, 25 St Stephen's Green, Dublin 2, Ireland
(a division of Penguin Books Ltd)
Penguin Group (Australia), 250 Camberwell Road, Camberwell, Victoria 3124, Australia
(a division of Pearson Australia Group Pty Ltd)
Penguin Books India Pvt Ltd, 11 Community Centre,
Panchsheel Park, New Delhi – 110 017, India
Penguin Group (NZ), 67 Apollo Drive, Rosedale, Auckland 0632, New Zealand
(a division of Pearson New Zealand Ltd)
Penguin Books (South Africa) (Pty) Ltd, 24 Sturdee Avenue,
Rosebank, Johannesburg 2196, South Africa

Penguin Books Ltd, Registered Offices: 80 Strand, London WC2R 0RL, England

13 15 17 19 20 18 16 14

First published in hardcover by Razorbill 2011
Published in this edition 2012

Copyright © 2011 Richelle Mead

ISBN 978-1-59514-473-7

Library of Congress Cataloging-in-Publication Data is available

Printed in the United States of America

The publisher does not have any control over and does not assume any responsibility for
author or third-party websites or their content.

For Katie, Morganna,
and other fans of Adrian.

CHAPTER 1

I COULDN'T BREATHE.

There was a hand covering my mouth and another shaking my shoulder, startling me out of a heavy sleep. A thousand frantic thoughts dashed through my mind in the space of a single heartbeat. It was happening. My worst nightmare was coming true.

They're here! They've come for me!

My eyes blinked, staring wildly around the dark room until my father's face came into focus. I stilled my thrashing, thoroughly confused. He let go and stepped back to regard me coldly. I sat up in the bed, my heart still pounding.

"Dad?"

"Sydney. You wouldn't wake up."

Naturally, that was his only apology for scaring me to death.

"You need to get dressed and make yourself presentable," he continued. "Quickly and quietly. Meet me downstairs in the study."

I felt my eyes widen but didn't hesitate with a response. There was only one acceptable answer. "Yes, sir. Of course."

"I'll go wake your sister." He turned for the door, and I leapt out of bed.

"Zoe?" I exclaimed. "What do you need her for?"

"Shh," he chastised. "Hurry up and get ready. And remember—be quiet. Don't wake your mother."

He shut the door without another word, leaving me staring. The panic that had only just subsided began to surge within me again. What did he need Zoe for? A late-night wake-up meant Alchemist business, and she had nothing to do with that. Technically, neither did I anymore, not since I'd been put on indefinite suspension for bad behavior this summer. What if that's what this was about? What if I was finally being taken to a re-education center and Zoe was replacing me?

For a moment, the world swam around me, and I caught hold of my bed to steady myself. Re-education centers. They were the stuff of nightmares for young Alchemists like me, mysterious places where those who grew too close to vampires were dragged off to learn the errors of their ways. What exactly went on there was a secret, one I never wanted to find out. I was pretty sure "re-education" was a nice way of saying "brainwashing." I'd only ever seen one person who had come back, and honestly, he'd seemed like half a person after that. There'd been an almost zombielike quality to him, and I didn't even want to think about what they might have done to make him that way.

My father's urging to hurry up echoed back through my mind, and I tried to shake off my fears. Remembering his other warning, I also made sure I moved silently. My mother was a light sleeper. Normally, it wouldn't matter if she caught us going off on

Alchemist errands, but lately, she hadn't been feeling so kindly toward her husband's (and daughter's) employers. Ever since angry Alchemists had deposited me on my parents' doorstep last month, this household had held all the warmth of a prison camp. Terrible arguments had gone down between my parents, and my sister Zoe and I often found ourselves tiptoeing around.

Zoe.

Why does he need Zoe?

The question burned through me as I scurried to get ready. I knew what "presentable" meant. Throwing on jeans and a T-shirt was out of the question. Instead, I tugged on gray slacks and a crisp, white button-down shirt. A darker, charcoal gray cardigan went over it, which I cinched neatly at my waist with a black belt. A small gold cross—the one I always wore around my neck—was the only ornamentation I ever bothered with.

My hair was a slightly bigger problem. Even after only two hours of sleep, it was already going in every direction. I smoothed it down as best I could and then coated it with a thick layer of hair spray in the hopes that it would get me through whatever was to come. A light dusting of powder was the only makeup I put on. I had no time for anything more.

The entire process took me all of six minutes, which might have been a new record for me. I sprinted down the stairs in perfect silence, careful, again, to avoid waking my mother. The living room was dark, but light spilled out past the not-quite-shut door of my father's study. Taking that as an invitation, I pushed the door open and slipped inside. A hushed conversation stopped at my entrance. My father eyed me from head to toe and showed his approval at my appearance in the way he knew best: by simply withholding criticism.

"Sydney," he said brusquely. "I believe you know Donna Stanton."

The formidable Alchemist stood near the window, arms crossed, looking as tough and lean as I remembered. I'd spent a lot of time with Stanton recently, though I would hardly say we were friends—especially since certain actions of mine had ended up putting the two of us under a sort of "vampire house arrest." If she harbored any resentment toward me, she didn't show it, though. She nodded to me in polite greeting, her face all business.

Three other Alchemists were there as well, all men. They were introduced to me as Barnes, Michaelson, and Horowitz. Barnes and Michaelson were my father and Stanton's age. Horowitz was younger, mid-twenties, and was setting up a tattooist's tools. All of them were dressed like me, wearing business casual clothing in nondescript colors. Our goal was always to look nice but not attract notice. The Alchemists had been playing Men in Black for centuries, long before humans dreamed of life on other worlds. When the light hit their faces the right way, each Alchemist displayed a lily tattoo identical to mine.

Again, my unease grew. Was this some kind of interrogation? An assessment to see if my decision to help a renegade half-vampire girl meant my loyalties had changed? I crossed my arms over my chest and schooled my face to neutrality, hoping I looked cool and confident. If I still had a chance to plead my case, I intended to present a solid one.

Before anyone could utter another word, Zoe entered. She shut the door behind her and peered around in terror, her eyes wide. Our father's study was huge—he'd built an addition on to our house for it—and it easily held all the occupants. But as I watched my sister take in the scene, I knew she felt stifled and trapped. I met her eyes and tried to send a silent message of sympathy. It must have worked because she scurried to my side, looking only fractionally less afraid.

"Zoe," said my father. He let her name hang in the air in this way he had, making it clear to both of us that he was disappointed. I could immediately guess why. She wore jeans and an old sweatshirt and had her brown hair in two cute but sloppy braids. By any other person's standards, she would have been "presentable"—but not by his. I felt her cower against me, and I tried to make myself taller and more protective. After making sure his condemnation was felt, our father introduced Zoe to the others. Stanton gave her the same polite nod she'd given me and then turned toward my father.

"I don't understand, Jared," said Stanton. "Which one of them are you going to use?"

"Well, that's the problem," my father said. "Zoe was requested . . . but I'm not sure she's ready. In fact, I know she isn't. She's only had the most basic of training. But in light of Sydney's recent . . . experiences . . ."

My mind immediately began to pull the pieces together. First, and most importantly, it seemed I wasn't going to be sent to a re-education center. Not yet, at least. This was about something else. My earlier suspicion was correct. There was some mission or task afoot, and someone wanted to sub in Zoe because she, unlike certain other members of her family, had no history of betraying the Alchemists. My father was right that she'd only received basic instruction. Our jobs were hereditary, and I had been chosen years ago as the next Alchemist in the Sage family. My older sister, Carly, had been passed over and was now away at college and too old. He'd taught Zoe as backup instead, in the event something happened to me, like a car accident or vampire mauling.

I stepped forward, not knowing what I was going to say until I spoke. The only thing I knew for sure was that I could *not* let Zoe get sucked into the Alchemists' schemes. I feared for her safety more than I did going to a re-education center—and I was pretty afraid of that. "I spoke to a committee about my actions after they happened," I said. "I was under the impression that they understood why I did the things I did. I'm fully qualified to serve in whatever way you need—much more so than my sister. I have real-world experience. I know this job inside and out."

"A little too much real-world experience, if memory serves," said Stanton dryly.

"I for one would like to hear these 'reasons' again," said Barnes, using his fingers to make air quotes. "I'm not thrilled about tossing a half-trained girl out there, but I also find it hard to believe someone who aided a vampire criminal is 'fully qualified to serve.'" More pretentious air quotes.

I smiled back pleasantly, masking my anger. If I showed my true emotions, it wouldn't help my case. "I understand, sir. But Rose Hathaway was eventually proven innocent of the crime she'd been accused of. So, I wasn't technically aiding a criminal. My actions eventually helped find the real murderer."

"Be that as it may, we—and you—didn't know she was 'innocent' at the time," he said.

"I know," I said. "But I believed she was."

Barnes snorted. "And there's the problem. You should've believed what the Alchemists told you, not run off with your own far-fetched theories. At the very least, you should've taken what evidence you'd gathered to your superiors."

Evidence? How could I explain that it wasn't evidence that had driven me to help Rose so much as a feeling in my gut that she was telling the truth? But that was something I knew they'd never understand. All of us were trained to believe the worst of her kind. Telling them that I had seen truth and honesty in her wouldn't help my cause here. Telling them that I'd been black-mailed into helping her by another vampire was an even worse explanation. There was only one argument that the Alchemists might possibly be able to comprehend.

"I . . . I didn't tell anyone because I wanted to get all the credit for it. I was hoping that if I uncovered it, I could get a promotion and a better assignment."

It took every ounce of self-control I had to say that lie straight-faced. I felt humiliated at making such an admission. As though ambition would really drive me to such extreme behaviors! It made me feel slimy and shallow. But, as I'd suspected, this was something the other Alchemists could understand.

Michaelson snorted. "Misguided, but not entirely unex-pected for her age."

The other men shared equally condescending looks, even my father. Only Stanton looked doubtful, but then, she'd wit-nessed more of the fiasco than they had.

My father glanced among the others, waiting for further comment. When none came, he shrugged. "If no one has any objections, then, I'd rather we use Sydney. Not that I even entirely understand what you need her for." There was a slightly accusing tone in his voice over not having been filled in yet. Jared Sage didn't like to be left out of the loop.

"I have no problem with using the older girl," said Barnes. "But keep the younger one around until the others get here, in case they have any objections." I wondered how many "others" would be joining us. My father's study was no stadium. Also, the more people who came, the more important this case probably was. My skin grew cold as I wondered what the assignment could possibly be. I'd seen the Alchemists cover up major disasters with only one or two people. How colossal would something have to be to require this much help?

Horowitz spoke up for the first time. "What do you want me to do?"

"Re-ink Sydney," said Stanton decisively. "Even if she doesn't go, it won't hurt to have the spells reinforced. No point in inking Zoe until we know what we're doing with her."

My eyes flicked to my sister's noticeably bare—and pale—cheeks. Yes. As long as there was no lily there, she was free. Once the tattoo was emblazoned on your skin, there was no going back. You belonged to the Alchemists.

The reality of that had only hit me in the last year or so. I'd certainly never realized it while growing up. My father had dazzled me from a very young age about the rightness of our duty. I still believed in that rightness but wished he'd also mentioned just how much of my life it would consume.

Horowitz had set up a folding table on the far side of my father's study. He patted it and gave me a friendly smile.

"Step right up," he told me. "Get your ticket."

Barnes shot him a disapproving look. "Please. You could show a little respect for this ritual, David."

Horowitz merely shrugged. He helped me lie down, and though I was too afraid of the others to openly smile back, I hoped my gratitude showed in my eyes. Another smile from him told me he understood. Turning my head, I watched as Barnes reverently set a black briefcase on a side table. The other Alchemists gathered around and clasped their hands together in front of them. He must be the hierophant, I realized. Most of what the Alchemists did was rooted in science, but a few tasks required divine assistance. After all, our core mission to protect humanity was rooted in the belief that vampires were unnatural and went against God's plan. That's why hierophants—our priests—worked side by side with our scientists.

"Oh Lord," he intoned, closing his eyes. "Bless these elixirs. Remove the taint of the evil they carry so that their life-giving power shines through purely to us, your servants."

He opened the briefcase and removed four small vials, each filled with dark red liquid. Labels that I couldn't read marked each one. With a steady hand and practiced eye, Barnes poured precise amounts from each vial into a larger bottle. When he'd used all four, he produced a tiny packet of powder that he emptied into the rest of the mix. I felt a tingle in the air, and the bottle's contents turned to gold. He handed the bottle to Horowitz, who stood ready with a needle. Everyone relaxed, the ceremonial part complete.

I obediently turned away, exposing my cheek. A moment later, Horowitz's shadow fell over me. "This will sting a little, but nothing like when you originally got it. It's just a touch-up," he explained kindly.

"I know," I said. I'd been re-inked before. "Thanks."

The needle pricked my skin, and I tried not to wince. It *did* sting, but like he'd said, Horowitz wasn't creating a new tattoo. He was simply injecting small amounts of the ink into my existing tattoo, recharging its power. I took this as a good sign. Zoe might not be out of danger yet, but surely they wouldn't go to the trouble of re-inking me if they were just going to send me to a re-education center.

"Can you brief us on what's happening while we're waiting?" asked my father. "All I was told was that you needed a teen girl." The way he said it made it sound like a disposable role. I fought back a wave of anger at my father. That's all we were to him.

"We have a situation," I heard Stanton say. Finally, I'd get some answers. "With the Moroi."

I breathed a small sigh of relief. Better them than the Strigoi. Any "situation" the Alchemists faced always involved one of the vampire races, and I'd take the living, non-killing ones any day. They almost seemed human at times (though I'd never tell anyone here that) and lived and died like we did. Strigoi, however, were twisted freaks of nature. They were undead, murderous vampires created either when a Strigoi forcibly made a victim drink its blood or when a Moroi purposely took the life of another through blood drinking. A situation with the Strigoi usually ended with someone dead.

All sorts of possible scenarios played through my mind as I considered what issue had prompted action from the Alchemists tonight: a human who had noticed someone with fangs, a feeder who had escaped and gone public, a Moroi treated by human doctors. . . . Those were the kinds of problems we Alchemists faced the most, ones I had been trained to handle and cover up with ease. Why they would need "a teenage girl" for any of those, however, was a mystery.

"You know that they elected their girl queen last month," said Barnes. I could practically see him rolling his eyes.

Everyone in the room murmured affirmatively. Of course they knew about that. The Alchemists paid careful attention to the political goings-on of the Moroi. Knowing what vampires were doing was crucial to keeping them secret from the rest of humanity—and keeping the rest of humanity safe from them. That was our purpose, to protect our brethren. *Know thy enemy* was taken very seriously with us. The girl the Moroi had elected queen, Vasilisa Dragomir, was eighteen, just like me.

"Don't tense," said Horowitz gently.

I hadn't realized I had been. I tried to relax, but thinking of Vasilisa Dragomir made me think of Rose Hathaway. Uneasily, I wondered if maybe I shouldn't have been so quick to assume I was out of trouble here. Mercifully, Barnes simply kept going with the story, not mentioning my indirect connection to the girl queen and her associates.

"Well, as shocking as that is to us, it's been just as shocking to some of their own people. There's been a lot of protests and dissidence. No one's tried to attack the Dragomir girl, but that's probably because she's so well guarded. Her enemies, it seems, have therefore found a work-around: her sister."

"Jill," I said, speaking before I could stop myself. Horowitz tsked me for moving, and I immediately regretted drawing attention to myself and my knowledge of the Moroi. Nevertheless, an image of Jillian Mastrano flashed into my mind, tall and annoyingly slim like all Moroi, with big, pale green eyes that always seemed nervous. And she had good reason to be. At fifteen, Jill had discovered she was Vasilisa's illegitimate sister, making her the only other member of their royal family's line. She too was tied to the mess I'd gotten myself into this summer.

"You know their laws," continued Stanton, after a moment of awkward silence. Her tone conveyed what we all thought of Moroi laws. An elected monarch? It made no sense, but what else could one expect from unnatural beings like vampires? "And Vasilisa must have one family member in order to hold her throne. Therefore, her enemies have decided if they can't directly remove her, they'll remove her family."

A chill ran down my spine at the unspoken meaning, and I again commented without thinking. "Did something happen to Jill?" This time, I'd at least chosen a moment when Horowitz was refilling his needle, so there was no danger of messing up the tattoo.

I bit my lip to prevent myself from saying anything else, imagining the chastisement in my father's eyes. Showing concern for a Moroi was the last thing I wanted to do, considering my uncertain status. I didn't have any strong attachment to Jill, but the thought of someone trying to kill a fifteen-year-old girl—the same age as Zoe—was appalling, no matter what race she belonged to.

"That's what's unclear," Stanton mused. "She was attacked, we know that much, but we can't tell if she received any real injury. Regardless, she's fine now, but the attempt happened at their own Court, indicating they have traitors at high levels."

Barnes snorted in disgust. "What can you expect? How their ridiculous race has managed to survive as long as they have without turning on each other is beyond me."

There were mutters of agreement.

"Ridiculous or not, though, we *cannot* have them in civil

war," said Stanton. "Some Moroi have acted out in protest, enough that they've caught the attention of human media. We can't allow that. We need their government stable, and that means ensuring this girl's safety. Maybe they can't trust themselves, but they can trust us."

There was no use in my pointing out that the Moroi didn't really trust the Alchemists. But, since we had no interest in killing off the Moroi monarch or her family, I supposed that made us more trustworthy than some.

"We need to make the girl disappear," said Michaelson. "At least until the Moroi can undo the law that makes Vasilisa's throne so precarious. Hiding Mastrano with her own people isn't safe at the moment, so we need to conceal her among humans." Disdain dripped from his words. "But it's imperative she also remains concealed *from* humans. Our race cannot know theirs exists."

"After consultation with the guardians, we've chosen a location we all believe will be safe for her—both from Moroi and Strigoi," said Stanton. "However, to make sure she—and those with her—remain undetected, we're going to need Alchemists on hand, dedicated solely to her needs in case any complications come up."

My father scoffed. "That's a waste of our resources. Not to mention unbearable for whoever has to stay with her."

I had a bad feeling about what was coming.

"This is where Sydney comes in," said Stanton. "We'd like her to be one of the Alchemists that accompanies Jillian into hiding."

"What?" exclaimed my father. "You can't be serious."

"Why not?" Stanton's tone was calm and level. "They're

13

close in age, so being together won't raise suspicion. And Sydney already knows the girl. Surely spending time with her won't be as 'unbearable' as it might be for other Alchemists."

The subtext was loud and clear. I wasn't free of my past, not yet. Horowitz paused and lifted the needle, allowing me the chance to speak. My mind raced. Some response was expected. I didn't want to sound too upset by the plan. I needed to restore my good name among the Alchemists and show my willingness to follow orders. That being said, I also didn't want to sound as though I were too comfortable with vampires or their half-human counterparts, the dhampirs.

"Spending time with any of them is never fun," I said carefully, keeping my voice cool and haughty. "Doesn't matter how much you do it. But I'll do whatever's necessary to keep us— and everyone else—safe." I didn't need to explain that "everyone" meant humans.

"There, you see, Jared?" Barnes sounded pleased with the answer. "The girl knows her duty. We've made a number of arrangements already that should make things run smoothly, and we certainly wouldn't send her there alone—especially since the Moroi girl won't be alone either."

"What do you mean?" My father still didn't sound happy about any of this, and I wondered what was upsetting him the most. Did he truly think *I* might be in danger? Or was he simply worried that spending more time with the Moroi would turn my loyalties even more? "How many of them are coming?"

"They're sending a dhampir," said Michaelson. "One of their guardians, which I really don't have a problem with. The location we've chosen should be Strigoi free, but if it's not, better *they* fight those monsters than us." The guardians were specially trained dhampirs who served as bodyguards.

"There you are," Horowitz told me, stepping back. "You can sit up."

I obeyed and resisted the urge to touch my cheek. The only thing I felt from his work was the needle's sting, but I knew powerful magic was working its way through me, magic that would give me a superhuman immune system and prevent me from speaking about vampire affairs to ordinary humans. I tried not to think about the other part, about where that magic came from. The tattoos were a necessary evil.

The others were still standing, not paying attention to me— well, except for Zoe. She still looked confused and afraid and kept glancing anxiously my way.

"There also may be another Moroi coming along," continued Stanton. "Honestly, I'm not sure why, but they were very insistent he be with Mastrano. We told them the fewer of them we had to hide, the better, but . . . well, they seemed to think it was necessary and said they'd make arrangements for him there. I think he's some Ivashkov. Irrelevant."

"Where *is* there?" asked my father. "Where do you want to send her?"

Excellent question. I'd been wondering the same thing. My first full-time job with the Alchemists had sent me halfway around the world, to Russia. If the Alchemists were intent on hiding Jill, there was no telling what remote location they'd send her to. For a moment, I dared to hope we might end up in my dream city: Rome. Legendary works of art and Italian food seemed like a good way to offset paperwork and vampires.

"Palm Springs," said Barnes.

"Palm Springs?" I echoed. That was *not* what I'd been expecting. When I thought of Palm Springs, I thought of movie stars and golf courses. Not exactly a Roman holiday, but not the Arctic either.

A small, wry smile tugged at Stanton's lips. "It's in the desert and receives a lot of sunlight. Completely undesirable for Strigoi."

"Wouldn't it be undesirable for Moroi too?" I asked, thinking ahead. Moroi didn't incinerate in the sun like Strigoi, but excessive exposure to it still made Moroi weak and sick.

"Well, yes," admitted Stanton. "But a little discomfort is worth the safety it provides. So long as the Moroi spend most of their time inside, it won't be a problem. Plus, it'll discourage other Moroi from coming and—"

The sound of a car door opening and slamming outside the window caught everyone's attention. "Ah," said Michaelson. "There are the others. I'll let them in."

He slipped out of the study and presumably headed toward the front door to admit whoever had arrived. Moments later, I heard a new voice speaking as Michaelson returned to us.

"Well, Dad couldn't make it, so he just sent me," the new voice was saying.

The study door opened, and my heart stopped.

No, I thought. *Anyone but him.*

"Jared," said the newcomer, catching sight of my father. "Great to see you again."

My father, who had barely spared me a glance all night, actually *smiled.* "Keith! I'd been wondering how you've been."

16

The two of them shook hands, and a wave of disgust rolled through me.

"This is Keith Darnell," said Michaelson, introducing him to the others.

"Tom Darnell's son?" asked Barnes, impressed. Tom Darnell was a legendary leader among the Alchemists.

"The same," said Keith cheerfully. He was about five years older than me, with blond hair a shade lighter than mine. I knew a lot of girls thought he was attractive. Me? I found him vile. He was pretty much the last person I'd expected to see here.

"And I believe you know the Sage sisters," added Michaelson.

Keith turned his blue eyes first to Zoe, eyes that were just fractionally different from each other in color. One eye, made of glass, stared blankly ahead and didn't move at all. The other one winked at her as his grin widened.

He can still wink, I thought furiously. *That annoying, stupid, condescending wink!* But then, why wouldn't he? We'd all heard about the accident he'd had this year, an accident that had cost him an eye. He'd still survived with one good one, but somehow, in my mind, I'd thought the loss of an eye would stop that infuriating winking.

"Little Zoe! Look at you, all grown up," he said fondly. I'm not a violent person, not by any means, but I suddenly wanted to hit him for looking at my sister that way.

She managed a smile for him, clearly relieved to see a familiar face here. When Keith turned toward me, however, all that charm and friendliness vanished. The feeling was mutual.

The burning, black hatred building up inside of me was so overwhelming that it took me a moment to formulate any sort of response. "Hello, Keith," I said stiffly.

Keith didn't even attempt to match my forced civility. He immediately turned toward the senior Alchemists. "What is *she* doing here?"

"We know you requested Zoe," said Stanton levelly, "but after consideration, we decided it would be best if Sydney fulfill this role. Her experience dwarfs any concerns about her past actions."

"No," said Keith swiftly, turning that steely blue gaze back on me. "There is no way she can come, no way I'm trusting some twisted *vamp lover* to screw this up for all of us. We're taking her sister."

CHAPTER 2

A COUPLE OF PEOPLE GASPED, no doubt over Keith's use of the term "vamp lover." Neither word was that terrible in and of itself, but together . . . well, they represented an idea that was pretty much anathema to all that the Alchemists stood for. We fought to protect humans from vampires. Being in league with those creatures was about the vilest thing any of us could be accused of. Even while questioning me earlier, the other Alchemists had been very careful with their choice of language.

Keith's usage was almost obscene. Horowitz looked angry on my behalf and opened his mouth as though he might make an equally biting retort. After a quick glance at Zoe and me, he seemed to reconsider, and stayed silent. Michaelson, however, couldn't help himself from muttering, "Protect us all." He made the sign against evil.

Yet it wasn't Keith's name-calling that really set me off (though that did certainly send a chill through me). It was

Stanton's earlier offhand comment. *We know you requested Zoe.*

Keith had requested Zoe for this assignment? My resolve to keep her out of it grew by leaps and bounds. The thought of her going off with him made me clench my fists. Everyone here might think Keith Darnell was some kind of poster child, but I knew better. No girl—let alone my sister—should be left alone with him.

"Keith," said Stanton, a gentle warning in her voice. "I can respect your feelings, but you aren't in a position to make that call."

He flushed. "Palm Springs is my post! I have every right to dictate what goes on in my territory."

"I can understand why you'd feel that way," said my father. Unbelievable. If Zoe or I had questioned authority like Keith had, our father wouldn't have hesitated to tell us our "rights"— or rather, he'd tell us that we *had* none. Keith had stayed with my family one summer—young Alchemists sometimes did that while training—and my father had grown to regard him like the son he'd never had. Even then, there'd been a double standard between Keith and us. Time and distance apparently hadn't diminished that.

"Palm Springs may be your post," said Stanton, "but this assignment is coming from places in the organization that are far above your reach. You're essential for coordination, yes, but you are by no means the ultimate authority here." Unlike me, I suspected Stanton had smacked a few people in her day, and I think she wanted to do that to Keith now. It was funny that she would become my defender, since I'd been pretty sure she didn't buy my story about using Rose to advance my career.

Keith visibly calmed himself, wisely realizing a childish out-burst wasn't going to get him anywhere. "I understand. But I'm simply worried about the success of this mission. I know both of the Sage girls. Even before Sydney's 'incident,' I had serious concerns about her. I figured she'd grow out of them, though, so I didn't bother saying anything at the time. I see now I was wrong. Back then, I actually thought Zoe would have been a far better choice for the family position. No offense, Jared." He gave my father what was probably supposed to be a charming smile.

Meanwhile, it was getting harder and harder to hide my incredulity. "Zoe was eleven when you stayed with us," I said. "How in the world could you have drawn those conclusions?" I didn't buy for an instant that he'd had "concerns" about me back then. No—scratch that. He'd probably had concerns the last day he stayed with us, when I confronted him about a dirty secret he'd been hiding. That, I was almost certain, was what all of this was about. He wanted me silenced. My adventures with Rose were simply an excuse to get me out of the way.

"Zoe was always advanced for her age," Keith said. "Some-times you can just tell."

"Zoe's never seen a Strigoi, let alone a Moroi! She'd prob-ably freeze up if she did. That's true of most Alchemists," I pointed out. "Whoever you send is going to have to be able to stand being around them, and no matter what you think of my reasons, I'm used to them. I don't like them, but I know how to tolerate them. Zoe hasn't had anything but the most basic of instruction—and that's all been in our home. Everyone keeps saying this is a serious assignment. Do you really want to risk its outcome because of inexperience and unsubstantiated fears?"

I finished, proud of myself for staying calm and making such a reasoned argument.

Barnes shifted uneasily. "But if Keith had doubts years ago . . ."

"Zoe's training is still probably enough to get by," said my father.

Five minutes ago, my father had endorsed me going instead of her! Was anyone here even listening to me? It was like I was invisible now that Keith was here. Horowitz had been busily cleaning and putting away his tattooing tools but looked up to scoff at Barnes's remark.

"You said the magic words: 'years ago.' Keith couldn't have been much older than these girls are now." Horowitz shut his tool case and leaned casually against the wall, arms crossed. "I don't doubt you, Keith. Not exactly. But I'm not really sure you can base your opinion of her off memories from when you were all children."

By Horowitz's logic, he was saying I was still a child, but I didn't care. He'd delivered his comments in an effortless, easy way that nonetheless left Keith looking like an idiot. Keith knew it, too, and turned bright red.

"I concur," said Stanton, who was clearly getting impatient. "Sydney wants this badly, and few would, considering it means she'll actually have to live with a vampire."

Want it badly? Not exactly. But I did want to protect Zoe at all costs and restore my credibility. If it meant thwarting Keith Darnell along the way, then so much the—

"Wait," I said, replaying Stanton's words. "Did you say *live* with a vampire?"

"Yes," said Stanton. "Even if she's in hiding, the Moroi girl still has to have some semblance of a normal life. We figured we'd kill two birds with one stone and enroll her in a private boarding school. Take care of her education *and* lodging. We would make arrangements for you to be her roommate."

"Wouldn't that mean . . . wouldn't that mean I'd have to go to school?" I asked, feeling a little puzzled now. "I already graduated." High school, at least. I'd made it clear a number of times to my father that I'd love to go to college. He'd made it equally clear that he didn't feel there was a need.

"You see?" said Keith, jumping on the opportunity. "She's too old. Zoe's a better age match."

"Sydney can pass for a senior. She's the right age." Stanton gave me a once-over. "Besides, you were homeschooled, right? This'll be a new experience for you. You can see what you were missing."

"It would probably be easy for you," said my father grudgingly. "Your education was superior to anything they can offer." *Nice backhanded compliment, Dad.*

I was afraid to show how uneasy this deal was making me. My resolve to look out for Zoe and myself hadn't changed, but the complications just kept growing. Repeat high school. Live with a vampire. Keep her in witness protection. And even though I'd talked up how comfortable I was around vampires, the thought of sharing a room with one—even a seemingly benign one like Jill—was unnerving. Another woe occurred to me.

"Would you be an undercover student too?" I asked Keith. The idea of lending him class notes made me nauseous again.

"Of course not," he said, sounding insulted. "I'm too old. I'll be the Local Area Mission Liaison." I was willing to bet he'd just made that title up on the spot. "My job is to help coordinate the assignment and report back to our superiors. And I'm not going to do it if *she's* the one there." He looked from face to face as he spoke that last line, but there was no question who *she* was. Me.

"Then don't," said Stanton bluntly. "Sydney is going. That's my decision, and I'll argue it to any higher authority you want to take it to. If you are so against her placement, Mr. Darnell, I will personally see that you are transferred out of Palm Springs and don't have to deal with her at all."

All eyes swiveled to Keith, and he hesitated. She'd caught him in a trap, I realized. I had to imagine that with its climate, Palm Springs didn't see a lot of vampire action. Keith's job there was probably pretty easy, whereas when I'd worked in St. Petersburg, I'd been constantly having to do damage control. That place was a vampire haven, as were some of the other places in Europe and Asia my father had taken me to visit. Don't even get me started about Prague. If Keith were transferred, he took the risk of not only getting a bigger workload but also of being in a much worse location. Because although Palm Springs wasn't desirable for vampires, it sounded kind of awesome for humans.

Keith's face confirmed as much. He didn't want to leave Palm Springs. "What if she goes there, and I have reason to suspect her of treason again?"

"Then report her," said Horowitz, shifting restlessly. He obviously wasn't impressed with Keith. "The same as you would anyone."

"I can increase some of Zoe's training in the meantime," said my father, almost as an apology to Keith. It was clear whose side

24

my father was on. It wasn't mine. It wasn't even Zoe's, really. "Then, if you find fault with Sydney, we can replace her."

I bristled at the thought of Keith being the one to decide if I had faults, but that didn't bother me nearly as much as the thought of Zoe still being tied to this. If my father was keeping her on standby, then she wasn't out of danger yet. The Alchemists could still have their hooks in her—as could Keith. I vowed then that no matter what it took, even if I had to hand-feed him grapes, I would make sure Keith had no reason to doubt my loyalties.

"Fine," he said, the word seeming to cause him a lot of pain. "Sydney can go . . . for now. But I'll be watching you." He fixed his gaze on me. "And I'm not going to cover for you. You'll be responsible for keeping that vampire girl in line and getting her to her feedings."

"Feedings?" I asked blankly. Of course. Jill would need blood. For a moment, all my confidence wavered. It was easy to talk about hanging out with vampires when none were around. Easier still when you didn't think about what it was that made vampires who they were. Blood. That terrible, unnatural need that fueled their existence. An awful thought sprang into my mind, vanishing as quickly as it came. *Am I supposed to give her my blood?* No. That was ridiculous. That was a line the Alchemists would never cross. Swallowing, I tried to conceal my brief moment of panic. "How do you plan on feeding her?"

Stanton nodded to Keith. "Would you explain?" I think she was giving him a chance to feel important, as a way of making up for his earlier defeat. He ran with it.

"There's only one Moroi we know of living in Palm Springs,"

said Keith. As he spoke, I noticed that his tousled blond hair was practically coated in gel. It gave his hair a slimy shine that I didn't think was attractive in the least. Also, I didn't trust any guy who used more styling products than I did. "And if you ask me, he's crazy. But he's harmless crazy—inasmuch as any of them are harmless. He's this old recluse who lives outside the city. He's got this hang-up about the Moroi government and doesn't associate with any of them, so he isn't going to tell anyone you guys are there. Most importantly, he's got a feeder he's willing to share."

I frowned. "Do we really want Jill hanging out with some anti-government Moroi? The whole purpose is to keep them stable. If we introduce her to some rebel, how do we know he won't try to use her?"

"That's an excellent point," said Michaelson, seeming surprised to admit as much.

I hadn't meant to undermine Keith. My mind had just jumped ahead in this way it had, spotting a potential problem and pointing it out. From the look he gave me, though, it was like I was purposely trying to discredit his statement and make him look bad.

"We won't tell him who she is, obviously," he said, a glint of anger in his good eye. "That would be stupid. And he's not part of any faction. He's not part of anything. He's convinced the Moroi and their guardians let him down, so he wants nothing to do with any of them. I've passed a story to him about how Jill's family has the same antisocial feelings, so he's sympathetic."

"You're right to be wary, Sydney," said Stanton. There was a look of approval in her eyes, like she was pleased at having defended me. That approval meant a lot to me, considering how fierce she often seemed. "We can't assume anything about any of them. Although we also checked out this Moroi with Abe Mazur, who concurs he's harmless enough."

"Abe Mazur?" scoffed Michaelson. He scratched at his graying beard. "Yes. I'm sure he'd be an expert on who's harmless or not."

My heart lurched at the name, but I tried not to show it. *Do not react, do not react,* I ordered my face. After a deep breath, I asked very, very carefully, "Is Abe Mazur the Moroi who's going with Jill? I've met him before . . . but I thought you said it was an Ivashkov who was going." If Abe Mazur was in residence in Palm Springs, that would alter things significantly.

Michaelson scoffed. "No, we'd never send you off with Abe Mazur. He's simply been helping with the organization of this plan."

"What's so bad about Abe Mazur?" asked Keith. "I don't know who he is."

I studied Keith very closely as he spoke, looking for some trace of deception. But, no. His face was all innocence, openly curious. His blue eyes—or eye, rather—held a rare look of confusion, contrasting with the usual know-it-all arrogance. Abe's name meant nothing to him. I exhaled a breath I hadn't realized I'd been holding.

"A scoundrel," said Stanton flatly. "He knows far too much about things he shouldn't. He's useful, but I don't trust him."

A scoundrel? That was an understatement. Abe Mazur was a Moroi whose nickname in Russia—*zmey*, the serpent—said it all. Abe had done a number of favors for me, ones I'd had to pay back at considerable risk to myself. Part of that payback had been helping Rose escape. Well, he'd called it payback; I called it blackmail. I had no desire to cross paths with him again, mostly because I was afraid of what he'd ask for next. The frustrating part was that there was no one I could go to for help. My superiors wouldn't react well to learning that, in addition to all my other solo activities with vampires, I was making side deals with them.

"None of them are to be trusted," my father pointed out. He made the Alchemist sign against evil, drawing a cross on his left shoulder with his right hand.

"Yes, well, Mazur's worse than most," said Michaelson. He stifled a yawn, reminding all of us that it was the middle of the night. "Are we all set, then?"

There were murmurs of assent. Keith's stormy expression displayed how unhappy he was at not getting his way, but he made no more attempts to stop me from going. "I guess we can leave anytime now," he said.

It took me a second to realize that the "we" meant him and me. "Right now?" I asked in disbelief.

He shrugged. "The vampires are going to be on their way soon. We need to make sure everything's set up for them. If we switch off driving, we can be there by tomorrow afternoon."

"Great," I said stiffly. A road trip with Keith. Ugh. But what else could I say? I had no choice in this, and even if I did, I was in no position to turn down anything the Alchemists asked of me now. I'd played every card I had tonight, and I had to believe being with Keith was better than a re-education center. Besides, I'd just fought a hard battle to prove myself and spare Zoe. I had to continue showing I was up for anything.

My father sent me off to pack with the same briskness he'd

ordered me to make myself presentable earlier. I left the others talking and scurried quietly up to my room, still conscious of my sleeping mother. I was an expert in packing quickly and efficiently, thanks to surprise trips my father had sprung on me throughout my childhood. In fact, I always had a bag of toiletries packed and ready to go. The problem wasn't so much in speed as it was in wondering how much to pack. The length of time for this assignment hadn't been specified, and I had the uneasy feeling that no one actually knew. Were we talking about a few weeks? An entire school year? I'd heard someone mention the Moroi wanting to repeal the law that endangered Jill, but that seemed like the kind of legal process that could take a while. To make things worse, I didn't even know what to wear to high school. The only thing I was certain of was that the weather would be hot. I ended up packing ten of my lightest outfits and hoped I'd be able to do laundry.

"Sydney?"

I was putting my laptop in a messenger bag when Zoe appeared in my doorway. She'd redone her braids so that they were neater, and I wondered if it had been an attempt to impress our father. "Hey," I said, smiling at her. She slipped into the room and shut the door behind her. I was glad she'd come to say goodbye. I would miss her and wanted her to know that—

"Why did you do that to me?" she demanded before I could get a word out. "Do you know how humiliated I am?"

I was taken aback, speechless for a few moments. "I . . . what are you talking about? I was trying to—"

"You made me sound incompetent!" she said. I was astonished to see the glint of tears in her eyes. "You went on and on about how I didn't have any experience and couldn't handle doing what you and Dad do! I looked like an idiot in front of all those Alchemists. And Keith."

"Keith Darnell is no one you need to worry about impressing," I said quickly, trying to control my temper. Seeing her stormy face, I sighed and replayed the conversation in the study. I hadn't been trying to make Zoe look bad so much as do whatever I could to make sure I was the one sent away. I'd had no clue she would take it like this. "Look, I wasn't trying to embarrass you. I was trying to protect you."

She gave a harsh laugh, and the anger sounded weird coming from someone as gentle as Zoe. "Is that what you call it? You even said yourself that you were trying to get a promotion!"

I grimaced. Yes, I had said that. But I could hardly tell her the truth. No human knew the truth about why I'd helped Rose. Lying to my own kind—especially my sister—pained me, but there was nothing I could do. As usual, I felt trapped in the middle. So, I dodged the comment.

"You were never intended to be an Alchemist," I said. "There are better things for you out there."

"Because I'm not as smart as you?" she asked. "Because I don't speak five languages?"

"That has nothing to do with it," I snapped. "Zoe, you're wonderful, and you'd probably make a great Alchemist! But believe me, the Alchemist life . . . you don't want any part of it." I wanted to tell her that she'd hate it. I wanted to tell her that she'd never be responsible for her own future or get to make her own decisions again. But my sense of duty prevented me, and I stayed silent.

"I'd do it," she said. "I'd help protect us from vampires . . .

if Dad wanted me to." Her voice wavered a little, and I suddenly wondered what was really fueling her desire to be an Alchemist.

"If you want to get close to Dad, find another way. The Alchemist cause might be a good one, but once you're in it, they own you." I wished I could explain to her how it felt. "You don't want this life."

"Because you want it all for yourself?" she demanded. She was a few inches shorter than me but filled with so much fury and fierceness right now that she seemed to take up the room.

"No! I don't—you don't understand," I finally said. I wanted to throw my hands up in exasperation but held back, as always.

The look she gave me nearly turned me to ice. "Oh, I think I understand perfectly." She turned around abruptly and hurried out the door, still managing to move quietly. Her fear of our father overpowered her anger at me.

I stared at where she'd been standing and felt terrible. How could she have thought I was really trying to steal all the glory and make her look bad? *Because that's exactly what you said,* a voice inside me pointed out. I supposed it was true, but I'd never expected her to be offended. I'd never known she had any interest in being one of the Alchemists. Even now, I wondered if her desire was more about being a part of something and proving herself to our father than it was about really wishing she'd been chosen for this task.

Whatever her reasons, there was nothing to be done for it now. I might not like the heavy-handed way the Alchemists had dealt with me, but I still fiercely believed in what they were doing to protect humans from vampires. And I definitely believed in keeping Jill safe from her own people if it meant avoiding a massive civil war. I could do this job and do it well. And Zoe—she would be free to pursue whatever she wanted in life.

"What took you so long?" my father asked when I returned to the study. My conversation with Zoe had delayed me a couple minutes, which was two minutes too long for him. I didn't attempt to answer.

"I'm ready to go whenever you are," Keith told me. His mood had shifted while I was upstairs. Friendliness oozed from him now, so strongly that it was a wonder everyone didn't recognize it as fake. He'd apparently decided to try a more pleasant attitude around me, either in the hopes of impressing the others or sucking up to me so that I wouldn't reveal what I knew about him. Yet even as he wore that plastic smile, there was a stiffness in his posture and the way he crossed his arms that told me—if no else—that he was no happier about being thrown together than I was. "I can even do most of the driving."

"I don't mind doing my share," I said, trying to avoid glancing at his glass eye. I also wasn't comfortable being driven by someone with faulty depth perception.

"I'd like to speak to Sydney in private before she goes, if that's all right," my father said.

No one had a problem with that, and he led me into the kitchen, shutting the door behind us. We stood quietly for a few moments, simply facing each other with arms crossed. I suddenly dared to hope that maybe he'd come to tell me he was sorry for how things had been between us this last month, that he forgave me and loved me. Honestly, I would've been happy if he'd simply wanted a private, fatherly goodbye.

He peered down at me intently, his brown eyes so identical to mine. I hoped mine never had such a cold look in them. "I don't have to tell you how important this is for you, for all of us."

So much for fatherly affection.

"No, sir," I said. "You don't."

"I don't know if you can undo the disgrace you brought down on us by running off with *them*, but this is a step in the right direction. Do not mess this up. You're being tested. Follow your orders. Keep the Moroi girl out of trouble." He sighed and ran a hand through his dark blond hair, which I'd also inherited. Strange, I thought, that we had so many things in common . . . yet were so completely different. "Thank God Keith is with you. Follow his lead. He knows what he's doing."

I stiffened. There was that note of pride in his voice again, like Keith was the greatest thing walking the earth. My father had seen to it that my training was thorough, but when Keith had stayed with us, my father had taken him on trips and lessons I'd never been part of. My sisters and I had been furious. We'd always suspected that our father regretted having only daughters, and that had been proof. But it wasn't jealousy that made my blood boil and teeth clench now.

For a moment, I thought, *What if I tell him what I know? What will he think of his golden boy then?* But staring into my father's hard eyes, I answered my own question: *No one would believe me.* That was immediately followed by the memory of another voice and a girl's frightened, pleading face staring at me with big brown eyes. *Don't tell, Sydney. Whatever you do, don't tell what Keith did. Don't tell anyone.* I couldn't betray her like that.

My father was still waiting for an answer. I swallowed and nodded. "Yes, sir."

He raised his eyebrows, clearly pleased, and gave me a rough pat on the shoulder. It was the closest he'd come to real affection in a while. I flinched, both from surprise and because of how rigid I was with frustration. "Good." He moved toward the kitchen door and then paused to glance back at me. "Maybe there's hope for you yet."

CHAPTER 3

THE DRIVE TO PALM SPRINGS WAS AGONY.

I was exhausted from being dragged out of bed, and even when Keith took over the wheel, I couldn't fall asleep. I had too much on my mind: Zoe, my reputation, the mission at hand. . . . My thoughts spun in circles. I just wanted to fix all the problems in my life. Keith's driving did nothing to make me less anxious.

I was also upset because my father hadn't let me say good-bye to my mom. He'd gone on and on about how we should just let her sleep, but I knew the truth. He was afraid that if she knew I was leaving, she'd try to stop us. She'd been furious after my last mission: I'd gone halfway around the world alone, only to be returned with no clue as to what my future held. My mom had thought the Alchemists had used me badly and had told my dad it was just as well they seemed to be done with me. I don't know if she really could've stood in the way of tonight's plans, but I didn't want to take my chances in case Zoe got sent instead of me. I certainly hadn't expected a warm and fuzzy farewell from him, but it felt strange leaving on such unsettled terms with my sister and mother.

When dawn came, briefly turning the desert landscape of Nevada into a blazing sea of red and copper, I gave up on sleep altogether and decided to just power through. I bought a twenty-four-ounce cup of coffee from a gas station and assured Keith I could drive us the rest of the way. He gladly gave up the wheel, but rather than sleep, he bought coffee as well and chatted me up for the remaining hours. He was still going strong with his new *we're-friends* attitude, almost making me wish for his earlier animosity. I was determined not to give him any cause to doubt me, so I worked hard to smile and nod appropriately. It was kind of hard to do while constantly gritting my teeth.

Some of the conversation wasn't so bad. I could handle business talk, and we had plenty of details to still work out. He told me all he knew about the school, and I ate up his description of my future home. Amberwood Preparatory School was apparently a prestigious place, and I idly wondered if maybe I could treat it as pretend college. By Alchemist standards, I knew all I needed for my job, but something in me always burned for more and more knowledge. I'd had to learn to content myself with my own reading and research, but still, college—or even just being around those who knew more and had something to teach me—had long been a fantasy of mine.

As a "senior," I would have off-campus privileges, and one of our first orders of business—after securing fake IDs—was to get me a car. Knowing I wouldn't be trapped at a boarding school made things a bit more bearable, even though it was obvious that half of Keith's enthusiasm for getting me my own transportation was to make sure I could shoulder any work that came along with the job.

Keith also enlightened me about something I hadn't realized—but probably should have. "You and that Jill girl are being enrolled as sisters," he said.

"*What?*" It was a measure of my self-control that my hold on the car never wavered. Living with a vampire was one thing—but being *related* to one? "Why?" I demanded.

I saw him shrug in my periphery. "Why not? It explains why you'll be around her so much—and is a good excuse for you to be roommates. Normally, the school doesn't pair students who are different ages, but . . . well . . . your 'parents' promised a hefty donation that made them change their normal policy."

I was so stunned that I didn't even have my normal gut reaction to slap him when he concluded with his self-satisfied chuckle. I'd known we'd be living together . . . but sisters? It was . . . weird. No, not just that. Outlandish.

"That's crazy," I said at last, still too shocked to come up with a more eloquent response.

"It's just on paper," he said.

True. But something about being cast as a *vampire relative* threw my whole order off. I prided myself on the way I'd learned to behave around vampires, but part of that came from the strict belief that I was an outsider, a business associate distinct and removed. Playacting as Jill's sister destroyed those lines. It brought about a familiarity that I wasn't sure I was ready for.

"Living with one of them shouldn't be so bad for you," Keith commented, drumming his fingers against the window in a way that put my nerves on edge. Something about the too-casual way he spoke made me think he was leading me into a trap. "You're used to it."

"Hardly," I said, choosing my words carefully. "I was with them for a week at most. And actually, most of my time was spent with dhampirs."

"Same difference," he replied dismissively. "If anything, the dhampirs are worse. They're abominations. Not human, but not full vampires. Products of unnatural unions."

I didn't respond right away and instead pretended to be deeply interested in the road ahead. What he said was true, by Alchemist teaching. I'd been raised believing that both races of vampires, Moroi and Strigoi, were dark and wrong. They needed blood to survive. What kind of person drank from another? It was disgusting, and just thinking about how I'd soon be ferrying Moroi to their feedings made me ill.

But the dhampirs . . . that was a trickier matter. Or at least, it was for me now. The dhampirs were half human and half vampire, created at a time when the two races had mingled freely. Over the centuries, vampires had pulled away from humans, and both of our races now agreed that those kinds of unions were taboo. The dhampir race had persisted against all odds, however, in spite of the fact that dhampirs couldn't reproduce with each other. They could with Moroi or humans, and plenty of Moroi were up to the task.

"Right?" asked Keith.

I realized he was staring at me, waiting for me to agree with him about dhampirs being abominations—or maybe he was hoping I would disagree. Regardless, I'd been quiet for too long.

"Right," I said. I mustered the standard Alchemist rhetoric. "In some ways, they're worse than the Moroi. Their race was never meant to exist."

"You scared me there for a second," Keith said. I was watching the road but had a sneaking suspicion he'd just winked at me. "I thought you were going to defend them. I should've known better than to believe the stories about you. I can totally get why you'd want to gamble at the glory—but man, that had to have been harsh, trying to work with one of them."

I couldn't explain how once you'd spent a little time with Rose Hathaway, it was easy to forget she was a dhampir. Even physically, dhampirs and humans were virtually indistinguishable. Rose was so full of life and passion that sometimes she seemed more human than I was. Rose certainly wouldn't have meekly accepted this job with a simpering, "Yes, sir." Not like me.

Rose hadn't even accepted being locked in jail, with the weight of the Moroi government against her. Abe Mazur's blackmail had been a catalyst that spurred me to help her, but I'd also never believed that Rose had committed the murder they'd accused her of. That certainty, along with our fragile friendship, had driven me to break Alchemist rules to help Rose and her dhampir boyfriend, the formidable Dimitri Belikov, elude the authorities. Throughout it all, I'd watched Rose with a kind of wonder as she battled the world. I couldn't envy someone who wasn't human, but I could certainly envy her strength—and refusal to back down, no matter what.

But again, I could hardly tell Keith any of that. And I still didn't believe for an instant, despite his sunny act, that he was suddenly okay with me coming along.

I gave a small shrug. "I thought it was worth the risk."

"Well," he said, seeing I wasn't going to offer anything more. "The next time you decide to go rogue with vampires and dhampirs, get a little backup so you don't get in as much trouble."

I scoffed. "I have no intention of going rogue again." That, at least, was the truth.

We reached Palm Springs late in the afternoon and got to work immediately with our tasks. I was dying for sleep by that point, and even Keith—despite his talkativeness—looked a little worn around the edges. But we'd gotten the word that Jill and her entourage were arriving tomorrow, leaving very little time to put the remaining details in place.

A visit to Amberwood Prep revealed that my "family" was expanding. Apparently, the dhampir coming with Jill was enrolling as well and would be playing our brother. Keith was also going to be our brother. When I questioned that, he explained that we needed someone local to act as our legal guardian should Jill or any of us need to be pulled from school or granted some privilege. Since our fictitious parents lived out of state, getting results from him would be faster. I couldn't fault the logic, even though I found being related to him more repulsive than having dhampirs or vampires in the family. And that was saying a lot.

Later on, a driver's license from a reputable fake ID maker declared that I was now Sydney Katherine Melrose, from South Dakota. We chose South Dakota because we figured the locals didn't see too many licenses from that state and wouldn't be able to spot any flaws in it. Not that I expected there to be. The Alchemists didn't associate with people who did second-rate work. I also liked the picture of Mount Rushmore on the license. It was one of the few places in the United States that I'd never been.

The day wrapped up with what I had most been looking forward to: a trip to a car dealer. Keith and I did almost as much haggling with each other as we did with the salesman. I'd been raised to be practical and keep my emotions in check, but I *loved* cars. That was one of the few legacies I'd picked up from my mom. She was a mechanic, and some of my best childhood memories were of working in the garage with her.

I especially had a weakness for sports cars and vintage cars, the kinds with big engines that I knew were bad for the environment—but that I guiltily loved anyway. Those were out of the question for this job, though. Keith argued that I needed something that could hold everyone, as well as any cargo—and that wouldn't attract a lot of attention. Once more, I conceded to his reasoning like a good little Alchemist.

"But I don't see why it has to be a station wagon," I told him.

Our shopping had led us down to a new Subaru Outback that met most of his requirements. My car instincts told me the Subaru would do what I needed. It would handle well and had a decent engine, for what it was. And yet . . .

"I feel like a soccer mom," I said. "I'm too young for that."

"Soccer moms drive vans," Keith told me. "And there's nothing wrong with soccer."

I scowled. "Does it have to be brown, though?"

It did, unless we wanted a used one. As much as I would've liked something in blue or red, the newness took precedence. My fastidious nature didn't like the idea of driving "someone else's" car. I wanted it to be *mine*—shiny, new, and clean. So, we made the deal, and I, Sydney Melrose, became the proud owner of a brown station wagon. I named it Latte, hoping my love of coffee would soon transfer to the car.

Once our errands were done, Keith left me for his apartment in downtown Palm Springs. He offered to let me stay there as well, but I'd politely refused and gotten a hotel room, grateful for the Alchemists' deep pockets. Honestly, I would've paid with my own money to save me from sleeping under the same roof as Keith Darnell.

I ordered a light dinner up to my room, relishing the alone time after all those hours in the car with Keith. Then I changed into pajamas and decided to call my mom. Even though I was glad to be free of my dad's disapproval for a while, I would miss having her around.

"Those are good cars," she told me after I began the call by explaining my trip to the dealership. My mother had always been a free spirit, which was an unlikely match for someone like my dad. While he'd been teaching me chemical equations, she'd showed me how to change my own oil. Alchemists didn't have to marry other Alchemists, but I was baffled by whatever forces had drawn my parents together. Maybe my father had been less uptight when he was younger.

"I guess," I said, knowing I sounded sullen. My mother was one of the few people I could be anything less than perfect or content around. She was a big advocate of letting your feelings out. "I think I'm just annoyed that I didn't have much say in it."

"Annoyed? I'm *furious* that he didn't even talk to me about it," she huffed. "I can't believe he just smuggled you out like that! You're my daughter, not some commodity that he can just move around." For a moment, my mother reminded me weirdly of Rose—both possessed that unflinching tendency to say what was on their minds. That ability seemed strange and exotic to me, but sometimes—when I thought about my own carefully controlled and reserved nature—I wondered if maybe *I* was the weird one.

"He didn't know all the details," I said, automatically defending him. With my father's temper, if my parents were mad at each other, then life at home would be unpleasant for Zoe—not to mention my mom. Better to ensure peace. "They hadn't told him everything."

"I hate them sometimes." There was a growl in my mom's voice. "Sometimes I hate him too."

I wasn't sure what to say to that. I resented my father, sure, but he *was* still my father. A lot of the hard choices he made were because of the Alchemists, and I knew that no matter how stifled I felt sometimes, the Alchemists' job was important. Humans had to be protected from the existence of vampires. Knowing vampires existed would create a panic. Worse, it could drive some weak-willed humans into becoming slaves to the Strigoi in exchange for immortality and the eventual corruption of their souls. It happened more often than we liked to admit.

"It's fine, Mom," I said soothingly. "I'm fine. I'm not in trouble anymore, and I'm in the U.S. even." Actually, I wasn't sure if the "trouble" part was really true, but I thought the latter would soothe her. Stanton had told me to keep our location in Palm Springs secret, but giving up that we were domestic wouldn't hurt too much and might make my mom think I had an easier job ahead of me than I likely did. She and I talked a little bit more before hanging up, and she told me she'd heard from my sister Carly. All was well with her at college, which I was relieved to hear. I wanted desperately to find out about Zoe as well but resisted asking to talk to her. I was afraid that if she got on the phone, I'd find out she was still mad at me. Or, worse, that she wouldn't speak to me at all.

I went to bed feeling melancholy, wishing I could have poured out all my fears and insecurities to my mom. Wasn't that what normal mothers and daughters did? I knew she would've welcomed it. I was the one who had trouble letting myself go, too wrapped up in Alchemist secrets to be a normal teenager.

After a long sleep, and with the morning sunlight streaming through my window, I felt a little better. I had a job to do, and having purpose shifted me out of feeling sorry for myself. I remembered that I was doing this for Zoe, for Moroi and humans alike. It allowed me to center myself and push my insecurities aside—at least, for now.

I picked up Keith around noon and drove us outside of the city to meet Jill and the recluse Moroi who'd be helping us. Keith had a lot to say about the guy, whose name was Clarence Donahue. Clarence had lived in Palm Springs for three years, ever since the death of his niece in Los Angeles, which had apparently had quite a traumatic effect on the man. Keith had met him a couple of times on past jobs and kept making jokes about Clarence's tenuous grip on sanity.

"He's a few pints short of a blood bank, you know?" Keith said, chuckling to himself. I bet he'd been waiting days to use that line.

The jokes were in poor taste—and stupid to boot—but as we got closer and closer to Clarence's home, Keith eventually became very quiet and nervous. Something occurred to me.

"How many Moroi have you met?" I asked as we pulled off the main road and turned into a long and winding driveway. The house was straight out of a Gothic movie, boxy and made of gray bricks that were completely at odds with most of the Palm Springs architecture we'd scene. The only reminder that we were in southern California was the ubiquitous palm trees surrounding the house. It was a weird juxtaposition.

"Enough," said Keith evasively. "I can handle being around them."

The confidence in his tone sounded forced. I realized that despite his brashness about this job, his comments on the Moroi and dhampir races, and his judgment of my actions, Keith was actually very, very uncomfortable with the idea of being around non-humans. It was understandable. Most Alchemists were. A large part of our job didn't even involve interacting with the vampiric world—it was the human world that needed tending. Records had to be covered up, witnesses bribed. The majority of Alchemists had very little contact with our subjects, meaning most Alchemists' knowledge came from the stories and teachings passed down through the families. Keith had said he'd met Clarence but made no mention of spending time with other Moroi or dhampirs—certainly not a group, like we were about to face.

I was no more excited to hang around vampires than he was, but I realized it didn't scare me nearly as much as it once would have. Rose and her companions had given me a tough skin. I'd even been to the Moroi Royal Court, a place few Alchemists had ever visited. If I'd walked away from the heart of their civilization intact, I was certain I could handle whatever was inside this house. Admittedly, it would've been a little easier if Clarence's house didn't look so much like a creepy haunted manor from a horror movie.

We walked up to the door, presenting a united front in our stylish, formal Alchemist attire. Whatever his faults, Keith cleaned up well. He wore khaki pants with a white button-up shirt and navy silk tie. The shirt had short sleeves, though I doubted that was helping much in the heat. It was early September, and the temperature had been pushing ninety when I left my hotel. I was equally hot in a brown skirt, tights, and a cap-sleeved blouse scattered with tan flowers.

Belatedly, I realized we kind of matched.

Keith lifted his hand to knock at the door, but it opened before he could do anything. I flinched, a bit unnerved despite the assurances I'd just given myself.

The guy who opened the door looked just as surprised to see us. He held a cigarette pack in one hand and appeared as though he'd been heading outside to smoke. He paused and gave us a once-over.

"So. Are you guys here to convert me or sell me siding?"

The disarming comment was enough to help me shake off my anxiety. The speaker was a Moroi guy, a little older than me, with dark brown hair that had undoubtedly been painstakingly styled to look messy. Unlike Keith's ridiculously over-gelled attempts, this guy had actually done it in a way that looked good. Like all Moroi, he was pale and had a tall, lean build. Emerald green eyes studied us from a face that could have been sculpted by one of the classical artists I so admired. Shocked, I dismissed the comparison as soon as it popped into my head. This was a vampire, after all. It was ridiculous to admire him the way I would some hot human guy.

"Mr. Ivashkov," I said politely. "It's nice to see you again."

He frowned and studied me from his greater height. "I know you. How do I know you?"

"We—" I started to say "met" but realized that wasn't quite right since we hadn't been formally introduced the last time I had seen him. He'd simply been present when Stanton and I had been hauled to the Moroi Court for questioning. "We ran into each other last month. At your Court."

Recognition lit his eyes. "Right. The Alchemist." He thought for a moment and then surprised me when he pulled up my name. With everything else that had been going on when I was at the Moroi Court, I hadn't expected to make an impression. "Sydney Sage."

I nodded, trying not to look flustered at the recognition. Then I realized Keith had frozen up beside me. He'd claimed he could "handle" being around Moroi, but apparently, that meant staring gape-mouthed and not saying a word. Keeping a pleasant smile on, I said, "Keith, this is Adrian Ivashkov. Adrian, this is my colleague, Keith Darnell."

Adrian held out his hand, but Keith didn't shake it. Whether that was because Keith was still shell-shocked or because he simply didn't want to touch a vampire, I couldn't say. Adrian didn't seem to mind. He dropped his hand and took out a lighter, stepping past us as he did. He nodded toward the doorway.

"They're waiting for you. Go on in." Adrian leaned close to Keith's ear and spoke in an ominous voice. "If. You. Dare." He poked Keith's shoulder and gave a "Muhahaha" kind of monster laugh.

Keith nearly leapt ten feet in the air. Adrian chuckled and strolled off down a garden path, lighting his cigarette as he walked. I glared after him—though it *had* been kind of funny—and nudged Keith toward the door. "Come on," I said. The coolness of air conditioning brushed against me.

If nothing else, Keith seemed to have come alive. "What was that about?" he demanded as we stepped into the house. "He nearly attacked me!"

I shut the door. "It was about you looking like an idiot. And he didn't do a thing to you. Could you have acted any more terrified? They know we don't like them, and you looked like you were ready to bolt."

Admittedly, I kind of liked seeing Keith caught off guard, but human solidarity left no question about which side I was on.

"I did not," argued Keith, though he was obviously embarrassed. We walked down a long hallway with dark wood floors and trim that seemed to absorb all light. "God, what is wrong with these people? Oh, I know. They *aren't* people."

"Hush," I said, a bit shocked at the vehemence in his voice. "They're right in there. Can't you hear them?"

Heavy French doors met us at the end of the hall. The glass was frosted and stained, obscuring what was inside, but a low murmur of voices could still be heard. I knocked on the door and waited until a voice called an entry. The anger on Keith's face vanished as the two of us exchanged brief, commiserating looks. This was it. The beginning.

We stepped through.

When I saw who was inside, I had to stop my jaw from dropping like Keith's had earlier.

For a moment, I couldn't breathe. I'd mocked Keith for

being afraid around vampires and dhampirs, but now, face-to-face with a group of them, I suddenly felt trapped. The walls threatened to close in on me, and all I could think about were fangs and blood. My world reeled—and not just because of the group's size.

Abe Mazur was here.

Breathe, Sydney. Breathe, I told myself. It wasn't easy, though. Abe represented a thousand fears for me, a thousand entanglements I'd gotten myself into.

Slowly, my surroundings crystallized, and I regained control. Abe wasn't the only one here, after all, and I made myself focus on the others and ignore him.

Three other people sat in the room with him, two of whom I recognized. The unknown, an elderly Moroi with thinning hair and a big white mustache, had to be our host, Clarence.

"Sydney!" That was Jill Mastrano, her eyes lighting up with delight. I liked Jill, but I hadn't thought I'd made enough of an impression on the girl to warrant such a welcome. Jill almost looked like she would run up and hug me, and I prayed that she wouldn't. I didn't need Keith to see that. More importantly, I didn't need Keith *reporting* about that.

Beside Jill was a dhampir, one I knew in the same way I knew Adrian—that is, I'd seen him but had never been introduced. Eddie Castile had also been present when I was questioned at the Royal Court and, if memory served, had been in some trouble of his own. For all intents and purposes, he looked human, with an athletic body and face that had spent a lot of time in the sun. His hair was a sandy brown, and his hazel eyes regarded me and Keith in a friendly—but wary—way. That's how it was with guardians. They were always on alert, always watching for the next threat. In some ways, I found it reassuring.

My survey of the room soon returned me to Abe, who had been watching and seemed amused by my obvious avoidance of him. A sly smile spread over his features.

"Why, Miss Sage," he said slowly. "Aren't you going to say hello to me?"

CHAPTER 4

ABE HAD THE KIND OF APPEARANCE that could leave many people speechless, even if they knew nothing about him.

Oblivious to the heat outside, the Moroi man was dressed in a full suit and tie. The suit was white, at least, but it still looked like it would be warm. His shirt and tie were purple, as was the rose tucked into his pocket. Gold glittered in his ears and at his throat. He was originally from Turkey and had more color to him than most Moroi but was still paler than humans like me and Keith. Abe's complexion actually reminded me of a tanned person who'd been sick for a while.

"Hello," I said stiffly.

His smile split into a full grin. "So nice to see you again."

"Always a pleasure." My lie sounded robotic, but hopefully it was better than sounding afraid.

"No, no," he said. "The pleasure's all mine."

"If you say so," I said. This amused him further.

Keith had frozen up again, so I strode over to the old Moroi man and extended my hand so that at least one of us would look like we had manners. "Are you Mr. Donahue? I'm Sydney Sage."

Clarence smiled and clasped my hand in his wrinkled one. I didn't flinch, even though the urge was there. Unlike most Moroi I'd met, he didn't conceal his fangs when he smiled, which almost made my facade crack. Another reminder that no matter how human they seemed at times, these were still vampires.

"I am so pleased to meet you," he said. "I've heard wonderful things about you."

"Oh?" I asked, arching an eyebrow and wondering who'd been talking about me.

Clarence nodded emphatically. "You are welcome in my home. It's delightful to have so much company."

Introductions were made for everyone else. Eddie and Jill were a little reserved, but both friendly. Keith didn't shake any hands, but he at least stopped acting like a drooling fool. He took a chair when offered and put on an arrogant expression, which was probably supposed to look like confidence. I hoped he wouldn't embarrass us.

"I'm sorry," said Abe, leaning forward. His dark eyes glittered. "Did you say your name was Keith Darnell?"

"Yes," said Keith. He studied Abe curiously, no doubt recalling the Alchemists' conversation back in Salt Lake City. Even through the bravado Keith was attempting to put on, I could see a sliver of unease. Abe had that effect. "Why?"

"No reason," said Abe. His eyes flicked to me and then to Keith. "It just sounds familiar, that's all."

"My father's a very important man among the Alchemists,"

said Keith loftily. He'd relaxed a little, probably thinking the stories about Abe were overrated. Fool. "You've undoubtedly heard of him."

"Undoubtedly," said Abe. "I'm sure that's what it is." He spoke so casually that no one would suspect he wasn't telling the truth. Only I knew the real reason Abe knew who Keith was, but I certainly didn't want that revealed. I also didn't want Abe dropping any more hints, which I suspected he was doing just to irk me.

I tried to steer the subject away—and get some answers for myself. "I wasn't aware you were joining us, Mr. Mazur." The sweetness in my voice matched his.

"Please," he said. "You know you can call me Abe. And I won't be staying, unfortunately. I simply came along to make sure this group arrived safely—and to meet Clarence in person."

"That's very nice of you," I said dryly, sincerely doubting Abe's motives were as simple as that. If I'd learned anything, it was that things were never simple when Abe Mazur was involved. He was a puppet master of sorts. He not only wanted to observe things, he also wanted to control them.

He smiled winningly. "Well, I always aim to help others in need."

"Yeah," a new voice suddenly said. "That's exactly what comes to mind when I think of you, old man."

I hadn't thought anyone could shock me more than Abe, but I was wrong. "Rose?" The name came out as a question from my lips, even though there could be no doubt about who this new-comer was. There was only one Rose Hathaway, after all.

"Hey, Sydney," she said, giving me a small, crooked smile as she entered the room. Her flashing, dark eyes were friendly, but they were also assessing everything in the room, much as Eddie's gaze was. It was a guardian thing. Rose was about my height and dressed very casually in jeans and a red tank top. But, as always, there was something exotic and dangerous about her beauty that made her stand out from everyone else. She was like a tropical flower in this dark, stuffy room. One that could kill you. I'd never seen her mother, but it was easy to tell that some of her looks came from Abe's Turkish influence, like her long, dark brown hair. In the dim lighting, that hair looked nearly black. Her eyes rested on Keith, and she nodded politely. "Hey, other Alchemist."

Keith stared at her wide-eyed, but whether that was a reaction to us being further outnumbered or simply a response to Rose's extraordinary nature, I couldn't say. "I-I'm Keith," he stammered at last.

"Rose Hathaway," she told him. His eyes bugged even more as he recognized the name. She strode across the room, toward Clarence, and I noted that half of her allure was simply in the way she dominated her surroundings. Her expression softened as she regarded the elderly man. "I checked the house's perimeter like you asked. It's about as safe as you can make it, though your back door's lock should probably be replaced."

"Are you sure?" asked Clarence in disbelief. "It's brand new."

"Maybe when this house was built," came yet another new voice. Looking over to the doorway, I realized now that someone else had been with Rose when she arrived, but I'd been too startled by her to notice. Again, that was a Rose thing. She always drew the attention. "It's been rusted since we moved here."

This newcomer was a Moroi, which set me on edge again. That brought the count up to four Moroi and two dhampirs. I was trying very hard not to adopt Keith's attitude—especially since I already knew some of the people here—but it was hard to shake that overwhelming sense of Us and Them. Moroi aged like humans, and at a guess, I thought this new guy was close to my age, maybe Keith's at most. He had nice features, I supposed, with black curling hair and gray eyes. The smile he offered seemed sincere, though there was a slight sense of uneasiness in the way he stood. His gaze was fixed on Keith and me, intrigued, and I wondered if maybe he didn't spend a lot of time with humans. Most Moroi didn't, though they didn't share the same fears about our race as we did about theirs. But then, ours didn't use theirs as food.

"I'm Lee Donahue," he said, extending his hand. Once again, Keith didn't take it, but I did and introduced us.

Lee looked back and forth between me and Keith, face full of wonder. "Alchemists, right? I've never met one of you. The tattoos you guys have are beautiful," he said, eyeing the gold lily on my cheek. "I've heard about what they can do."

"Donahue?" asked Keith. He glanced between Lee and Clarence. "Are you related?"

Lee gave Clarence an indulgent look. "Father and son."

Keith frowned. "But you don't live here, do you?" I was surprised that this, of all things, would draw him out. Maybe he didn't like the idea that his intel was faulty. He was Palm Springs' Alchemist, after all, and he'd believed Clarence was the only Moroi in the area.

"Not regularly, no," said Lee. "I go to college in LA, but

my schedule's just part-time this semester. So, I want to try to spend more time with Dad."

Abe glanced at Rose. "You see that?" he said. "Now that's devotion." She rolled her eyes at him.

Keith looked like he had more questions about this, but Clarence's mind was still back in the conversation. "I could've sworn I had that lock replaced."

"Well, I can replace it soon for you if you want," said Lee. "Can't be that hard."

"I think it's fine." Clarence rose unsteadily to his feet. "I'm going to take a look."

Lee hurried to his side and shot us an apologetic look. "Does it have to be right now?" When it appeared that it did, Lee said, "I'll go with you." I got the impression that Clarence frequently followed his whims, and Lee was used to it.

I used the Donahues' absence to get some answers I'd been dying to know. I turned to Jill. "You didn't have any problems getting here, did you? No more, um, incidents?"

"We ran into a couple dissidents before we left Court," said Rose, a dangerous note in her voice. "Nothing we couldn't handle. The rest was uneventful."

"And it's going to stay that way," said Eddie matter-of-factly. He crossed his arms over his chest. "At least if I have anything to do with it."

I glanced between them, puzzled. "I was told there'd be *a* dhampir along . . . did they decide to send two?"

"Rose invited herself along," said Abe. "Just to make sure the rest of us didn't miss anything. Eddie's the one who will be joining you at Amberwood."

Rose scowled. "I should be the one staying. I should be Jill's roommate. No offense, Sydney. We need you for the paperwork, but I'm the one who's gotta kick anyone's ass who gives Jill trouble."

I certainly wasn't going to argue against that.

"No," said Jill, with surprising intensity. She'd been quiet and hesitant the last time I'd seen her, but her eyes grew fierce at the thought of being a burden to Rose. "You need to stay with Lissa and keep her safe. I've got Eddie, and besides, no one even knows I'm here. Nothing else is going to happen."

The look in Rose's eyes said she was skeptical. I also suspected she didn't truly believe anyone could protect either Vasilisa or Jill as well as she could. That was saying something, considering the young queen was surrounded in bodyguards. But even Rose couldn't be everywhere at once, and she must have had to choose. Her words made me turn my attention back to Jill.

"What *did* happen?" I asked. "Were you hurt? We heard stories about an attack but no confirmation."

There was a heavy pause in the room. Everyone except Keith and me seemed distinctly uncomfortable. Well, we were uncomfortable—but for other reasons.

"I'm fine," said Jill at last, after a sharp look from Rose. "There was an attack, yeah, but none of us were hurt. I mean, not seriously. We were in the middle of a royal dinner when we were attacked by Moroi—like, Moroi assassins. They made it look like they were going for Lis—for the queen, but instead came for me." She hesitated and dropped her eyes, letting her long, curly brown hair fall forward. "I was saved, though, and the guardians rounded them up." There was a nervous energy to Jill that I remembered from before. It was cute and made her seem very much like the shy teenager she was.

"But we don't think they're all gone, which is why we have to stay away from Court," explained Eddie. Even as he directed his words to Keith and me, he radiated a protectiveness toward Jill, daring anyone to challenge the girl he was in charge of keeping safe. "And we don't know where the traitors in our own ranks are. So, until then, here we all are."

"Hopefully not for long," said Keith. I gave him a warning look, and he seemed to realize his comment could be perceived as rude. "I mean, this place can't be all that fun for you guys, with the sun and everything."

"It's safe," said Eddie. "That's what counts."

Clarence and Lee returned, and there was no more mention of Jill's background or the attack. As far as father and son knew, Jill, Eddie, and Adrian had simply fallen out of favor with important royal Moroi and were in exile here. The two Moroi men didn't know who Jill really was and believed that the Alchemists were helping her due to Abe's influence. It was a web of lies but a necessary one. Even if Clarence was in self-imposed exile, we couldn't risk him (or Lee now) accidentally letting outsiders know the queen's sister was holed up here.

Eddie glanced over at the older Moroi. "You said you've never heard of any Strigoi being around here, right?"

Clarence's eyes went unfocused for a moment as his thoughts turned inward. "No . . . but there are worse things than Strigoi . . ."

Lee groaned. "Dad, please. Not that."

Rose and Eddie were on their feet in an instant, and it was

a wonder they didn't pull out weapons. "What are you talking about?" demanded Rose.

"What other dangers are there?" asked Eddie, his voice like steel.

Lee was actually blushing. "Nothing . . . please. It's a delusion of his, that's all."

"'Delusion?'" asked Clarence, narrowing his eyes at his son. "Was your cousin's death a delusion? Is the fact that those high-ups at Court let Tamara go unavenged a delusion?"

My mind spun back to a conversation I'd had with Keith in the car. I gave Clarence what I hoped was a reassuring look. "Tamara was your niece, right? What happened to her, sir?"

"She was killed," he said. There was a dramatic pause. "By vampire hunters."

"I'm sorry, by what?" I asked, certain I'd misheard.

"Vampire hunters," repeated Clarence. Everyone in the room looked as surprised as I felt, which was a small relief. Even some of Rose and Eddie's fierceness wavered. "Oh, you won't find that anywhere—not even in *your* records. We were living in Los Angeles when they got her. I reported it to the guardians, demanded they hunt the culprits down. Do you know what they said?" He peered at each person in turn. "Do you?"

"No," said Jill meekly. "What did they say?" Lee sighed and looked miserable.

Clarence snorted. "They said there was no such thing. That there was no evidence to support my claim. They ruled it a Strigoi killing and said there was nothing anyone could do, that I should be grateful she wasn't turned."

I looked at Keith, who again seemed startled by this story. He apparently didn't know Clarence as well as he'd claimed.

Keith had known the old man had a hang-up involving his niece, but not the extent of it. Keith gave me a small shrug that seemed to say, *See? What did I tell you? Crazy.*

"The guardians are very thorough," said Eddie. His tone and words were both clearly chosen with care, striving not to offend. He sat back down next to Jill. "I'm sure they had their reasons."

"Reasons?" asked Clarence. "If you consider denial and living a delusional life reasons, then I suppose so. They just don't want to accept that vampire hunters are out there. But tell me this. If my Tamara was killed by Strigoi, why did they cut her throat? It was cut cleanly with a blade." He made a slashing motion under his chin. Jill flinched and cowered into her chair. Rose, Eddie, and Abe also looked taken aback, which surprised me because I didn't think anything would make that group squeamish. "Why not use fangs? Makes it easier to drink. I pointed that out to the guardians, and they said that since about half of her blood had been drunk, it was obviously a Strigoi. But I say a vampire hunter did it and made it *look* like they took her blood. Strigoi would have no reason to use a knife."

Rose started to speak, paused, and then began again. "It *is* strange," she said calmly. I had a feeling she'd probably been about to blurt out how ridiculous this conspiracy theory was, but had thought better of it. "But I'm sure there's another explanation, Mr. Donahue."

I wondered if mentioning that the Alchemists had no records of vampire hunters—not in several centuries, at least—would be helpful or not. Keith suddenly took the conversation in an unexpected direction. He met Clarence's gaze levelly.

"It might seem strange for Strigoi, but they do all

BLOODLINES

sorts of vicious things for no reason. I know from personal experience."

My stomach sank. *Oh no.* All eyes turned to Keith.

"Oh?" asked Abe, smoothing his black goatee. "What happened?"

Keith pointed to his glass eye. "I was attacked by Strigoi earlier this year. They beat me up and ripped out my eye. Then they left me."

Eddie frowned. "Without drinking or killing? That *is* really weird. That doesn't sound like normal Strigoi behavior."

"I'm not sure you can really expect Strigoi to do anything 'normal,'" pointed out Abe. I gritted my teeth, wishing he wouldn't engage Keith in this. *Please don't ask about the eye,* I thought. *Let it go.* That was too much to expect, of course, because Abe's next question was, "They only took the one eye? They didn't try for both?"

"Excuse me." I rose before Keith could answer. I couldn't sit through this conversation and listen to Abe bait Keith, simply for the fun of tormenting me. I needed to escape. "I . . . I don't feel well. I'm going to get some air."

"Of course, of course," said Clarence, looking as though he wanted to rise as well. "Should I have my housekeeper get you some water? I can ring the bell—"

"No, no," I said, moving toward the door. "I just . . . I just need a minute."

I hurried out and heard Abe saying, "Such delicate sensibilities. You'd think she wouldn't be so squeamish, considering her profession. But you, young man, seem like you can handle talking about blood . . ."

Abe's ego-stroking worked, and Keith launched into the

one story I most definitely didn't want to hear. I went back down the dark hallway and emerged outside. The fresh air was welcome, even if it was more than twenty degrees warmer than what I'd come from. I took a deep, steadying breath, forcing myself to stay calm. Everything was going to be okay. Abe would be leaving soon. Keith would return to his own apartment. I would go back to Amberwood with Jill and Eddie, who really didn't seem like bad companions, considering who I could have ended up with.

With no real destination in mind, I decided to walk around and scope out Clarence's home—more like an estate, really. I picked a side of the house at random and walked around, admiring the detailed sculpting of the house's exterior. Even if it was hopelessly out of place in the southern California landscape, it was still impressive. I had always loved studying architecture—a subject my father thought was pointless—and was impressed by my surroundings. Glancing around, I noted that the grounds didn't match the rest of what we'd driven through to get here. A lot of the land in this region had gone brown from summer and lack of rain, but Clarence had clearly spent a fortune to keep his sprawling yard lush and green. Non-native trees—beautiful and full of flowers—were artfully arranged to make walking paths and courtyards.

After several minutes of my nature stroll, I turned around and headed back toward the front of the house. I came to a stop when I heard someone.

"Where are you?" a voice asked. Abe. Great. He was looking for me.

"Over here," I just barely heard Adrian say. His voice came from the far side of the house, opposite the side I was on. I heard someone walk across the gravel driveway, the footsteps coming to a halt when they reached what I gauged to be the back door where Abe stood.

I bit my lip and stayed where I was, concealed by the house. I was almost afraid to breathe. With their hearing, Moroi could pick up the tiniest detail.

"Were you ever coming back?" asked Abe, amused.

"Didn't see the point," was Adrian's laconic response.

"The point is politeness. You could have made an effort to meet the Alchemists."

"They don't want to meet me. Especially the guy." There was concealed laughter in Adrian's voice. "You should have seen his face when I ran into him at the door. I wish I'd had a cape on. The girl's at least got some nerve."

"Nevertheless, they play a crucial role in your stay here— and Jill's. You know how important it is that she remain safe."

"Yeah, I get that. And I get why she's here. What I don't get is why *I'm* here."

"Don't you?" asked Abe. "I'd assume it's obvious to both Jill and you. You have to stay near her."

There was a pause. "That's what everyone says . . . but I'm still not sure it's necessary. I don't think she needs me close by, no matter what Rose and Lissa claim."

"You have something better to do?"

"That's not the point." Adrian sounded annoyed, and I was glad that I wasn't the only one Abe had that effect on.

"That's exactly the point," Abe said. "You were wasting away at Court, drowning in your own self-pity—among other things. Here, you have a chance to be useful."

"To you."

"To yourself as well. This is an opportunity for you to make something of your life."

"Except you won't tell me what it is I'm supposed to do!" said Adrian irritably. "Aside from Jill, what is this great task you have for me?"

"Listen. Listen and watch." I could perfectly picture Abe stroking his chin in that mastermind way of his again as he spoke. "Watch *everyone*—Clarence, Lee, the Alchemists, Jill and Eddie. Pay attention to every word, every detail, and report it to me later. It may all be useful."

"I don't know that that really clears things up."

"You have potential, Adrian. Too much potential to waste. I'm very sorry for what happened with Rose, but you have to move on. Maybe things don't make sense now, but they will later. Trust me."

I almost felt bad for Adrian. Abe had once told me to trust him too, and look how things had turned out.

I waited until the two Moroi returned inside and then followed a minute later. In the living room, Keith was still wearing his cocky attitude but looked relieved to have me back. We discussed more details and worked out a schedule for feedings, one I was in charge of maintaining since I'd have to drive Jill (and Eddie, since he didn't want to let her out of his sight) back and forth to Clarence's.

"How are you going to get to feedings?" I asked Adrian. After hearing his conversation with Abe, I was now more curious than ever about his role here.

Adrian was standing against the wall, on the opposite side of the room. His arms were crossed defensively, and there was a rigidness to his posture that conflicted with the lazy smile he wore. I couldn't be sure, but it looked as though he was purposely positioning himself as far from Rose as possible. "By walking down the hall."

Seeing my puzzled look, Clarence explained, "Adrian will be staying here with me. It will be nice to have someone else in these old walls."

"Oh," I said. To myself, I muttered, "How very *Secret Garden.*"

"Hmm?" asked Adrian, tilting his head toward me.

I flinched. Their hearing *was* good. "Nothing. I was just thinking of a book I read."

"Oh," said Adrian dismissively, glancing away. The way he said the word seemed to be a condemnation of books everywhere.

"Don't forget me," said Lee, grinning at his father. "I told you I'll be around more."

"Maybe young Adrian here will keep you out of trouble, then," declared Clarence.

No one said anything to that, but I saw Adrian's friends exchange a few amused glances.

Keith didn't look nearly as freaked out as he had when we'd arrived, but there was a new air of impatience and irritability in him that I didn't quite understand. "Well," he said, after clearing his throat. "I need to get home and take care of some business. And since you're my ride, Sydney . . ."

He left the words hanging but looked at me meaningfully. From what I'd learned, I was more convinced than ever that Palm Springs was the least active vampire area anywhere. I couldn't honestly figure out what "business" Keith would have to take care of, but we had to leave here sooner or later. Eddie and Jill went to gather their luggage, and Rose used the opportunity to pull me aside.

"How have you been?" she asked in a low voice. Her smile was genuine. "I've been worried about you, ever since . . . well, you know. No one would tell me what happened to you." The last time I'd seen her, I'd been held prisoner in a hotel by guardians while the Moroi tried to figure out how big my role had been in Rose's escape.

"I was in a little trouble at first," I said. "But it's past." What was a small lie between friends? Rose was so strong that I couldn't stand the thought of looking weak in front of her. I didn't want her to know that I still lived in fear of the Alchemists, forced to do whatever it took to get back in their good graces.

"I'm glad," she said. "They told me originally it was your sister that was going to be here."

Those words reminded me again how Zoe could replace me at any moment. "It was a mix-up."

Rose nodded. "Well, I feel a little better with you here, but it's still hard . . . I still feel like I should protect Jill. But I need to protect Lissa too. They think Jill's the easier target, but they're still going after Lissa." The inner turmoil shone in her dark eyes, and I felt a pang of pity. This was what I'd had trouble explaining to the other Alchemists, how dhampirs and vampires could seem so human at times. "It's been crazy, you know. Ever since Lissa took the throne? I thought I'd finally get to relax with Dimitri." Her smile broadened. "I should've known nothing's ever simple with us. We've spent all our time looking out for Lissa and Jill."

"Jill will be okay. As long as the dissidents don't know she's here, it should all be easy. Boring, even."

She was still smiling, but her smile had dimmed a little. "I hope so. If you only knew what had happened . . ." Her expression changed as some memory seized her. I started to insist she tell me what had happened, but she shifted the subject before I could. "We're working on changing the law—the one that says Lissa needs one family member in order to stay queen. Once that's done, both she and Jill will be out of danger. But that just means those who want to take out Jill are more insane than ever, because they know the clock's ticking."

"How long?" I asked. "How long will it take to change the law?"

"I don't know. A few months, maybe? Legal stuff . . . well, it's not my thing. Not the details of it, at least." She grimaced briefly and then became battle tough again. She tossed her hair over one shoulder. "Crazy people who want to hurt my friends? That *is* my thing, and believe me, I know how to deal with it."

"I remember," I said. It was weird. I thought of Rose as one of the strongest people I knew, yet it seemed as though she needed my assurance. "Look, you go do what you do, and I'll do what I do. I'll make sure Jill blends in. You guys got her out without anyone knowing. She's off the grid now."

"I hope so," Rose repeated, voice grim. "Because if she's not, your little group here doesn't stand a chance against those crazy rebels."

CHAPTER 5

AND ON THAT NOTE, Rose left me so she could tell the others goodbye.

Her words left me chilled. For half a second, I wanted to demand a reassessment of this mission. I wanted to insist that they send no less than a dozen guardians here with Jill, in the event her attackers came back. Soon, I dismissed that thought. One of the key parts of this plan working was simply not attracting attention. So long as her whereabouts were secret, Jill was safer if she blended in. A squadron of guardians would hardly be discreet and could attract notice from the larger Moroi community. We were doing the right thing. So long as no one knew we were here, all would be well.

Surely if I told myself that often enough, it would become true.

Yet why Rose's ominous statement? Why Eddie's presence? Had this mission really been bumped from "inconvenient" to "life-threatening"?

Knowing how close Jill and Rose were, I kind of expected their goodbye to be more tearful. Instead, it was Adrian whom Jill had the most difficulty leaving. She flung herself at him in a giant hug, fingers clinging to his shirt. The young Moroi girl had remained quiet for most of the visit, simply watching the rest of us in that curious, nervous way of hers. The most I'd heard her talk was when Lee had tried to draw her out earlier. Her goodbye display seemed to surprise Adrian too, though the snarky look he'd worn on his face softened into something like affection as he awkwardly patted her shoulder.

"There, there, Jailbait. I'll see you again soon."

"I wish you were coming with us," she said in a small voice.

He crooked her a grin. "No, you don't. Maybe the rest of them can get away with playing back-to-school, but I'd be thrown out on my first day. At least here, I won't corrupt any-one . . . unless it's Clarence and his liquor cabinet."

"I'll be in touch," promised Jill.

His smile twitched, and he gave her a knowing look that was both amused and rueful. "So will I."

This small moment between them was odd. With his flippant, arrogant nature and her sweet shyness, they seemed like an unlikely pair of friends. Yet there was obvious affection between them. It didn't seem romantic but had a definite intensity I couldn't quite understand. I remembered the conversation I'd overheard between Abe and Adrian, where Abe had said it was imperative Adrian stay near Jill. Something told me there was a connection between that and what I was witnessing now, but I didn't have enough information to put it all together. I filed this mystery away for later.

I was sad to leave Rose but glad that our departure meant parting ways with Abe and Keith. Abe left with his typically cryptic remarks and a knowing look for me that I didn't appreciate. I dropped Keith off at his place before going on to Amberwood, and he told me he'd keep me updated. Honestly, I wondered what exactly he had to update *me* on, since I was doing most of the work around here. As far as I could tell, he really had nothing to do except lounge around in his downtown apartment. Still, it was worth it to be rid of him. I never thought I'd be so happy to drive off with a vampire and a dhampir.

Jill still seemed troubled during the car ride to the school. Eddie, sensing this, tried to soothe her. He peered back at her from the passenger seat.

"We'll see Adrian soon."

"I know," she said with a sigh.

"And nothing else bad is going to happen. You're safe. They can't find you here."

"I know that too," she said.

"How bad was it?" I asked. "The attack, I mean. No one's getting into details." Out of the corner of my eye, I saw Eddie glance back at Jill again.

"Bad enough," he said grimly. "But everyone's okay now; that's what matters."

Neither of them said any more, and I quickly picked up on the hint that no more details would be forthcoming. They acted as though the attack had been no big deal, that it was done and over with, but they were being *too* evasive. Something had happened that I didn't know about—that the Alchemists likely didn't know about—something that they were working to keep secret. My guess was that it had to do with Adrian being here. He had mentioned an "obvious reason" for coming to Palm Springs, and then Abe had hinted at some ulterior motive that Adrian himself didn't know about. It was all kind of annoying, seeing as I was risking my life here. How did they expect me to adequately do my job if they insisted on making this a tangle of secrets?

Alchemists dealt in secrets, and despite my rocky past, I was still Alchemist enough to resent being denied answers. Fortunately, I was also Alchemist enough to hunt those answers down myself.

Of course, I knew grilling Jill and Eddie right away wasn't going to get me anywhere. I needed to play it friendly and get them to relax around me. They might not harbor the secret belief that humans were creatures of darkness, but that didn't mean they trusted me yet. I didn't blame them. After all, I certainly didn't trust them either.

It was well into evening when we arrived at Amberwood. Keith and I had scoped out the school earlier, but Eddie and Jill took it in with wide eyes. Whereas Clarence's home had seemed old-fashioned, the school was bright and modern, consisting of stucco buildings that were so typical of California and southwest architecture. Palm trees skirted along lush green lawns. In the fading light, students were still strolling, in pairs and groups, along the many walking paths that wove throughout the grounds.

We'd picked up fast food along the way, but the late hour meant Jill and I had to split from Eddie. At eighteen, with a car and "parental permission," I had a lot of freedom to come and go, but I had to answer to curfew just like everyone else when night came. Eddie was uneasy about leaving Jill, particularly when he realized how far away from her he'd be.

Amberwood Prep's sprawling grounds were divided into three campuses: East, West, and Central. East Campus housed the girls' dorm while West contained the boys'. Central, the largest of the three, was where the administrative, academic, and recreational facilities were. The campuses were about a mile apart from each other and served by a shuttle bus that ran throughout the day, though walking was always an option for those who could stand the heat.

Eddie had to have known he couldn't stay in the girls' dorm, though I suspected that if he had his way, he would have slept at the foot of Jill's bed like a loyal dog. Watching the two of them was kind of amazing. I'd never observed a guardian-Moroi pairing before. When I'd been with Rose and Dimitri, they'd been simply trying to keep themselves alive—plus, they were both dhampirs. Now, I was finally able to see the system in action and understood why dhampirs trained so hard. You'd have to, to remain that vigilant. Even in the most mundane moments, Eddie always watched our surroundings. Nothing escaped his notice.

"How good is the security system here?" he demanded when we stepped inside the girls' dorm. He'd insisted on seeing it before going to his own. The lobby was quiet at this hour, and only a couple of students wandered through with boxes and suitcases as they finished last-minute move-ins. They gave us curious looks as they passed, and I had to quell the knot of anxiety rising in me. Considering everything else going on for me, high school social life shouldn't scare me—but it did. The Alchemists didn't cover that in their lessons.

"Security's good enough," I said, keeping my voice low as I turned back to Eddie. "They aren't worried about vampire assassins, but they certainly want their students safe. I know there are security guards that patrol the grounds at night."

Eddie eyed the dorm matron, a stout, gray-haired woman who supervised the lobby from her desk. "Do you think she has any kind of combat training? Do you think she could subdue an intruder?"

"I bet she could wrestle down a guy sneaking into a girl's room," joked Jill. She rested a hand on his arm, making him jump. "Relax. This place is safe."

In some ways, Eddie's concern was comforting and made me feel secure. At the same time, I couldn't help but think again about *why* he was so watchful. He'd been there for the attack that no one would tell me about. He knew the threats because he'd seen them firsthand. If he was this on edge, even now, then how much danger were we still in? The Alchemists had led me to believe that once we were hidden here at Amberwood, all would be well and it would just become a waiting game. I'd had that very conversation with Rose and tried to convince her of the same. Eddie's attitude was concerning.

The dorm room I shared with Jill was small by my standards. I'd always had my own room growing up and never had to worry about sharing space or closets. During my time in St. Petersburg, I'd even had my own apartment. Still, our one window had a sweeping view of the dorm's back courtyard. Everything inside the room was airy and bright, with maple-finished furniture that looked new: beds, desks, and dressers. I had no experience with dorm rooms—but I could only assume by Jill's reaction that we'd gotten a good one. She swore that the room was larger than the one she'd had at her Moroi school, St. Vladimir's Academy, and was quite happy.

I half-wondered if she thought our room was big simply because we had so little to put in it. Neither of us had been able to do much packing with such swift departures. The furniture gave everything a warm, golden feel, but without personal decorations or other touches, the room could've come straight from a catalog. The dorm matron, Mrs. Weathers, had been astonished when she saw us and our minimal luggage. The girls I'd observed moving in earlier had arrived with cars packed to bursting. I hoped we didn't look suspicious.

Jill paused to stare out the window as we got ready for bed. "It's so dry here," she murmured, more to herself than me. "They keep the lawn green, but it's so strange not to feel the moisture in the air." She glanced over at me sheepishly. "I'm a water user."

"I know," I said, not sure what else to add. She was referring to the magical abilities all Moroi possessed. Each Moroi specialized in one of the elements, either the physical four—earth, air, water, and fire—or the more intangible and psychic element of spirit. Hardly anyone wielded that last one, though I'd heard Adrian was one of the few. If Jill couldn't access her magic easily, I wasn't going to be disappointed. Magic was one of those things, like the blood drinking, that served as a slap-in-the-face reminder that these people I was laughing and eating with were not human.

If I wasn't still exhausted from the drive with Keith, I probably would've lain awake agonizing over the fact that I was sleeping close to a vampire. When I'd first met Rose, I hadn't even been able to stay in the same room with her. Our hectic escape together had changed that a little, and by the end, I'd been able to let my guard down. Now, some of that old fear came back in the darkness. *Vampire, vampire.* Sternly, I told myself it was just Jill. I had nothing to worry about. Eventually, fatigue triumphed fear, and I slept.

When morning came, I couldn't help looking in the mirror to make sure I had no bite marks or other sign of vampire harm. When I'd finished, I immediately felt foolish. With the difficulty Jill was currently having waking up, it made no sense to imagine her sneaking up on me in the night. As it was, I had a hard time getting her out the door in time for orientation. She was groggy, with bloodshot eyes, and kept complaining about a headache. I guessed I didn't have to worry about nighttime attacks from my roommate.

Nonetheless, she managed to get up and around. We left our dorm and found Eddie, gathering with other new students near a fountain on Central Campus. Most of the crowd appeared to be freshmen like Jill. Only a few were the same age as me and Eddie, and I was surprised to see him easily chatting with those around him. With how vigilant he'd been the day before, I would've expected him to be more on guard, less capable of normal social interaction—but he fit right in. As we walked up, however, I caught him glance around stealthily at his surroundings. He might be playing a student, like me—but he was still a dhampir.

He was just telling us about how he hadn't met his roommate yet when a smiling guy with bright blue eyes and reddish hair strode up to them.

"Hey there," he said. Up close, I could see a smattering of freckles. "Are you Eddie Melrose?"

"Yes, I'm—" Eddie had spun around with that guardian efficiency, ready to take on this potential threat. When he saw the newcomer, Eddie went perfectly still. His eyes widened slightly, and whatever he'd been about to say faded away.

"I'm Micah Vallence. I'm your roommate—also your orientation leader." He nodded toward the other mingling students and grinned. "But I wanted to come say hi first since I just got here this morning. My mom pushed our vacation to the limits."

Eddie was still staring at Micah as though he'd seen a ghost. I studied Micah too, wondering what I was missing. He seemed normal to me. Whatever was going on, Jill was also out of the loop because she was regarding Micah with a perfectly ordinary expression too, no alarm or surprise.

"Nice to meet you," said Eddie at last. "These are my, uh, sisters—Jill and Sydney."

Micah smiled at each of us in turn. He had a manner about him that made me feel easy, and I could see why he'd been drafted as an orientation leader. I wondered why Eddie was reacting so strangely.

"What grades are you in?" he asked us.

"Senior," I said. Remembering the cover story, I added, "Eddie and I are twins."

"I'm a freshman," said Jill.

Looking over our "family," I noticed that Eddie and I could probably pass for siblings pretty easily. Our coloring was similar, and of course, there was the fact that we both looked human. While a human wouldn't necessarily look at Jill and say "vampire!" she still possessed certain features that marked her as unusual. Her build and paleness were definite contrasts to me and Eddie.

If Micah noticed the lack of family resemblance, he didn't let on. "Nervous about starting high school?" he asked Jill.

She shook her head and smiled back. "I'm ready for the challenge."

"Well, if you need anything, let me know," he said. "For now, I've gotta get this party started. Talk to you guys later."

From the way his attention focused solely on her, it was obvious that the "if you need anything" was directed at Jill, and her blush showed that she knew too. She smiled, holding his gaze a moment, and then looked away shyly. I would've found it cute, if not for the alarming prospect it presented. Jill was in a school full of humans. It was absolutely out of the question for her to date one, and guys like Micah couldn't be encouraged. Eddie didn't appear to care about the comment, but it seemed to be more because he was still troubled about Micah in general.

Micah called our group to attention and began the orientation. The first part of it was simply a tour of the grounds. We followed him around, in and out of air conditioning, as he showed us the important buildings. He explained the shuttle system, and we rode it up to West Campus, which was almost a mirror of East. Boys and girls were allowed in each other's dorms, with limitations, and he explained those rules as well, which caused some grumbling. Recalling the formidable Mrs. Weathers, I felt sorry for any boy that tried to break her dorm rules.

Both dorms had their own cafeterias, where any student was welcome to eat, and our orientation group had lunch while we were still on West Campus. Micah joined my "siblings" and me, going out of his way to talk to each of us. Eddie responded politely, nodding and asking questions, but his eyes still looked vaguely haunted. Jill was shy at first, but once Micah starting joking around with her, she eventually warmed up to him.

How funny, I thought, that it was easier for Eddie and Jill to adapt to this situation than it was for me. They were in a strange environment, with a different race, but were still among familiar things, like cafeterias and lockers. They slipped right into the roles and procedures with no difficulty. Meanwhile, despite having traveled and lived all over the world, I felt out of place in what was for everyone else an ordinary setting.

Regardless, it didn't take me long to figure out how the school ran. Alchemists were trained to observe and adapt, and even though school was foreign to me, I quickly picked up on the routine. I wasn't afraid to talk to people either—I was used to striking up conversations with strangers and explaining my way out of situations. One thing, however, I knew I would have to work on.

"I heard her family might be moving to Anchorage." We were at orientation lunch, and a couple of freshmen girls sitting near me were discussing a friend of theirs who hadn't shown up today.

The other girl's eyes widened. "Seriously? I would *die* if I had to move there."

"I don't know," I mused, moving my food around my plate. "With all the sun and UV rays here, it seems like Anchorage might actually provide a longer life span. You don't need as much sunblock, so it's a more economical choice as well."

I'd thought my comment was helpful, but when I looked up, I was met with gaping stares. It was obvious from the looks the girls were giving me that I probably couldn't have picked a weirder comment.

"I guess I shouldn't say everything that comes to mind," I murmured to Eddie. I was used to being direct in social situations, but it occurred to me that simply saying "Yeah, totally!" would've probably been the correct response. I'd had few friends my own age and was out of practice.

Eddie grinned at me. "I don't know, sis. You're pretty entertaining as you are. Keep it up."

After lunch, our group returned to Central Campus, where we parted ways to meet with academic advisors and plan our class schedules. When I sat down with my advisor, a cheery young woman named Molly, I wasn't surprised to see that the Alchemists had sent along academic records from a fictitious school in South Dakota. They were even fairly consistent with what I had studied in my homeschooling.

"Your grades and tests have placed you in our most advanced math and English classes," Molly said. "If you do well in them, you can receive college credit." *Too bad there's no chance I'll get to go to college,* I thought with a sigh. She flipped through a few pages in my file. "Now, I don't see any records of foreign language here. It's an Amberwood requirement that everyone learn at least one language."

Oops. The Alchemists had messed up there in faking my records. I'd actually studied a number of languages. My father had made sure I had lessons from an early age, since an Alchemist never knew where he or she might end up. Scanning Amberwood's list of offered languages, I hesitated and wondered if I should lie. Then I decided I really didn't want to sit through conjugations and tenses I'd already learned.

"I already know all of these," I told Molly.

Molly regarded me skeptically. "All of these? There are five languages here."

I nodded and added helpfully, "But I only studied Japanese for two years. So I suppose I could learn more."

Molly still didn't seem to buy this. "Would you be willing to take proficiency tests?"

And so, I ended up spending the rest of my afternoon laboring over foreign languages. It wasn't how I wanted to spend my day, but I supposed it would pay off later—the tests were a breeze.

When I finally finished all five languages three hours later, Molly hurried me out to get fitted for my uniform. Most of the other new students had long gone through already, and she was concerned that I might have already missed the woman doing the fittings. I moved as fast as I could without running down the halls and nearly bumped into two girls rounding a corner.

"Oh!" I exclaimed, feeling like an idiot. "I'm sorry—I'm late for my fitting—"

One of them laughed good-naturedly. She was dark-skinned with an athletic build and wavy black hair. "Don't worry about it," she said. "We just walked past the room. She's still there."

The other girl had blond hair a shade lighter than mine that she wore in a high ponytail. Both of them had the easy assurance of those who knew their way around this world. These weren't new students.

"Mrs. Delaney always takes longer than she thinks she will with the fittings," the blond girl said knowingly. "Every year, it's—" Her jaw dropped, her words freezing up for a few moments. "Where . . . where did you get that?"

I had no clue what she meant, but the other girl soon noticed and leaned closer to me. "That's amazing! Is that what they're doing this year?"

"Your tattoo," explained the blonde. I must have still looked clueless. "Where'd you get it?"

"Oh. That." My fingers absentmindedly touched my cheek. "In, um, South Dakota. Where I'm from."

Both girls looked disappointed. "I guess that's why I've never seen it," said the dark-haired girl. "I thought Nevermore was doing something new."

"Nevermore?" I asked.

The girls exchanged silent glances, and some message passed between them. "You're new, right? What's your name?" asked the blond girl. "I'm Julia. This is Kristin."

"Sydney," I said, still mystified.

Julia was smiling again. "Have lunch with us at East tomorrow, okay? We'll explain everything."

"Everything about what?" I asked.

"It's a long story. Just get to Delaney for now," added Kristin, starting to move away. "She'll stay late, but not forever."

When they were gone, I continued on my way—much more slowly—wondering what that had been about. Had I just made friends? I really wasn't sure how one went about it in a school like this, but that whole exchange had seemed pretty weird.

Mrs. Delaney was just packing up when I arrived. "What size do you wear, dear?" she asked, catching sight of me in the doorway.

"Two."

A number of articles were produced: skirts, pants, blouses, and sweaters. I doubted the sweaters would see much wear, unless a freak apocalyptic blizzard hit Palm Springs. Amberwood wasn't particularly fussy about which ensemble students wore, as long as it came from the approved pool of fashion. The colors were burgundy, dark gray, and white, which I actually thought looked kind of nice together.

Watching me button a white blouse, Mrs. Delaney tsked, "I think you need a size four."

I froze mid-button. "I wear a two."

"Oh, yes, you can fit into them, but look at the arms and the skirt length. I think you'll be more comfortable in a four. Try these." She handed over a new stack and then laughed. "Don't look so mortified, girl! A four's nothing. You're still a twig." She patted her ample stomach. "We could fit three of you into my clothes!"

Despite my many protests, I was still sent away with the size-four clothing. I rode back to my dorm, dejected, and found Jill lying on her bed and reading. She sat up at my arrival.

"Hey, I wondered what had happened to you."

"Got delayed," I said with a sigh. "Are you feeling better?"

"Yeah. A lot." Jill watched as I put away the uniforms. "They're pretty terrible, right? We didn't have uniforms at St. Vladimir's. It's going to be so boring wearing the same thing every day." I didn't want to tell her that as an Alchemist, I might have worn an outfit like this anyway.

"What size did you get?" I asked, to change the subject. I was kind of a glutton for punishment.

"Two."

A twinge of annoyance shot through me as I hung my uniforms in the closet beside hers. I felt huge by comparison. How were all those Moroi so skinny? Genetics? Low-carb blood diet?

Maybe it was just because they were all so tall. All I knew was that whenever I spent time around them, I felt frumpy and awkward and wanted to eat less.

When I finished unpacking, Jill and I compared schedules. Not surprisingly, considering the difference in grades, we had almost nothing in common. The only thing we shared was a multi-grade PE class. All students were required to take it every semester, since fitness was considered part of a well-rounded student's experience. Maybe I could lose a few pounds and get back into my normal size.

Jill smiled and handed my schedule back. "Eddie went and demanded to be in our PE class since it's pretty much the only one we could share. It conflicts with his Spanish class, though, and they wouldn't let him. I don't think he can handle going the whole school day without seeing that I'm alive. Oh, and Micah's with us in PE."

I'd stalked off to my bed, still irritated about the uniforms. Jill's words caught my attention. "Hey, do you know why Eddie seemed weirded out around Micah?"

Jill shook her head. "No, I didn't get a chance to ask, but I noticed it too—especially at first. Later—while you were testing—and we were waiting for uniforms, Eddie seemed to chill out. A little. Every once in a while, I'd see him giving Micah a strange look, though."

"You don't think he thinks Micah's dangerous, do you?"

Jill shrugged. "He didn't seem dangerous to me, but I'm no guardian. If Eddie did think he was some kind of threat, it seems like he'd be acting differently. More aggressive. He mostly seems nervous around Micah. Almost—but not quite—afraid. And that's weirdest of all because guardians *never* look scared. Not that Eddie's technically a guardian. But you know what I mean."

"I do," I said, smiling despite my grumpy intentions. That cute, rambling nature cheered me up a little. "What do you mean Eddie's *technically* not a guardian? Isn't he assigned to protect you here?"

"Yeah, he is," said Jill, toying with one of her light brown curls. "But . . . well, it's kind of weird. He got in some trouble with the guardians for helping Rose and for, um, killing a guy."

"He killed a Moroi that attacked Vasilisa, right?" It had come up at my interrogation.

"Yeah," said Jill, lost in her own memories. "It was self-defense—well, and defense of Lissa, but everyone was shocked at him killing a Moroi. Guardians aren't supposed to do that, but then, you know, Moroi aren't supposed to attack each other either. Anyway, he was put on suspension. No one knew what to do with him. When I got . . . attacked, Eddie helped protect me. Later, Lissa said it was stupid to keep him off duty when he could be helpful and that considering Moroi were behind this attack too, she said everyone was going to have to get used to the idea of Moroi being the enemy. Hans—the guardian in charge at Court—finally agreed and sent Eddie here with me, but I think officially, Eddie's not restored yet. It's weird." Jill had delivered the whole speech without pausing and now stopped to catch a breath.

"Well, I'm sure it'll be sorted out," I said, trying to be reassuring. "And it seems like he'll get points for keeping a princess alive."

Jill looked at me sharply. "I'm no princess."

I frowned and tried to remember the complexities of Moroi law. "The prince or princess is the oldest member of a family. Since Vasilisa's queen, the title rolls over to you, right?"

"On paper," said Jill, looking away. Her tone was hard to read, an odd mixture of what seemed like bitterness and sorrow. "I'm not a princess, not really. I'm just someone who happens to be related to the queen."

Jill's mother had briefly been mistress to Eric Dragomir, Vasilisa's father, and had kept Jill's existence a secret for years. It had only come out recently, and I'd played a big role in helping Rose track Jill down. With all the fallout in my own life, as well as the emphasis on Jill's safety, I hadn't spent much time wondering how she had adapted to her new status. That had to be a serious lifestyle change.

"I'm sure there's more to it than that," I said gently. I wondered if I was going to be spending a lot of time playing therapist to Jill during this assignment. The prospect of actually *comforting* a vampire still seemed so strange to me. "I mean, you're obviously important. Everyone's gone to a lot of trouble to keep you safe here."

"But is it for me?" asked Jill. "Or is it to help Lissa keep the throne? She's hardly spoken to me since she found out we were sisters."

This conversation was steering into uncomfortable waters, into interpersonal matters that I didn't really know how to deal with. I couldn't imagine being in either Vasilisa or Jill's place. The only thing I felt certain of was that it couldn't be easy for any of them.

"I'm sure she cares about you," I said, though not really

sure at all. "But it's probably strange for her—especially with all the other changes in her life too. Give it time. Focus on the important things first—staying here and staying alive."

"You're right," said Jill. She lay back on her bed and stared up at the ceiling. "I'm nervous about tomorrow, about being around everyone, in classes all day. What if they notice? What if someone finds out the truth about me?"

"You did fine at orientation," I assured her. "Just don't show your fangs. And besides, I'm pretty good at convincing people they didn't see what they think they saw."

The grateful expression on her face reminded me uncomfortably of Zoe. They were so alike in many ways, shy and uncertain—yet intensely fierce and desperately wanting to prove themselves. I'd tried to protect Zoe—and only failed in her eyes. Now, being here for Jill made me feel conflicted. In some ways, I could make up for what I hadn't been able to do for Zoe. Yet even as I thought that, some inner voice kept saying, *Jill is not your sister. She's a vampire. This is business.*

"Thanks, Sydney. I'm glad you're here." She smiled, and the guilt only twisted further inside me. "You know, I'm kind of jealous of Adrian. He thinks it's so boring at Clarence's, but he doesn't have to worry about meeting new people or getting used to a new school. He just gets to hang out, watch TV, play pool with Lee, sleep in . . . it sounds amazing." She sighed.

"I suppose," I said, a little surprised at the detail. "How do you know all that? Have you . . . have you talked to him since we left?" Even as I said that, the idea seemed unlikely. I'd been with her most of the day.

The smile dropped from her face. "Oh no. I mean, I just figure that's what's going on. He mentioned some of it earlier, that's all. Sorry. I'm being melodramatic and rambling. Thanks for listening to me . . . it really does make me feel better."

I smiled tightly and said nothing. I still couldn't get over the fact that I was starting to feel so warmly toward a vampire. First Rose, now Jill? It didn't matter how likable she was. I had to keep our relationship professional so that no Alchemist could accuse me of getting attached. Keith's words echoed in my head: *vamp lover . . .*

That's ridiculous, I thought. There was nothing wrong with being nice to those in my care. It was normal, a far cry from "getting too close" to them. Right? Pushing my worries aside, I concentrated on finishing unpacking and thinking about our new life here. I sincerely hoped tomorrow would go as smoothly as I'd assured Jill it would.

Unfortunately, it didn't.

CHAPTER 6

To be fair, the day started off great.

Sunlight was streaming in through the windows when we woke up, and I could already feel the heat even though it was early morning. I chose my lightest ensemble from the uniform selection: a gray skirt, paired with a short-sleeved white blouse. "Simple jewelry" was allowed, so I kept the gold cross on. My hair was having one of its difficult days—which seemed to be more often than not in this new climate. I wished I could pull it in a ponytail, like Jill did with hers, but it had too many layers to do that neatly. Eyeing where they hit my shoulders at different lengths, I wondered if maybe it was time to grow it out.

After a breakfast neither of us really ate, we rode the shuttle bus up to Central Campus, which was suddenly packed with people. Only about a third of the students were boarders. The rest were locals, and they had all turned out today. Jill barely spoke throughout the entire ride and seemed to be sick again. It was hard to say, but I thought she looked paler than usual.

Her eyes were bloodshot once more, heavy with dark circles. I'd woken up once in the night and seen her fast asleep, so I wasn't entirely sure what the problem was. Those dark circles were actually the first flaw I'd ever seen in any Moroi's skin—it was always perfect, porcelain. No wonder she could usually sleep in late. She didn't have to bother with the powder and concealer I used.

As the morning progressed, Jill kept biting her lip and looking worriedly around. Maybe she was just nervous about immersing herself in a world populated entirely with humans. She didn't seem at all concerned about the logistics of getting to the right rooms and completing work. That was the aspect that still scared me a little. *Just get from one class to another,* I told myself. *That's all you have to do.*

My first class was ancient history. Eddie was in it too, and he practically ran me down when he saw me. "Is she okay? Have you seen her?"

"Well, we share a room, so yeah." We sat down at neighboring desks. I smiled at Eddie. "Relax. She's fine. She seemed nervous, but I can't really blame her."

He nodded but still looked uncertain. He gave his full attention to the front of the room when the teacher stepped up, but there was a restlessness about Eddie as he sat there, like he could just barely stop himself from springing up to go check on Jill.

"Welcome, welcome." Our instructor was a forty-something woman with white-streaked, wiry black hair and enough nervous energy to rival Eddie—and if her giant coffee cup was any indication, it wasn't hard to figure out why. I was also a little jealous and wished we were allowed to have beverages in class—particularly since the dorm cafeteria didn't serve coffee. I didn't know how I was going to survive the next few months with caffeine-free days. Her wardrobe favored argyle. "I am Ms. Terwilliger, your illustrious guide on the wondrous journey that is ancient history." She spoke in a sweeping, grandiose voice that made a few of my classmates break into snickers. She gestured to a young man who'd been sitting behind her, near the large desk. He'd been watching the class with a bored expression, but when she turned to him, he perked up. "And this is my co-guide, Trey, whom I believe some of you may know. Trey is my student aide for this period, so he'll mostly be skulking in corners and filing papers. But you should be nice to him since he may very well be the one entering your grades into my computer."

Trey gave a small wave and grinned at some of his friends. He had deeply tanned skin and black hair whose length flirted with the dress code's rules. The neatly pressed Amberwood uniform gave him the illusion of all business, but there was a mischievous glint in his dark eyes that made me think he didn't really take being an aide seriously.

"Now," continued Ms. Terwilliger. "History is important because it teaches us about the past. And by learning about the past, you come to understand the present, so that you may make educated decisions about the future."

She paused dramatically to let those words sink in. Once she was convinced we were awed, she moved over to a laptop that was wired up to a projector. She pushed a few keys, and an image of a white-pillared building appeared on the screen at the front of the room.

"Now, then. Can anyone tell me what this is?"

"A temple?" someone called out.

"Very good, Mr.—?"

"Robinson," the boy supplied.

Ms. Terwilliger produced a clipboard and scanned a list. "Ah, there you are. Robinson. Stephanie."

"*Stephan*," corrected the boy, flushing as some of his friends giggled.

Ms. Terwilliger pushed her glasses up her nose and squinted. "So you are. Thank goodness. I was just thinking how difficult your life must be with such a name. My apologies. I broke my glasses in a freak croquet accident this weekend, forcing me to bring my old ones today. So, Stephan-not-Stephanie, you're correct. It's a temple. Can you be more specific?"

Stephan shook his head.

"Can anyone else offer any insight?"

When only silence met Ms. Terwilliger, I took a deep breath and raised my hand. Time to see what it was like to be a real student. She nodded toward me.

"It's the Parthenon, ma'am."

"Indeed it is," she said. "And your name is?"

"Sydney."

"Sydney . . ." She checked the clipboard and looked up in astonishment. "Sydney Melbourne? My goodness. You don't sound Australian."

"Er, it's Sydney Melrose, ma'am," I corrected.

Ms. Terwilliger scowled and handed the clipboard to Trey, who seemed to think my name was the funniest thing ever. "You take over, Mr. Juarez. Your youthful eyes are better than mine. If I keep at this, I'll keep turning boys into girls and perfectly nice young ladies into the descendants of criminals. So." Ms.

Terwilliger focused back on me. "The Parthenon. Do you know anything about it?"

The others were watching me, mostly with friendly curiosity, but I still felt the pressure of being the center of attention. Focusing solely on Ms. Terwilliger, I said, "It's part of the Acropolis, ma'am. In Athens. It was built in the fifth century BC."

"No need to call me 'ma'am,'" Ms. Terwilliger told me. "Though it is refreshing to get a bit of respect for a change. And brilliantly answered."

She glanced over the rest of the room. "Now, tell me this. Why on earth should we care about Athens or anything that took place over fifteen hundred years ago? How can that be relevant to us today?"

More silence and shifting eyes. When the unbearable quiet dragged on for what felt like hours, I started to raise my hand again. Ms. Terwilliger didn't notice and glanced back at Trey, who was resting his feet on the teacher's desk. The boy instantly dropped his legs and straightened up.

"Mr. Juarez," declared Ms. Terwilliger. "Time to earn your keep. You took this class last year. Can you tell them why the events of ancient Athens are relevant to us today? If you don't, then I'm going to have to call on Miss Melbourne again. She looks like she knows the answer, and think how embarrassing that will be for you."

Trey's eyes flicked to me and then back to the teacher. "Her name is Melrose, not Melbourne. And democracy was founded in Athens in the sixth century. A lot of the procedures they set into place are still in effect with our government today."

Ms. Terwilliger clasped her hand over her heart dramatically.

"You *were* paying attention last year! Well, almost. Your date is off." Her gaze fell on me. "I bet you know the date democracy was started in Athens."

"The fifth century," I answered immediately.

That earned me a smile from the teacher and a glare from Trey. The rest of the class proceeded in much the same way. Ms. Terwilliger continued on with her flamboyant style and highlighted a number of important times and places that we were going to study in more detail. I found I could answer any question she asked. Some part of me said I should ration myself, but I couldn't help it. If no one knew the answer, I felt compelled to provide it. And each time I did, Ms. Terwilliger would say, "Trey, did you know that?" I winced. I really didn't want to make enemies on my first day. The other students watched me curiously when I spoke, which made me a little self-conscious. I also saw a few of them exchange knowing looks each time I answered, as though they were in on some secret I wasn't. That concerned me more than irritating Trey did. Did it sound like I was showing off? I was too unsure of the social politics here to understand what was normal and what wasn't. This was an academically competitive school. Surely it wasn't a bad thing to be educated?

Ms. Terwilliger left us with an assignment to read the first two chapters of our textbook. The others groaned, but I was excited. I loved history, specifically the history of art and architecture. My homeschooling had been aggressive and well rounded, but that particular subject wasn't one my father had thought we needed to spend a lot of time on. I'd had to study it on my own time, and it was both startling and luxurious to think I now had a class whose sole purpose was to learn about this *and* that my knowledge would be valued—by the teacher, at least.

I parted ways with Eddie after that and went off to AP Chemistry. While I was waiting for class to start, Trey slid into a desk beside me.

"So, Miss Melbourne," he said, imitating Ms. Terwilliger's voice. "When will you be starting up your own history class?"

I was sorry Ms. Terwilliger had picked on him, but I didn't like his tone. "Are you actually taking this class? Or are you going to lounge around some more and pretend to be helping the teacher?"

This brought a grin to his face. "Oh, I'm in this one, unfortunately. And I was Ms. T's best student last year. If you're as good at chemistry as you are in history, then I'm nabbing you for a lab partner. I'll be able to take the whole semester off."

Chemistry was a crucial part of the Alchemists' trade, and I doubted there was anything in this class I didn't already know. The Alchemists had arisen in the Middle Ages as "magical scientists" trying to turn lead into gold. From those early experiments, they'd gone on to discover the special properties of vampire blood and how it reacted with other substances, eventually branching out into the crusade to keep vampires and humans separate from one another. That earlier scientific background, and our current work with vampire blood, made chemistry one of the main subjects of my childhood education. I'd received my first chemistry set when I was six. When other kids were practicing the alphabet, my father was grilling me with acid and base flash cards.

Unable to admit as much to Trey, I averted my eyes and casually brushed hair from my face. "I'm okay in it."

His gaze moved to my cheek, and a look of understanding came over him. "Ah. So that's it."

"What's it?" I asked.

He pointed to my face. "Your tattoo. *That's* what it does, huh?"

In moving my hair, I'd revealed the gold lily. "What do you mean?" I asked.

"You don't have to play coy with me," he said, rolling his dark eyes. "I get it. I mean, it seems like cheating to me, but I guess not everyone cares about honor. Pretty ballsy to have it on your face, though. They're against the dress code, you know—not that that stops anyone."

I shifted and let my hair fall back into place. "I know. I meant to put makeup on it and forgot. But what do you mean about cheating?"

He simply shook his head in a way that clearly said I'd been dismissed. I sat there feeling helpless, wondering what I'd done wrong. Soon, my confusion was replaced by dismay as our instructor gave us an introduction to the class and its setup. I had a chemistry set back in my room that was more extensive than Amberwood's. Oh well. I supposed a little elementary review wouldn't hurt me.

My other classes progressed in a similar way. I was on top of all my subjects and found myself answering every question. This got me in good with my teachers, but I couldn't gauge the rest of my classmates' reactions. I still saw a lot of rueful head shakes and intrigued expressions—but only Trey actually condemned. I didn't know if I should hold back or not.

I ran into Kristin and Julia a couple of times, and they reminded me to join them for lunch. I did, finding them sitting in a corner table in East's cafeteria. They waved me over, and as I wove through the rows of tables, I did a quick scan, hoping to see Jill. I hadn't run into her all day, but that wasn't too shocking, considering our schedules. Presumably, she was eating over at the other cafeteria, maybe with Eddie or Micah.

Kristin and Julia were friendly, chatting me up about how my first day had gone and imparting wisdom about certain teachers they'd had before. They were seniors like me, and we shared a couple classes. We spent most of lunch exchanging basic info, like where we were all from. It wasn't until lunch was winding down that I began to get answers to some of the questions that had been bugging me all day. Although it required wading through still more questions first.

"So," said Kristin, leaning across the table. "Does it just give you a super memory? Or does it like, I don't know, actually change your brain and make you smarter?"

Julia rolled her eyes. "It can't make you smarter. It's gotta be memory. What I want to know is, how long does it last?"

I glanced back and forth between them, more confused than ever. "Whatever you're talking about can't be making me smarter, because I'm so lost right now."

Kristin laughed at that. "Your tattoo. I heard you answering all the hardest questions in math. And a friend of mine is in your history class and said you were dominating there too. We're trying to figure out how the tattoo helps you."

"Helps me . . . answer questions?" I asked. Their faces confirmed as much. "It doesn't. That stuff . . . that's just, well, me. I just know the answers."

"No one's that smart," argued Julia.

"It's not that crazy. I'm no genius. I guess I've just learned a lot. I was homeschooled part of the time, and my dad was really . . . strict," I added, thinking that might help.

"Oh," said Kristin, toying with a long braid. I'd noticed she wore her dark hair in very practical ways while blond Julia's was always teased and tousled. "I guess that could be it . . . but then, what does your tattoo do?"

"It doesn't do anything," I said. Yet even as I spoke the words, I felt a slight tingle in my flesh. The tattoo had a kind of magic in it that stopped me from speaking about anything Alchemist-related to those who weren't part of the inner circle. This was the tattoo stopping me from saying too much, not that there was any need. "I just thought it was cool."

"Oh," said Julia. Both girls looked inexplicably disappointed.

"Why on earth would you think the tattoo is making me smart?" I asked.

The warning bell interrupted further conversation, reminding us all it was time to get to our next class. There was a pause as Kristin and Julia considered something. Kristin seemed to be the leader of the two because she was the one who gave a decisive nod. I had the distinct feeling I was being assessed.

"Okay," she said finally, giving me a big smile. "We'll fill you in more on everything later."

We set up a time to hang out and study later, then parted ways. My impression was that more socialization than studying would go on, which was fine with me, but I made a mental note to get my homework done first. The rest of the day went quickly, and I received a note in one class from Molly the advisor. As expected, I'd passed out of all of my language courses, and she wanted me to come by and discuss matters during the last period, when I technically had no class. This meant that my school day would officially wrap up with PE.

I changed into my assigned gym clothes, shorts and an Amberwood T-shirt, and trekked outside into the hot sun with the others. I'd felt a little of the heat ducking between classes today, but it wasn't until I actually had to stand outside for any length of time that I really and truly appreciated the fact that we were out in the desert. Glancing around at my classmates, who were guys and girls of all grades, I saw that I wasn't the only one sweating. I rarely burned but reminded myself to pick up sunscreen to be safe. Jill would need it too.

Jill!

I peered around. I'd nearly forgotten that Jill was supposed to be in the same class. Except, where was she? There was no sign of her. When our instructor, Miss Carson, called attendance, she didn't even say Jill's name. I wondered if there'd been a last-minute schedule change.

Miss Carson believed in jumping right into the action. We were divided into teams for volleyball, and I found myself standing beside Micah. His fair, freckled complexion was growing pink, and I almost wanted to suggest sunscreen to him as well. He gave me one of his friendly smiles.

"Hey," I said. "You haven't seen my sister today, have you? Jill?"

"No," he said. A slight frown crossed his forehead. "Eddie was looking for her at lunch. He figured she was eating with you over at your dorm."

I shook my head, a queasy feeling welling in my stomach. What was going on? Nightmare scenarios flashed through my mind. I'd thought Eddie was overreacting with his vigilance, but had something happened to Jill? Was it possible that, despite all our planning, one of Jill's enemies had slipped in and stolen her out from under us? Was I going to have to tell the Alchemists—and my father—that we'd lost Jill on the first day? Panic flashed through me. If I wasn't about to be sent to a re-education center before, I definitely was on my way to one now.

"Are you okay?" Micah asked, studying me. "Is Jill okay?"

"I don't know," I said. "Excuse me." I broke out of my team formation and jogged over to where Miss Carson was supervising.

"Yes?" she asked me.

"I'm sorry to bother you, ma'am, but I'm worried about my sister. Jill Melrose. I'm Sydney. She's supposed to be in here. Do you know if she changed classes?"

"Ah, yes. Melrose. I got a note from the office, just before class, that she wouldn't be attending today."

"Did they say why?"

Miss Carson shook her head apologetically and barked an order to some guy who was slacking off. I rejoined my team, mind spinning. Well, at least someone had seen Jill today, but why on earth would she not be attending?

"Is she okay?" Micah asked me.

"I . . . I guess. Miss Carson seemed to know she wouldn't be in class but doesn't know why."

"Is there anything I can do?" he asked. "To help her? Er, you guys?"

"No, thanks. That's nice of you to ask." I wished there was a clock around. "I'll check on her as soon as class is over." A thought suddenly occurred to me. "But Micah? Don't say anything to Eddie."

Micah gave me a curious look. "Why not?"

"He's overprotective. He'll worry when it's probably nothing."

Also, he'll tear the school apart looking for her.

When class ended, I quickly showered and changed clothes before heading to the administrative building. I was desperate to run back to the dorm first to see if Jill was there, but I couldn't be late for the appointment. As I walked down a hallway to Molly's office, I passed by the main one—and an idea came to me. I stopped in to talk to the attendance secretary before going to my appointment.

"Jill Melrose," the secretary said, nodding. "She was sent back to her dorm."

"Sent back?" I exclaimed. "What does that mean?"

"I'm not at liberty to say." Melodramatic much?

Annoyed and more confused than ever, I went to Molly's office, taking comfort in the fact that even if Jill's absence was mysterious, at least it was sanctioned by the school. Molly told me I could either take another elective or engage in some kind of independent study in place of a language, if I got a teacher to sponsor me. An idea popped into my head.

"Can I check in with you tomorrow?" I asked. "I need to talk to someone first."

"Sure," said Molly. "Just decide soon. You can go back to your dorm now, but we can't have you wandering around every day during this time."

I assured her she'd have an answer soon and headed back. The shuttle bus didn't run very often during classes, so I just walked the mile back. It only took fifteen minutes but felt twice as long in the heat. When I finally reached the dorm room, relief flooded me. Hanging out in our room as if nothing strange had happened was Jill.

"You're all right!"

Jill was lying on the bed, reading her book again. She looked up morosely. "Yeah. Kind of."

I sat down on my own bed and kicked off my shoes. "What happened? I had a panic attack when you weren't in class. If Eddie knew—"

Jill sat bolt upright. "No, don't tell Eddie. He'll freak out."

"Okay, okay. But tell me what happened. They said you got *sent* here?"

"Yeah." Jill made a face. "Because I was kicked out of my first class."

I was speechless. I couldn't imagine what sweet, shy Jill could have possibly done to warrant that. *Oh, God. I hope she didn't bite someone.* I was the one everyone expected to have trouble fitting into a school schedule. Jill should have been a pro.

"What were you kicked out for?"

Jill sighed. "For having a hangover."

More speechlessness. *"What?"*

"I was sick. Ms. Chang—my teacher—took one look at me and said she could spot a hangover a mile away. She sent me to the office for breaking school rules. I told them I was just sick, but she kept saying she *knew*. The principal finally said there was no way to prove that's why I was sick, so I didn't get punished, but I wasn't allowed to go to the rest of my classes. I had to stay here for the rest of the school day."

"That's . . . that's idiotic!" I shot to my feet and began pacing. Now that I'd recovered from my initial disbelief, I was simply outraged. "I was with you last night. You slept here. I should know. I woke up once, and you were out cold. How can Ms. Chang even make an accusation like that? She had no proof! The school didn't either. They had no right to send you out of class. I should go to the office right now! No, I'm going to talk to Keith and the Alchemists and have our 'parents' file a complaint."

"No, wait, Sydney." Jill jumped up and caught ahold of my arm, as though afraid I would march out then and there. "Please. Don't. Just let it go. I don't want to cause any more trouble. I didn't get any bad marks. I wasn't really punished."

"You're behind in your classes," I said. "That's punishment enough."

Jill shook her head, eyes wide. She was afraid, I realized, but I had no idea why she wouldn't want me to tell. She was the victim here. "No, it's fine. I'll catch up. There are no long-term consequences. Please don't make a big deal out of this. The other teachers probably just thought I was sick. They probably don't even know about the accusations."

"It's not right, though," I growled. "I can do something about it. It's what I'm here for, to help you."

"No," said Jill adamantly. "Please. Let it go. If you really want to help . . ." She averted her eyes.

"What?" I asked, still filled with righteous fury. "What do you need? Name it."

Jill looked back up. "I need you . . . I need you to take me to Adrian."

CHAPTER 7

"ADRIAN?" I SAID IN SURPRISE. "What's he have to do with any of this?"

Jill simply shook her head and looked at me beseechingly. "Please. Just take me to him."

"But we'll be back there in a couple days for your feeding."

"I know," said Jill. "But I need to see him *now*. He's the only one who will understand."

I found that hard to believe. "You're saying I wouldn't? Or that even Eddie wouldn't?"

She groaned. "No. You *can't* tell Eddie. He'll flip out."

I tried not to frown as I mulled everything over. Why would Jill need to see Adrian after this mishap at school? Adrian couldn't do anything to help that I couldn't. As an Alchemist, I was in the best position to file a complaint. Did Jill just want moral support? I remembered how Jill had hugged Adrian goodbye and suddenly wondered if she had a crush on him. Because surely, if Jill needed to feel protected by someone, Eddie would be a better source to turn to. Or would he? Eddie was likely to go throwing office desks around in his outrage. Keeping this from him might not be a bad idea.

"Okay," I said at last. "Let's go."

I signed us out for off-campus travel, which took a little finagling. Mrs. Weathers was quick to point out that Jill had been banished to her dorm for the rest of the school day. I was equally quick to point out that classes were almost done, technically meaning the school day was almost finished. Mrs. Weathers couldn't fault the logic but still made us wait the full ten minutes until the last bell rang. Jill sat there, tapping her foot anxiously against the chair.

We drove the half hour to Clarence's estate in the hills, saying little. I didn't really know what kind of small talk to make. "How was your first day of school?" was hardly an appropriate topic. And anyway, each time I thought about it, I just grew angrier. I couldn't believe any teacher would have the audacity to accuse Jill of drinking and having a hangover. There was really no way to prove something like that, and besides, you could tell after spending five minutes with her that it was impossible.

A middle-aged human woman greeted us at the door. Her name was Dorothy, and she was Clarence's housekeeper and feeder. Dorothy was pleasant enough, if a little distracted, and wore a stiff gray dress with a high collar to hide the bite marks on her neck. I smiled back at her and maintained my professional mode but couldn't help a shudder when I thought about what she was. How could anyone do that? How could anyone offer their blood up willingly like that? My stomach lurched, and I found myself keeping my distance from her. I didn't even want to accidentally brush her arm when I walked past.

Dorothy escorted us back to the room we'd all been sitting in the day before. There was no sign of Clarence, but Adrian was lying on a plush green couch, watching a TV that had been cleverly concealed inside an ornate wooden cabinet last time. When he saw us, he turned the TV off with a remote control and sat up. Dorothy excused herself and shut the French doors behind her.

"Well, this is a nice surprise," he said. He looked us over. Jill had changed into her normal clothes during her isolation today, but I still had on the Amberwood blouse and skirt. "Sage, aren't you guys supposed to have uniforms? This looks like what you usually wear."

"Cute," I said, suppressing an eye roll.

Adrian gave me a mock bow. "Careful. You almost smiled." He reached for a bottle of brandy sitting on a nearby table. Small glasses were arranged around it, and he poured himself a generous amount. "You guys want one?"

"It's the middle of the afternoon," I said incredulously. Not that it'd really matter for me what time of day it was.

"I've got a wicked hangover," he declared, giving us a mock toast. "This is just the thing to cure it."

"Adrian, I need to talk to you," said Jill earnestly.

He looked over at her, the smirk fading from his face. "What's up, Jailbait?"

Jill glanced uneasily at me. "Would you mind . . ."

I took the hint and tried not to let on how irritated I was by all the secrets. "Sure. I'll just . . . I'll just go outside again." I didn't like the idea of being exiled, but no way was I going to wander the halls of the old house. I'd face the heat.

I hadn't gotten very far down the hall when someone

stepped out in front of me. I let out a small scream and nearly jumped three feet in the air. A heartbeat later, I realized it was Lee—not that it reassured me much. No matter how ostensibly friendly I was with this group, old defenses inside me kicked up at being alone with a new vampire. Running into him didn't help matters either because my brain processed it as *an attack!* Lee just stood there, staring at me. From the expression on his face, he was just as startled to find me in his house—though perhaps not quite as alarmed about it as I was.

"Sydney?" asked Lee. "What are you doing here?"

Within moments, my fear became embarrassment, like I'd been caught prowling. "Oh . . . I'm here with Jill. She had kind of a rough day and needed to talk to Adrian. I wanted to give them some privacy and was going to just . . . uh, go outside."

Lee's confusion transformed into a smile. "You don't have to do that. No need for exile. Come on, I was going to get a snack in the kitchen." My face must have shown abject horror because he laughed. "Not the human kind."

I blushed and followed along with him. "Sorry," I said. "It's instinct."

"No problem. You Alchemists are kind of jumpy, you know."

"Yeah." I laughed uncomfortably. "I know."

"I've always wanted to meet one of you, but you guys certainly aren't what I expected." He opened the door to a spacious kitchen. The rest of the house might be antique and gloomy, but inside here, everything was bright and modern. "If it makes you feel any better, you're not as bad as Keith. He was here earlier today and was so nervous, he literally kept looking over his shoulder." Lee paused thoughtfully. "I think it might have been because Adrian kept laughing like a mad scientist at those old black-and-white movies he was watching."

I came to an abrupt stop. "Keith was here—today? What for?"

"You'd have to ask Dad. That's who he talked to the most." Lee opened the refrigerator and produced a can of Coke. "Want one?"

"I—uh, no. Too much sugar."

He grabbed another can. "Diet?"

I hesitated only a moment before taking it. "Sure. Thanks." I hadn't intended to eat or drink anything in this house, but the can seemed safe enough. It was sealed and looked like it had come straight from a human grocery store, not some vampiric cauldron. I opened it and took a sip as my mind spun. "You have no idea at all what it was about?"

"Huh?" Lee had added an apple to his menu and hoisted himself up so he sat on the counter. "Oh, Keith? No. But if I had to guess, it was about me. Like he was trying to figure out if I'm staying here or not." He took a giant bite into the apple, and I wondered if having fangs made that harder at all.

"He just likes his facts straight," I said neutrally. As much as I disliked Keith, I still wanted a unified human front. I wasn't entirely inaccurate, though. I was pretty sure Keith felt undermined at learning there was one extra Moroi in "his territory" and was now making sure he was in on everything. Part of it was good Alchemist business, sure, but most was probably Keith's wounded pride.

Lee didn't seem to think much of it and kept chewing his apple, though I could feel his eyes studying me. "You said Jill had a bad day? Is everything okay?"

"Yeah, I think so. I mean, I don't know. I'm not even sure how things got messed up. She wanted to see Adrian for some reason. Maybe he can help."

"He's Moroi," said Lee pragmatically. "Maybe it's just something only he could understand—something you and Eddie couldn't. No offense."

"None taken," I said. It was only natural that Jill and I would have distinct differences—I was a human, and she was a vampire, after all. We couldn't be more different if we tried, and in fact, I kind of preferred it that way. "You go to college . . . in Los Angeles? A human school?" It wasn't that weird a behavior for Moroi. Sometimes they stuck together in their own communities; sometimes they tried to blend into large human cities.

Lee nodded. "Yup. And it was hard for me at first too. I mean, even without others obviously knowing you're a vampire . . . well, there's just a sense of *otherness* you're always aware of. I eventually adjusted . . . but I know what she's going through."

"Poor Jill," I said, suddenly realizing I'd come at this situation all wrong. Most of my energy had been fixed on the school believing Jill's illness was a hangover. I should've focused on why she was sick in the first place. Anxiety over this new life change had to be taking its toll. I'd battled my own uneasiness, trying to figure out friendships and social cues—but at least I was still dealing with my own race. "I didn't really think about what she's going through."

"Do you want me to talk to her?" asked Lee. He set the apple core aside. "Not that I'm sure I have that much wisdom to share."

"Anything might help," I said honestly.

A silence fell between us, and I began to feel uneasy. Lee seemed very friendly, but my old fears were too ingrained. Part of me felt like he didn't so much want to get to know me as *study* me. Alchemists were clearly a novelty to him. "Do you mind me asking . . . the tattoo. It gives you special powers, right?"

It was nearly a repeat of the conversation at school, except Lee actually knew the truth behind it. I absentmindedly touched my cheek. "Not powers, exactly. There's compulsion in it to keep us from talking about what we do. And I get a good immune system out of it. But the rest? I'm nothing special."

"Fascinating," he murmured. I looked away uneasily and tried to casually brush my hair back into my face.

Adrian stuck his head in just then. All his earlier humor was gone. "Ah, there you are. Can I talk to you in private for a sec?"

The question was directed to me, and Lee jumped off the counter. "I'll take the cue. Is Jill still in the den?" Adrian nodded, and Lee glanced at me questioningly. "Do you want me to . . . ?"

I nodded. "That'd be great. Thank you."

Lee left, and Adrian glanced back at me curiously. "What was that about?"

"Oh, we thought Lee might be able to help Jill with her problems," I explained. "Since he can relate."

"Problems?"

"Yeah, you know. Adjusting to living with humans."

"Oh," said Adrian. He produced a pack of cigarettes and, to my complete astonishment, lit up right in front of me. "That. Yeah, I guess that's good. But that's not what I wanted to talk to you about. I need you to get me out of this place."

I was startled. This wasn't about Jill?

"Out of Palm Springs?" I asked.

"No! Out of *this* place." He gestured around him. "It's like living in a retirement home! Clarence is taking a nap right now, and he eats at five. It's *so* boring."

"You've only been here for two days."

"And that's more than enough. The only thing keeping me alive is that he keeps a hefty supply of liquor on hand. But at the rate I'm going, that'll be gone by the weekend. Jesus Christ, I'm climbing the walls." His eyes fell on the cross at my neck. "Oh. Sorry. No offense to Jesus."

I was still too baffled by the unexpected topic to feel much offense. "What about Lee? He's here, right?"

"Yes," agreed Adrian. "Sometimes. But he's busy with . . . hell, I don't know. School stuff. He's going back to Los Angeles tomorrow, and that'll be another boring night for me. Besides . . ." He looked around conspiratorially. "Lee's nice enough, but he's not . . . well, he's not really into having fun. Not the way I am."

"That might be a good thing," I pointed out.

"No morality lectures, Sage. And hey, like I said, I like him okay, but he's not here enough. When he is, he keeps to himself. He's always checking himself out in the mirror, even more than I do. I heard him worrying about gray hair the other day."

I didn't care about Lee's eccentricities. "Where would you even want to go? You don't want . . ." A very unpleasant thought came to me. "You don't want to enroll at Amberwood, do you?"

"What, and play *21 Jump Street* with the rest of you? No, thank you."

"Twenty-one what?"

"Never mind. Look." He put out the cigarette—on the counter—which I thought was kind of ridiculous since he'd hardly smoked any of it. Why bother with such a filthy habit if you weren't going to use it all? "I need my own place, okay? You guys make things happen. Can't you get me some swank bachelor's pad like Keith has downtown so I can party with all the rich vacationers? Drinking alone is sad and pathetic. I need people. Even human people."

"No," I said. "I'm not authorized to do that. You aren't . . . well, you aren't really my responsibility. We're just taking care of Jill—and Eddie, since he's her bodyguard."

Adrian scowled. "What about a car? Can you do that?"

I shook my head.

"What about *your* car? What if I drop you guys back off at the school and then borrow it for a while?"

"No," I said swiftly. That was probably the craziest suggestion he could've made. Latte was my baby. I certainly wasn't about to lend it out to a heavy drinker—especially to one who also happened to be a vampire. If there was ever a vampire who seemed particularly irresponsible, it was Adrian Ivashkov.

"You're killing me here, Sage!"

"I'm not doing anything."

"Exactly my point."

"Look," I said, growing irritated. "I told you. You're not my responsibility. Talk to Abe if you want things changed. Isn't he the reason you're here?"

Adrian's annoyance and self-pity shifted to wariness. "What do you know about that?"

Right. He didn't know I'd overheard their conversation.

"I mean, he's the one who brought you guys here and made

the arrangements with Clarence, right?" I hoped that would be convincing enough—and maybe yield me a little information on what Abe's master plan was.

"Yes," Adrian said, after several seconds of intense scrutiny. "But Abe *wants* me to stay in this tomb. If I got my own place, we'd have to keep it secret from him."

I scoffed. "Then I'm definitely not helping, even if I could. You couldn't pay me to cross Abe."

I could see Adrian bracing for another argument and decided to make my exit. Turning my back on him and any further protests, I headed out of the kitchen and back to the living room. There, I found Jill and Lee talking, and she wore the first genuine smile I'd seen in a while. She laughed at some comment he made and then looked up at my entrance.

"Hey, Sydney," she said.

"Hey," I said. "Are you about ready to go?"

"Is it time?" she asked. Both she and Lee looked disappointed, but then she answered her own question. "I guess it is. You probably have homework, and Eddie's probably worried already."

Adrian entered the room behind me, looking pouty. Jill glanced at him, and for a moment, her gaze turned inward, like her mind had gone somewhere else. Then she turned back to me. "Yeah," she said. "We should go. I hope we can talk later, Lee."

"Me too," he said, standing up. "I'll be around here, off and on."

Jill hugged Adrian goodbye, clearly reluctant to be leaving him too. With Lee, she'd looked mostly like she was sad to leave something that had just gotten interesting. With Adrian, there was more of a sense like she wasn't sure how she was going to get by. Her next scheduled feeding was in two days, and Adrian was encouraging, telling her she was strong enough to get through the next school day. Despite how much he kept annoying me, I was moved by his compassion for the younger girl. Anyone who was that nice to Jill couldn't be *that* bad. He was starting to surprise me.

"You look better," I told her as we drove toward Vista Azul.

"Talking to Adrian . . . to both of them . . . it was helpful."

"Do you think you'll be okay tomorrow?"

"Yeah." Jill sighed and leaned back against the seat. "It was just nerves. That, and I didn't eat much breakfast."

"Jill . . ." I bit my lip, hesitant to plunge forward. Confrontation wasn't my strong suit, particularly with awkward personal topics. "You and Adrian . . ."

Jill gave me a wary look. "What about us?"

"Is there anything . . . I mean, are you guys . . . ?"

"No!" Out of the corner of her eye, I saw Jill turn bright pink. It was the most color I had ever seen in a vampire's face. "Why would you say that?"

"Well. You were sick this *morning*. And then really adamant about seeing Adrian. You're always sad to leave him too . . ."

Jill gaped. "Do you think I'm pregnant?"

"Not exactly," I said, realizing it was kind of a nonsensical answer. "I mean, maybe. I don't know. I'm just considering all the possibilities . . ."

"Well, don't consider that one! There's nothing going on between us. *Nothing*. We're friends. He'd never be interested in me." She said it with a dismal certainty—and maybe even a little wistfully.

113

"That's not true," I said, fumbling to undo the damage. "I mean, you're younger, yeah, but you're cute . . ." Yes, this was a terrible conversation. I was just babbling now.

"Don't," said Jill. "Don't tell me I'm nice and pretty and have a lot to offer. Or whatever. None of that matters. Not when he's still hung up on *her*."

"Her? Oh. Rose."

I'd nearly forgotten. The trip to Court had been the first time I'd seen Adrian in person, but I'd actually seen him once before on security camera footage when he'd been at a casino with Rose. The two of them had dated, though I wasn't entirely sure how serious the relationship had been. When I'd helped Rose and Dimitri escape, the chemistry between those two had been off the charts, even if they'd both been in denial of it. Even I'd been able to spot it a mile away, and I knew next to nothing about romance. Seeing as Rose and Dimitri were officially a couple now, I had to assume things with Adrian hadn't ended well.

"Yeah. Rose." Jill sighed and stared vacantly ahead. "She's all he sees when he closes his eyes. Flashing dark eyes and a body full of fire and energy. No matter how much he tries to forget her, no matter how much he drinks . . . she's always there. He can't escape her."

Jill's voice dripped with astonishing bitterness. I might have written it off as jealousy, except that she talked as though she'd been personally been wronged by Rose too.

"Jill? Are you okay?"

"Huh? Oh." Jill shook her head, like she was shaking off the cobwebs of a dream. "Yeah, fine. Sorry. It's been a weird day. I'm a little out of it. Didn't you say we could pick up some things?" A sign for the next exit advertised a shopping center.

I rolled with the change in subject, glad to be away from personal matters, though I was still pretty confused. "Uh, yeah. We need sunscreen. And maybe we can get a little TV for the room."

"That'd be great," said Jill.

I left it at that and took the next exit. Neither of us spoke about Adrian for the rest of the night.

CHAPTER 8

"ARE YOU GOING TO EAT THAT?" asked Eddie.

Eddie might not have known about all the shenanigans that went down with Jill on the first day of school, but not seeing her all day had unnerved him. So, when she and I came downstairs for the second day, we found him waiting in our dorm lobby, ready to go with us to breakfast.

I pushed my plate and its half a bagel across the table. He'd already polished off a bagel of his own, as well as pancakes and bacon, but was quick to accept my offering. Maybe he was an unnatural hybrid creature, but from what I could tell, his appetite was the same as any human teenage guy.

"How are you feeling?" he asked Jill, once he'd swallowed a mouthful of bagel. Since he'd eventually hear she hadn't been in class, we'd simply told Eddie that Jill had been sick from nerves yesterday. The hangover allegations still infuriated me, but Jill insisted on letting them go.

"Fine," she said. "A lot better."

I didn't comment on that but secretly had my doubts. Jill *did* look better this morning, but she'd hardly had a solid night's sleep.

In fact, she'd woken in the middle of the night, screaming.

I'd leapt out of my bed, expecting no less than a hundred Strigoi or Moroi assassins to come bursting through our window. But when I'd looked over, there'd only been Jill, thrashing and screaming in her sleep. I'd hurried over and finally woken her up with some difficulty. She'd sat up gasping, drenched in sweat, and clutching her chest. Once she'd calmed down, she'd told me it was only a nightmare, but there'd been something in her eyes . . . the echo of something *real*. I knew because it reminded me of the many times I'd woken up thinking the Alchemists were coming to take me to the re-education centers.

She'd insisted she was fine, and when morning came, the only acknowledgment she gave of her nightmare was to insist that we not mention it to Eddie.

"It's only going to worry him," she said. "And besides, it's not a big deal."

I conceded that point, but when I tried to ask what had happened, she brushed me off and wouldn't talk about it.

Now, at breakfast, there was a definite edge to her, but for all I knew, it had more to do with finally facing her first day in a human school. "I still can't get over how different I am from everyone," she said in a low voice. "I mean, for one thing, I'm taller than almost every girl here!" It was true. It wasn't uncommon for Moroi women to push six feet in height. Jill wasn't quite there, but her long, slim build gave the illusion of being taller than she was. "And I'm really bony."

"You are not," I said.

"I'm too skinny—compared to them," Jill argued.

"Everyone's got something," countered Eddie. "That girl over there has a ton of freckles. That guy shaved his head. There's no such thing as 'normal.'"

Jill still looked dubious but doggedly went off to class when the first warning bell rang, promising to meet Eddie for lunch and me in PE.

I made it to my history class a few minutes early. Ms. Terwilliger stood at her desk, shuffling some papers around, and I hesitantly approached.

"Ma'am?"

She glanced up at me, pushing her glasses up her nose as she did. "Hmm? Oh, I remember you. Miss Melbourne."

"Melrose," I corrected.

"Are you sure? I could've sworn you were named after some-place in Australia."

"Well, my first name is Sydney," I said, not sure if I should be encouraging her.

"Ah. Then I'm not crazy. Not yet, at least. What can I do for you, Miss Melrose?"

"I wanted to ask you . . . well, you see, I have a gap in my schedule because I passed out of the language requirement. I wondered if maybe you needed another teacher aide . . . like Trey." The aforementioned Trey was already there, sitting at a desk allotted to him and collating papers. He glanced up at the mention of his name and eyed me warily. "It's last period, ma'am. So, if there was any extra work you needed . . ."

Her eyes studied me for several moments before she answered. I'd made sure to cover up my tattoo today, but it felt like she was staring right through to it. "I don't need another teacher aide," she said bluntly. Trey smirked. "Mr. Juarez, despite his many limitations, is more than capable of sorting all my stacks of paper." His smirk disappeared at the backhanded compliment.

I nodded and started to turn away, disappointed. "Okay. I understand."

"No, no. I don't think you do. You see, I'm writing a book." She paused, and I realized she was waiting for me to look impressed. "On heretical religion and magic in the Greco-Roman world. I've lectured on it at Carlton College before. Fascinating subject."

Trey stifled a cough.

"Now, I could really use a research assistant to help me track down certain information, run errands for me, that sort of thing. Would you be interested in that?"

I gaped. "Yes, ma'am. I would be."

"For you to get credit for an independent study, you'd have to do some project alongside it . . . research and a paper of your own. Not nearly the length of my book, of course. Is there anything from that era that interests you?"

"Er, yes." I could hardly believe it. "Classical art and architecture. I'd love to study it more."

Now she looked impressed. "Really? Then it seems we're a perfect match. Or, well, nearly. Pity you don't know Latin."

"Well . . ." I averted my eyes. "I, um, actually . . . I *can* read Latin." I dared a glance back at her. Rather than impressed, she mostly looked stunned.

"Well, then. How about that." She gave a rueful head shake. "I'm afraid to ask about Greek." The bell rang. "Go ahead and take your seat, then come find me at the end of the day. Last period is also my planning period, so we'll have plenty of time to talk and fill out the appropriate paperwork."

I returned to my desk and received an approving fist bump from Eddie. "Nice work. You don't have to take a real class. Of course, if she's got you reading Latin, maybe it'll be worse than a real class."

"I like Latin," I said with absolute seriousness. "It's fun."

Eddie shook his head and said in a very, very low voice: "I can't believe you think *we're* the strange ones."

Trey's comments for me in my next class were less complimentary. "Wow, you sure have Terwilliger wrapped around your finger." He nodded toward our chemistry instructor. "Are you going to go tell her that you split atoms in your free time? Do you have a reactor back in your room?"

"There's nothing wrong with—" I cut myself off, unsure what to say. I'd nearly said "being smart," but that sounded egotistical. "There's nothing wrong with knowing things," I said at last.

"Sure," he agreed. "When it's legitimate knowledge."

I remembered the crazy conversation with Kristin and Julia yesterday. Because I'd had to take Jill to Adrian, I'd missed the study session and couldn't follow up on my tattoo questions. Still, I at least now knew where Trey's disdain was coming from—even though it seemed absurd. No one else at school had specifically mentioned my tattoo being special, but a number of people had approached me already, asking where I'd gotten it. They'd been disappointed when I said South Dakota.

"Look, I don't know where this idea's coming from about my tattoo making me smart, but if that's what you think, well . . . don't. It's just a tattoo."

"It's gold," he argued.

"So?" I asked. "It's just special ink. I don't get why people would believe it has some mystical properties. Who believes in that stuff?"

He snorted. "Half this school does. How are you so smart, then?"

Was I really that much of a freak when it came to academics that people had to turn to supernatural explanations? I went with my stock answer. "I was homeschooled."

"Oh," said Trey thoughtfully. "That would explain it."

I sighed.

"I bet your homeschooling didn't do much in the way of PE, though," he added. "What are you going to do about your sport requirement?"

"I don't know; I hadn't thought about it," I said, feeling a little uneasy. I could handle Amberwood's academics in my sleep. But its athletics? Unclear.

"Well, you better decide soon; the deadline's coming up. Don't look so worried," he added. "Maybe they'll let you start a Latin club instead."

"What's that supposed to mean?" I asked, not liking the tone. "I've played sports."

He shrugged. "If you say so. You don't seem like the athletic type. You seem too . . . neat."

I wasn't entirely sure if that was a compliment or not. "What's your sport?"

Trey held his chin up, looking very pleased with himself. "Football. A real man's sport."

A guy sitting nearby overheard him and glanced back. "Too bad you won't make quarterback, Juarez. You came so close last year. Looks like you're going to graduate without fulfilling yet another dream."

I'd thought Trey didn't like *me*—but as he turned his attention to the other guy, it was like the temperature dropped ten degrees. I realized in that moment that Trey just liked giving me a hard time. But this other guy? Trey completely despised him.

"I don't remember you even being in the running, Slade," returned Trey, eyes hard. "What makes you think you're going to take it this year?"

Slade—it wasn't clear to me if that was his first or last name—exchanged knowing glances with a couple friends. "Just a feeling." They turned away, and Trey scowled.

"Great," he muttered. "Slade finally got the money for one. You want to know about tattoos? Go talk to him."

My thirty-second impression told me Slade was no one I wanted to talk to, but Trey provided no additional explanation. Class soon started, but as I tried to focus on the lesson, all I could think about was Amberwood's apparent obsession with tattoos. What did it mean?

When PE came, I was relieved to see Jill in the locker room. The Moroi girl gave me a weary smile as we walked outside. "How's your day been?" I asked.

"Fine," Jill said. "Not great. Not terrible. I haven't really gotten to know many people." She didn't say it, but Jill's tone implied, "See? I told you I would stand out."

Yet as the class started, I realized that the problem was that Jill *didn't* stand out. She avoided eye contact, letting her nerves get the best of her, and made no effort to talk to people. No one openly shunned her, but with the vibes she gave off, no one went out of their way to talk to her either. I certainly wasn't the most social person in the world, but I still smiled and tried to chat with my classmates as we did more volleyball drills. It was enough to foster the sparks of friendship.

I also soon noticed another problem. The class had been divided into four teams, playing two concurrent matches. Jill was in the other game, but I still occasionally caught sight of her. She looked miserable and tired within ten minutes, without even having done much in the game. Her reaction time was bad too. A number of balls went past her, and those she did notice were met with clumsy maneuvers. Some of her team-mates exchanged frustrated looks behind her back.

I returned to my own game, worried for her, just as the opposing team spiked the ball into a zone that wasn't well guarded by my team. I didn't have the reaction time that, say, a dhampir had, but in that split second, my brain knew I could block the ball if I made a hard and fast move. Doing so went against my natural instincts, the ones that said, *Don't do anything that will hurt or get you dirty.* I'd always carefully reasoned through my actions, never acting on impulse. Not this time. I was going to stop that ball. I dove for it, hitting it into range of another teammate who was able to then spike it back over the net and out of danger. The volley pushed me to a hard landing on my knees. It was ungraceful and jarred my teeth, but I'd stopped the opposition from scoring. My teammates cheered, and I was surprised to find myself laughing. I'd always been trained that everything I did had to have a greater, practical purpose. Sports were sort of antithetical to the Alchemist way of life, because they were just for fun. But maybe fun wasn't so bad once in a while.

"Nice, Melrose," said Miss Carson, strolling by. "If you want to defer your sport until winter and be on the volleyball team, come talk to me later."

"Well done," said Micah, and offered me his hand. I shook my head and stood up on my own. I was dismayed to see a scrape on one of my legs but was still grinning from ear to ear. If anyone had told me two weeks ago that I'd be so happy about rolling around in the dirt, I wouldn't have believed it. "She doesn't give out compliments very often."

It was true. Miss Carson had already been on Jill a number of times and was now halting our game to correct a teammate's sloppy form. I took advantage of the break to watch Jill, whose game was still in action. Micah followed my gaze.

"Doesn't run in the family, huh?" he asked sympathetically.

"No," I murmured. My smile faded. I felt a pang of guilt in my chest over exalting so much in my own triumph when Jill was obviously struggling. It didn't seem fair.

Jill still looked exhausted, and her curly hair was drenched in sweat. Pink spots had appeared on her cheeks, giving her a feverish look, and it seemed to take all her effort to remain upright. It was strange that Jill would have so much difficulty. I'd overheard a brief conversation in which she and Eddie had discussed combat and defensive moves, giving me the impression that Jill was fairly athletic. She and Eddie had even talked about practicing later that night and—

"The sun," I groaned.

"Huh?" asked Micah.

I'd mentioned my concerns about the sun to Stanton, but she'd dismissed them. She'd just advised that Jill be careful to stay inside—which Jill did. Except, of course, when school requirements made her take a class that kept her outside. Forcing her to play sports out in the full blaze of the Palm Springs sun was cruel. It was a wonder she was still standing.

I sighed, making a mental note to call the Alchemists later. "We're going to have to get her a doctor's note."

"What are you talking about?" asked Micah. The game was back on, and he shifted into position beside me.

"Oh. Jill. She's . . . she's sensitive to the sun. Kind of like an allergic thing."

As though on cue, we heard Miss Carson exclaim from the other court: "Melrose Junior! Are you blind? Did you not see that coming right toward you?"

Jill swayed on her feet but took the criticism meekly.

Micah watched them with a frown, and as soon as Miss Carson was off picking on someone else, he darted out of formation and ran over to Jill's game. I hastily tried to cover both his and my own positions. Micah ran up to a guy beside Jill, whispered something, and pointed back at me. A moment later, the guy ran over to my team and Micah took the spot beside Jill.

As class continued, I realized what was happening. Micah was good at volleyball—very good. So much so that he was able to defend his spot *and* Jill's. Without seeing any blatant blunders, Miss Carson kept her attention elsewhere, and Jill's team grew a little less hostile toward her. When the game ended, Micah caught hold of Jill's arm and quickly walked her over to a shaded spot. From the way she staggered, he seemed to be all that was holding her upright.

I was about to join them when I heard loud voices beside me.

"I'm getting it tonight. The guy I talked to swears it's gonna be badass." It was Slade, the guy who'd sparred with Trey earlier. I hadn't realized it out in the sun in the middle of the game, but he was the player Micah had swapped places with. "It better be," continued Slade, "for how much he's charging me."

Two of Slade's friends joined him as they began heading toward the locker room. "When are tryouts, Slade?" one of his friends asked. In chemistry, I'd learned Slade's first name was Greg, but everyone seemed to refer to him by his last name, even teachers.

"Friday," Slade said. "I'm going to *kill*. Like totally destroy them. I'm gonna rip Juarez's spine out and make him eat it."

Charming, I thought, watching them go. My initial assessment of Slade had been correct. I turned toward Jill and Micah and saw that he'd gotten ahold of a water bottle for her. They seemed okay for the moment, so I caught Miss Carson's attention as she walked by.

"My sister gets sick in the sun," I said. "This is really hard on her."

"Lots of kids have trouble in the heat at first," said Miss Carson knowingly. "They just need to toughen up. You handled yourself okay."

"Yeah, well, she and I are pretty different," I said dryly. *If only she knew.* "I don't think she's going to 'toughen up.'"

"Nothing I can do," said Miss Carson. "If I let her sit out, do you have any idea how many other kids would suddenly 'feel tired in the sun'? Unless she's got a doctor's note, she's got to stick it out."

I thanked her and went to join Jill and Micah. As I approached, I heard Micah saying, "Get cleaned up, and I'll walk you to your next class. We can't have you fainting in the halls." He paused and considered. "Of course, I'm totally happy to catch you if you do faint."

Jill was understandably dazed but was with it enough to thank him. She told him she'd meet him soon and walked to the girls' locker room with me. I eyed the grin on Micah's face, and a troubling thought occurred to me. Jill seemed stressed enough so I decided not to say anything, but my concern grew when we left for last period. Micah walked with Jill, as promised, and told her that later, when evening came, he'd tutor her in volleyball if she wanted.

As we stood outside the classroom, a girl with long red hair and a haughty attitude walked by, trailed by an entourage of other girls. She paused when she saw Micah and tossed her hair over one shoulder, flashing him a big smile. "Hey, Micah."

Micah was engrossed with Jill and barely glanced in the other girl's direction. "Oh, hey, Laurel." He walked away, and Laurel watched him go, her expression turning dark. She shot a dangerous look at Jill, whipped her long hair over her shoulder, and stormed off.

Uh-oh, I thought as I watched her stalk down the hall. *Is that going to come back and haunt us?* It was one of those moments when I could have used a lesson in social cues.

I went to Ms. Terwilliger's classroom afterward and spent most of that initial meeting setting up the semester's goals and outlining what I'd be doing for her. I was in store for a lot of reading and translation, which suited me just fine. It also appeared as though half of my job would be keeping her organized—something else I excelled at. The time flew by, and as soon as I was free, I hurried off to find Eddie. He was waiting with a group of other boys at the shuttle stop to go back to their dorm.

When he saw me, his response was the usual: "Is Jill okay?"

"Fine . . . well, kind of. Can we talk somewhere?"

Eddie's face darkened, no doubt thinking there was a legion of Strigoi on their way to hunt Jill. We stepped back inside one of the academic buildings, finding chairs in a private corner that enjoyed the full force of air conditioning. I gave him a quick update on Jill and her sunny PE misadventures.

"I didn't think it would be this bad," said Eddie grimly, echoing my thoughts. "Thank God Micah was there. Is there anything you can do?"

"Yeah, we should be able to get something from our 'parents' or a doctor." As much as I hated to, I added, "Keith might be able to expedite it."

"Good," said Eddie fiercely. "We can't have her getting beat up out there. I'll go talk to that teacher myself, if that's what it takes."

I hid a smile. "Well, hopefully it won't come to that. But there is something else . . . nothing dangerous," I amended quickly, seeing that warrior look cross his face again. "Just something . . ." I tried not to say the words that were popping into my mind. *Horrifying. Wrong.* "Concerning. I think . . . I think Micah likes Jill."

Eddie's face went very still. "Of course he likes her. She's nice. He's nice. He likes everyone."

"That's not what I mean, and you know it. He *likes* her. In the more-than-friends way. What are we going to do about that?"

Eddie stared off across the hall for a few moments before turning back to me. "Why do we have to do anything?"

"How can you ask that?" I exclaimed, shocked by the response. "You know why. Humans and vampires can't be together! It's disgusting and wrong." The words flew out of my mouth before I could stop them. "Even a dhampir like you should know that."

He smiled ruefully. "'Even a dhampir like me?'"

I supposed I'd been a little insulting, but it couldn't be helped. Alchemists—myself included—never believed dhampirs and Moroi worried enough about the same problems we did. They might acknowledge a taboo like this, but years of training said that only we humans really took it seriously. That was why the Alchemist job was so important. If we didn't look after these matters, who would?

"I mean it," I told him. "This is something all of us agree on."

His smile faded. "Yeah, it is."

Even Rose and Dimitri, who had a high tolerance for craziness, had been shocked at meeting the Keepers, rogue Moroi who intermingled freely with dhampirs and humans. It was a taboo the three of us shared, and we'd worked hard to tolerate the custom while with the Keepers. They lived hidden in the Appalachian Mountains and had provided excellent refuge when Rose was on the run. Ignoring their savage ways had been an acceptable price for the security they'd offered us.

"Can you talk to him?" I asked. "I don't think Jill has any strong feelings. She's got too many other things going on. She probably knows better anyway . . . but it'd still be best if you could discourage him. We can stop this before she gets involved."

"What do you expect me to say?" Eddie asked. He sounded

at a loss, which struck me as funny, considering he'd been ready to go make all sorts of demands to Miss Carson on Jill's behalf.

"I don't know. Play the big brother card. Act protective. Say she's too young."

I expected Eddie to agree, but he once more averted his eyes. "I don't know if we should say anything."

"What? Are you insane? Do you think it's okay to—"

"No, no." He sighed. "I'm not advocating it. But look at it this way. Jill's stuck in a school full of humans. It's not fair that she be banned from hanging out with any guys."

"I think Micah wants to do more than hang out."

"Well, why shouldn't she get to go on a date now and then? Or go to a dance? She should get to do all the normal things a girl her age does. She's already had her life radically changed. We shouldn't make it any harder."

I eyed him in disbelief, trying to figure out why he was so laid back about this. Admittedly, he didn't face the same consequences I did. If my superiors found out I was "encouraging" human and vampire dating, it'd be more evidence against me and my alleged bias. After all, my reputation wasn't yet restored with the Alchemists. Still, I knew Eddie's people didn't like the idea of dating, either. So what was the problem? A strange answer suddenly came to me. "I feel like you just don't want to confront Micah."

Eddie looked right at me. "It's complicated," he said. Something in his face told me I'd hit the mark. "Why don't *you* talk to Jill? She knows the rules. She'll understand that she can be with him without getting serious."

"I think it's a bad idea," I said, still unable to believe he was taking this stance. "We're creating a gray area here that's eventually going to cause confusion. We should keep it black and white and ban her from dating while she's here."

That wry smile returned. "Everything's black and white with you Alchemists, isn't it? Do you think you can really stop her from doing anything? You should know better. Even *your* childhood couldn't have been that abnormal."

With that slap in the face, Eddie stalked off, leaving me aghast. What had just happened? How could Eddie—who was so adamant about doing the right thing for Jill—be okay with her casually dating Micah? There was something weird going on here, something connected to Micah, though I couldn't figure out what. Well, I refused to let this matter go. It was too important. I'd talk to Jill and make sure she knew right from wrong. If necessary, I'd also talk to Micah—though I still felt *that* conversation would be better coming from Eddie.

And, I realized, thinking of how I had to go hunt down a doctor's note, there was one more source I could appeal to, one that had a lot of influence over Jill.

Adrian.

Looked like I'd be paying him another visit.

CHAPTER 9

CONSIDERING I WAS ONLY SUPPOSED to visit Clarence's twice a week for feedings, I was kind of amazed that I seemed to be here practically every day. Not only that, this was my first time visiting the estate alone. Before, I'd been with Keith or Jill and had a very well-defined goal. Now, I was on my own. I hadn't realized how much that would freak me out until I was approaching the house, which became even more looming and dark than usual.

There's nothing to be afraid of, I told myself. *You've been with a vampire and dhampir all week. You should be used to it.* Besides, really, the scariest thing about this place was the old house itself. Clarence and Lee weren't all that intimidating, and Adrian . . . well, Adrian was pretty much the least scary vampire I'd ever met. He was too bratty for me to feel any real fear, and actually . . . as much as I hated to admit it, I kind of looked forward to seeing him. It made no sense, but something about his infuriating nature made me forget about my other worries. Weirdly, I felt like I could relax around him.

Dorothy escorted me in, and I expected to be taken to the sitting room again. Instead, the housekeeper led me through a few twists and turns of the dark halls, finally landing in a billiards room that looked like it could have been straight out of *Clue*. More dark wood lined the room, and stained glass windows let in filtered sunlight. Most of the room's illumination came from a hanging light centered over a rich green pool table. Adrian was lining up a shot as I shut the door behind me.

"Oh," he said, knocking a red ball into a hole. "It's you."

"You were expecting someone else?" I asked. "Am I interrupting your social calendar?" I made a big show of glancing around the empty room. "I don't want to keep you from the mob of fans beating down your door."

"Hey, a guy can hope. I mean, it's not impossible that a car full of scantily clad sorority girls might break down outside and need my help."

"That's true," I said. "Maybe I can put a sign out front that says, 'ATTENTION ALL GIRLS: FREE HELP HERE.'"

"'ATTENTION ALL HOT GIRLS,'" he corrected, straightening up.

"Right," I said, trying not to roll my eyes. "That's an important distinction."

He pointed at me with the pool stick. "Speaking of hot, I like that uniform."

This time, I did roll my eyes. After Adrian had teased me last time about my uniform looking like my normal clothes, I'd made sure to change out of it before coming today. Now I wore dark jeans and a black-and-white printed blouse with a ruffled collar. I should have known the outfit change wouldn't save me from his snark.

"Are you the only one here?" I asked, noting his solo game.

"Nah. Clarence is around doing . . . I don't know. Old man stuff. And I think Lee's fixing that lock before he heads to LA. It's kind of funny. He seems upset that he needs to use tools. He keeps thinking the strength of his own hands should be more than enough."

I couldn't help a smile. "I don't suppose you offered to help?"

"Sage," Adrian declared. "These hands don't do manual labor." He knocked another ball into a hole. "You want to play?"

"What? With you?"

"No, with Clarence." He sighed at my dumbfounded look. "Yes, of course with me."

"No. I need to talk to you about Jill."

He was silent for a few moments and then returned to the game as though nothing had happened. "She wasn't sick today." He said that with certainty, though there was a funny, bitter tone to his words.

"No. Well, not in the same way. She got sick out in the sun during PE. I'm going to see Keith after this to see if we can get a medical excuse." I'd actually tried calling him earlier, with no luck. "But that's not why I'm here. There's a guy who likes Jill—a human guy."

"Have Castile rough him up."

I leaned back against the wall and sighed. "That's the thing. I asked him to. Well, not rough him up, exactly. It's Eddie's roommate. I asked Eddie to tell him to back off and make up some reason for staying away from Jill—like that she's too young." Fearing

Adrian would be as lax as Eddie in this, I asked, "You understand why it's important, right? No Moroi and human dating?"

He was watching the table, not me. "Yup, I'm with you there, Sage. But I still don't see the problem."

"Eddie won't do it. He says he doesn't think Jill should be denied the chance to date and go to dances. That it's okay if she and Micah hang out, so long as it doesn't get serious."

Adrian was good at hiding his feelings, but this looked like it'd caught him by surprise. He straightened up and spun the base of the pool stick on the floor as he thought. "That is weird. I mean, I get the logic, and there's something to it. She shouldn't be forced into isolation while she's here. I'm just surprised Castile came up with it."

"Yeah, but that's a hard concept to live by. Where do you draw the 'casual' line? Honestly, I get this feeling Eddie just didn't want to confront Micah—the roommate. Which is crazy, because Eddie doesn't seem like the type to be afraid of anything. What is there about Micah that would make Eddie so uneasy?"

"Is Micah some big, hulking guy?"

"No," I said. "He's built, I guess. Good at sports. Really friendly and easygoing—not the type you'd have to be afraid would turn on you if you warned him away from your sister."

"Then you can talk to him. Or just talk to Jailbait and explain things to her." Adrian seemed satisfied he'd solved the matter and knocked in the last ball.

"That was my plan. I just wanted to make sure you'd back me. Jill listens to you, and I thought it'd be easier if she knew you agreed with me. Not that I even know how she feels. For all I know, this is all overkill."

"Can't hurt to be too careful with her," said Adrian. He stared off, lost in his own thoughts. "And I'll let her know how I feel about it."

"Thank you," I said, kind of surprised at how easy this had been.

His green eyes danced mischievously. "*Now* will you play a round with me?"

"I don't really—"

The door opened, and Lee walked in, dressed casually in jeans and a T-shirt. He was carrying a screwdriver. "Hey, Sydney. I thought I saw your car out there." He glanced around. "Is, uh, Jill with you?"

"Not today," I said. New insight struck me as I recalled that Lee attended school in Los Angeles. "Lee, have you ever dated a human girl at your school?"

Adrian arched an eyebrow. "Are you asking him out, Sage?"

I scowled. "No!"

Lee turned thoughtful. "No, not really. I have some human friends, and we go out as a group and hang out . . . but I've never done more than that. LA's a big place, though. There are Moroi girls around, if you know where to look."

Adrian perked up. "Oh?"

My hope that Lee might tell Jill he too had to avoid dating faded. "Well, that would make your dating situation much easier than Jill's."

"What do you mean?" asked Lee.

I recapped everything to him about Micah and Eddie. Lee nodded along thoughtfully.

"That is hard," he admitted.

"Can we go back to the part about Moroi girls hanging out

in LA?" asked Adrian hopefully. "Can you direct me to some of the . . . oh, let's say, more open-minded ones?"

Lee's attention was on me, however. His easy smile grew uncertain, and he glanced at his feet. "This might seem kind of weird . . . but I mean, I wouldn't mind asking Jill out."

Adrian was on that before I could even think of a response. "What, do you mean like on a *date*? You son of a bitch! She's only fifteen." You never would've guessed he'd been talking about easy Moroi girls only moments before.

"Adrian," I said. "I'm guessing Lee's definition of a date is a little different than yours."

"Sorry, Sage. You've got to trust me when it comes to dating definitions. Last I checked, you aren't an expert in social matters. I mean, when was the last time you were even on a date?" It was just another of the witty barbs he tossed around so easily, but it stung a little. Was my lack of social experience *that* obvious?

"But," I added, ignoring Adrian's question, "there *is* an age difference." I honestly had no idea how old Lee was. His being in college gave me some clue, but Clarence seemed awfully old. Having a child late in life wasn't that weird, though, for humans or Moroi.

"There is," said Lee. "I'm nineteen. Not a huge gap—but big enough. I shouldn't have said anything." He looked embarrassed, and I felt both sorry for him and confused for myself. Matchmaking wasn't in the Alchemist handbook.

"Why would you want to ask her out?" I asked. "I mean, she's great. But are you just doing this to distract her from Micah and give her a safe dating alternative? Or do you, um, like her?"

"Of course he likes her," said Adrian, quick to defend Jill's honor.

I had a feeling that there was really no good way for Lee to answer at this point. If he expressed interest in her, Adrian's bizarre chivalric instincts were going to kick in. If Lee wasn't interested, Adrian would no doubt demand to know why Lee didn't want to marry her then and there. It was one of those fascinating—but weird—quirks of Adrian's personality.

"I like her," said Lee bluntly. "I've only talked to her a couple of times, but . . . well, I'd really like to get to know her better."

Adrian scoffed, and I shot him a glare. "Once again," I said. "I think you guys have different definitions for the same words."

"Not true," said Adrian. "All guys mean the same thing when they want to 'get to know a girl better.' You're a well-bred young lady, so I understand why you'd be too innocent to understand. Good thing you've got me here to interpret."

I turned back to Lee, not even bothering to respond to Adrian. "I think it's fine if you go out with her."

"Assuming she'd even be interested," said Lee, looking uncertain.

I remembered her smile when he'd stopped to talk to her yesterday. That had seemed pretty promising. But then, so had her enthusiasm over Micah. "I bet she would."

"So you're just going to let her go off alone?" asked Adrian, giving me a look that told me not to question him. This time, his concern was legitimate. I shared it. Jill was in Palm Springs to be safe. She was enrolled at Amberwood because it was also safe. Suddenly going out with a guy we hardly knew would not meet either Alchemist or guardian protocols for safety.

"Well, she can't even leave campus," I said, thinking aloud. "Not without me."

"Whoa," said Adrian, "if you get to come along as a chaperone, so do I."

"If we both do, then Eddie will want to as well," I pointed out. "Doesn't sound like much of a date."

"So?" Adrian's brief moment of seriousness and concern had vanished in the face of what he saw as social fun. How could anyone's mood flip so quickly? "Think of it as less of a date than a faux-family outing. One that will entertain me while protecting her virtue."

I put my hands on my hips and turned toward him. This seemed to amuse him more. "Adrian, we're focusing on Jill here. This isn't about your personal entertainment."

"Not true," he said, green eyes sparkling. "Everything's about my personal entertainment. The world is my stage. Keep it up—you're becoming a star performer in the show."

Lee glanced between us with a comically helpless look. "Do you guys want to be alone?"

I flushed. "Sorry." Adrian made no apologies, of course.

"Look," said Lee, who kind of seemed like he was beginning to regret bringing this up at all. "I like her. If it means bringing your whole group so I can be with her, then that's fine."

"Maybe it's better this way," I mused. "Maybe if we do more things as a group—aside from her feedings—she won't be in danger of wanting to go out with a human guy." Who we didn't even know for sure that she was interested in. We didn't even know if she was interested in Lee either. We were being awfully heavy-handed with her love life, I realized.

"This is kind of what I wanted before," Adrian said to me. "Just more of a social life."

I thought back to yesterday's conversation, in which he'd demanded I find him lodging. "That's not quite what you asked for."

"If you want to get out more," said Lee, "you should come back to LA with me tonight. I'll be back here after class tomorrow anyway, so it'd just be a quick trip."

Adrian brightened so much that I wondered if Lee had suggested it to try to smooth over any tension remaining about his interest in Jill. "Will you introduce me to those girls?" asked Adrian.

"Unbelievable," I said. Adrian's double standard was ridiculous.

I didn't notice the door opening until Keith was completely in the room. I was never exactly happy to see him, but it was good luck that he was suddenly here, right when I needed to talk to him about Jill and her problems with PE. My best plan had been to show up at his apartment and hope to catch him there. He'd saved me the trouble.

Keith looked at all three of us—but he didn't share our smiles. No winks or pretty boy charm from him today. "I saw your car out there, Sydney," he said sternly, turning to me. "What are you doing here?"

"I had to talk to Adrian," I said. "Did you get my message? I tried calling earlier."

"I've been busy," he said crisply. His expression was hard, his tone chilling the room. Adrian and Lee had lost their smiles, and both now looked confused as they tried to figure out why Keith was so annoyed. I shared their curiosity. "Let's talk. In private."

I suddenly felt like a naughty child without knowing why. "Sure," I said. "I . . . I was just leaving anyway." I moved to join Keith at the door.

"Wait," said Lee. "What about—" Adrian nudged him and shook his head, murmuring something I couldn't hear. Lee stayed quiet.

"See you around," said Adrian cheerfully. "Don't worry—I'll remember what we talked about."

"Thanks," I said. "See you guys later."

Keith left without a word, and I followed him out of the house and into the late-afternoon heat. The temperature had gone down since the ill-fated PE class but not by much. Keith trudged through the gravel driveway, coming to a halt beside Latte. His car was parked nearby.

"That was rude," I told him. "You didn't even say goodbye to them."

"Sorry if I don't bring out my best manners for vampires," snapped Keith. "I'm not as *close* to them as you are."

"What's that supposed to mean?" I demanded, crossing my arms. Staring him down, I felt all my old animosity bubble up. It was hard to believe that I'd been laughing just a minute ago.

Keith sneered. "Just that you seemed awfully cozy with them in there—hanging out, having a good time. I didn't know this was where you spent your free time after school."

"How dare you! I came here on business," I growled.

"Yeah, I could tell."

"I did. I had to talk to Adrian about Jill."

"I don't recall him being her guardian."

"He cares about her," I argued. "Just like any of us would for a friend."

"Friend? They're not like us at all," said Keith. "They're god-less and unnatural, and you have no business being *friends* with any of them."

I wanted to shout back that from what I'd observed, Lee was a hundred times more decent of a person than Keith would ever be. Even Adrian was. It was only at the last second that my training kicked in. *Don't raise a fuss. Don't contradict your superiors.* No matter how much I hated it, Keith was in charge here. I took a deep breath.

"It was hardly fraternizing. I simply came by to talk to Adrian, and Lee happened to be here. It wasn't like we'd all been planning some big party." Best not to mention the group date plan.

"Why didn't you just call Adrian if you had a question? You called me."

Because being face-to-face with him is less sickening than being around you.

"It was important. And when I couldn't get ahold of you, I figured I'd have to drive over to your place anyway."

Hoping to shift away from my "bad behavior," I jumped in and recapped everything that had happened today, including Jill's sun exposure and Micah's attentions.

"Of course she can't date him," he exclaimed, after I'd explained about Micah. "You have to put a stop to that."

"I'm trying. And Adrian and Lee said they'd help."

"Oh, well, I feel a lot better now." Keith shook his head. "Don't be naive, Sydney. I told you. They don't care about this stuff as much as we do."

"I think they do," I argued. "Adrian seemed to get it, and he has a lot of influence over Jill."

"Well, he's not the one the Alchemists are going to come after and send off to re-education for playing around with vampires when she should be disciplining them."

I could only stare. I wasn't sure which part of what he'd just said was more offensive: the well-worn insinuation that I was a "vamp lover" or that I was capable of "disciplining" any of them. I should've known his false friendliness wouldn't last.

"I'm doing my job here," I said, still keeping my voice level. "And from what I can see, I'm doing more work than *you*, since I'm the one who's been putting out fires all week."

I knew it was an illusion, seeing as the glass eye couldn't really stare, but I felt like he was glaring at me with both eyes. "I'm doing plenty. Don't even think to criticize me."

"What were you doing here?" I asked, suddenly realizing how weird that was. He'd accused me of "socializing" but had never explained his motives.

"I had to see Clarence, not that it's any of your business."

I wanted more details but refused to let on how curious I was. He'd been here yesterday too, according to Lee. "Will you call the school tomorrow and get Jill excused from PE?"

Keith gave me a long and heavy look. "No."

"What? Why not?"

"Because being out in the sun won't kill her."

Again, I bit down on my anger and tried for the diplomacy I'd been schooled in. "Keith, you didn't see her. Maybe it won't kill her, but it was miserable for her. She was in agony."

"I don't really care if they're miserable or not," Keith said. "And neither should you. Our job is to keep her alive. There was no mention of making sure she's happy and comfortable."

"I wouldn't think anyone would *have* to tell us," I said,

aghast. Why was he so upset? "I'd think being sensitive human beings, we could just do it."

"Well, now you can. You can either get someone above us to issue a note to the school or you can give her ice baths after gym class. I really don't care what you do, but maybe it'll keep you busy enough that you'll stop coming over here unannounced and throwing yourself at creatures of darkness. Don't let me hear about this happening again."

"You are unbelievable," I said. I was too upset and at a loss for words to manage anything more eloquent.

"I'm looking out for your soul," he said loftily. "It's the least I can do for your dad. Too bad you aren't more like your sisters."

Keith turned his back on me and unlocked the car door without another word. He got in and drove off, leaving me staring. Tears threatened my eyes, and I swallowed them back. I felt like an idiot—but not because of his accusations. I didn't believe for an instant that I'd done anything wrong by coming over here. No, I was mad—mad at myself—because I'd let him walk away with the last word and because I hadn't had the nerve to say anything back. I'd stayed silent, just like everyone always told me to.

I kicked the gravel in my anger, sending a spray of it into the air. A few small rocks hit my car, and I winced. "Sorry."

"Would he accuse you of being evil for talking to an inanimate object?"

I spun around, heart racing. Adrian was leaning against the house, smoking. "Where did you come from?" I demanded. Even though I knew everything there was to know about vampires, it was hard to shake superstitious fears of them appearing out of thin air.

"Other door," he explained. "I went out to smoke and over-heard the commotion."

"It's rude to eavesdrop," I said, knowing I sounded unbear-ably prim but unable to stop myself.

"It's rude to be an asshole like that." Adrian nodded toward where Keith had driven away. "Are you going to be able to get Jill out of class?"

I sighed, suddenly feeling tired. "Yeah, I should be able to. It'll just take a little longer while I get some other Alchemist to be our fake parents. Would've been a lot faster if Keith had done it."

"Thanks for looking out for her, Sage. You're okay. For a human."

I almost laughed. "Thanks."

"You can say it too, you know."

I walked over to Latte and paused. "Say what?"

"That I'm okay . . . for a vampire," he explained.

I shook my head, still smiling. "You'll have a hard time get-ting any Alchemist to admit that. But I can say you're okay for an irreverent party boy with occasional moments of brilliance."

"Brilliant? You think I'm brilliant?" He threw his hands sky-ward. "You hear that, world? Sage says I'm brilliant."

"That's *not* what I said!"

He dropped the cigarette and stamped it out, giving me a devil-may-care grin. "Thanks for the ego boost. I'm going to go tell Clarence and Lee all about your high opinion."

"Hey, I didn't—"

But he was already gone. As I drove away, I decided the Alchemists needed an entire department devoted to handling Adrian Ivashkov.

When I got back to my dorm room, I found Jill sitting sur-rounded in textbooks and papers, undoubtedly trying to catch up from yesterday.

"Wow," I said, thinking of the homework that waited for me too. "You've got a whole command center set up."

Rather than smile at my joke, Jill looked up with an icy gaze. "Do you think," she said, "that maybe next time you want to mess with my dating life, you could talk to *me* first?"

I was speechless. Adrian had said he'd talk to Jill. I just hadn't realized it'd be so quickly.

"You don't have to go behind my back to keep me away from Micah," she added. "I'm not stupid. I know I can't date a human."

So Adrian had apparently told her that much.

"And," Jill continued, still in that cold tone, "you don't have to set me up with the only eligible Moroi within a hundred miles in order to keep me out of trouble."

Okay . . . Adrian had apparently told her *everything*. I would've expected more discretion from him, especially with the Lee part.

"We . . . we weren't setting you up," I said lamely. "Lee wanted to ask you out anyway."

"But rather than talk to me, he asked permission from you guys! You don't control my life."

"I know that," I said. "We weren't trying to!" How had this just blown up right in front of me? "Lee acted on his own."

"Just like you did when you went to talk to Adrian behind my back." Her eyes glittered with angry tears, daring me to deny it. I couldn't and only now realized the wrongness of what I'd done. Ever since she found out she was royal, Jill had watched other people dictate her life for her. Maybe my intentions to get Adrian to talk to her about Micah were good, but I'd addressed them in the wrong way.

"You're right," I said. "I'm sorry that I—"

"Forget it," she said, slipping a pair of headphones on. "I don't want to hear any more. You made me look stupid in front of both Adrian and Lee. Not that they'll even think twice about me in Los Angeles tonight." She waved a hand at me and looked down at the book in front of her. "I'm done with you."

Whether she couldn't hear me because of the music or simply because she'd now chosen to ignore me, I couldn't say. All I knew was that I once again found myself comparing her to Zoe. Just like with Zoe, I'd tried to do something good for Jill, and it had backfired. Just like with Zoe, I'd ended up hurting and humiliating the one I'd tried to protect.

Sorry, Sage. Last I checked, you aren't an expert in social matters.

That, I thought bitterly, was the saddest part of all—that Adrian Ivashkov was right.

CHAPTER 10

MY PHONE RANG JUST THEN, saving me from the awkwardness of figuring out what to do about Jill. I answered without
bothering to check the caller ID.

"Miss Melbourne? Your services are needed immediately."

"Ma'am?" I asked in surprise. Ms. Terwilliger's frantic voice
was not what I'd been expecting. "What's wrong?"

"I need you to get me a caramel sauce cappuccino from
Spencer's. There is absolutely *no way* I can finish translating
this document if you don't."

There were a million responses I could make to that, none
of which were very polite, so I went with the obvious point of
logic.

"I don't think I can," I said.

"You have off-campus privileges, don't you?"

"Well, yes, ma'am, but it's almost campus curfew. I don't
know where Spencer's is, but I don't think I can make it back
in time."

"Nonsense. Who's running your dorm? That Weathers woman? I'll call down and get you an exception. I'm working in one of the library offices. Meet me there."

Despite my personal devotion to coffee, getting an "exception" to the school's curfew seemed kind of excessive for an errand like this. I didn't like to bend the rules. On the other hand, I was Ms. Terwilliger's assistant. Wasn't this part of my job description? All the old Alchemist instincts to follow orders kicked in.

"Well, yes, ma'am, I suppose I—"

She disconnected, and I stared at the phone in astonishment. "I have to go," I told Jill. "Hopefully I'll be back soon. Maybe very soon since I'll be surprised if she remembers to call Mrs. Weathers." She didn't look up. With a shrug, I packed my laptop and some homework, just in case Ms. Terwilliger thought of something else for me to do.

With coffee on the line, my teacher's memory was good, and I found I did indeed have clearance to leave when I went downstairs. Mrs. Weathers even gave me directions to Spencer's, a coffee shop that was a few miles away. I got the cappuccino, wondering if I'd be reimbursed, and picked up something for myself as well. The library staff at Amberwood gave me a hard time about carrying in beverages when I returned, but when I explained my errand, they waved me on through to the back offices. Apparently, Ms. Terwilliger's addiction was well known.

The library was surprisingly busy, and I quickly deduced why. After a certain point each night, guys and girls were banned from each other's dorms. The library was open later, so this was the place to go to hang out with the opposite sex. Lots of people were just there to study too, including Julia and Kristin.

"Sydney! Over here!" called Kristin in a stage whisper.

"Break free of Terwilliger," added Julia. "You can do it."

I held up the coffee as I passed them. "Are you kidding? If she doesn't get her caffeine soon, there'll be no escaping her. I'll come back if I can."

As I continued walking through, I saw a small cluster of students gathered around someone—and heard a familiar and annoying voice. Greg Slade's.

Curious in spite of myself, I walked over to the edge of the crowd. Slade was showing off something on his upper arm: a tattoo.

The design itself was nothing special. It was an eagle in flight, the kind of generic art all tattoo shops had in stock and copied en masse. What caught my attention was the color. It was all done in a rich, metallic silver. Metallics like that weren't easy to pull off, not with that sheen and intensity. I knew the chemicals that went into my own gold tattoo, and the formula was complex and composed of several rare ingredients.

Slade made a halfhearted effort to keep his voice low—tattoos were forbidden around here, after all—but it was clear he was enjoying the attention. I observed quietly, glad others were asking some of my questions for me. Of course, those questions only left me with more questions.

"That's brighter than the ones they used to do," one of his friends noted.

Slade tilted his arm so the light caught it. "Something new. They say these are better than the ones from last year. Not sure if that's true, but it wasn't cheap, I can tell you that."

The friend who'd spoken grinned. "You'll find out at tryouts."

Laurel—the red-haired girl who'd been interested in Micah—stretched out her leg beside Slade, revealing a slim ankle adorned with a faded butterfly tattoo. No metallics there. "I might get mine touched up, maybe for homecoming if I can get the money from my parents. Do you know if the celestial ones are better this year too?" She tossed back her hair as she spoke. From what I'd observed in my brief time at Amberwood, Laurel was very vain about her hair and made sure to throw it around at least every ten minutes.

Slade shrugged. "Didn't ask."

Laurel noticed me watching. "Oh, hey. Aren't you vampire girl's sister?"

My heart stopped. "Vampire?"

"Vampire?" echoed Slade.

How did she find out? What am I going to do? I had just begun making a list of the Alchemists I had to call when one of Laurel's friends snickered.

Laurel looked at them and laughed haughtily, then turned back to me. "That's what we've decided to call her. No one *human* could possibly have skin that pale."

I nearly sagged in relief. It was a joke—one that hit painfully close to the truth, but a joke nonetheless. Still, Laurel didn't seem like someone to cross, and it'd be better for all of us if it was a joke soon forgotten. I admittedly blurted out the first distracting comment that came to mind. "Hey, stranger things have happened. When I first saw you, I didn't think anyone could have hair that long or that red. But you don't hear me talking about extensions or dye."

Slade nearly doubled over with laugher. "I knew it! I knew it was fake!"

Laurel flushed nearly as red as her hair. "It is not! It's real!"

"Miss Melbourne?"

I jumped at the voice behind me and found Ms. Terwilliger there, watching me with bemusement. "You aren't getting credit for chatting, especially when my coffee's on the line. Come on."

I skulked away, though hardly anyone noticed. Laurel's friends were having too much fun teasing her. I hoped I had diffused the vampire jokes. Meanwhile, I couldn't get the image of Greg's tattoo out of my mind. I let my thoughts wander to the mystery of what components would be needed for that silver color. I almost had it figured out—at least, I had one possibility figured out—and wished I had access to Alchemist ingredients to do some experiments. Ms. Terwilliger took the coffee grate-fully when we reached a small workroom.

"Thank God," she said, after taking a long sip. She nodded at mine. "Is that a backup one? Excellent thinking."

"No, ma'am," I said. "It's mine. Do you want me to start in on those?" A familiar stack of books sat on the table, ones I'd seen in her classroom. They were core parts of her research, and she'd told me I'd eventually need to outline and document them for her. I reached for the top one, but she stopped me.

"No," she said, moving toward a large briefcase. She rifled through papers and assorted office supplies, finally digging out an old leather book. "Do this one instead."

I took the book. "Can I work out there?" I was hoping if I went back to the main study area, I could talk to Kristin and Julia.

Ms. Terwilliger considered. "The library won't let you have the coffee. You should probably leave it in here."

I waffled, debating whether my desire to talk to Kristin and Julia outweighed the likelihood that Ms. Terwilliger would drink my coffee before I got back. I decided to take the risk and bid my coffee a painful farewell as I hauled my books and gear back out to the library.

Julia eyed Ms. Terwilliger's beat-up book with disdain. "Isn't that just on the internet somewhere?"

"Probably not. I'm guessing no one's even looked at this since before the internet was invented." I opened the cover. Dust fluttered out. "*Way* before."

Kristin had math homework open in front of her but didn't look particularly interested in it. She tapped a pen absentmindedly against the textbook's cover. "So you saw Slade's tattoo?"

"Hard not to," I said, getting out my laptop. I glanced across the screen. "He's still showing it off."

"He's wanted one for a while but never had the money," explained Julia. "Last year, all the big athletes had them. Well, except for Trey Juarez."

"Trey almost doesn't need one," pointed out Kristin. "He's that good."

"He will now—if he wants to keep up with Slade," said Julia.

Kristin shook her head. "He still won't do it. He's against them. He tried reporting them to Mr. Green last year, but no one believed him."

I looked back and forth between them, more lost than ever. "Are we still talking about tattoos? About Trey 'needing' one or not?"

"You really haven't found out yet?" asked Julia.

"It's my second day," I pointed out with frustration.

Remembering I was in a library, I spoke more softly. "The only people who have really talked about them are Trey and you guys—and you haven't said much of anything."

They had the grace to look embarrassed by that, at least. Kristin opened her mouth, paused, and then seemed to change what she was going to say. "You're *sure* yours doesn't do anything?"

"Positive," I lied. "How is that even possible?"

Julia cast a glance around the library and twisted in her chair. She rolled her shirt up a little, exposing her lower back—and a faded tattoo of a swallow in flight. Satisfied that I'd seen it, she turned back around. "I got this last spring break—and it was the best spring break ever."

"Because of the tattoo?" I asked skeptically.

"When I got it, it didn't look like this. It was metallic . . . not like yours. Or Slade's. More like . . ."

"Copper," provided Kristin.

Julia thought about it and nodded. "Yeah, like reddish-goldish. The color only lasted a week, and while it did, it was *amazing*. Like, I have never felt that good. It was inhumanly good. The best high ever."

"I swear, there's some kind of drug in those celestials," said Kristin. She was trying to sound disapproving, but I thought I detected a note of envy.

"If you had one, you'd understand," Julia told her.

"Celestials . . . I heard that girl over there talk about them," I said.

"Laurel?" asked Julia. "Yeah, that's what they call the copper ones. Because they make you feel out of this world." She looked almost embarrassed about her enthusiasm. "Stupid name, huh?"

"Is that what Slade's does?" I asked, stunned at what was unfolding before me.

"No, he's got a steel one," said Kristin. "Those give you a big athletic boost. Like, you're stronger, faster. Stuff like that. They last longer than the celestials—more like two weeks. Sometimes three, but the effect fades. They call them steel because they're tough, I guess. And maybe because there's steel in them."

Not steel, I thought. *A silver compound*. The art of using metal to bind certain properties in skin was one the Alchemists had perfected a long time ago. Gold was the absolute best, which was why we used it. Other metals—when formulated in the proper ways—achieved similar effects, but neither silver nor copper would bind the way gold could. The copper tattoo was easy to understand. Any number of feel-good substances or drugs could be combined with that for a short-term effect. The silver one was more difficult for me to understand—or rather, the effects of the silver one. What they were describing sounded like some kind of athletic steroid. Would silver hold that? I'd have to check.

"How many people have these?" I asked them, awestruck. I couldn't believe that such complicated tattoos were so popular here. It was also beginning to sink in just how wealthy the student body here really was. The materials alone would cost a fortune, let alone any of the alleged side effects.

"Everyone," said Julia.

Kristin scowled. "Not everyone. I've almost got enough saved up, though."

"I'd say half the school's at least tried a celestial," said

Julia, flashing her friend a comforting look. "You can get them touched up again later—but it still costs money."

"Half the school?" I repeated incredulously. I looked around, wondering how many shirts and pants concealed tattoos. "This is crazy. I can't believe a tattoo can do any of that." I hoped I was doing an okay job of hiding how much I really knew.

"Get a celestial," said Julia with a grin. "Then you'll believe."

"Where do you get them?"

"It's a place called Nevermore," said Kristin. "They're selective, though, and don't give them out easily." Not that selective, I thought, if half the school had them. "They got a lot more cautious after Trey tried to turn them in." There was Trey's name again. It now made sense that he'd been so disdainful of my tattoo when we met. But I wondered *why* he cared so much—enough to try to get them shut down. That wasn't just a casual disagreement.

"I guess he thinks it's unfair?" I offered diplomatically.

"I think he's just jealous that he can't afford one," said Julia. "He's got a tattoo, you know. It's a sun on his back. But it's just a regular black one—not gold like yours. I've never seen anything like yours."

"So that's why you thought mine made me smart," I said.

"That could've been really useful during finals," said Julia wistfully. "You're sure that's not why you know so much?"

I smiled, despite how appalled I was by what I'd just learned. "I wish. It might make getting through this book easier. Which," I added, glancing at the clock. "I should get to." It was on Greco-Roman priests and magicians, a kind of grimoire detailing the kinds of spells and rituals they'd worked with. It wasn't terrible reading material, but it was long. I'd thought Ms. Terwilliger's research was more focused on mainstream religions in that era, so the book seemed like a weird choice. Maybe she was hoping to include a section on alternative magical practices. Regardless, who was I to question? If she asked, I'd do it.

I outlasted both Kristin and Julia in the library, since I had to stay as long as Ms. Terwilliger stayed, which was until the library closed. She seemed pleased that I'd gotten so far with the notes and told me she'd like the whole book completed in three days.

"Yes, ma'am," I said automatically, as if I didn't have any other classes at this school. Why did I always agree without thinking?

I returned to East Campus, bleary-eyed from all the work I'd done and exhausted over the thought of the homework remaining. Jill was fast asleep, which I took as a small blessing. I wouldn't have to face her accusing stare or figure out how to handle the awkward silence. I got ready for bed quickly and quietly and fell asleep almost as soon as I hit the pillow.

I woke at around three to the sound of crying. Shaking off my sleepy haze, I was able to make out Jill sitting up in her bed, her face buried in her hands. Great, shaking sobs racked her body.

"Jill?" I asked uncertainly. "What's wrong?"

In the faint light coming in from outside, I saw Jill raise her head and look at me. Unable to answer, she shook her head and began crying once more, this time more loudly. I got up and came to sit on the edge of her bed. I couldn't quite bring myself to hug or touch her for comfort. Nonetheless, I felt terrible. I knew this had to be my fault.

"Jill, I'm so sorry. I never should have gone to see Adrian.

When Lee mentioned you, I should've just stopped it there and told him to talk to you if he was interested. I should've just talked to you in the first place . . ." The words came out in a jumble. When I looked at her, all I could think of was Zoe and her horrible accusations on the night I'd left.

Somehow, my help always backfired.

Jill sniffled and managed to get out a few words before breaking down again. "It's not . . . it's not that . . ."

I stared helplessly at her tears, frustrated at myself. Kristin and Julia thought I was superhumanly smart. Yet I guaranteed one of them would've been able to comfort Jill a hundred times better than I could. I reached out my hand and nearly patted her arm—but pulled back at the last moment. No, I couldn't do that. That Alchemist voice in me, the voice that always warned me to keep my distance from vampires, wouldn't let me touch one in a way that was so personal.

"Then what is it?" I asked at last.

She shook her head. "It's not . . . I can't tell . . . you wouldn't understand."

With Jill, I thought, any number of things could be wrong. The uncertainty of her royal status. The threats against her. Being sent away from all her family and friends, trapped among humans in the perpetual sun. I really didn't know where to start. Last night, there had been a chilling, desperate terror in her eyes when she woke up. But this was different. This was sorrow. This was from the heart.

"What can I do to help?" I asked at last.

It took her a few moments to pull herself together. "You're already doing plenty," she managed. "We all appreciate it—really. Especially after what Keith said to you." Was there nothing

Adrian hadn't told her? "And I'm sorry—I'm sorry I was so bitchy to you earlier. You didn't deserve that. You were just trying to help."

"No . . . don't apologize. I messed up."

"You don't have to worry, you know," she added. "About Micah. I understand. I only want to be his friend."

I was pretty sure that I still wasn't doing a great job at making her feel better. But I had to admit, apologizing to me at least seemed to be distracting her from whatever had woken her to so much pain.

"I know," I said. "I should never have worried about you."

She assured me again that she was fine, with no more explanation about why she'd woken up crying. I felt like I should have done more to help, but instead, I made my way back to my own bed. I didn't hear any more sobs for the rest of the night, but once, when I woke up a couple hours later, I stole a glance at her. Her features were just barely discernible in the early light. She lay there, eyes wide open and staring off into nothingness, a haunted look on her face.

CHAPTER 11

BEFORE CLASS THE NEXT DAY, I left a message with someone at the Alchemists' office, telling them I needed "Mr. and Mrs. Melrose" to send a note excusing Jill from PE—or at least from outdoor activities. I hoped they'd move quickly on this. The Alchemists were fast when they wanted to be, but they sometimes had odd ideas of what took priority. I hoped they didn't have the same attitude toward Jill's misery as Keith did.

But I knew not to expect any action that day, so Jill had to suffer through another PE class—and I had to suffer through watching her suffer. What was really terrible was that Jill didn't whine or try to get out of anything. She didn't even show any sign of last night's breakdown. She came in with determination and optimism, as though maybe *this* would be the day the sun wouldn't affect her. Yet, before long, she began to wane just as she had last time. She looked sick and tired, and my own performance faltered a little because I kept watching her, afraid she'd pass out.

Micah was the saving grace. Once again, he fearlessly switched teams—this time from the very start of class. He covered for her just as he had last time, allowing her to escape the notice of teacher and classmates—well, except for Laurel, who seemed to notice—and get annoyed by—everything he did. Her eyes flicked angrily between him and Jill, and she kept flinging her hair over her shoulder to get his attention. I was a little amused to note that Micah's attention remained solely on keeping the ball away from Jill.

Micah also jumped immediately to her side when class ended and had a water bottle ready, which she accepted gratefully. I was grateful too, but seeing his concern for her dredged up all my old worries. She was good to her word, however. She returned his attentions in a friendly way, but you definitely couldn't call it flirting. He made no secret of his intentions, though, and I still worried that it would be better if she didn't have to deal with them. I'd meant it when I said I trusted her, but I couldn't help but think it'd be a lot easier on everyone if he laid off in his advances. This would require A Talk.

Dreading what I had to do, I caught up with Micah outside the locker rooms. We were both waiting for Jill to finish up, and I took advantage of the alone time with him.

"Hey, Micah," I said, "I need to talk to you . . ."

"Hey," he returned brightly. His blue eyes were wide and excited. "I had an idea I wanted to run past you. If you guys aren't able to get a note for her, maybe you could see about getting her schedule switched around? If she took PE first period, it wouldn't be nearly as hot out yet. Maybe it wouldn't be as hard on her. I mean, she seems like she'd like to participate in some of this stuff."

"She would," I said slowly. "And that's a really good idea."

"I know some people who work in the office. I'll ask them to run some options and see if it's even possible with the rest of her classes." He faked a pout. "I'll be sad not to have her in class, but it'd be worth it to know she's not so miserable."

"Yeah," I agreed weakly, suddenly feeling at a loss. He really had come up with a good idea. He was even unselfish enough to give up the chance to be with her in order to promote the greater good. How could I have "the talk" with him now? How could I suddenly say, "Leave my sister alone," when he was going out of his way to be so nice? I was as bad as Eddie, avoiding confrontation with Micah. This guy was too likable for his own good.

Before I could manage a response, Micah then went off in an unexpected direction. "You really should get her to a doctor, though. I don't think she has a sun allergy."

"Oh?" I asked in surprise. "Have you *not* been watching her suffer through class each day?"

"No, no, believe me, she's definitely got an issue with the sun," he assured me quickly. "But she might be misdiagnosed. I read up on sun allergies, and people usually get rashes with them. This overall weakness she gets . . . I don't know. I think it might be something else."

Oh no. "Like what?"

"I don't know," he mused. "But I'll keep researching theories and let you know."

Wonderful.

PE also gave me my first glimpse at one of Amberwood's metallic tattoos in action. Greg Slade was impossible not to watch during class, and I wasn't the only one who got distracted. Just as Kristin and Julia had said, he really was faster and stronger. He made dives no one else was quick enough to react to. When he hit the ball, it was a wonder we didn't hear a sonic boom shortly thereafter. This earned him praise at first, but soon, I noticed something. There was a sloppy edge to his game. He was filled with ability, yes, but sometimes it was unfocused. Those powerful hits didn't always help because he'd blast the ball out of bounds. And in running to make a shot, he rarely considered those around him. When a guy from my English class got knocked down flat on his back, simply for being in the path of Slade and the ball, Miss Carson stopped the game and roared her displeasure about Slade's aggression. He took it in with a sulky smirk.

"Too bad Eddie's not in this class," Jill said afterward. "He'd be a total match for Slade."

"Maybe it's better no one notices," I remarked. Eddie, from what I'd heard, was already a shining star in his PE class. It was part of a dhampir's natural athleticism, and I knew he was actually working hard not to be *too* good at everything.

I checked in with Ms. Terwilliger after PE, happy to find my teacher fully stocked with coffee of her own. I spent most of the period going through the book and taking notes on my laptop. Partway through, she came over to check my work.

"You're very organized," she said, looking over my shoulder. "Headings and subheadings and sub-subheadings."

"Thank you," I said. Jared Sage had been very particular in teaching his children research skills.

Ms. Terwilliger took a sip of coffee and continued reading the screen. "You didn't list the ritual and spell steps," she pointed out moments later. "You just summarize them in a couple lines."

Well, yes, that was the point of note-taking. "I cite all the page numbers," I said. "If you need to check the actual components, there's an easy reference."

"No . . . go back and put all the steps and ingredients in your notes. I want to be able to have them all in one place."

You do have them in one place, I wanted to say. *In the book.* Notes were about condensing the material, not retyping the original text word for word. But Ms. Terwilliger had already wandered away, staring at her filing cabinet absentmindedly as she muttered to herself about a misplaced folder. With a sigh, I flipped back to the beginning of the book, trying not to think about how this was going to set me back. At least I was only doing this for credit and not a grade.

I stayed past the late bell in an effort to make up some lost time. When I got back to my room, I had to wake up Jill, who was sound asleep after her exhausting day.

"Good news," I told her as she blinked at me with sleepy eyes. "It's feeding day."

Definitely words I *never* thought I'd say.

I also didn't think I'd be excited for it. And sure, I certainly wasn't thrilled about the idea of Jill biting into Dorothy's neck. I was, however, feeling pretty bad for Jill and was glad she'd get some nourishment. Being on such a limited supply of blood had to make things doubly hard for her.

We met up with Eddie downstairs when it was time to go. He looked Jill over worriedly. "Are you okay?"

"I'm fine," she said with a smile. She looked nowhere near as bad as she had earlier. I shuddered to think what Eddie would've done if he'd actually been in our class and seen her at her worst.

"Why is this still going on?" he asked me. "Weren't you going to talk to Keith?"

"We're a little delayed," I said evasively, leading them to where Latte was parked in the student lot. "We'll make it happen." If the Alchemists didn't come through with the note, I was going to try to act on Micah's suggestion and get her switched into morning PE.

"We know you will," said Jill. I could just barely pick out the sympathy in her voice, reminding me that she knew about my fight with Keith yesterday. I hoped she wouldn't mention it in front of Eddie and was saved when she switched to a more random and surprising topic. "Do you think we can pick up some pizza along the way? Adrian doesn't want any more of Dorothy's cooking."

"How terrible for him," remarked Eddie, getting into the backseat and letting Jill ride shotgun. "Having a personal chef on hand to make him whatever he wants. I don't know how he gets by."

I laughed, but Jill seemed outraged on Adrian's behalf. "It's not the same! She cooks really super-gourmet stuff."

"Still waiting for the problem," said Eddie.

"She tries to also make it really healthy. She says it's better for Clarence. So, there's never any salt and pepper or butter." Jeez, how often did she and Adrian talk? "There's no flavor or anything. It's driving him crazy."

"Everything seems to be driving him crazy," I remarked, remembering his plea for new lodging. "And he can't have it too bad. Didn't he go to LA last night?" Jill's only answer was a frown.

Nonetheless, I had a feeling we'd be hanging out at

Clarence's for a while, and I personally didn't want to eat anything prepared in that house. So, it was more for selfish reasons that I agreed to stop at a takeout place en route and buy a few pizzas. Adrian's face was radiant when we entered the sitting room, which—pool games aside—seemed to be his primary hangout at Clarence's.

"Jailbait," he declared, leaping up. "You're a saint. A goddess, even."

"Hey," I said, "I'm the one who paid for them."

Adrian carried off one of the boxes to the couch, much to Dorothy's dismay. She hurried off muttering about plates and napkins. Adrian gave me a conciliatory nod.

"You're okay too, Sage," he said.

"Well, well, what have we here?" Clarence came tottering into the room. I hadn't noticed before, but he used a cane to get around. It had a crystal snake head on top, which was both impressive and scary. Just the kind of thing you'd picture for an old vampire. "Looks like a party."

Lee was with him, greeting us with smiles and nods. His eyes lingered briefly on Jill, and he made a point of sitting near her—but not too near. Jill perked up more than she had in days. Everyone was just starting to dive into the pizza when Dorothy appeared in the doorway with a new guest. I felt my eyes widen. It was Keith.

"What are you doing here?" I asked, keeping my voice neutral.

He winked. "Came to check in on everybody and make sure all's well. That's my job—to look after everyone."

Keith was chipper and friendly as he helped himself to the

pizza, with no indication of the fight we'd gotten into last time. He smiled and talked to everyone as though they were all best friends, leaving me totally bewildered. No one else seemed to think anything odd about his behavior—but then, why would they? None of them had my history with Keith.

No—that wasn't quite true. Despite being deep in conversation with Eddie, Adrian paused to give me a curious look, silently asking about yesterday's fight. He glanced at Keith and then back to me. I shrugged helplessly, letting him know I was just as confused by the change of heart. Maybe Keith regretted his outburst from yesterday. Of course, that would've been much easier to accept if it had come with, oh, an apology.

I nibbled on a piece of cheese pizza, but mostly I observed the others. Jill was animatedly recounting her first couple of days to Adrian, noticeably leaving out any of the negative parts. He listened to her indulgently, nodding and interjecting with occasional witty quips. Some of the stuff she told him was pretty basic, and I was surprised it hadn't come up in their phone conversations. Maybe he just had so much to say at those times that there'd been no chance for her. As it was, he made no mention of his boredom or other grievances.

Clarence occasionally chatted with Eddie and Lee, but his eyes constantly strayed to Jill. There was a wistful look in his gaze, and I remembered that his niece had only been a little older than Jill. I wondered if perhaps part of the reason he'd been so willing to take us all on was in an effort to reclaim some part of the family life that had been lost to him.

Keith had sat down near me, at first making me uncomfortable but then later giving me a reason to pick his brain. Seeing the others engaged in conversation, I asked him softly, "Have you ever heard of knockoff Alchemist tattoos making it into the general population?"

He gave me a startled look in return. "I don't even know what that means."

"At Amberwood, there's this trend. There's apparently some-place in town that gives metallic tattoos, and they have special properties—kind of like ours. Some just kind of give off a high. Others kind of have a steroid effect."

He frowned. "They're not bound with gold, are they?"

"No. Silver and copper. So, they don't last. Probably so the people giving them can make more money."

"But they can't be ours, then," he argued. "We haven't used those metals for tattoos in centuries."

"Yeah, but someone may be using Alchemist technology to create these."

"Just to get people high?" he asked. "I wouldn't even know how you'd go about that with metallic agents."

"I have some ideas," I said.

"And let me guess. They involve narcotic mixtures." When I nodded, he sighed and gave me a look like I was ten years old. "Sydney, it's most likely someone's found a crude tattooing method that's like ours but has no connection. If so, there's nothing we can do about it. Drugs happen. Bad things hap-pen. If it isn't mixed with Alchemist business, then it isn't our business."

"But what if it is connected to Alchemist business?" I asked.

He groaned. "See? This is why I was worried about you coming, this tendency you have of running off with tangents and wild theories."

"I don't—"

"Please don't embarrass me," he hissed, casting a glance at the others. "Not with them, not with our superiors."

His rebuke silenced me, mostly from surprise. What did he mean about this "tendency" I had? Was he actually suggesting he had made some deep psychological analysis of me years ago? The idea that *I* would embarrass *him* was ludicrous . . . and yet his words planted a seed of doubt in me. Maybe the tattoos at Amberwood were just an unrelated fad.

"How's PE?" Adrian's words dragged me from my own thoughts. He was still getting the summary of school from Jill. She made a face at the question.

"Not great," she admitted, giving a recap of some of the worse moments. Eddie shot me a meaningful look, similar to the one from earlier.

"You can't go on like that," exclaimed Lee. "The sun around here's brutal."

"I agree," said Keith, of all people. "Sydney, why didn't you tell me how bad it was?"

I think my jaw hit the floor. "I did! That's why I was trying to get you to contact the school."

"You didn't really give me the whole story." He flashed one of his sugary smiles at Jill. "Don't worry. I'll take care of this for you. I'll get in touch with school officials—and the Alchemists."

"I already talked to them," I argued.

But I might as well have not said anything. Keith had already switched topics and was talking to Clarence about something irrelevant. Where had this about-face come from? Yesterday, Jill's discomfort had been low priority. Today, Keith was her knight in shining armor. And in the process, he was suggesting that I was the one who'd screwed up. *That's his plan,* I realized. *He doesn't want me here. He never has.* And then something even worse occurred to me.

He's going to use this to start building a case against me.

Across the room, Adrian caught my eye again. He knew. He'd been eavesdropping when I talked to Keith in the driveway. Adrian started to speak, and I knew he was going to call Keith out on his lie. It was gallant but not what I wanted. I would deal with Keith myself.

"How was LA?" I asked quickly before Adrian had a chance to say anything. He looked at me curiously, no doubt wondering why I wouldn't let him be a witness to my case. "You went there with Lee last night, right?"

Adrian looked confused, but a grin smoothed over his face. "Yeah," he said at last. "It was great. Lee showed me college life."

Lee laughed. "I wouldn't go that far. I don't know where you were half the night."

Adrian got this look on his face that was somehow charming but made me want to slap him at the same time. "We parted ways. I was getting to know some of the other Moroi in the area."

Even Eddie couldn't stay silent at that. "Oh, is that what you call it?"

Jill abruptly stood up. "I'm going to get my blood now. Is that okay?"

There was a moment of awkward silence, largely because I don't think anyone really knew who she was asking permission from. "Of course, my dear," said Clarence, stepping into his role as host. "I believe Dorothy's in the kitchen."

Jill gave a curt nod and hurried out of the room. The rest of us exchanged puzzled glances.

"Is something wrong?" asked Lee, looking worried. "Should I . . . should I go talk to her?"

"She's still just stressed," I said, not daring to mention the screaming or crying episodes.

"I thought of something that might be fun for her . . . for all of us to do," he said tentatively. He glanced around and then settled his gaze on me. I guess I was the designated mother here. "If you think it's okay. I mean . . . it's kind of silly, but I thought we could go mini-golfing in the evening. They've got all these fountains and pools on the course. She's a water user, right? She must be missing it out here."

"She does," said Eddie, frowning. "She mentioned it yesterday."

I shivered. Keith had been texting on his phone and froze. No matter our differences, we still shared a core of similar training, and both of us were uneasy with the idea of Moroi magic.

"She'd probably like that a lot," said Adrian. He sounded reluctant to admit it. I think he was still uneasy with the idea of Lee being interested in Jill, no matter how friendly the two guys were. Lee's idea was both innocent and conscientious. Hard to find fault with.

Lee tilted his head thoughtfully. "You have a later curfew on the weekends, right? Do you want to go tonight?"

It was Friday, granting us an extra hour extension at our dorm. "I'm game," said Adrian. "Literally and figuratively."

"If Jill's there, I'm there," said Eddie.

They looked at me. I was trapped. I wanted to go back and catch up on homework. Saying that sounded pathetic, though, and I supposed I had to represent as Jill's only female chaperone. Besides, I reminded myself, this assignment wasn't about me and my academics, no matter how much I pretended it was. It was about Jill.

"I can go," I said slowly. Thinking that this sounded very much like fraternizing with vampires, I glanced uneasily at Keith. He'd gone back to texting now that magic wasn't being discussed. "Keith?" I asked by way of permission.

He looked up. "Huh? Oh, I can't go. I have to be somewhere."

I tried not to grimace. He'd misread me and thought I was inviting him. On the bright side, he also wasn't objecting to the rest of us going.

"Ah, how nice," said Clarence. "An outing for you young people. Perhaps you'll share a glass of wine with me first?" Dorothy was just entering with a bottle of red wine, Jill trailing behind her. Clarence smiled at Adrian. "I know you'd like a glass."

Adrian's expression said he most definitely would. Instead, Adrian took a deep breath and shook his head. "I'd better not."

"You should," said Jill gently. Even after a short drink of blood, she looked full of life and energy.

"Can't," he said.

"It's the weekend," she told him. "It's not that big of a deal. Especially if you're careful."

The two locked gazes and then at last, he said, "All right. Pour me a glass."

"Pour me one too, please," said Keith.

"Really?" I asked him. "I didn't know you drank."

"I'm twenty-one," he countered.

Adrian accepted his from Dorothy. "Somehow, I'm thinking that's not Sage's concern. I thought Alchemists avoided alcohol the same way they do primary colors."

I glanced down. I was wearing gray. Keith was wearing brown.

"One glass won't hurt," said Keith.

I didn't argue with him. It wasn't my place to babysit Keith. And the Alchemists didn't have rules against drinking per se. We had strong religious beliefs about what it meant to live a good and pure lifestyle, and drinking was generally looked down upon. Was it forbidden? No. It was a custom, one I considered important. If he didn't, I guessed that was his choice.

Keith was just bringing the glass to his lips when Adrian said, "Mmm. O positive, my favorite."

Keith sprayed out the wine he'd just drunk and promptly started coughing. I was relieved that none got on me. Jill burst into giggles, and Clarence stared at his glass wonderingly.

"Is it? I thought it was a cabernet sauvignon."

"So it is," said Adrian, straight-faced. "My mistake."

Keith gave Adrian a tight smile, like he too thought it was a funny joke, but I wasn't fooled. Keith was mad at having been mocked, and no matter how friendly he pretended to be with everyone, his views against vampires and dhampirs were as harsh as they'd ever been. Of course, Adrian probably wasn't helping matters any. I thought it was pretty funny, honestly, and worked to hide my smile so that Keith wouldn't get mad at me again. It was hard to do because shortly thereafter, Adrian flashed me a secret, knowing smile that seemed to say, *That's payback for earlier.*

Eddie glanced at Jill. "I'm glad you got your blood today. I know you've been wanting to learn some defense moves, but I wanted to wait until you were back up to strength."

Jill lit up. "Can we do it tomorrow?"

"Of course," he said, looking nearly as delighted by this as she did.

Keith frowned. "Why should she learn to fight when she's got you around?"

Eddie shrugged. "Because she wants to, and she should have every edge she can get." He didn't specifically mention the attempts on her life—not in front of Lee and Clarence—but the rest of us understood.

"I thought Moroi weren't good at fighting, though," said Keith.

"Mostly because they haven't trained for it. They aren't as strong as us, sure, but their reflexes are better than yours," explained Eddie. "It's just a matter of learning the skills and having a good teacher."

"Like you?" I teased.

"I'm not bad," he said modestly. "I can train anyone who wants to learn." He elbowed Adrian, who was reaching for the wine and a refill. "Even this guy."

"No, thank you," said Adrian. "These hands don't sully themselves with fighting."

"Or with manual labor," I remarked, recalling past comments of his.

"Exactly," he said. "But maybe you should have Castile show you how to throw a punch, Sage. It might come in handy. Seems like a skill a plucky young woman like yourself should possess."

"Well, thanks for the vote of confidence, but I'm not really sure when I'd need it," I said.

"Of course she needs to learn!"

Clarence's exclamation caught all of us by surprise. I'd actually thought he was dozing off since he'd had his eyes closed moments ago. But now, he was leaning forward with a zealous expression. I cringed under the intensity of his stare.

"You *must* learn to protect yourself!" He pointed at me, then moved on to Jill. "*And* you. Promise me you'll learn to defend yourself. Promise me."

Jill's light green eyes went wide with shock. She tried to give him a reassuring smile, though it was tinged with uneasiness.

"Of course, Mr. Donahue. I'm trying to. And until then, I've got Eddie to protect me from Strigoi."

"Not Strigoi!" His voice dropped to a whisper. "The vampire hunters."

None of us said anything. Lee looked mortified.

Clarence squeezed his wineglass so tightly that I worried it would break. "No one talked about this back then—about defending ourselves. Maybe if Tamara had learned something, she wouldn't have been killed. It's not too late for you—for either of you."

"Dad, we've been over this," said Lee.

Clarence ignored him. The old man's gaze flicked between me and Jill, and I wondered if he even knew I was human. Or maybe it didn't matter. Maybe he just had a slightly deranged protective instinct toward all girls the same age as Tamara. I kind of expected Keith to tactlessly point out that there were no such things as vampire hunters, but he was uncharacteristically quiet. Eddie was the one who finally spoke, his words soothing and kind. He so often gave off the impression of a do-or-die warrior that it was surprising to realize he was actually very compassionate.

"Don't worry," said Eddie. "I'll help them. I'll keep them safe and make sure nothing bad happens to them, okay?"

Clarence still looked agitated but focused on Eddie hopefully. "You promise? You won't let them kill Tamara again?"

"I promise," said Eddie, in no way indicating how weird the request was.

Clarence studied Eddie a few more seconds and then nodded. "You're a good boy." He reached for the wine bottle and topped off his glass. "More?" he asked Adrian, as though nothing had happened.

"Yes, please," said Adrian, holding out his glass.

We continued the conversation as though nothing had happened, but the shadow of Clarence's words continued to hang over me.

CHAPTER 12

WHEN WE LEFT on our group date or family outing or whatever it was, Lee couldn't stop apologizing for his father.

"I'm sorry," he said, slumping miserably in the backseat of Latte. "There's no reasoning with him anymore. We tried to tell him that Tamara was killed by Strigoi, but he won't believe it. He doesn't want to. He can't take revenge on a Strigoi. They're immortal. Invincible. But some human vampire hunter? Somehow, in his head, that's something he can go after. And if he can't, then he can focus his energy on how the guardians won't go after these nonexistent vampire hunters."

I just barely heard Eddie mutter, "Strigoi aren't that invincible."

In the rearview mirror, I saw Jill's face filled with compassion. She was seated between Lee and Eddie. "Even if it's a fantasy, maybe it's better this way," she suggested. "It gives him comfort. I mean, kind of. Having something tangible to hate is what gets him through. Otherwise he'd just give in to despair.

He's not hurting anyone with his theories. I think he's sweet." She caught her breath in that way she did when she'd said a whole lot all at once.

My eyes were back on the road, but I could swear Lee was smiling. "That's nice of you," he told her. "I know he likes having you around. Turn right up here."

That was to me. Lee had been giving me directions ever since we left Clarence's. We were just outside of Palm Springs proper, nearing the very impressive-looking Desert Gods Golf Course and Resort. Further guidance from him led us to the Mega-Fun Mini-Golf Center, which was adjacent to the resort. I searched for a parking spot and heard Jill gasp when she caught sight of the golf course's crowning glory. There, in the center of a cluster of gaudily decorated putting greens, was a huge fake mountain with an artificial waterfall spouting from its top.

"A waterfall!" she exclaimed. "It's amazing."

"Well," said Lee, "I wouldn't go that far. It's made of water that's been pumped over and over and has God only knows what in it. I mean, I wouldn't try to drink or swim in it."

Before I even had the car to a stop, Adrian was out the door, lighting a cigarette. We'd gotten in an argument on the way over, despite me telling him three times that Latte was a strictly no-smoking car. The rest of us soon got out as well, and I wondered what I'd signed up for here as we strolled toward the entrance.

"I've actually never been mini-golfing," I remarked.

Lee came to a halt and stared. "Never?"

"Never."

"How does that happen?" asked Adrian. "How is it possible that you've never played mini-golf?"

"I had kind of an unusual childhood," I said at last.

Even Eddie looked incredulous. "You? I was practically raised at an isolated school in the middle of nowhere Montana, and even I've played mini-golf."

Saying I was homeschooled was no excuse this time, so I just let it go. Really, it just came down to having a childhood more focused on chemical equations than on fun and recreation.

Once we started playing, I soon got the hang of it. My first few attempts were pretty bad, but I soon understood the weight of the club and how the angles on each course could be maneuvered. From there, it was pretty simple to calculate distance and force to make accurate shots.

"Unbelievable. If you'd been playing since you were a child, you'd be a pro by now," Eddie told me as I knocked my ball into a gaping dragon's mouth. The ball rolled out the back, down a tube, bounced off a wall, and into the hole. "How'd you do that?"

I shrugged. "It's simple geometry. You're not that bad either," I pointed out, watching him make his shot. "How do *you* do it?"

"I just line it up and putt."

"Very scientific."

"I just rely on natural talent," said Adrian, strolling up to the start of the Dragon's Lair. "When you have such a wealth of it to draw from, the danger comes from having too much."

"That makes no sense whatsoever," said Eddie.

Adrian's response was to pause and take out a silver flask from his inner coat pocket. He unscrewed it and took a quick drink before leaning in to line up his shot.

"What was that?" I exclaimed. "You can't have alcohol out here."

"You heard Jailbait earlier," he countered. "It's the weekend."

He lined up his ball and shot. The ball went directly for the dragon's eye, bounced off it, and shot back toward Adrian. It rolled and came to a stop at his feet, nearly where it had started.

"Natural talent, huh?" asked Eddie.

I leaned forward. "I think you broke the dragon's eye."

"Just like Keith," said Adrian. "I figured you'd appreciate that, Sage."

I gave him a sharp look, wondering if there was any hidden meaning behind that. Mostly, Adrian seemed amused by his own wit. Eddie mistook my expression.

"That was inappropriate," he told Adrian.

"Sorry, Dad." Adrian shot again and managed not to maim any statues this time. A couple more shots, and he sank the ball. "There we go. Three."

"Four," said Eddie and I in unison.

Adrian looked at us incredulously. "It was three."

"You're forgetting about your first one," I said. "The one where you blinded the dragon."

"That was just the warm-up," Adrian argued. He put on a smile I think he hoped would charm me. "Come on, Sage. You understand how my mind works. You said I was brilliant, remember?"

Eddie glanced at me in surprise. "You did?"

"No! I never said that." Adrian's smile was infuriating. "Stop telling people that."

Since I was in charge of the scorecard, his play was logged as four, despite his many further protests. I started to move forward, but Eddie held out a hand to stop me, his hazel eyes gazing over my shoulder.

"Hold up," he said. "We need to wait for Jill and Lee."

I followed his gaze. The two of them had been in deep conversation since we arrived, so much so that they'd slowed and lagged behind the rest of us. Even during his bantering with Adrian and me, Eddie had continually checked on her—and our surroundings. It was kind of amazing the way he could multitask. Thus far, Jill and Lee had only been one hole behind us. Now it was nearly two, and that was too far for Eddie to keep her in his sight. So, we waited while the oblivious couple meandered their way toward the Dragon's Lair.

Adrian took another drink from his flask and shook his head in awe. "You had nothing to worry about, Sage. She went right for him."

"No thanks to you," I snapped. "I can't believe you told her every detail of my visit that night. She was so mad at me for interfering behind her back with you, Lee, and Micah."

"I hardly told her anything," argued Adrian. "I just told her to stay away from that human guy."

Eddie glanced between our faces. "Micah?"

I shifted uncomfortably. Eddie didn't know about how I'd gone proactive. "Remember when I wanted you to say something to him? And you wouldn't?" I proceeded to tell him how I'd then sought out Adrian's help and found out about Lee's interest in Jill. Eddie was aghast.

"How could you not tell me any of this?" he demanded.

"Well," I said, wondering if everything I did was going to result in the wrath of a Moroi or dhampir, "it didn't involve you."

"Jill's safety does! If some guy likes her, I need to know."

Adrian chuckled. "Should Sage have passed you a note in class?"

"Lee's fine," I said. "He obviously adores her, and it's not like she'll ever be alone with him."

"We don't know for sure that he's fine," said Eddie.

"Whereas Micah's a hundred percent okay? Did you do a background check or something?" I asked.

"No," said Eddie, looking embarrassed. "I just know. It's a feeling I get about him. There's no problem with him spending time with Jill."

"Except that he's human."

"They wouldn't have gotten serious."

"You don't know that."

"Enough, you two," interrupted Adrian. Jill and Lee had finally reached the start of the Dragon's Lair, meaning we could move on. Adrian lowered his voice. "Your argument's useless. I mean, look at them. That human boy doesn't enter into it."

I looked. Adrian was right. Jill and Lee were clearly enthralled with each other. Some guilty part of me wondered if I should be a doing a better job of looking out for Jill. I was so relieved that she was interested in a Moroi that I hadn't stopped to wonder if she should even be dating anyone. Was fifteen old enough? I hadn't dated at fifteen. I'd actually, well, never dated.

"There is an age difference between them," I admitted, more to myself.

Adrian scoffed. "Believe me, I've seen age differences. Theirs is nothing."

He walked off, and a few moments later, Eddie and I went to join him. Eddie maintained his simultaneous vigil of Jill, but this time, I got the impression the danger he was watching out for was right beside her. Adrian's laughter rang out ahead of us.

"Sage!" he called. "You have *got* to see this."

Eddie and I reached the next green and stared in astonishment. Then I burst out laughing.

We had reached Dracula's Castle.

A huge, multi-towered black castle guarded the hole some distance away. A tunnel was cut out through the center of it with a narrow bridge meant for the ball to go over. If the ball fell off the sides before getting through the castle, it was returned back to the starting point. An animatronic Count Dracula stood off to the castle's side. He was pure white, with red eyes, pointed ears, and slicked-back hair. He jerkily kept raising his arms to show off a batlike cape. Nearby, a speaker blasted eerie organ music.

I couldn't stop laughing. Adrian and Eddie looked at me as though they'd never seen me before.

"I don't think I've ever heard her laugh," Eddie told him.

"Certainly not the reaction I was expecting," mused Adrian. "I'd been counting on abject terror, judging from past Alchemist behavior. I didn't think you liked vampires."

Still grinning, I watched Dracula raise his cape up and down. "This isn't a vampire. Not a real one. And that's what makes it so funny. It's pure Hollywood camp. Real vampires are terrifying and unnatural. This? This is hilarious."

It was clear from their expressions that neither really understood why this would appeal to my sense of humor so much. Adrian did, however, offer to take a picture with my cell phone when I asked him. I posed by Dracula and put on a big smile.

Adrian managed to snap the shot just as Dracula was raising his cape. When I viewed the picture, I was pleased to see it had come out perfectly. Even my hair looked good.

Adrian gave the picture a nod of approval before handing me the phone. "Okay, even I can admit that's pretty cute."

I found myself overanalyzing the comment. What had he meant in saying *even he* could admit it? That I was cute for a human? Or that I had just met some kind of Adrian hot-girl criteria? Moments later, I had to forcibly stop thinking about it. *Let it go, Sydney. It's a compliment. Accept it.*

We played through the rest of the course, finally finishing off with the waterfall itself. That was a particularly challenging hole, and I took my time lining up the shot—not that I needed to. I was beating everyone pretty handily. Eddie was the only one who came close. It was clear Jill and Lee didn't even have their attention on the game, and as for Adrian and his natural talent . . . well, they were very solidly in last place.

Eddie, Adrian, and I were still ahead of the other two, so we waited for them by the waterfall. Jill practically ran to it when she had the chance, gazing up at it with enchanted eyes. "Oh," she breathed. "This is wonderful. I haven't seen this much water in days."

"Remember what I said about the toxicity," teased Lee. But it was clear he found her reaction endearing. As I glanced at the other two guys, I saw that they shared the same feelings. Well, not exactly the same. Adrian's affection was clearly brotherly. Eddie's? It was hard to read, kind of a mix of the other two. Maybe it was a kind of guardian fondness.

Jill made a gesture to the waterfall, and suddenly, part of it broke off from the tumbling cascade. The chunk of water shaped itself into a braid, then twisted high into the air, making spirals before shattering into a million drops that misted over us all. I had been staring wide-eyed and frozen, but those drops hitting me shocked me awake.

"Jill," I said in a voice I barely recognized as my own. "Don't do that again."

Jill, eyes bright, barely spared me a glance as she made another piece of water dance in the air. "No one's around to see, Sydney."

That wasn't what had me so upset. That wasn't what filled me with so much panic that I could barely breathe. The world was doing that thing where it started to spin, and I worried I was going to faint. Stark, cold fear ran through me, fear at the unknown. The unnatural. The laws of my world had just been broken. This was vampire magic, something foreign and inaccessible to humans—inaccessible because it was forbidden, something no mortal was meant to delve into. I had only once seen magic used, when two spirit users had turned on each other, and I never wanted to see it again. One had forced the plants of the earth to do her bidding while the other telekinetically hurled objects meant to kill. It had been terrifying, and even though I hadn't been the target, I'd felt trapped and overwhelmed in the face of such otherworldly power. It was a reminder that these weren't fun, easy people to hang out with. These were creatures wholly different from me.

"Stop it," I said, feeling the panic rise. I was afraid of the magic, afraid it would touch me, afraid of what it might do to me. "Don't do it anymore!"

Jill didn't even hear me. She grinned at Lee. "You're air, right? Can you create fog over the water?"

Lee stuffed his hands in his pockets and looked away. "Ah, well, it's probably not a good idea. I mean, we're in public . . ."

"Come on," she pleaded. "It won't take any effort for you at all."

He actually appeared nervous. "Nah, not right now."

"Not you too." She laughed. Above her and in front of her, that demon water was still spinning, spinning, spinning . . .

"Jill," said Adrian, a harsher note in his voice than I'd ever heard before. In fact, I couldn't recall him ever addressing her by her actual name. "Stop."

It was all he said, but it was like a wave of something went through Jill. She flinched, and the water spirals disappeared, falling away in droplets. "Fine," she said, looking confused.

There was a moment of awkwardness, and then Eddie said, "We should hurry. We're going to be pushing curfew."

Lee and Jill set out to make their shots and soon were laughing and flirting again. Eddie continued watching them in his concerned way. Only Adrian paid any attention to me. He was the only one who really understood what had happened, I realized. His green eyes studied me, with no trace of their usual bitter humor. I wasn't fooled, though. I knew there had to be some witty quip coming, mocking my reaction.

"Are you okay?" he asked quietly.

"I'm fine," I said, turning from him. I didn't want him to see my face. He'd already seen too much, seen my fear. I didn't want any of them to know how afraid of them I was. I heard him take a few steps toward me.

"Sage—"

"Leave me alone," I snapped back. I hurried off toward the course's exit, certain he wouldn't follow me. I was right.

I waited for them to finish the game, using the alone time to calm myself down. By the time they caught up to me, I was fairly certain I had wiped most of the emotions from my face. Adrian still watched me with concern, which I didn't like, but at least he didn't say anything else about my breakdown.

Surprising to no one, the final score showed that I had won and Adrian had lost. Lee had come in third, which seemed to trouble him. "I used to be a lot better," he muttered, frowning. "I used to be perfect at this game." Considering he'd spent most of the time paying attention to Jill, I thought third was a pretty respectable performance.

I dropped him and Adrian off first and then just barely got Eddie, Jill, and me back to Amberwood on time. I was more or less back to normal by then, not that anyone would've noticed. Jill was floating on a cloud as we went into our dorm room, talking nonstop about Lee.

"I had no idea he'd traveled so much! He's maybe been more places than you, Sydney. He keeps telling me that he'll take me to all of them, that we'll spend the rest of our lives traveling and doing whatever we want. And he's taking all sorts of classes in college because he's not sure what he wants to major in. Well, not all sorts this semester. He's got a light schedule so that he can spend more time with his father. And that's good for me. For us, I mean."

I stifled a yawn and nodded wearily. "That's great."

She paused from where she'd been searching her dresser for pajamas. "I'm sorry, by the way."

I froze. I didn't want an apology for the magic. I didn't even want to remember it had happened.

"For yelling at you the other night," she continued. "You

187

didn't set me up with Lee. I should never have accused you of interfering. He really has liked me all along, and, well . . . he's really great."

I let out the breath I'd been holding and attempted a weak smile. "I'm glad you're happy."

She returned cheerfully to her tasks and to talking about Lee until I left to go down to the bathroom. Before brushing my teeth, I stood in front of the sink and washed my hands and arms over and over, scrubbing as hard as I could to wash away the magical drops of water I swore I could still feel on my skin.

CHAPTER 13

MY CELL PHONE RANG at the crack of dawn the next morning. I was already up, being an early riser, but Jill rolled over in bed and put her pillow over her head.

"Make it stop," she groaned.

I answered and found Eddie on the other end of the line.

"I'm downstairs," he said. "Ready to practice some self-defense before it gets too hot."

"You're going to have to do it without me," I said. I had a feeling Eddie was taking his promise to Clarence about training us very seriously. I felt no such obligation. "I've got a ton of homework to do. That, and I'm sure Ms. Terwilliger's going to make me do a coffee run today."

"Well, then send Jill down," said Eddie.

I glanced over to the cocoon of blankets on her bed. "That might be easier said than done."

Surprisingly, she managed to rouse herself enough to brush her teeth, take aspirin for a headache, and throw on some workout clothes. She bid me farewell, and I promised to check on them later. Not long after that, Ms. Terwilliger called with her coffee demand, and I prepared myself for another day of trying to fit in my own work with hers.

I drove over to Spencer's and didn't even notice Trey until I was standing right in front of him.

"Ms. Terwilliger's?" he asked, pointing to the caramel sauce cappuccino.

"Huh?" I looked up. Trey was my cashier. "You work here?"

He nodded. "Gotta make spending money somehow."

I handed him some cash, noting that he'd charged me half price. "Don't take this the wrong way, but you don't look so great," I told him. He looked tired and worn out around the edges. Closer inspection showed bruises and cuts as well.

"Yeah, well, I had kind of a rough day yesterday."

I hesitated. That was a leading comment, but there was no one in line behind me. "What happened?" I asked, knowing it was expected.

Trey scowled. "That asshole Greg Slade wreaked havoc in football tryouts yesterday. I mean, the results aren't up yet, but it's pretty obvious he's going to get quarterback. He was like a machine, just plowing guys over." He extended his left hand, which had some bandage-wrapped fingers. "He stepped on my hand too."

I winced, remembering Slade's out-of-control athleticism in PE. The politics of high school football and who was quarterback weren't that important to me. True, I felt sorry for Trey, but it was the source behind the tattoos that intrigued me. Keith's warnings about not causing trouble rang back to me, but I was unable to stop myself.

"I know about the tattoos," I said. "Julia and Kristin told me about them. And I get now why you were suspicious of mine—but it's not what you think. Really."

"That's not what I've heard. Most people think you're just saying that because you don't want to tell where you got it."

I was a little taken aback by that. I was pretty sure Julia and Kristin had believed me. Were they actually spreading around the opposite? "I had no idea."

He shrugged, a small smile on his lips. "Don't worry. I believe you. There's something kind of naively charming about you. You don't seem like the cheating type."

"Hey," I scolded. "I'm not naive."

"It was a compliment."

"How long have these tattoos been around?" I asked, deciding it was best to move in. "I heard since last year."

He handed me my coffee, thinking. "Yeah, but it was the end of last year. School year, I mean."

"And they come from a placed called Nevermore?"

"As far as I know." Trey eyed me suspiciously. "Why?"

"Just curious," I said sweetly.

A couple of college kids dressed like rich hobos got in line behind me and regarded us impatiently. "Can we get some service here?"

Trey gave them a stiff smile and then rolled his eyes at me as I moved away. "See you around, Melbourne."

I headed back to Amberwood and delivered Ms. Terwilliger's coffee. I wasn't in the mood to stay leashed to her all day, so I asked if I could go elsewhere if I kept my cell phone handy. She agreed. The library had too much activity and—ironically—noise for me today. I wanted the solitude of my room.

As I was cutting across the lawn to catch the shuttle, I spotted some familiar figures behind a cluster of trees. I changed direction and found Jill and Eddie squaring off in a small clearing. Micah sat cross-legged on the ground, watching avidly. He waved at me as I approached.

"I didn't realize your brother was a kung-fu master," he remarked.

"It's not kung fu," said Eddie gruffly, never taking his eyes off Jill.

"Same difference," said Micah. "It's still pretty badass."

Eddie feinted, like he was going to strike at Jill's side. She responded fairly quickly with a block, though not quite fast enough to match him. Had he been serious, he would have hit her. Still, he seemed pleased with her response time.

"Good. That would deflect part of a hit, though you'd still feel it. Best is if you can duck and dodge altogether, but that takes a little more work."

Jill nodded obediently. "When can we work on that?"

Eddie regarded her with pride. That expression softened after a few moments of study. "Not today. Too much sun."

Jill started to protest and then stopped herself. She had that worn-out-from-the-light look again and was sweating heavily. She glanced up at the sky for a moment, as though begging it to give us some cloud cover. It remained unresponsive, so she nodded at Eddie.

"All right. But we're doing this tomorrow at the same time? Or earlier maybe. Or maybe tonight! Could we do both? Practice tonight when the sun's going down and then again in the morning? Would you mind?"

Eddie grinned, amused at her enthusiasm. "Whatever you want."

Smiling back, Jill sat down beside me, getting into as much shade as possible. Eddie regarded me expectantly. "What?" I asked.

"Aren't you supposed to learn to throw a punch?"

I scoffed. "No. When would I ever need to do that?"

Jill nudged me. "Do it, Sydney!"

Reluctantly, I allowed Eddie to give me a quick lesson on throwing a punch without injuring my hand in the process. I barely paid attention and felt like I was mostly providing entertainment for the others. When Eddie finished with me, Micah asked, "Hey, would you mind showing me some ninja moves too?"

"They have nothing to do with ninjas," protested Eddie, still smiling. "Come on up."

Micah leapt to his feet, and Eddie walked him through some rudimentary steps. More than anything, it seemed like Eddie was sizing up Micah and his capabilities. After a while, Eddie grew comfortable and let Micah practice some offensive moves to get rid of an attacker.

"Hey," protested Jill when Eddie landed a kick on Micah. Micah shrugged it off in a guy kind of way. "No fair. You wouldn't hit me when we were practicing."

Eddie was caught off guard enough that Micah actually got a hit in. Eddie gave him a look of grudging respect and then said to Jill, "That was different."

"Because I'm a girl?" she demanded. "You never held back with Rose."

193

"Who's Rose?" asked Micah.

"Another friend," explained Eddie. To Jill, he said: "And Rose has had years more experience than you."

"She's had more than Micah too. You were going easy on me."

Eddie flushed and kept his eyes on Micah. "Was not," he said.

"Were too," she muttered. As the boys sparred again, she said quietly to me, "How am I ever going to learn if he's afraid of breaking me?"

I watched the guys, analyzing what I knew of Eddie so far. "I think it's more complicated than that. I think he also just believes you shouldn't have to take the risk—that if he's doing a good enough job, you shouldn't have to defend yourself."

"He's doing a great job. You should have seen him at the attack." Her face got that haunted look it did whenever the attack that had driven her into hiding was mentioned. "But I still need to learn." She lowered her voice even more. "I really want to learn to use my magic to fight too, not that I'll get much practice in this desert."

I shuddered, recalling her display from the night before. "There'll be time," I said vaguely.

I stood up, saying I had to go get some work done. Micah asked Eddie and Jill if they wanted to get lunch. Eddie said yes immediately. Jill looked to me for help.

"It's just lunch," said Eddie meaningfully. I knew he still thought Micah was harmless. I didn't know, but after seeing how infatuated Jill was with Lee, I figured Micah would have to make some pretty aggressive moves to get anywhere.

"I'm sure it's fine," I said.

Jill looked relieved, and the group headed off. I spent the day finishing off that miserable book for Ms. Terwilliger. I still thought having to copy the archaic spells and rituals verbatim was a waste of time. The only point I could see for it was that if she ever did need to reference them for her research, she would have an easy computer file to check and not risk damage to the ancient book.

It was evening by the time I finished that and my other homework. Jill still wasn't back, and I decided to use the opportunity to check on something that had been bothering me. Earlier in the day, Jill had mentioned Eddie defending her in the attack. I'd felt from the beginning that there was something strange about that initial attack, something that they weren't telling me. So, I logged onto the Alchemists' network and pulled up everything we had on the Moroi rebels.

Naturally, it was all documented. We had to keep track of important events among the Moroi, and this ranked pretty high. Somehow, the Alchemists had gotten pictures of the Moroi Court, with protesters lined up outside one of the administrative buildings. Dhampir guardians were easy to pick out as they mingled and kept order. To my surprise, I recognized Dimitri Belikov—Rose's boyfriend—among those doing crowd control. He was easy to spot since he was almost always taller than everyone around him. Dhampirs look very human, and even I could admit that he was pretty good-looking. There was a rugged handsomeness to him, and even in a still photograph, I could see a fierceness as he watched the crowd.

Other protest pictures confirmed what I knew. By far, most people supported the young queen. Those against her were a minority—but a loud and dangerous one. A video from a human news show in Denver showed two Moroi guys nearly getting in a bar fight. They were shouting about queens and justice, most of which wouldn't make sense to a human observer. What made this video special was that the guy who'd filmed it—some random human with a cell phone camera—claimed he'd seen fangs on both men in the argument. The videographer had submitted his recording claiming he'd witnessed a vampire fight, but no one gave it much credibility. It was too grainy for anything to show up. Still, it was a reminder of what could happen if the Moroi situation spun out of control.

A status check showed me that Queen Vasilisa was indeed trying to get a law passed so that her rule was no longer dependent on there being at least one other person in her royal family. Alchemist experts guessed it would take three months, which was about what Rose had said. The number loomed in my head like a ticking time bomb. We needed to keep Jill safe for three months. And for three months, Vasilisa's enemies would be trying harder than ever to get to Jill. If Jill died, Vasilisa's rule would end—along with her attempts to fix the system.

Yet none of this was what had really driven me to research. I wanted to know about Jill's initial attack, the one that no one talked about. What I found wasn't much help. No Alchemists had been there at the time, of course, so our information was based on what Moroi sources had reported. All we knew was that "the queen's sister had been viciously and severely attacked—but had made a full recovery." From what I'd observed, that was certainly true. Jill showed no signs of injury, and the attack had occurred a week before she came to Palm Springs. Was that enough time to heal from a "vicious and severe" attack? And was an attack like that enough to make her wake screaming?

I didn't know but still couldn't shake my suspicions. When Jill came home later, she was in such a good mood that I couldn't bear to interrogate her. I also remembered too late that I'd meant to research the case of Clarence's niece and her bizarre death by throat-slitting. Jill's situation had distracted me. I let the matter go and called it an early night.

Tomorrow, I thought drowsily. *I'll do it all tomorrow.*

Tomorrow came much more quickly than I expected. I was woken out of a heavy sleep by someone shaking me, and for a split second, the old nightmare was there, the one about Alchemists carrying me away in the night. Recognizing Jill, I just barely stopped myself from screaming.

"Hey, hey," I scolded. There was light outside, but it was purplish. Barely after sunrise. "What's going on? What's the matter?"

Jill looked at me, face grim and eyes wide with fear. "It's Adrian. You have to rescue him."

CHAPTER 14

"FROM HIMSELF?"

I couldn't help it. The joke was out before I could stop it.

"No." She perched on the edge of the bed and bit her lower lip. "Maybe 'rescue' isn't the right word. But we have to go get him. He's trapped in Los Angeles."

I rubbed my eyes as I sat up and then waited a few moments, just in case this was all a dream. Nope. Nothing changed. I picked up my cell phone from my bedside table and groaned when I read the display.

"Jill, it's not even six yet." I started to question if Adrian was even awake this early but then remembered he was probably on a nocturnal schedule. Left to their own devices, Moroi went to bed around what was late morning for the rest of us.

"I know," she said in a small voice. "I'm sorry. I wouldn't ask if it wasn't important. He got a ride there last night because he wanted to see those . . . those Moroi girls again. Lee was supposed to be in LA too, so Adrian figured he could get a ride home. Only, he can't get ahold of Lee, so now he can't get back. Adrian, that is. He's stranded and hung over."

I started to lie back down. "I don't have a lot of sympathy for that. Maybe he'll learn a lesson."

"Sydney, *please*."

I put an arm over my eyes. Maybe if I looked like I was asleep, she'd leave me alone. A question suddenly popped into my head, and I jerked my arm away.

"How do you know any of this? Did he call?" I wasn't a super-light sleeper, but I still would've heard her phone ring.

Jill looked away from me. Frowning, I sat up.

"Jill? How do you know any of this?"

"Please," she whispered. "Can't we just go get him?"

"Not until you tell me what's going on." A weird feeling was crawling along my skin. I'd felt for a while that I was being excluded from something big, and now, I suddenly knew I was about to find out what the Moroi had been hiding from me.

"You can't tell," she said, finally meeting my eyes again.

I tapped the tattoo on my cheek. "I can hardly tell anyone anything as it is."

"No, not anyone. Not the Alchemists. Not Keith. Not any other Moroi or dhampirs who don't already know."

Not tell the Alchemists? That would be a problem. Among all the other craziness in my life, no matter how much my assignments infuriated me or how much time I'd spent with vampires, I'd never questioned who my loyalty was to. I *had* to tell the Alchemists if something was going on with Jill and the others. It was my duty to them, to humanity.

Of course, part of my duty to the Alchemists was looking after Jill, and whatever was plaguing her now obviously was connected to her welfare. For half a second, I considered lying to her and immediately dismissed the idea. I couldn't do it. If I was going to keep her secret, I would keep it. If I wasn't going to keep it, then I would let her know up front.

"I won't tell," I said. I think the words surprised me as much as her. She studied me in the dim light and must have at last decided I was telling the truth. She gave a slow nod.

"Adrian and I are bound. Like, with a spirit bond."

I felt my eyes widen in disbelief. "How did that—" Everything suddenly clicked together, the missing pieces. "The attack. You—you—"

"Died," said Jill bluntly. "There was so much confusion when the Moroi assassins came. Everyone thought they were coming for Lissa, so most of the guardians went to surround her. Eddie was the only one who came for me, but he wasn't fast enough. This man, he . . ." Jill touched a spot in the center of her chest and shuddered. "He stabbed me. He . . . he killed me. That's when Adrian came along. He used spirit to heal me and bring me back, and now we're bound. Everything happened so fast. No one there even realized what he did."

My mind was reeling. A spirit bond. Spirit was a troubling element to the Alchemists, mostly because we had so few records of it. Our world was documents and knowledge, so any gap made us feel weak. Signs of spirit use had been recorded over the centuries, but no one had really realized it was its own element. Those events had been written off as random magical phenomena. It was only recently, when Vasilisa Dragomir had exposed herself, that spirit had been rediscovered, along with its myriad psychic effects. She and Rose had had a spirit bond, the only modern one we had documented. Healing was one of spirit's most notable attributes, and Vasilisa had brought Rose back from a car accident. It had forged a psychic connection between them, one that had only been shattered when Rose had had a second near-death experience.

"You can see in his head," I breathed. "His thoughts. His feelings." So much began to come together. Like how Jill always knew everything about Adrian, even when he claimed he hadn't told her.

She nodded. "I don't want to. Believe me. But I can't help it. Rose said in time, I'll learn the control to keep his feelings out, but I can't do it now. And he has so much, Sydney. So much feeling. He feels everything so strongly—love, grief, anger. His emotions are up and down, all over the place. What happened between him and Rose . . . it tears him apart. It's hard to stay focused on me sometimes with all of that going on in him. At least it's only some of the time. I can't really control when it happens."

I didn't say it but wondered if some of those volatile feelings were part of spirit's tendency to drive its users insane. Or maybe it was just part of Adrian's innate personality. All irrelevant, for now.

"But he can't feel you, right? It's only one way?" I asked. Rose had been able to read Vasilisa's thoughts and see her experiences in everyday life—but not the other way around. I assumed it was the same now, but with spirit, one couldn't take anything for granted.

"Right," she agreed.

"That's how . . . that's how you always know things about him. Like my visits. And when he wanted pizza. That's why he's here, what Abe wanted him here for."

Jill frowned. "Abe? No, it was kind of a group choice for Adrian to come along. Rose and Lissa thought it would be best if we were together while we were getting used to the bond, and I wanted him nearby too. What made you think Abe was involved?"

"Er, nothing," I said. Abe instructing Adrian to stay at Clarence's must not have been something Jill observed. "I was just mixed up about something."

"Can we go now?" she begged. "I answered your questions."

"Let me make sure I understand something first," I said. "Explain how he ended up in Los Angeles and why he's stuck."

Jill clasped her hands together and looked away again, a habit I was coming to associate with when she had information that she knew wasn't going to be received well.

"He, um, left Clarence's last night. Because he was bored. He hitchhiked into town—to Palm Springs—and ended up partying with some people who were going to LA. So, he went with them. And while he was in a club, he found those girls—some Moroi girls—and so he went home with them. And then he spent the night and kind of passed out. Until now. Now he's awake. And he wants to go home. To Clarence's."

With all this talk of clubbing and girls, an unsettling thought was building in my mind. "Jill, just how much of that did you actually experience?"

She was still avoiding my gaze. "It's not important."

"It is to me," I said. The night Jill had woken in tears . . . that had been when Adrian was with those girls too. Was she living his sex life? "What was he thinking? He knows you're there, that you're living everything he does, but he never stops to—oh

God. The first day of school. Ms. Chang was right, wasn't she? You *were* hung over. Vicariously, at least." And almost every other morning, she woke up feeling semi-sick—because Adrian was hung over too.

Jill nodded. "There was nothing physical they could've tested—like blood or anything—to prove that's what it was, but yeah. I might as well have had one. I certainly felt like it. It was awful."

I reached out and turned her face toward mine so that she had to look at me. "And you are now too." There was more light in the room as the sun rose higher, and I could see the signs again. The sickly paleness and bloodshot eyes. I wouldn't have been surprised if her head and stomach hurt too. I dropped my hand and shook my head in disgust. "He can stay there."

"Sydney!"

"He deserves it. I know you feel . . . something . . . for him." Whether it was sisterly or romantic affection, it really didn't matter. "But you can't baby him and run to every need and request he sends to you."

"He's not asking me, not exactly," she said. "I can just feel that he wants it."

"Well, he should've thought of that before he got himself into this mess. He can figure out his own way back."

"His cell phone died."

"He can borrow one from his new 'friends.'"

"He's in agony," she said.

"That's how life is," I said.

"*I'm* in agony."

I sighed. "Jill—"

"No, I'm serious. And it's not just the hangover. I mean,

yeah, part of it's the hangover. And as long as he's sick and not taking anything, then so am I! Plus . . . his thoughts. Ugh." Jill rested her forehead in her hands. "I can't get rid of how unhappy he is. It's like . . . like a hammer banging in my head. I can't get away from it. I can't do anything else except think about how miserable he is! And that makes me miserable. Or think I'm miserable. I don't know." She sighed. "Please, Sydney. Can we go?"

"Do you know where he is?" I asked.

"Yes."

"All right, then. *I'll* go." I slid over to the edge of the bed. She stood up with me.

"I'll come too."

"No," I said. "You go back to bed. Take some aspirin and see if you can make yourself feel better." I also had a few things I wanted to say to Adrian in private. Admittedly, if she was constantly connected to him, she'd "overhear" our conversation, but it'd be a lot easier to tell him what I wanted to when she wasn't actually there in the flesh, looking at me with those big eyes.

"But how will you—"

"I don't want you getting sick in the car. Just call me if something changes or if he leaves or whatever."

Jill's further protests were halfhearted, either because she didn't feel up to them or was just willing to be grateful for anyone "rescuing" Adrian. She didn't have an exact address, but she had a very vivid description of the condo he was at, which was right next door to a notable hotel. When I looked it up, I saw the hotel was actually in Long Beach, meaning I'd have to go past Los Angeles proper. I had a two-hour drive ahead of me. Coffee would be required.

It was a pretty day, at least, and there was almost no traffic out so early on a Sunday. Looking at the sun and blue skies, I kept thinking about how nice it would be if I were making this drive in a convertible, with the top down. It would also be nice if I had been making this drive for any other reason besides retrieving a stranded vampire party boy.

I was still having a hard time wrapping my mind around the idea that Jill and Adrian were spirit bound. The notion of someone bringing another back from the dead was not one that meshed well with my religious beliefs. It was just as troubling as another of spirit's feats: restoring Strigoi. We had two documented cases of that happening too, two Strigoi magically changed by spirit users back to their original form. One was a woman named Sonya Karp. The other was Dimitri Belikov. Between that and all this resurrection, spirit was really starting to freak me out. That much power just didn't seem right.

I reached Long Beach right on schedule and had no problem finding the condo complex. It was right across the street from an oceanfront hotel called the Cascadia. Since Jill hadn't called with a change of location, I assumed Adrian was still holed up. Street parking was easy to find at this time of day, and I paused outside to stare at the blue-gray expanse of the Pacific on the western horizon. It was breathtaking, especially after my first week in the desert of Palm Springs. I almost wished Jill had come. Maybe being near so much water would have made her feel better.

The condos were in a peach stucco building with three floors, two units on each floor. From Adrian's memories, Jill remembered going to the top of the building and turning right. I retraced those steps and came to a blue door with a heavy brass knocker. I knocked.

When no answer came after almost a minute, I tried again more loudly. I was nearly on the verge of a third attempt when I heard the lock unclick. The door opened a crack, and a girl peeked out.

She was clearly Moroi, with a skinny runway model build and pale, perfect skin that seemed particularly irritating today, considering I was pretty sure a pimple was going to break out on my forehead soon. She was my age, maybe a little older, with sleek black hair and deep blue eyes. She looked like some otherworldly doll. She was also half-asleep.

"Yeah?" She looked me over. "Are you selling something?" Next to this tall, perfect Moroi, I suddenly felt self-conscious and frumpy in my linen skirt and button-down top.

"Is Adrian here?"

"Who?"

"Adrian. Tall. Brown hair. Green eyes."

She frowned. "Do you mean Jet?"

"I . . . I'm not sure. Does he smoke like a chimney?"

The girl nodded sagely. "Yup. You must mean Jet." She glanced behind her and yelled, "Hey, Jet! There's some sales-woman here to see you."

"Send her out," called a familiar voice.

The Moroi opened the door wider and beckoned me in. "He's on the balcony."

I walked through a living room that served as a caution-ary tale of what would ever happen if Jill and I lost all sense of housekeeping and self-respect. The place was a disaster. A girl disaster. Laundry piles littered the floor, and dirty dishes covered every square inch that wasn't occupied by empty beer bottles. A knocked-over bottle of nail polish had created a bubblegum pink splotch on the carpet. On the couch, tangled in blankets, a blond Moroi girl peered at me drowsily and then went back to sleep.

Stepping around everything, I made my way to Adrian through a patio door. He stood on a balcony, leaning against its railing, his back to me. The morning air was warm and clear, so naturally, he was trying to ruin it by smoking.

"Tell me this, Sage," he said, without turning back to face me. "Why the hell would someone put a building near the beach but not have the balconies face the water? They were built to look at hills behind us. Unless the neighbors start doing something interesting, I'm ready to declare this structure a total waste."

I crossed my arms and glared at his back. "I'm so glad I've got your valuable opinion on that. I'll be sure and note it when I file my complaint to the city council for their inadequate ocean views."

He turned around, the hint of a smile twisting his lips. "What are you doing here? I figured you'd be in church or something."

"What do you think? I'm here because of the pleas of a fifteen-year-old girl who doesn't deserve what you put her through."

Any trace of a smile vanished. "Oh. She told you." He turned back around.

"Yes, and you all should have told me sooner! This is serious . . . monumental."

"And no doubt something the Alchemists would *love* to study." I could envision his sneer perfectly.

"I promised her I wouldn't tell. But you still should've filled me in. It's kind of important information to have since I'm the one who has to babysit all of you."

"'Babysit' is kind of an extreme term, Sage."

"Considering the current scenario? No, not really."

Adrian said nothing, and I gave him a quick assessment. He wore high-quality, dark-washed jeans and a red cotton shirt that must have been slept in, judging from the wrinkles. His feet were bare.

"Did you bring a coat?" I asked.

"No."

I went back inside and did a search among the clutter. The blond Moroi girl was fast asleep, and the one who'd let me in was sprawled on an unmade bed in another room. I finally found Adrian's socks and shoes tossed in a corner. I rushed to retrieve them, then headed back outside and dropped them next to him on the balcony.

"Put those on. We're leaving."

"You aren't my mom."

"No, yours is serving a sentence for perjury and theft, if memory serves."

It was a mean, mean thing to say, but it was also the truth. And it got his attention.

Adrian's head whipped around. Anger glinted in the depths of his green eyes, the first I'd ever truly seen in him. "Don't you ever mention her again. You have no idea what you're talking about."

His anger was a little intimidating, but I held my ground. "Actually, I was the one in charge of tracking down the records she stole."

"She had her reasons," he said through gritted teeth.

"You're so willing to defend someone who was convicted of a crime, yet you don't have any consideration for Jill—who's done nothing."

"I have plenty of consideration for her!" He paused to light a cigarette with trembling hands, and I suspected he was also trying to get a grip on his emotions. "I think about her all the time. How could I not? She's there . . . I can't feel it, but she's always there, always listening to things in my head, listening to things *I* don't even want to hear. Feeling things I don't want to feel." He inhaled on the cigarette and turned to look at the view, though I doubted he actually saw it.

"If you're so aware of her, then how come you do stuff like this?" I gestured around us. "How could you drink when you know it affects her too? How could you do"—I grimaced—"whatever you did with those girls, knowing she could 'see' it? She's *fifteen*."

"I know, I know," he said. "I didn't know about the drinking—not at first. When she came over after school and told me that day, I stopped. I really did. But then . . . when you guys were over on Friday, she told me to go ahead since it was the weekend. I guess she wasn't as worried about getting sick. So, I said to myself, 'I'll just have a couple.' Only last night, it turned into more than that. And then things got kind of crazy, and I ended up here and—what am I doing? I don't have to justify my actions to you."

"I don't think you can justify them to anyone." I was furious, my blood boiling.

"You're one to talk, Sage." He pointed an accusing finger. "At least I *take* action. You? You let the world go by without you. You stand there while that asshole Keith treats you like crap and just smile and nod. You have no spine. You don't fight back. Even old Abe seems to push you around. Was Rose right that he's got something on you? Or is he just someone else you won't fight back against?"

I worked hard not to let him know just how deeply those words struck me. "You don't know the first thing about me, Adrian Ivashkov. I fight back plenty."

"You could've fooled me."

I gave him a tight smile. "I just don't make a spectacle of myself when I do it. It's called being responsible."

"Sure. Whatever helps you sleep at night."

I threw up my hands. "Well, that's the thing: I don't sleep at night anymore because I have to come save you from your own idiocy. Can we leave now? Please?"

As an answer, he put out the cigarette and began putting on his socks and shoes. He looked up at me as he did, the anger totally gone. His moods were changed as easily as flipping a light switch.

"You have to get me out of there. Out of Clarence's." His voice was level and serious. "He's a nice enough guy, but I'm going to go crazy if I stay there."

"As opposed to your excellent behavior when you aren't there?" I glanced back into the condo. "Maybe your two groupies have room for you."

"Hey, show some respect. They're real people with names. Carla and Krissy." He frowned. "Or was it Missy?"

I sighed. "I told you before, I don't have any control over your living arrangement. How hard is it for you to go get your own place? Why do you need me?"

"Because I have almost no money, Sage. My old man cut

me off. He gives me an allowance that's barely enough for cigarettes."

I considered suggesting he quit, but that probably wouldn't be a useful turn in the conversation. "I'm sorry. I really am. If I think of something, I'll let you know. Besides, doesn't Abe want you to stay there?" I decided to come clean. "I overheard you two on the first day. How he wanted you to do something for him."

Adrian straightened up, shoes secured. "Yeah, I don't know what that's all about. Did you hear how totally vague he was too? I think he's just trying to screw with me, keep me busy because somewhere in that messed-up heart of his, he feels bad about what happened with—"

Adrian shut his mouth, but I could hear the unspoken name: *Rose.* A terrible sadness crossed his features, and his eyes looked lost and haunted. I remembered when I'd been in the car with Jill, and she'd slipped into a tirade about Rose, about how the memory of her tormented Adrian. Knowing what I knew now about the bond, I had a feeling there'd been very little of Jill in those words. That had been a direct line to Adrian. Looking at him, I could barely understand the scope of that pain, nor did I know how to help. I just knew that I suddenly understood a tiny bit better why he would want to drown his sorrows so much, not that that made it any healthier.

"Adrian," I said awkwardly, "I'm—"

"Forget it," he said. "You don't know what it's like to love someone like that, then to have that love thrown back in your face—"

An ear-splitting scream suddenly pierced the air. Adrian flinched more than me, proving the downside of vampire hearing: annoying sounds were that much more annoying.

As one, we hurried back inside the condo. The blond girl was sitting upright on the couch, as startled as we were. The other girl, the one who had let me in, stood in the doorway to the bedroom, pale as death, a cell phone clutched in her hand.

"What's the matter?" I asked.

She opened her mouth to speak and then did a double take at me, seeming to remember that I was human.

"It's okay, Carla," said Adrian. "She knows about us. You can trust her."

That was all Carla needed. She threw herself into Adrian's arms and began crying uncontrollably. "Oh, Jet," she said between sobs. "I can't believe it happened to her. How did this happen?"

"*What* happened?" asked the other Moroi girl, rising unsteadily to her feet. Like Adrian, she looked like she'd slept in her clothes. I dared to hope that Jill hadn't been subjected to as much as indecency as I'd originally imagined.

"Tell us what happened, Carla," said Adrian in a gentle voice I'd only ever heard him use around with Jill.

"I'm Krissy," she sniffed. "And our friend—our friend." She wiped at her eyes as more tears came to her eyes. "I just got the call. Our friend—another Moroi who goes to our college—she's *dead*." Krissy looked up at the other girl, whom I guessed was Carla now. "It was Melody. She was killed by Strigoi last night."

Carla gasped and began crying, triggering more tears from Krissy. I met Adrian's eyes, both of us aghast. Even if we had no idea who this Melody was, a Strigoi killing was still a terrible, tragic thing. Immediately, my Alchemist mind kicked into action. I needed to make sure the crime scene was secure and the murder kept secret from humans.

"Where?" I asked. "Where did it happen?"

"West Hollywood," said Carla. "Out behind some club."

I relaxed a little, though I was still shaken by the tragedy of it all. That was a busy, populated region, one that would definitely be on the Alchemists' radar. If any humans had found out, the Alchemists would have long since taken care of it.

"At least they didn't turn her," said Carla forlornly. "She can rest in peace. Of course, those monsters still couldn't rest without mutilating her body."

I stared, feeling cold all over. "What do you mean?"

She rubbed her nose on Adrian's shirt. "Melody. They didn't just drink from her. They slit her throat too."

CHAPTER 15

ADRIAN SLEPT for a lot of the way back to Palm Springs. Apparently, his late-night partying with Carla and Krissy had resulted in very little rest. Thinking about it made me uncomfortable. Thinking about Jill experiencing it through him made me ill.

There'd been little we could do for Carla and Krissy except offer our sympathies. Strigoi attacks happened. It was tragic and terrible, but the only way most Moroi could protect themselves was to exercise caution, keep their whereabouts secure, and stay with guardians if possible. For non-royal Moroi living and going to school in the world like Carla and Krissy were, guardians weren't an option. Plenty of Moroi got by like that; they just had to be careful.

The two of them thought the circumstances surrounding their friend's death were awful. That was true. They were. But neither girl thought much past that or felt there was anything odd about the throat-slitting. I wouldn't have either if I hadn't heard Clarence's account of his niece's death.

I brought Adrian back to Amberwood with me and signed him in briefly as a guest, figuring Jill would feel better about seeing him in the flesh. Sure enough, she was already waiting for us in the dorm when we arrived. She hugged him and flashed me a grateful look. Eddie was with her, and though he said nothing, there was a look of exasperation on his face that said I wasn't the only one who thought Adrian had behaved ridiculously.

"I was so worried," Jill said.

Adrian ruffled her hair, which made her duck away. "Nothing to worry about, Jailbait. So long as the wrinkles come out of this shirt, there's no harm done."

No harm done, I thought, feeling anger kindle within me. *No harm except Jill has to watch Adrian hook up with other girls and endure his drinking binges.* It didn't matter if Lee had supplanted her old crush on Adrian. She was just too young to witness anything like that. Adrian had been selfish.

"Now," Adrian continued, "if Sage would be kind enough to keep playing chauffeur, I'll take us all out to lunch."

"I thought you didn't have any money," I pointed out.

"I said I don't have *very much* money."

Jill and Eddie exchanged looks. "We, um, were going to meet Micah for lunch," Jill said.

"Bring him along," said Adrian. "He can meet the family."

Micah showed up shortly thereafter and was happy to meet our other "brother." He shook Adrian's hand and smiled. "Now I see some family resemblance. I was starting to wonder if Jill was adopted, but you two kind of look like each other."

"So does our mailman back in North Dakota," said Adrian.

"South," I corrected. Fortunately, Micah didn't seem to think there was anything weird about the slip.

"Right," said Adrian. He studied Micah thoughtfully. "There's something familiar about *you*. Have we met?"

Micah shook his head. "I've never been to South Dakota."

I was pretty sure I heard Adrian murmur, "That makes two of us."

"We should go," said Eddie hastily, moving toward our dorm's door. "I've got some homework to catch up on later."

I frowned, puzzled by the attitude change. Eddie wasn't a bad student by any means, but it had been obvious to me since coming to Amberwood that he didn't take the same interest in the school that I did. This was a repeated year for him, and he was content to just play along and only do what was necessary to stay in good standing.

If anyone else thought his behavior was odd, they didn't show it. Micah was already talking to Jill about something, and Adrian still looked like he was trying to place Micah. Adrian's generous offer to buy lunch only extended to fast food, so our meal was quick. After a week of dorm food, though, I appreciated the change, and Adrian had long since made his views clear on Dorothy's "healthy" cooking.

"You should've just gotten a kids' meal," Adrian told me, pointing to my half-eaten burger and fries. "You could have saved me a lot of money. And gotten a toy."

"'A lot' is kind of an exaggeration," I said. "Besides, now you have leftovers to help get you by."

He rolled his eyes and stole a fry off my plate. "You're the one who should take the leftovers home. How do you even function on so little food?" he demanded. "One of these days, you're just going to blow away."

"Stop it," I said.

"Just telling it like it is," he said with a shrug. "You could stand to gain about ten pounds."

I stared at him incredulously, too shocked to even come up with a response. What did a Moroi know about weight gain? They had perfect figures. They didn't know what it was like to look in the mirror and see inadequacy, to never feel good enough. It was effortless for them, whereas no matter how hard I worked, I never seemed to match their inhuman perfection.

Adrian's eyes drifted over to where Jill, Eddie, and Micah were animatedly talking about practicing more self-defense together.

"They're kind of cute," said Adrian in a voice pitched just for my ears. He played with his straw as he studied the group. "Maybe Castile was on to something about letting her date at the school."

"Adrian," I groaned.

"Kidding," he said. "Lee would probably challenge him to a duel. He couldn't stop talking about her, you know. When we got back from mini-golfing, Lee just kept going on with, 'When can we all go out again?' And yet, he dropped off the face of the earth when he was in LA and I needed him."

"Had you made plans to meet up?" I asked. "Had he agreed to take you home?"

"No," Adrian admitted. "But what else was he really doing?"

Just then, a gray-haired man passed by, bumping into Jill's chair as he balanced a tray of burgers and sodas. Nothing spilled, but Eddie jumped to his feet with lightning speed, ready to fly across the table and defend her. The man backed up and mumbled an apology.

Adrian shook his head in amazement. "Just send *him* as a chaperone with whoever she goes out with, and we'll never have to worry."

Knowing what I knew now about Adrian and Jill's bond, I was able to regard Eddie's protectiveness in a different light. Oh, sure, I knew his guardian training had instilled that nature into him, but there always seemed to be something a little stronger there. Something almost . . . personal. At first, I'd wondered if maybe it was because Jill was just part of his larger circle of friends, like Rose. Now, I kept thinking it might go further than that. Jill had said Eddie had been the only one to try to protect her the night of the attack. He'd failed, most likely through timing and not because of a lack of skill.

But what kind of mark must that have left on him? He was someone whose sole purpose in life was to defend others—and he'd had to watch someone die on his watch. Now that Adrian had brought her back to life, was it almost like a second chance for Eddie? An opportunity to redeem himself? Maybe that's why he was so vigilant.

"You look confused," said Adrian.

I shook my head and sighed. "I think I'm just overthinking things."

He nodded solemnly. "That's why I try to never do it."

An earlier question popped into my head. "Hey, how come you told those girls your name was Jet?"

"Standard practice if you don't want chicks to find you later, Sage. Besides, I figured I was protecting our operation here."

"Yeah, but why Jet? Why not . . . I don't know . . . Travis or John?"

Adrian gave me a look that said I was wasting his time. "Because Jet sounds badass."

After lunch, we returned Adrian to Clarence's, and the rest of us went back to Amberwood. Jill and Micah went off to do their own thing, and I convinced Eddie to go to the library with me. There, we staked out a table, and I brought out my laptop.

"So, we found out something interesting when I picked up Adrian today," I told Eddie, keeping my voice library soft.

Eddie gave me a wry look. "I'm guessing the whole experience of picking up Adrian was interesting—at least from what Jill told me."

"It could've been worse," I speculated. "At least he was dressed when I got there. And there were only two other Moroi there. I didn't stumble into a sorority house full of them or anything."

That made him laugh. "You might have had a harder time getting Adrian out of there if that was the case."

My laptop screen flared to life, and I began the complicated process of logging into the Alchemists' mega-secure database.

"Well, as we were leaving, the girls he was with found out that a friend of theirs was killed by Strigoi the other night."

All humor vanished from Eddie's face. His eyes went hard. "Where?"

"In LA, not here," I added. I should've known better than to open up the conversation like that without clearly stating beforehand that he didn't need to be on the lookout for Strigoi on campus. "As far as we know, everyone's right—Strigoi don't want to hang out in Palm Springs."

Eddie became about one percent less tense.

"Here's the thing," I continued. "This Moroi girl—this friend of theirs—was allegedly killed like Clarence's niece."

Eddie's eyebrows rose. "With the slit throat?"

I nodded.

"That's weird. Are you sure that's what happened—to either of them? I mean, we're just going off of Clarence's report, right?" Eddie drummed a pencil against the table as he pondered this. "Clarence is nice enough, but come on. We all know he's not quite there."

"That's why I brought you here. And why I wanted to check this database. We keep track of most Strigoi-related deaths."

Eddie peered over my shoulder as I brought up an entry on Tamara Donahue from five years ago. Sure enough, she'd been found with a cut throat. Another search on Melody Croft—Krissy and Carla's friend—also turned up a report from last night. My people had been on the scene and quick to log the information. Melody too had had her throat slit. There had been other reported Strigoi murders in LA—it was a big city, after all—but only two matched this profile.

"Are you still thinking about what Clarence said—about vampire hunters?" Eddie asked me.

"I don't know. I just thought it was worth checking these out."

"Guardians weighed in on both of these cases," said Eddie, pointing at the screen. "They also declared them Strigoi attacks—there was blood taken from both girls. That's what a Strigoi does. I don't know what a vampire hunter does, but I just don't see drinking blood as part of their goal."

"I wouldn't think so either. But neither of these girls was drained."

"Strigoi don't always finish drinking from their victims. Especially if they're interrupted. This girl Melody was killed near a club, right? I mean, if her killer heard someone coming, they'd just take off."

"I suppose. But what about the throat-slitting?"

Eddie shrugged. "We have tons of accounts of Strigoi doing crazy things. Just look at Keith and his eye. They're evil. You can't apply logic to them."

"Um, let's leave his eye out of this." Keith wasn't a case I wanted brought up. I sat back in my chair and sighed. "There's just something bugging me about all the killings. The half-drinking. The throat-slitting. They're both strange things happening together. And I don't like strange things."

"Then you're in the wrong profession," said Eddie, his smile returning.

I smiled back, my mind still turning everything over. "I suppose so."

When I didn't say anything else, he gave me a surprised look. "You're not actually . . . you don't think there are vampire hunters, do you?"

"No, not really. We have no evidence to think they exist."

"But . . ." Eddie prompted.

"But," I said. "Doesn't the idea freak you out a little? I mean, right now, you know who to look out for. Other Moroi. Strigoi. They stand out. But a human vampire hunter?" I gestured to the students gathered and working in the library. "You wouldn't know who's a threat."

Eddie shook his head. "It's pretty easy, actually. I just treat everyone as a threat."

I couldn't decide if that made me feel better or not.

When I returned to my dorm later, Mrs. Weathers flagged me down. "Ms. Terwilliger dropped something off for you."

"She brought *me* something?" I asked in surprise. "It's not money, is it?" So far, none of my coffee purchases had been reimbursed.

By way of answer, Mrs. Weathers handed over a leather-covered book. At first, I thought it was the one I'd just finished. Then I looked more closely at the cover and read *Volume 2*. A yellow sticky note attached to the book had Ms. Terwilliger's spidery writing on it: *Next*. I sighed and thanked Mrs. Weathers. I'd do any task my teacher asked of me, but I was kind of hoping she'd assign me a book that was more of a historical account than recipes for spells.

As I was walking down my hall, I heard a few exclamations of alarm from the far end. I could see an open door and a few people huddled around it. Hurrying past my own room, I went to see what the problem was. It was Julia and Kristin's room. Although I wasn't sure I really had the right, I pushed my way past some of the frightened onlookers. No one stopped me.

I found Kristin lying on her bed, twitching violently. She was sweating profusely, and her pupils were so large, there was hardly any discernible iris. Julia sat near her on the bed, as did a couple girls I didn't know so well. She looked up at my approach, her face filled with fear.

"Kristin?" I cried. "Kristin, are you okay?" When no response came, I turned to the others. "What's the matter with her?"

Julia anxiously refolded a wet cloth and placed it on Kristin's forehead. "We don't know. She's been like this since this morning."

I stared incredulously. "Then she needs to see a doctor! We need to call someone now. I'll get Mrs. Weathers—"

"No!" Julia jumped up and caught hold of my arm. "You can't. The reason she's like this . . . well, we think it's because of the tattoo."

"Tattoo?"

One of the other girls caught hold of Kristin's wrist and turned it so that I could see the inside. There, tattooed in glittering coppery ink on her dusky skin, was a daisy. I remembered Kristin pining for a celestial tattoo, but last I knew, she couldn't afford it. "When did she get this?"

"Earlier today," said Julia. She looked abashed. "I lent her the money."

I stared at that sparkling flower, so pretty and seemingly harmless. I had no doubt it was what was causing this fit. Whatever was mixed with the ink to provide the high wasn't reacting correctly with her system.

"She needs a doctor," I said firmly.

"You can't. We'll have to tell them about the tattoos," said the girl who had been holding Kristin's hand. "No one believed Trey, but if they saw something like this . . . well, everything at Nevermore could be shut down."

Good! I thought. But to my astonishment, her words were met with nods from the other gathered girls. Were they crazy? How many of them had those ridiculous tattoos? And was protecting them really more important than Kristin's life?

223

Julia swallowed and sat back down on the edge of the bed. "We were hoping this might pass. Maybe she needs a little time to adjust."

Kristin moaned. One of her legs trembled like it was having a muscle spasm and then stilled. Her eyes and their large pupils stared off blankly, and her breathing was shallow.

"She's had all day!" I pointed out. "You guys, she could die."

"How do you know?" asked Julia in astonishment.

I didn't, not for sure. But every once in a while, Alchemist tattoos didn't take either. In ninety-nine percent of the cases, human bodies accepted the vampire blood used in an Alchemist tattoo, allowing its properties to infuse with our own, kind of like a low-grade dhampir. We gained good stamina and long life, though hardly got the amazing physical abilities dhampirs received. The blood was too diluted for that. Even so, there was always the occasional person who got sick from an Alchemist tattoo. The blood poisoned them. It was made worse because the gold and other chemicals worked to keep the blood infused in the skin, so it never had a chance to leave. Those left untreated died.

Vampire blood wouldn't cause a euphoric high, so I didn't believe there was any in this tattoo. But the treatment we used for Alchemist tattoos relied on breaking down the metallic components of the tattoo in order to release the blood, allowing the body then to clear it naturally. I had to assume the same principle would work here. Only, I didn't know the exact formula for the Alchemist compound and wasn't even sure it would break down copper like it did gold.

I bit my lip, thinking, and finally made a decision. "I'll be right back," I told them, racing to my room. All the while, an inner voice chastised me for foolishness. I had no business attempting what I was about to. I should go straight to Mrs. Weathers.

Instead, I opened my room door and found Jill with her laptop. "Hey, Sydney," she said, smiling. "I'm IM-ing with Lee and—" She did a double take. "What's wrong?"

I turned on my own laptop and set it on the bed. While it booted up, I reached for a small metal suitcase I'd carefully packed but never expected to use. "Can you go get me some water? Quickly?"

Jill hesitated only a moment before nodding. "Be right back," she said, jumping off her bed.

While she was gone, I unlocked the case with a key I always kept on me. Inside it were small amounts of dozens of Alchemist compounds, the kinds of substances we mixed together and used as part of our jobs. Some ingredients—like the ones I used to dissolve Strigoi bodies—I had lots of. Others, I had only a sampling of. My laptop finished booting up, and I logged onto the Alchemist database. A few searches and I soon had the formula for anti-tattoo treatment pulled up.

Jill returned then, carrying a cup brimming with water. "Is this enough? If we were in any other climate, I could've pulled it straight from the air."

"It's fine," I said, glad the climate had kept her from magic.

I scanned the formula, analyzing which ingredients did what. I mentally deleted the ones I was certain were specific to gold. A couple I didn't even have, but I was pretty sure they were simply for skin comfort and weren't requisite. I began pulling out ingredients from my kit, carefully measuring them—though still moving as quickly as possible—into another cup. I made substitutions where necessary and added an ingredient I was certain would break down copper, though the amount required was only a guess on my part. When I finished, I took the water from Jill and added the same amount that was in the original instructions. The final result was a liquid that reminded me of iodine.

I lifted it up and felt a little like a mad scientist. Jill had watched me without comment the entire time, sensing the urgency. Her face was filled with concern, but she was biting back all the questions I knew she had. She followed me when I left the room and headed back to Kristin's. More girls were there than before, and it was honestly a wonder Mrs. Weathers didn't just hear the racket. For a group so intent on protecting their precious tattoos, they weren't being particularly covert.

I returned to Kristin's bedside, finding her unchanged. "Expose her wrist again, and hold her arm as still as possible for me." I didn't direct the command to anyone but put enough force into it that I felt certain someone would obey. I was right. "If this doesn't work, we get a doctor." My voice left no room for argument.

Julia looked paler than Jill but gave a weak a nod of acceptance. I took the washcloth she'd been using and dipped it into my cup. I'd never actually seen this done and had to guess about how to apply it. I made a silent prayer and then pressed the washcloth against the tattoo on Kristin's wrist.

She let out a strangled cry, and her whole body bucked up. A couple nearby girls instinctively helped hold her down. Tendrils of smoke curled up from where I was holding the washcloth against her, and I smelled a sharp, acrid odor. Waiting what I hoped was an acceptable amount of time, I finally removed the washcloth.

The pretty little daisy was mutating before our eyes. Its clean lines began to run and blur. The coppery color began to shift, darkening into a bluish green. Before long, the design was unrecognizable. It was an amorphous blob. Around it, red welts appeared on her skin, though they seemed to be more of a superficial irritation than anything dire.

Still, the whole thing looked terrible, and I stared in horror. What had I done?

Everyone else was silent, no one knowing what to do. A couple minutes passed, but they felt like hours. Abruptly, Kristin stopped twitching. Her breathing still seemed labored, but she blinked, her eyes focusing as though suddenly seeing the world for the first time. Her pupils were still huge, but she managed to look around and at last focus on me.

"Sydney," gasped out Kristin. "Thank you."

CHAPTER 16

I EXPLAINED AWAY my chemistry experiment by saying that it was just a substance I had on hand from when I received my tattoo, in the event I had an allergic reaction. I certainly didn't let on that I'd mixed it myself. I think they would've bought that cover story, if not for the fact that a few days later, I was able to get ahold of a formula that helped treat the chemical burns on Kristin's skin. The mixture did nothing for the ink stain—that seemed to be permanent, barring some tattoo laser removal—but her welts did fade a little bit.

After that, word got around that Sydney Melrose was the new on-site pharmacist. Because I had extra left over from Kristin, I gave the remainder of the skin cream to a girl with severe acne since it worked on that as well. That probably didn't do me any favors. People approached me for all sorts of things and even offered to pay me. Some requests were pointless, like cures for headaches. Those people I simply told to buy some aspirin. Other requests were out of my power and nothing I wanted to deal with, like birth control.

Aside from the weird requests, I actually didn't mind the increase in my daily social interaction. I was used to people needing things from me, so that was familiar territory. Some people just wanted to know more about me as a person, which was new and more enjoyable than I'd expected. And still others wanted . . . different things from me.

"Sydney."

I was waiting for my English class to start and was startled to see one of Greg Slade's friends standing over my desk. His name was Bryan, and although I didn't know much about him, he'd never come across as obnoxious as Slade, which was a point in Bryan's favor.

"Yes?" I asked, wondering if he wanted to borrow notes from me.

He had shaggy brown hair that seemed to be purposely grown unkempt and was actually kind of cute. He ran a hand over it as he picked his words. "Do you know anything about silent films?"

"Sure," I said. "The first ones were developed in the late nineteenth century and sometimes had live musical accompaniment, though it wasn't until the 1920s that sound become truly incorporated into films, eventually making silent ones obsolete in cinema."

Bryan gaped, as though that was more than he'd been expecting. "Oh. Okay. Well, um, there's a silent film festival downtown next week. Do you think you'd want to go?"

I shook my head. "No, I don't think so. I respect it as an art form but really don't get much out of watching them."

"Huh. Okay." He smoothed his hair back again, and I could almost see him groping for thoughts. Why on earth was he asking me about silent films? "What about *Starship 30*? It opens Friday. Do you want to see that?"

"I don't really like sci-fi either," I said. It was true, I found it completely implausible.

Bryan looked ready to rip that shaggy hair out. "Is there *any* movie out there you want to see?"

I ran through a mental list of current entertainment. "No. Not really." The bell rang, and with a shake of his head, Bryan slunk back to his desk. "That was weird," I muttered. "He has bad taste in movies." Glancing beside me, I was startled to see Julia with her head down on her desk while she shook with silent laughter. "What?"

"That," she gasped. "That was hilarious."

"What?" I said again. "Why?"

"Sydney, he was asking you out!"

I replayed the conversation. "No, he wasn't. He was asking me about cinema."

She was laughing so hard that she had to wipe away a tear. "So he could find out what you wanted to see and take you out!"

"Well, why didn't he just say that?"

"You are so adorably oblivious," she said. "I hope I'm around the day you actually notice someone is interested in you." I continued to be mystified, and she spent the rest of class bursting out with spontaneous giggles.

While I became an object of fascination, Jill's popularity fell. Part of it was her own shyness. She was still so conscious and worried about being different that she assumed everyone else was aware of her otherness too. She continued holding back from connecting with people out of fear, making her come across as aloof. Surprisingly making this worse, Jill's "doctor's note" had finally come through from the Alchemists. The school wouldn't put her into a different elective that was already in progress. Freshmen weren't allowed to be teacher's aides like Trey. After consultation with Miss Carson, they'd finally decided that Jill would participate in all indoor PE activities and do "alternate assignments" when we were outdoors. This usually meant writing reports on things like the history of softball. Unfortunately, sitting out half the time only managed to isolate Jill more.

Micah continued to dote on her, even in the face of adversity.

"Lee texted me this morning," she told me at lunch one day. "He wants to take me out to dinner this weekend. Do you think . . . I mean, I know you guys would have to go too . . ." She glanced uncertainly between Eddie and me.

"Who's Lee?" asked Micah. He had just sat down with our group.

A few moments of awkward silence fell. "Oh," said Jill, averting her eyes. "He's this, um, guy we know. He doesn't go here. He goes to college. In Los Angeles."

Micah processed this. "He asked you on a date?"

"Yeah . . . we actually went out before. I guess we're, well, kind of dating."

"Not seriously," piped in Eddie. I wasn't sure if he was saying this to spare Micah's feelings or if it was some protective way to stop Jill from getting too close to anyone.

Micah was good at hiding his emotions, I'd give him that. After a bit more thought, he finally gave Jill a smile that only seemed slightly forced. "Well, that's great. I hope I can meet him." After that, the conversation turned to the upcoming football game, and no one mentioned Lee again.

Finding out about Lee changed how Micah acted around Jill, but he still hung out with us all the time. Maybe it was in the hopes that Lee and Jill would break up. Or it could've simply been because Micah and Eddie spent a lot of time together, and Eddie was one of Jill's few friends. But the problem wasn't Micah. It was Laurel.

I didn't think Micah would've been interested in Laurel even if Jill hadn't been in the picture, but Laurel still saw Jill as a threat—and went out of her way to make her miserable. Laurel spread rumors about her and made pointed comments in the halls and during class about Jill's pale skin, height, and skinniness—Jill's biggest insecurities.

Once or twice, I heard the name *vampire girl* whispered in the halls. It made my blood run cold, no matter how many times I reminded myself it was a joke.

"Jill isn't what's keeping Laurel and Micah apart," I remarked to Julia and Kristin one day. They were amused by my continued efforts to apply logic and rationality to social behaviors in the school. "I don't understand. He just doesn't like Laurel."

"Yeah, but it's easier for her to think Jill's the problem, when really, Laurel's just a bitch and Micah knows it," explained Julia. Ever since the awkward encounter with Bryan, she and Kristin had taken it upon themselves to try to educate me in the ways "normal" humans behaved.

"Plus, Laurel just likes having someone to pick on," said Kristin. She rarely spoke about the tattoo but had been serious and sober ever since.

"Okay," I said, trying to follow the logic, "but *I* was the one who called her out about dying her hair. She's hardly said a word to me."

Kristin smiled. "No fun picking on you. You talk back. Jill doesn't defend herself much and doesn't have many people to stick up for her either. She's an easy target."

One positive thing did happen, at least. Adrian was staying on good behavior after the Los Angeles mishap, though I had to wonder how long it would last. Based on what I gathered from Jill, he was still bored and unhappy. Lee's schedule was erratic, and it wasn't his job to look after Adrian anyway. There didn't seem to be any good solution for her, really. If Adrian gave in to his vices, she suffered the effects of his hangovers and "romantic interludes." If he didn't, then he was miserable, and that attitude slowly trickled into her as well. The only hope they had was that Jill would eventually learn the control to block him out of her mind, but from what Rose had told her, that could take a very long time.

When the next feeding came around, I was disappointed to see Keith's car parked in Clarence's driveway. If he wasn't going to actually do anything active to help this assignment, I kind of wished he'd just stay away from it altogether. He apparently thought these "supervising" visits counted as work and continued to justify his presence. Except when we met up with Adrian in the living room, Keith was nowhere in sight. Neither was Clarence.

"Where are they?" I asked Adrian.

Adrian was lounging on the couch and put down a book he'd been reading. I had a feeling reading was a rare activity for him and almost felt bad for the interruption. He stifled a yawn. There was no alcohol in sight, but I did see what looked like three empty cans of energy drink.

He shrugged. "I don't know. Off talking somewhere. Your friend's got a sick sense of humor. I think he's feeding Clarence's paranoia about vampire hunters."

I glanced uneasily at Lee, who had immediately begun talking to Jill. Both were so caught up in each other, they didn't even realize what the rest of us were discussing. I knew how much the vampire hunter talk bothered Lee. He wouldn't appreciate Keith encouraging it.

"Does Clarence know about the killing in LA?" asked Eddie. There was no reason Keith wouldn't, since it was open Alchemist knowledge, but I wasn't sure if he would've made the connection to Clarence or not.

"He hasn't mentioned it," said Adrian. "I swear Keith's just doing it because he's bored or something. Even I haven't sunk that low."

"Is that what you've been doing instead?" I asked. I sat down across from him and pointed at the energy drinks.

"Hey, it's not vodka or brandy or . . . well, anything good." Adrian sighed and upended one can, drinking the last few drops. "So give me some credit."

Eddie glanced at the cans. "Didn't Jill say she had trouble sleeping last night?"

"Adrian," I said with a groan. Eddie was right. I'd noticed Jill tossing and turning constantly. Vicarious caffeine would certainly explain it.

"Hey, I'm trying," Adrian said. "If you could get me out of here, Sage, then I wouldn't be forced to drown my sorrows in taurine and ginseng."

"She can't, Adrian, and you know it," said Eddie. "Can't you . . . I don't know. Find a hobby or something?"

"Being charming is my hobby," said Adrian obstinately. "I'm the life of a party—even without drinking. I wasn't meant to be alone."

"You could get a job," said Eddie, settling into a corner chair. He smiled, amused by his own wit. "Solve both your problems—make some money *and* be around people."

Adrian scowled. "Careful, Castile. There's only one comedian in this family."

I straightened up. "That's actually not a bad idea."

"It's a terrible idea," said Adrian, glancing between me and Eddie.

"Why?" I asked. "Is this the part where you tell us your hands don't do manual labor?"

"It's more like the part where I don't have anything to offer society," he countered.

"I could help you," I offered.

"Are you going to do the work and give me the paycheck?" Adrian asked hopefully. "Because that actually could help."

"I can give you a ride to your interviews," I said. "And I can make you a resume that would get you any job." I eyed him and reconsidered. "Well, within reason."

Adrian stretched back out. "Sorry, Sage. Just not feeling it."

Clarence and Keith entered just then. Clarence's face was exuberant. "Thank you, thank you," he was saying. "It's so nice to talk to someone who understands my concerns about the hunters."

I hadn't been aware that Keith understood anything except his own self-serving nature. Lee's face darkened when he realized Keith was furthering the old man's irrationality. Nonetheless, the Moroi withheld the comments he undoubtedly wanted to make. It was the first time I'd seen any sort of dark emotion on Lee's face. Looked like Keith could bring down even the most cheerful person.

Clarence was happy to see us, as was Dorothy. Humans who gave blood to vampires weren't just disgusting because of the act itself. What was also appalling was the addiction that resulted. Vampires released endorphins into those they drank from, endorphins that created a pleasurable sort of high. Human feeders who lived among Moroi spent their entire days in that high, becoming heavily dependent on it. Someone like Dorothy, who had lived only with Clarence for years, hadn't experienced enough bites to really get addicted. Now, with Jill and Adrian around, Dorothy was getting an increased amount of endorphins in her daily life. Her eyes lit up when she saw Jill, showing she was eager for more.

"Hey, Sage," said Adrian. "I don't want an interview, but do you think you could give me a ride to get some cigarettes?"

I started to tell him I wasn't going to help with such a filthy habit and then noticed him looking meaningfully at Dorothy. Was he trying to get me out of here? I wondered. Give me an excuse to not be around for the feeding? From what I understood, Moroi normally didn't hide their feedings from each other. Jill and Dorothy just usually left the room for my comfort. I knew they'd probably do it again but decided I'd take the opportunity to get away. Of course, I glanced at Keith for confirmation, expecting him to protest. He merely shrugged. It looked like I was the last thing on his mind.

"Okay," I said, standing up. "Let's go."

In the car, Adrian turned to me.

"I changed my mind," he said. "I'll take you up on helping me get a job."

I almost swerved into oncoming traffic. Few things from him could have surprised me more—and he said pretty surprising things on a regular basis. "That was fast. Are you serious?"

"As much as I ever am. Will you still help me?"

"I suppose so, though there's only so much I can do. I can't actually get you the job." I ran down my mental list of what I knew about Adrian. "I don't suppose you have any idea of what you'd actually like to do?"

"I want something entertaining," he said. He thought some more. "And I want to make lots of money—but do as little work as possible."

"Lovely," I muttered. "That narrows it down."

We reached downtown, and I managed a flawless parallel-parking job that didn't impress him nearly as much as it should have. We were right in front of a convenience store, and I stood outside while he went in. Evening shadows were falling. I was off campus all the time, but so far, my trips had all been to Clarence's, mini-golf courses, and fast-food joints. It turned out that the city of Palm Springs was really pretty. Boutiques and restaurants lined the streets, and I could've spent hours people-watching. Retirees in golfing getups strolled alongside young glamorous socialites. I knew a lot of celebrities came here too, but I wasn't in tune enough with the entertainment world to know who was who.

"Man," said Adrian, emerging from the store. "They raised the price on my normal brand. I had to buy some crappy one."

"You know," I said. "Quitting would also be a really great way to save some—"

I froze as I spotted something down the street. Three blocks away, through the leaves of some palm trees, I could just barely make out a sign that read *Nevermore* in ornate Gothic lettering. That was the place. The source of the tattoos running rampant through Amberwood. Ever since Kristin's incident, I'd wanted to delve into this more but hadn't been sure how. Now I had my chance.

For a moment, I remembered Keith telling me not to get involved with anything that might raise attention or cause trouble. Then I thought about the way Kristin had looked during her overdose. This was my opportunity to actually *do* something. I made a decision.

"Adrian," I said. "I need your help."

I pulled him toward the tattoo parlor, filling him in on the situation. For a moment, he seemed so interested in high-inducing tattoos that I thought he'd want one. When I told him about Kristin, though, his enthusiasm faded.

"Even if it's not Alchemist technology, they're still doing something dangerous," I explained. "Not just to Kristin. What Slade and those guys are doing—using the steroids to be better at football—is just as bad. People are getting hurt." I thought, suddenly, of Trey's cuts and bruises.

A small alley separated the tattoo parlor from a neighboring restaurant, and we stopped just before it. A door opened inside the alley, on the parlor side, and a man stepped out and lit a cigarette. He'd taken only two steps when another man stuck his head out the side door and called, "How long are you going to be gone?" I could see shelves and tables behind him.

"Just running down to the store," said the man with the cigarette. "I'll be back in ten."

The other guy went back inside, shutting the door. A few moments later, we saw him through the window at the front of the store, tidying up something on the counter.

"I have to get back there," I said to Adrian. "Into that door."

He arched an eyebrow. "What, like sneaking in? How very black ops of you. And oh, you know—dangerous and foolish."

"I know," I said, surprised at how calm I sounded as I admitted that. "But I have to know something, and this may be my only chance."

"Then I'll go with you in case that guy comes back," he said with a sigh. "Never let it be said Adrian Ivashkov doesn't help damsels in distress. Besides, did you see him? He looked like some insane biker. They both did."

"I don't want you to—wait." Inspiration hit. "*You* talk to the guy inside."

"Huh?"

"Go in the front. Distract him so that I can look around. Talk to him about . . . I don't know. You'll think of something."

We quickly hashed out a plan. I sent Adrian on his way while I ducked into the alley and approached the door. I pulled the handle and found it—locked.

"Of course," I muttered. What business would leave a remote door like this exposed and unlocked? My brilliant plan started to crumble until I remembered I had my Alchemist "essentials" in my purse.

My full kit was rarely needed, high school acne crises aside, so it was usually kept at home. But Alchemists were always on call, no matter where they were, to cover up vampire sightings. And so, we always kept a couple of things on us at all times.

One was the substance that could dissolve a Strigoi body in under a minute. The other was almost equally efficient at dissolving metal.

It was a type of acid, and I kept it in a protected vial in my purse. Quickly, I fished it out and unscrewed the top. A bitter scent hit me and made me wrinkle my nose. With the bottle's glass dropper, I very carefully leaned down and placed a few drops right in the center of the lock. I immediately stepped back as a white mist rose up from the contact. Within thirty seconds, it had all dissipated, and there was a hole in the middle of the door's handle. One of the nice things about this stuff, which we called quickfire, was that its reaction occurred extremely fast. It was now inert and posed no danger to my skin. I pushed down on the handle, and it released.

I only opened the door a crack, just to ascertain that there was no one else around. Nope. Empty. I crept inside and quietly shut the door behind me, fastening an inside bolt to make sure it stayed locked. As I'd seen from the outside, the place was a storage room, filled with all sorts of tools of the tattoo trade. Three doorways surrounded me. One led to a bathroom, one to a darkened room, and another to the store's front and main counter. Light spilled in from that doorway, and I could hear Adrian's voice.

"My friend's got one," he was saying. "I've seen it, and he said this is the place he got it. Come on, don't play me."

"Sorry," came the gruff response. "No idea what you're talking about."

I slowly began scanning the cupboards and drawers, reading labels and looking for anything suspicious. There were a lot of supplies and not much time.

"Is it a money thing?" asked Adrian. "Because I've got enough. Just tell me how much it costs."

There was a long pause, and I hoped Adrian wouldn't be asked to show any cash since the last of his money had gone to promoting cancer.

"I don't know," the guy said at last. "If I was able to do this copper tattoo you're talking about—and I'm not saying I can—you probably couldn't afford it."

"I'm telling you," said Adrian. "Just name your price."

"What is it you're interested in exactly?" the man asked slowly. "Just the color?"

"I think we both know," said Adrian cunningly. "I want the color. I want the 'bonus effects.' And I want it to look badass. You probably can't even do the design I want."

"That's the least of your worries," said the guy. "I've been doing this for years. I can draw anything you want."

"Yeah? Can you draw a skeleton riding a motorcycle with flames coming out of it? And I want a pirate hat on the skeleton. And a parrot on his shoulder. A skeleton parrot. Or maybe a ninja skeleton parrot? No, that would be overkill. But it'd be cool if the biker skeleton could be shooting some ninja throwing stars. That are on fire."

Meanwhile, I'd still seen no sign of what I needed, but there were a million nooks and crannies left to explore. Panic began to rise in me. I was going to run out of time. Then, seeing the darkened room, I hurried over to it. With a quick glance toward the store's front, I flipped on the light and held my breath. No one must have noticed anything because the conversation continued where it had left off.

241

"That's the most ridiculous thing I've ever heard," said the tattooist.

"That's not what the ladies are going to say," said Adrian.

"Look, kid," said the guy. "It's not even about money. It's about availability. That's a lot of ink you're talking about, and I don't have that much in stock."

"Well, when will your supplier deliver next?" asked Adrian.

I stared in awe at what I had found: I was in the room where the tattooing took place. There was a lounging chair—much more comfortable than the table I'd received *my* tattoo on—and a small side table covered with what appeared to be freshly used implements.

"I've already got some people wait-listed ahead of you. I don't know when there'll be more."

"Can you call me when you know?" Adrian asked. "I'll give you my info. My name's Jet Steele."

If not for my own tense situation, I would've groaned. Jet Steele? Really? Before I could think much more about it, I finally found what I'd been looking for. The tattoo gun on the table had its own ink container, but sitting nearby were several smaller vials. All of them were empty, but some still had enough metallic residue of their former ingredients to tip me off. Without even thinking twice, I quickly began recapping them and putting them in my purse. Nearby, I noticed some sealed vials full of dark liquid. I froze for a moment. Carefully, I picked one up, opened it, and took a sniff.

It was what I'd feared.

I screwed the lid back on and added those vials to my purse.

Just then, I heard a rattling behind me. Someone was trying

to open the back door. I'd bolted it behind me, however, and it didn't give. Still, it meant my time for snooping was up. I was just zipping up my purse when I heard the store's front door open.

"Joey, why's the back door locked?" an angry voice demanded.

"It's always locked."

"No, the bolt was on. From the inside. It wasn't when I left."

Cue my exit. I flipped off the light and began hurrying back through the storage room.

"Wait!" exclaimed Adrian. There was an anxious note to his voice, like he was trying to get someone's attention. I had the uneasy feeling that the two guys who worked here were headed back behind the counter to investigate. "I need to know something else about the tattoo. Can the parrot also be wearing a pirate's hat? Like a miniature one?"

"In a minute. We have to check something." The voice was louder than before. Closer.

My hands fumbled as I unlatched the bolt. I managed it and opened the door, hurrying out just as I heard voices behind me. Without pausing to glance back, I shut the door and ran out the alley and up the street, back toward where I'd parked. I was pretty sure the guys hadn't gotten a good look at me. I think I'd just been a figure darting out the door. Still, I was grateful for the crowds of people on the street. I was able to blend in as I turned my attention to my car and unlocked the door. My hands were sweaty and shaking as I fumbled with the keys.

I wanted badly to look behind me but was afraid of attracting the attention of the two men, if they were out searching the street. As long as they had no reason to suspect me—

A hand suddenly grabbed my arm and jerked me away. I gasped.

"It's me," said a voice.

Adrian. I breathed a sigh of relief.

"Don't look back," he said calmly. "Just get in the car."

I obeyed. Once we were both safely inside, I took a deep breath, overwhelmed by the pounding of my heart. Fear-born adrenaline surged in my chest, so strongly it hurt. I closed my eyes and leaned back.

"That was too close," I said. "And you did good, by the way."

"I know," he said proudly. "And actually, I kind of want that tattoo now. Did you find what you were looking for?"

I opened my eyes and sighed. "I did. And a whole lot more."

"So, what is it? They're putting drugs in tattoos?"

"Worse," I said. "They're using vampire blood."

CHAPTER 17

MY DISCOVERY KICKED the tattoo problem up to a whole new level. Before, I'd just thought I was fighting against people using techniques similar to Alchemist methods to expose Amberwood to drugs. It had been a moral issue. Now, with blood on the line—it was an Alchemist issue. Our whole purpose was to protect humans from the existence of vampires. If someone was illicitly putting vampire blood into humans, they'd crossed the line we worked hard, every day, to maintain.

I knew I should immediately report this. If someone had gotten their hands on vampire blood, the Alchemists needed to send a force here and investigate. If I followed the normal chain of command, I supposed the thing would be to tell Keith and let him tell our superiors. If he did, however, I had no doubt he'd claim all the credit for uncovering this. I couldn't let that happen—and not because I wanted the glory for myself. Too many Alchemists erroneously believed Keith was an upstanding person. I didn't want to fuel that.

But before I did anything, I needed to figure out the rest of the vials' contents. I could make guesses at the metallic residues but wasn't sure if, like the blood, they came straight from the Alchemist catalog or were just knockoffs. And if they were our formulas, it wasn't obvious at a glance which were which. The silver powder in one vial, for example, could have been a few different Alchemist compounds. I had the means to do some experiments and figure it out, but one substance eluded me. It was clear, slightly thick liquid that had no discernable odor. My guess was that it was the narcotic used in the celestial tattoos. Vampire blood wouldn't cause that high, though it would absolutely explain the crazy athleticism of the so-called steel tattoos. So, I began running what experiments I could, while going on with the normal routines of school.

We were playing basketball inside in PE this week, so Jill was participating—and being subjected to Laurel's biting comments. I kept hearing her say things like, "You'd think she'd be a lot better since she's so tall. She can practically touch the basket without jumping. Or maybe she should turn into a bat and fly up there."

I winced. I had to keep telling myself not to make a big deal of the jokes, but every time I heard one, panic seized me. I had to hide it, though. If I wanted to help Jill, I needed the teasing stopped as a whole—not just the vampire stuff. Drawing more attention to those comments wouldn't help.

Micah tried to comfort Jill after each attack, which clearly infuriated Laurel more. Laurel's weren't the only comments reaching my ears. Since my raid of the tattoo parlor, I'd been hearing a fair amount of interesting information from Slade and his friends.

"Well, did he say when?" Miss Carson was taking attendance,

and Slade was interrogating a guy named Tim about a recent trip to the parlor.

Tim shook his head. "No. They're having some trouble with their shipment. It sounds like the supplier's got it but doesn't want to give it up for the same price."

"Damn it," growled Slade. "I need a touch-up."

"Hey," said Tim. "What about me? I don't even have my first one."

It wasn't the first comment I'd overheard from someone who already had a celestial and needed a touch-up. Addiction in action.

Jill's face was hard when PE ended, and I had the feeling she was trying not to cry. I tried talking to her in the locker room, but she simply shook her head and headed off for the showers. I was about to go there myself when I heard a shriek. Those of us who were still by the lockers raced to the shower room to see what was happening.

Laurel jerked the curtain back from her stall and came running out, oblivious to the fact that she was naked. I gaped. Her skin was covered in a fine sheen of ice. Water droplets from the shower had frozen solid on her skin and in her hair, though in the steamy heat of the rest of the room, they were already starting to melt. I glanced over to the shower itself and noticed that the water coming out of the faucet was also frozen solid.

Laurel's screams brought Miss Carson running in—shocked as the rest of us at the seemingly impossible thing we'd just witnessed. She finally declared it was some kind of freak problem with the pipes and the water heater. That was typical of my fellow humans. They'd always reach for far-fetched scientific explanations before delving into fantastic ones.

But I had no problem with that. It made my job easier.

Miss Carson tried to get Laurel to go into a different shower to get the ice off, but she refused. She waited for it all to melt and then toweled herself off. Her hair was atrocious when she finally left for her next class, and I smirked. I guessed there'd be no hair-tossing today.

"Jill," I called, catching sight of her trying to blend in to the group of girls leaving the locker room. She glanced guiltily over her shoulder but didn't otherwise acknowledge that she'd heard me. I followed close behind her. "Jill!" I called out again. She was definitely avoiding me.

In the hall, Jill spotted Micah and hurried over to him. Smart. She knew I wouldn't ask any dangerous questions with him around.

She managed to avoid me for the rest of the day, but I staked out our room until she finally came home, just before curfew.

"Jill," I exclaimed as soon as she walked through the door. "What were you thinking?"

She threw her books down and turned toward me. I had a feeling I wasn't the only one who'd been preparing a speech today.

"I was thinking I'm sick of listening to Laurel and her friends talk about me."

"So you froze her shower?" I asked. "How is that going to stop her? It's not like you can claim credit for it."

Jill shrugged. "It made me feel better."

"*That's* your excuse?" I could hardly believe it. Jill had always seemed so reasonable. She'd survived becoming a princess and *dying* with a clear head. This was what broke her. "Do you know what you risked? We're trying to *not* attract attention here!"

"Miss Carson didn't think it was weird."

"Miss Carson came up with a flimsy excuse to reassure herself! That's what people do. All it's going to take is some janitor investigating and saying pipes don't randomly freeze—especially in Palm Springs!"

"So what?" Jill demanded. "What then? Is their next leap going to be that it was vampire magic?"

"Of course not," I said. "But people are going to talk. You've raised their suspicions."

She eyed me carefully. "Is that what's really upsetting you? Or is it that I used magic at all?"

"Isn't it the same thing?"

"No. I mean, you're upset that I used magic because *you* don't like magic. You don't like anything to do with vampires. I think this is personal. I know what you think of us."

I groaned. "Jill, I do like you. You're right that magic makes me a little uneasy." Okay, a *lot* uneasy. "But my personal feelings aren't what's going to make people wonder what could have caused water to freeze like that."

"It isn't right that she can keep doing that!"

"I know. But you have to be better than her."

Jill sat on the bed and sighed. Like that, her anger seemed to melt into despair. "I hate it here. I want to go back to St. Vladimir's. Or Court. Or Michigan. Anywhere but here." She looked at me pleadingly. "Hasn't there been any news about when I can go back?"

"No," I said, unwilling to tell her it might be a while.

"Everyone's having a great time here," she said. "You love it. You have tons of friends."

"I don't—"

"Eddie likes it too. He's got Micah and some other guys in their dorm to hang out with. Plus, he's got me to look after, which gives him a purpose." I'd never thought of it like that but realized she was right. "But me? What do I have? Nothing except this stupid bond that just makes me more depressed because I have to listen to Adrian feel sorry for himself."

"I'm taking Adrian job-hunting tomorrow," I said, not sure if that would really help.

Jill nodded bleakly. "I know. His life'll probably be great now too."

She was sinking into melodrama and her own self-pity, but in light of everything, I kind of felt like she was entitled to it right now.

"You have Lee," I said.

That brought a smile to her face. "I know. He's great. I like him a lot, and I can't believe . . . I mean, it just seems crazy that he'd like me too."

"Not that crazy."

Her brightness faded. "Did you know Lee told me he thinks I can be a model? He says I've got the figure human fashion designers really like and knows this designer downtown who's looking for models. But when I told Eddie, he said it was a terrible idea because I can't risk having my picture taken. He said if it leaked out, others could find me."

"That's true," I said. "On all counts. You do have a model's figure—but it'd be too dangerous."

She sighed, looking defeated. "See? Nothing works out for me."

"I'm sorry, Jill. I really am. I know it's hard. All I can ask is that you keep trying to stay strong. You've done really great so far. Just hang in there a little longer, okay? Just keep thinking of Lee."

My words sounded hollow, even to me. I almost wondered if I should bring her along with Adrian and me but finally decided against it. I didn't think Adrian needed any distractions. I also wasn't sure how interesting it would be for her. If she was really that eager to watch Adrian go through job interviews, she could "listen in" through the bond.

I met up with Adrian after school the next day, and for the first time in ages, neither Lee nor Keith was around the old house. Clarence was, however, and he practically ran me down when I entered.

"Did you hear?" he demanded. "Did you hear about that poor girl?"

"What girl?" I asked.

"The one killed in Los Angeles a couple weeks ago."

"Oh, yeah," I said, relieved there was no new death. "It was tragic. We're lucky there are no Strigoi here."

He gave me a surprisingly knowing look. "It wasn't Strigoi! Haven't you paid attention? It was *them*. The vampire hunters."

"But they drank her blood, sir. Didn't you say vampire hunters are human? No human would have any reason to drink Moroi blood."

He turned away from me and paced the living room. I glanced around, wondering where Adrian was.

"Everyone keeps saying that!" said Clarence. "As though I don't already know that. I can't explain why they do what they do. They're a strange lot. They worship the sun and have weird beliefs about evil and honor—more unusual than even *your* beliefs." Well, that was something. At least he knew I was human. Sometimes I wasn't sure. "They also have strange views on which vampires should die. They kill all Strigoi without question. With Moroi and dhampirs, they're more selective."

"You sure know a lot about them," I said.

"I've made it my business to, ever since Tamara." He sighed and suddenly seemed very, very old. "At least Keith believes me."

I kept my face expressionless. "Oh?"

Clarence nodded. "He's a good young man. You should give him a chance."

My control slipped, and I knew I was scowling. "I'll try, sir." Adrian entered just then, much to my relief. Being alone with Clarence was freaky enough without him actually *praising* Keith Darnell.

"Ready?" I asked.

"You bet," said Adrian. "I can't wait to be a productive member of society."

I gave his outfit a once-over and had to bite off any comments. It was nice, but of course, his clothes always were. Jill had claimed I had an expensive wardrobe, but Adrian's blew mine away. Today he wore black jeans and a burgundy button-down shirt. The shirt looked like it was some sort of silk blend, and he wore it loose and unbuttoned. His hair was carefully styled to look like he'd just rolled out of bed. Too bad he didn't have my hair's texture. My hair did that without any styling at all.

I had to admit, he looked great—but he didn't look like he was going to a job interview. He looked like he was about to go clubbing. This left me kind of conflicted. I found myself admiring him nonetheless and was again reminded of that impression I got from him sometimes, like he was some kind of work of art. It was a little disconcerting, particularly since I had to keep telling myself that vampires were *not* attractive in the same way humans were. Fortunately, the practical part of me soon took over, chastising me that it didn't matter if he looked good or not. What mattered was that he looked inappropriate for job interviews. I shouldn't have been surprised, though. This was Adrian Ivashkov.

"So what's on the agenda?" he asked me once we were on the road. "I really think 'Chairman Ivashkov' has a nice ring to it."

"There's a folder in the backseat with our itinerary, Chairman."

Adrian twisted around and retrieved the folder. After a quick scan of it, he declared, "You get points for variety, Sage. But I don't think any of these are going to keep me in the lifestyle I'm accustomed to."

"Your resume's in the back. I did my best, but we're operating within limited parameters here."

He flipped through the papers and found the resume. "Wow. I was an educational assistant at St. Vladimir's?"

I shrugged. "It was the closest you had to a job."

"And Lissa was my supervisor, huh? I hope she gives me a good referral."

When Vasilisa and Rose were still in school, Adrian had lived there and worked with Vasilisa on learning spirit. "Educational assistant" was kind of a stretch, but it made him sound like he could multitask and show up for work on time.

He shut the folder and leaned back against the seat,

closing his eyes. "How's Jailbait? She seemed down the last time I saw her."

I considered lying but figured he'd probably find out the truth eventually, either from her directly or through his own deductions. Adrian's judgment might be questionable, but I'd discovered he was excellent at reading people. Eddie claimed it came from being a spirit user and had mentioned something about auras, which I wasn't quite sure I believed in. The Alchemists had no hard evidence that they were real.

"Not good," I said, giving him the full report as we drove.

"That shower thing was hilarious," he said when I finished.

"It was irresponsible! Why can't anyone see that?"

"But that bitch had it coming."

I sighed. "Have you guys forgotten why you're here? You of all people! You saw her die. Don't you get how important it is for her to stay safe and keep a low profile?"

Adrian was quiet for several moments, and when I glanced over, his face was uncharacteristically serious. "I know. But I don't want her to be miserable either. She . . . she doesn't deserve it. Not like the rest of us."

"I don't think we do either."

"Maybe you don't," he said with a small smile. "What with your pure lifestyle and all. I don't know. Jill's just so . . . innocent. It's why I saved her, you know. I mean, part of it."

I shivered. "When she died?"

He nodded, a troubled look in his eyes. "When I saw her there, bloody and not moving . . . I didn't think about the consequences of what I was doing. I just knew I had to save her. She had to live. I acted without question, not even knowing for sure if I could do it."

"It was brave of you."

"Maybe. I don't know. I do know she's gone through a lot. I don't want her to go through any more."

"Neither do I." I was touched at the concern. He kept surprising me in weird ways. Sometimes it was hard to imagine Adrian really caring about anything, but a softer side of him surfaced when he talked about Jill. "I'll do what I can. I know I should talk to her more . . . be more of a friend or even a fake sister. It's just . . ."

He eyed me. "Is it really so terrible being around us?"

I blushed. "No," I said. "But . . . it's complicated. I've been taught certain things my entire life. Those are hard to shake."

"The greatest changes in history have come because people were able to shake off what others told them to do." He looked away from me, out the window.

The statement annoyed me. It sounded good, of course. It was the kind of thing people said all the time without really understanding the implications. *Be yourself, fight the system!* But people who said them—people like Adrian—hadn't lived my life. They hadn't grown up in a system of beliefs so rigid, it was like being imprisoned. They hadn't been forced to give up their ability to think for themselves or make their own choices. His words didn't just annoy me, I realized. They made me angry. They made me jealous.

I scoffed and threw out a comment worthy of him. "Should I add motivational speaker to your resume?"

"If the pay's right, I'm in. Oh." He straightened up. "I finally placed him. That Micah guy you're so worried about."

"Placed him?"

"Yeah. Why he looks so familiar. Micah's a dead ringer for Mason Ashford."

"Who?"

"A dhampir that went to St. Vladimir's. He dated Rose for a while." Adrian scoffed and rested his cheek against the glass. "Well, inasmuch as anyone ever dated her. She was crazy for Belikov, even then. Just like she was when we dated. Don't know if Ashford ever knew or if she was able to fool him the whole time. I hope so. Poor bastard."

I frowned. "Why do you say that?"

"He died. Well, was killed, I should say. Did you know about that? A bunch of them were captured by Strigoi last year. Rose and Castile made it out. Ashford didn't."

"No," I said, making a mental note to look into this. "I didn't. Eddie was there too?"

"Yup. Physically, at least. The Strigoi kept feeding off him, so he was useless for most of it. You want to talk about emotional damage? Look no further."

"Poor Eddie," I said. Suddenly, a lot about the dhampir was beginning to make sense to me.

We arrived at the first place, a law firm that was looking for an office assistant. The title sounded more glamorous than it really was and would probably involve a lot of the same errands Trey and I ran for Ms. Terwilliger. But out of the three positions I'd found, this one also had the most potential for future advancement.

The firm was obviously doing well, judging from the lobby we waited in. Orchids grew in giant, well-placed vases, and there was even a fountain in the middle of the room. Three others waited in the lobby with us. One was a very nicely dressed woman in her forties. Opposite her was a man about the same age, sitting with a much younger woman whose low-cut blouse would've gotten her thrown out of Amberwood. Each time I looked at her, I wanted to cover her cleavage up with a cardigan. The three of them obviously knew each other, however, because they kept making eye contact and trading glares.

Adrian studied each of them in turn and then turned to me. "This law firm," he said in a low voice. "It specializes in divorce, doesn't it?"

"Yes," I said.

He nodded and took a few moments to process the information. Then, to my horror, he leaned over me and said to the older woman, "He was a fool, clearly. You're a stunning, classy woman. Just wait. He'll be sorry."

"Adrian!" I exclaimed.

The woman flinched in surprise but didn't look entirely offended. Meanwhile, on the other side of the room, the younger woman straightened up from where she'd been cuddling against the man.

"Sorry?" she demanded. "What's that supposed to mean?"

I willed the earth to swallow me up and save me. Fortunately, the next-best thing came when the receptionist called the three-some in to meet with a lawyer.

"Really?" I asked when they were gone. "Did you have to say that?"

"I speak my mind, Sage. Don't you believe in telling the truth?"

"Of course I do. But there's a time and place! Not with perfect strangers who are obviously in a bad situation."

"Whatever," he said, looking extremely pleased with himself. "I totally made that lady's day."

Just then, a woman in a black suit and very high heels emerged from an inner office. "I'm Janet McCade, the office manager," she said. She glanced between the two of us uncertainly, and then she decided on me. "You must be Adrian."

The name mistake was understandable, but the mix-up didn't bode well for him. My assessment of his clubbing outfit had been correct. My brown skirt and ivory blouse apparently seemed more appropriate for an interview.

"This is Adrian," I said, pointing. "I'm just his sister, here for moral support."

"Very kind of you," said Janet, looking a little perplexed. "Well, then. Shall we go talk, Adrian?"

"You bet," he said, standing. He started to follow her, and I jumped up.

"Adrian," I whispered, catching his sleeve. "You want to tell the truth? Do it in there. Do not embellish or make up crazy claims that you were a district attorney."

"Got it," he said. "This is going to be a breeze."

If by breeze he meant fast, then he was right. He emerged from the office door five minutes later.

"I don't suppose," I said, once we were in the car, "that she just gave you the job based on looks alone?"

Adrian had been staring off but now flashed me a big smile. "Why, Sage, you sweet talker."

"That's not what I meant! What happened?"

He shrugged. "I told the truth."

"Adrian!"

"I'm serious. She asked me what my greatest strength was. I said getting along with people."

"That's not bad," I admitted.

"Then she asked what my greatest weakness was. And I said, 'Where should I start?'"

"Adrian!"

"Stop saying my name like that. I told her the truth. By the time I was on the fourth one, she told me I could go."

I groaned and resisted the urge to beat my head on the steering wheel. "I should've coached you. That's a standard trick question. You're supposed to answer with things like 'I get too devoted to my work' or 'I'm a perfectionist.'"

He snorted and crossed his arms. "That's total bullshit. Who'd say something like that?"

"People who get jobs."

Since we had extra time now, I did my best to prep him with answers before the next interview. It was actually at Spencer's, and I'd gotten Trey to pull a few strings. While Adrian was interviewing in the back, I got a table and some coffee. Trey came to visit me after about fifteen minutes.

"Is that really your brother?" he demanded.

"Yes," I said, hoping I sounded convincing.

"When you said he was looking for a job, I pictured a male version of you. I figured he'd want to color code the cups or something."

"What's your point?" I asked.

Trey shook his head. "My point is that you'd better keep looking. I was just back there and overhead him talking with my manager. She was explaining the cleanup he would have to do each night. Then he said something about his hands and manual labor."

I wasn't the swearing type, but in that moment, I wished I was.

The last interview was at a trendy bar downtown. I'd taken it on faith that Adrian probably knew every drink in the world and had made up a fake credential for the resume, claiming he'd taken a bartending class. I stayed in the car for this one and sent him in alone, figuring he had the best chance here. At the very least, his outfit would be appropriate. When he came out in ten minutes, I was aghast.

"How?" I demanded. "How could you have screwed this one up?"

"When I got in, they said the manager was on the phone and would be a few minutes. So, I sat down and ordered a drink."

This time, I did lean my forehead against the steering wheel. "What did you order?"

"A martini."

"A martini." I lifted my head. "You ordered a martini before a job interview."

"It's a bar, Sage. I figured they'd be cool with it."

"No, you didn't!" I exclaimed. The volume of my voice surprised both of us, and he cringed a little. "You aren't stupid, no matter how much you pretend to be! You know you can't do that. You did it to screw around with them. You did it to screw around with me! That's what this has all been about. You haven't taken any of this seriously. You wasted these people's time and *mine*, just because you had nothing better to do!"

"That's not true," he said, though he sounded uncertain. "I do want a job . . . just not these jobs."

"You're in no position to pick and choose. You want out of Clarence's? These were your tickets. You should've been able to get any of them if you'd just put in a little effort. You're charming when you want to be. You could've talked yourself into a job." I started the car. "I'm done with this."

"You don't understand," he said.

"I understand that you're going through a tough time. I understand that you're hurting." I refused to look at him and gave all my attention to the road. "But that doesn't give you the right to play around with other people's lives. Try taking care of your own for a change."

He made no response until we were back at Clarence's, and even then, I didn't want to hear it.

"Sage—" he began.

"Get out," I said.

He hesitated like he might disagree but finally conceded with a swift nod. He left the car and strode toward the house, lighting a cigarette as he went. Fury and frustration burned within me. How could one person continually send me on such emotional highs and lows? Whenever I was starting to like him and feel like we were actually connecting, he would go and do something like *this*. I was a fool to ever start letting myself feel friendly toward him. Had I really thought he was a work of art earlier? More like a piece of work.

My feelings were still churning when I arrived back at Amberwood. I particularly cringed at the thought of running into Jill in our room. I had no doubt she'd know everything that had happened with Adrian, and I had no desire to hear her defend him.

But when I walked into my dorm, I never made it past the

front desk. Mrs. Weathers was in the lobby, along with Eddie and a campus security officer. Micah hovered nearby, face pale. My heart stopped. Eddie sprinted toward me, panic written all over him.

"There you are! I couldn't get ahold of you or Keith."

"M-my phone was off." I looked over at Mrs. Weathers and the officer and saw the same worry on their faces as his. "What's wrong?"

"It's Jill," said Eddie grimly. "She's missing."

CHAPTER 18

"WHAT DO YOU MEAN 'MISSING'?" I asked.

"She was supposed to meet us a couple hours ago," Eddie said, exchanging glances with Micah. "I thought maybe she was with you."

"I haven't seen her since PE." I was trying hard not to kick into panic mode yet. There were too many variables at play and not enough evidence to start thinking crazy Moroi dissidents had kidnapped her. "This is a really big place—I mean, three campuses. Are you sure she isn't just holed up studying somewhere?"

"We've done a pretty exhaustive search," said the security officer. "And teachers and workers are on alert looking for her. No sightings yet."

"And she isn't answering her cell phone," added Eddie.

I finally let true fear overtake me, and my face must have shown it. The officer's expression softened. "Don't worry. I'm sure she'll turn up." It was the kind of conciliatory thing people in his profession had to say to family members. "But do you have any other ideas of where she might be?"

"What about your other brothers?" asked Micah.

I'd been afraid it would come to that. I was almost one hundred percent sure she wasn't with Keith, but he should still probably be notified about her disappearance. It wasn't something I looked forward to because I knew there'd be a lecture in it for me. It would also be a sign of my failure in the eyes of other Alchemists. I should have stayed by Jill's side. That was my job, right? Instead, I'd—foolishly—been helping someone run errands. Not just anyone—a vampire. That's how the Alchemists would see it. *Vamp lover.*

"I was just with Adrian," I said slowly. "I suppose she could've somehow gotten to Clarence's and waited for him. I didn't actually go inside."

"I tried Adrian too," said Eddie. "No answer."

"Sorry," I said. "We were doing his interviews, so he must have turned his phone off. Do you want to try him again?" I certainly didn't want to.

Eddie stepped aside to call Adrian while I talked with Mrs. Weathers and the officer. Micah paced around, looking worried, and I felt guilty for always wanting to keep him from Jill. The race thing was a problem, but he really did care about her. I told the officer all the places Jill liked to frequent on campus. They confirmed that they'd already checked them all.

"You got ahold of him?" I asked when Eddie returned.

He nodded. "She's not there. I feel kind of bad, though. He's pretty worried now. Maybe we should've waited to tell him."

"No . . . actually, it might be a good thing." I met Eddie's eyes and saw a spark of understanding. Adrian's emotions seemed to intrude on Jill when they were running strong. If he was panicked enough, she'd hopefully realize people were concerned and show back up. That was assuming she was just hiding out or had gone somewhere we couldn't find. I tried not to consider the alternative: that something had happened where she *couldn't* contact us.

"Sometimes students just sneak off," said the officer. "It's inevitable. Usually they try to sneak back in before curfew. Hopefully that's just the case now. If she doesn't show up then—well, then we'll call the police."

He walked off to radio the rest of security for a status check, and we thanked him for his help. Mrs. Weathers returned to the front desk, but it was clear she was worried and agitated. She came across as gruff sometimes, but I had the feeling she actually cared about her students. Micah left us to find a few friends of his who worked on campus, in case they'd seen anything.

That left Eddie and me. Without conferring, we turned toward some chairs in the lobby. Like me, I think he wanted to stake out the door in order to see Jill the instant she showed up.

"I shouldn't have left her," he said.

"You had to," I said reasonably. "You can't be with her in classes or her room."

"This place was a bad idea. It's too big. Too hard to secure." He sighed. "I can't believe this."

"No . . . it was a good idea. Jill needs some semblance of a normal life. You could've locked her in a room somewhere and cut her off from all interaction, but what good would that do? She needs to go to school and be with people."

"She hasn't done much of that, though."

"No," I admitted. "She's had a rough time with it. I kept hoping it'd get better."

"I just wanted her to be happy."

"Me too." I straightened up as something alarming hit me. "You don't think . . . you don't think she would've run away and gone back to her mom, do you? Or Court or somewhere?"

His face grew even more bleak. "I hope not. Do you think things have been that bad?"

I thought about our fight after the shower incident. "I don't know. Maybe."

Eddie buried his face in his hands. "I can't believe this," he repeated. "I failed."

When it came to Jill, Eddie was usually all fierceness and anger. I'd never seen him so close to depression. I'd been living with the fear of my *own* failure since coming to Palm Springs but only now realized that Eddie had just as much on the line. I recalled Adrian's words about Eddie and his friend Mason, how Eddie felt responsible. If Jill didn't come back, would this be history repeating itself? Would she be someone else he'd lost? I'd thought this mission might be redemption for him. Instead, it could turn into Mason all over again.

"You didn't fail," I said. "You've been in charge of protecting her, and you've done that. You can't control her happiness. If anything, I'm to blame. I gave her a lecture for the shower incident."

"Yeah, but I destroyed her hopes when I told her the modeling idea Lee had wouldn't work."

"But you were right about—Lee!" I gasped. "That's it. That's where she is. She's with Lee, I'm certain of it. Do you have his number?"

Eddie groaned. "I'm such an idiot," he said, taking out his cell phone and scanning for the number. "I should've thought of that."

I touched the cross around my neck, saying a silent prayer that this would all be solved easily. As long as it meant Jill was alive and well, I could've handled her and Lee eloping.

"Hey, Lee? It's Eddie. Is Jill with you?"

There was a pause as Lee responded. Eddie's body language answered the question before I heard another word. His posture relaxed, and relief flooded his features.

"Okay," said Eddie a few moments later. "Well, get her back here. Now. Everyone's looking for her." Another pause. Eddie's face hardened. "We can talk about that later." He disconnected and turned to me. "She's okay."

"Thank God," I breathed. I stood up, only then realizing how tense I'd been. "I'll be right back."

I found Mrs. Weathers and the security officer and relayed the news. The officer immediately spread the word to his colleagues and soon left. To my surprise, Mrs. Weathers almost looked like she was on the verge of tears.

"Are you okay?" I asked.

"Yes, yes." She turned flustered, embarrassed at being so emotional. "I was just so worried. I—I didn't want to say anything and scare you all, but every time a student's missing . . . well, a few years ago, another girl disappeared. We thought she'd just sneaked off—like Matt said, it happens. But it turned out . . ." Mrs. Weathers grimaced and looked away. "I shouldn't be telling you this."

As if she could stop with that kind of intro. "No, please. Tell me."

She sighed. "The police found her a couple days later—dead. She'd been abducted and killed. It was terrible, and they never caught her killer. Now I just think of that whenever someone disappears. It's never happened again, of course. But something like that scars you."

I could imagine so. And as I returned to Eddie, I thought about him and Mason again. It seemed like everyone was carrying baggage from past events. I certainly was. Now that Jill's safety wasn't a concern, all I kept thinking was: *What will the Alchemists say? What will my father say?* Eddie was just hanging up his phone again when I approached.

"I called Micah to tell him everything's okay," he explained. "He was really worried."

All signs of Mrs. Weathers's past trauma vanished the instant that Jill and Lee walked through the door. Jill actually looked upbeat until she saw all of our faces. She came to a halt. Beside her, Lee already looked grim. I think he knew what was coming.

Eddie and I hurried forward but didn't have a chance to speak right away. Mrs. Weathers immediately demanded to know where they'd been. Rather than cover it up, Jill confessed and told the truth: she and Lee had gone off campus, into Palm Springs. She was careful to make sure Lee didn't get accused of any kidnapping charges, swearing he didn't know she could only leave with approved family members. I confirmed this—though Lee was hardly off the hook in my opinion.

"Will you wait outside?" I asked him politely. "I'd like to speak to you privately later."

Lee started to obey, flashing Jill a look of apology. He lightly brushed her hand in farewell and turned away. It was Mrs. Weathers who stopped him.

"Wait," she said, peering at him curiously. "Do I know you?"

Lee looked startled. "I don't think so. I've never been here before."

"There's something familiar about you," she insisted. Her frown deepened a few moments more. At last, she shrugged. "It can't be. I must be mistaken."

Lee nodded, met Jill's eyes in sympathy again, and left.

Mrs. Weathers wasn't done with Jill. She launched into a lecture about how dangerous and irresponsible they'd been. "If you were going to sneak off and break rules, you could've at least confided in your siblings. They've been scared to death for you." It was almost funny, her advising on "responsible" rule-breaking. Considering how panicked I'd been, I couldn't find anything amusing just then. She also told Jill that she'd be written up and punished.

"For now," said Mrs. Weathers, "you are confined to your room for the rest of the night. Come see me after breakfast, and we'll find out if the principal thinks this warrants suspension."

"Excuse me," said Eddie. "Can we have a few minutes alone here with her before she goes upstairs? I'd like to talk to her."

Mrs. Weathers hesitated, apparently wanting Jill's punishment immediately enforced. Then she gave Eddie a double take. The look on his face was hard and angry, and I think Mrs. Weathers knew there was punishment of a different sort coming from Jill's big brother.

"Five minutes," said Mrs. Weathers, tapping her watch. "Then up you go."

"Don't," said Jill, the instant we were alone. Her face was a mixture of fear and defiance. "I know what I did was wrong. I don't need a lecture from you guys."

"Don't you?" I asked. "Because if you knew it was wrong, you wouldn't have done it!"

Jill crossed her arms over her chest. "I *had* to get out of here. On my own terms. And not with you guys."

The comment rolled right off of me. It sounded young and petty. But to my surprise, Eddie actually looked hurt.

"What's that supposed to mean?" he asked.

"It means that I just wanted to be away from this place without *you* always telling me what I'm doing wrong." That was directed to me. "And *you* jumping at every shadow." That, of course, was to Eddie.

"I just want to protect you," he said, looking hurt. "I'm not trying to smother you, but I can't have anything happen to you. Not again."

"I'm in more danger from Laurel than any assassins!" Jill exclaimed. "Do you know what she did today? We were working in the computer lab, and she 'accidentally' tripped over my power cord. I lost half my work and didn't finish in time, so now I'm going to get a lower grade."

A lesson on backing up work probably wouldn't be useful just then. "Look, that's really terrible," I said. "But it's not in the same category as getting yourself killed. Not by a long shot. Where exactly did you go?"

For a moment, she looked as though she wasn't going to give up the info. Finally, she said, "Lee took me to Salton Sea." Seeing our blank looks, she added, "It's a lake outside of town. It was wonderful." An almost-dreamy expression crossed her features. "I haven't been around that much water in so long. Then we went downtown and just walked around, shopping and eating ice cream. He took me to that boutique, with the designer who's looking for models and—"

"Jill," I interrupted. "I don't care how awesome your day was. You *scared* us. Don't you get that?"

"Lee shouldn't have done this," growled Eddie.

"Don't blame him," said Jill. "I talked him into it—I made him think you guys wouldn't mind. And he doesn't know the real reason I'm here or the danger."

"Maybe dating was a bad idea," I muttered.

"Lee's the best thing that's happened to me here!" she said angrily. "I deserve to be able to go out and have fun like you guys."

"'Fun'? That's kind of an exaggeration," I said, recalling my afternoon with Adrian.

Jill needed a target for her frustration, and I won the honor. "Doesn't seem like it to me. You're always gone. And when you aren't, you just tell me what I'm doing wrong. It's like you're my mom."

I'd been wading through all of this calmly, but suddenly, something about that comment made me snap. My finely tuned control shattered.

"You know what? I kind of feel that way too. Because as far as I can tell, I am the *only* one in this group behaving like an adult. You think I'm out there having fun? All I'm doing is babysitting you guys and cleaning up your messes. I spent my afternoon—*wasted* my afternoon—driving Adrian around so that he could blow off the interviews that *I* set up. Then I get here and have to deal with the aftermath of *your* 'field trip.' I get that Laurel's a pain—although maybe if Micah had been

271

warned off from the beginning, these problems with her never would've happened." I directed that last comment at Eddie. "I don't get why I'm the only one who sees how serious everything is. Vampire-human dating. Your lives on the line. These aren't the kinds of things you can screw around with! And yet . . . somehow, you all still do. You leave me to do the hard stuff, to pick up after you . . . and all the while, I've got Keith and the other Alchemists breathing down my neck, waiting for *me* to screw up because no one trusts me since helping your pal Rose. You think this is fun? You want to live my life? Then do it. Step right up, and *you* start taking responsibility for a change."

I hadn't yelled, but my volume had certainly gone up. I'd pretty much delivered my speech without taking a breath and now paused for some oxygen. Eddie and Jill stared at me, wide-eyed, as though they didn't recognize me.

Mrs. Weathers returned to us just then. "That's enough for tonight. You need to go upstairs now," she told Jill.

Jill nodded, still a little stunned, and hurried away without saying goodbye to any of us. Mrs. Weathers walked her to the stairs, and Eddie turned to me. His face was pale and solemn.

"You're right," he said. "I haven't been pulling my share."

I sighed, suddenly feeling exhausted. "You're not as bad as they are."

He shook his head. "Still. You might be right about Micah. Maybe he'll keep some distance if I talk to him, and then Laurel will lay off Jill. I'll ask him tonight. But . . ." He frowned, choosing his words carefully. "Try not to be too hard on Adrian and Jill. This is stressful for her, and sometimes I think a little of Adrian's personality is leaking into her through the bond. I'm sure that's why she ran off today. It's something he'd do in her situation."

"No one forced her to do it," I said. "Least of all Adrian. The fact that she coaxed Lee and didn't tell us shows that she knew it was wrong. That's free will. And Adrian has no such excuses."

"Yeah . . . but he's Adrian," said Eddie lamely. "Sometimes I don't know how much of what he does is him and how much is spirit."

"Spirit users can take antidepressants, can't they? If he's worried about it becoming a problem, then he needs to step up and take charge. He has a choice. He's not helpless. There are no victims here."

Eddie studied me for several seconds. "And I thought *I* had a harsh view on life."

"You have a harsh life," I corrected. "But yours is built around the idea that you always have to take care of other people. I was raised to believe that's necessary sometimes but that everyone still needs to try to take care of themselves."

"And yet here you are."

"Tell me about it. You want to come talk to Lee with me?"

All apology vanished from Eddie's face. "Yes," he said fiercely.

We found Lee sitting on a bench outside, looking miserable. He jumped up when we approached. "You guys, I'm so sorry! I shouldn't have done it. She just sounded so sad and so lost that I wanted to—"

"You know how protective we are of her," I said. "How could you have not thought that this would worry us?"

"And she's a minor," said Eddie. "You can't just take her away and do whatever you want with her!"

I admit, I was a little surprised that the threat to Jill's virtue was what he chose to bring up. Don't get me wrong—I was also conscious of her age. But after he saw her literally die, it seemed like Eddie would be worried about more than making out.

Lee's gray eyes went wide. "Nothing happened! I would never do anything like that to her. I promise! I'd never take advantage of someone so trusting. I can't ruin this. She means more to me than any other girl I've dated. I want us to be together forever."

I thought being "together forever" was extreme at their ages, but there was a sincerity in his eyes that was touching. It still didn't excuse what he'd done. He took our lecturing seriously and promised there would never be a repeat.

"But please . . . can I still see her when you're around? Can we still do group things?"

Eddie and I exchanged glances. "If she's even allowed to leave campus after this," I said. "I really don't know what's going to happen."

Lee left after a few more apologies, and Eddie also returned to his dorm. I was walking upstairs when my phone rang. Glancing down, I was startled to see my parents' number in Salt Lake City on the caller ID.

"Hello?" I asked. For a frantic moment, I hoped it was Zoe.

"Sydney."

My father. My stomach filled with dread.

"We need to talk about what's happened."

Panic shot through me. How had he found out about Jill's disappearance already? Keith jumped out as the obvious culprit.

But how had Keith found out? Had he been at Clarence's when Eddie called Adrian? Despite his flaws, I couldn't imagine Adrian telling Keith what had happened.

"Talk about what?" I asked, playing for time.

"Your behavior. Keith called me last night, and I must say, I'm very disappointed."

"Last night?" This wasn't about Jill's disappearance. So what was it about?

"You're supposed to be coordinating efforts for that Moroi girl to blend in. You aren't supposed to be out socializing with them and having a good time! I could hardly believe it when Keith said you took them out bowling."

"It was mini-golf, and Keith okayed it! I asked him first."

"And then I hear you're helping all these other vampires run errands and whatnot. Your duty is only to the girl, and that is to do only what's necessary for her survival—which I also hear you aren't doing. Keith tells me there was an incident where you didn't properly handle her difficulties in the sun?"

"I reported that immediately!" I cried. I'd *known* Keith was planning to use that against me. "Keith—" I paused, thinking about the best way to handle this. "Misunderstood my initial report." Keith had blown off my initial report, but telling my father his protégé had lied would just put my father's defenses up. He wouldn't believe me. "And Keith's one to talk! He's always hanging out with Clarence and won't say why."

"Probably to make sure he remains stable. I understand the old man isn't all there."

"He's obsessed with vampire hunters," I explained. "He thinks there are humans out there that killed his niece."

"Well," said my father, "there *are* some humans out there

275

who catch on to the vampire world, those whom we can't dissuade. Hardly hunters. Keith's doing his duty by enlightening Clarence. You, however, are misguided."

"That's not a fair comparison!"

"Honestly, I blame myself," he said. Somehow I doubted that. "I shouldn't have let you go. You weren't ready—not after what you went through. Being with these vampires is confusing you. That's why I'm recalling you."

"*What?*"

"If I had my way, it'd be right now. Unfortunately, Zoe won't be ready for another two weeks. The Alchemists want her to undergo some testing before she gets her tattoo. Once she does, we'll send her in your place and get you . . . some help."

"Dad! This is crazy. I'm doing fine here. Please, don't send Zoe—"

"I'm sorry, Sydney," he said. "You've left me no choice. Please don't get into trouble in your remaining time."

He disconnected, and I stood in the hall, my heart sinking. Two weeks! Two weeks and they were sending Zoe. And me . . . where were they sending me? I didn't want to think about it, but I knew. I needed to stop this from happening. Wheels were already in motion. *The tattoos,* I suddenly thought. If I could finish my tests on the stolen substances and find out info about the blood supplier, I would earn the Alchemists' regard—hopefully enough to take away the taint that Keith had put on me.

And why had he done it? Why now? I knew he'd never wanted me along. Maybe he had just been biding his time, building up evidence against me until he could get me ousted in one fell swoop. I wouldn't let him, though. I'd bust open this tattoo case and prove who the stellar Alchemist was. I had enough evidence now to get their attention and would simply turn in what I had if nothing new came to light within a week.

The decision filled me with resolve, but I still had trouble sleeping when I went to bed later. My father's threat hung over me, as did my fear of the re-education centers.

After about an hour of tossing and turning I finally dozed off. But even that was fitful and troubled. I woke up after only a few hours and then had to fall asleep all over again.

This time, I dreamed.

In the dream, I stood in Clarence's living room. Everything was neat and in place, the dark wood and antique furniture giving the space its usual ominous feel. The details were surprisingly vivid, and it was like I could even smell the dusty books and leather on the furniture.

"Huh. It worked. Wasn't sure if it would with a human."

I spun around and found Adrian leaning against the wall. He hadn't been there a moment ago, and I had a flash of that childhood fear of vampires appearing out of nowhere. Then I remembered this was a dream, and these kinds of things happened.

"What weren't you sure about?" I asked.

He gestured around him. "If I could reach you. Bring you here into this dream." I didn't quite follow what he meant and said nothing. He arched an eyebrow. "You don't know, do you? Where you are?"

"At Clarence's," I said reasonably. "Well, in reality I'm asleep in my bed. This is just a dream."

"You're half right," he said. "This is a spirit dream. This is real."

I frowned. A spirit dream. Since most of our information

about spirit was sketchy, we had hardly anything on spirit dreams. I'd learned most of what I knew about them from Rose, who had been frequently visited by Adrian in them. According to her, the dreamer and the spirit user were actually together, in a meeting of the minds, communicating across long distances. It was hard for me to fully grasp that, but I'd seen Rose wake up with information she wouldn't have otherwise had. Still, I had no evidence to suggest I was really in a spirit dream now.

"This is just a regular dream," I countered.

"Are you sure?" he asked. "Look around. Concentrate. Doesn't it *feel* different? Like a dream . . . but not like a dream. Not quite like real life either. Call it what you want, but the next time we see each other in the waking world, I'll be able to tell you exactly what happened here."

I looked around the room, studying it as he'd suggested. Again, I was struck by the vividness of even the smallest details. It certainly felt real, but dreams often did . . . right? You usually never knew you were dreaming until you woke up. I closed my eyes and took a deep breath, trying to still my mind. And like that, I *felt* it. I understood what he meant. Not quite like a dream. Not quite like real life. My eyes flew open.

"Stop it," I cried, backing away from him. "Make it end. Get me out of here."

Because in accepting that this really was a spirit dream, I'd had to acknowledge something else: I was surrounded in vampire magic. My mind was ensnared in it. I felt claustrophobic. The magic was pressing on me, crushing the air.

"Please." My voice grew more and more frantic. "Please let me go."

Adrian straightened up, looking surprised. "Whoa, Sage. Calm down. You're okay."

"No. I'm not. I don't want this. I don't want the magic touching me."

"It won't hurt you," he said. "It's nothing."

"It's wrong," I whispered. "Adrian, stop it."

He reached out a hand, like he might try to comfort me, and then thought better of it. "It won't hurt you," he repeated. "Just hear me out, and then I'll dissolve it. I promise."

Even in the dream, my pulse was racing. I wrapped my arms around myself and backed up against the wall, trying to make myself small. "Okay," I whispered. "Hurry."

"I just wanted to say . . ." He stuffed his hands in his pockets and glanced away uncomfortably before looking at me again. Were his eyes greener here than in real life? Or was it just my imagination? "I wanted to . . . I wanted to apologize."

"For what?" I asked. I couldn't process anything beyond my own terror.

"For what I did. You were right. I wasted your time and your work today."

I forced my mind to dredge up memories from this afternoon. "Thank you," I said simply.

"I don't know why I do these things," he added. "I just can't help it."

I was still terrified, still suffocating in the magic surrounding me. Somehow, I managed to echo my earlier conversation with Eddie.

"You can take control of yourself," I said. "You aren't a victim."

Adrian had been gazing off, troubled by his thoughts. He suddenly jerked his gaze back to me. "Just like Rose."

"What?"

Adrian held out his hand, and a thorny red rose suddenly materialized there. I gasped and tried to back up farther. He twirled the stem around, careful not to prick his fingers.

"She said that. That I was playing the victim. Am I really that pathetic?"

The rose wilted and crumpled before my eyes, turning to dust and then vanishing altogether. I made the sign against evil on my shoulder and tried to remember what we were talking about.

"*Pathetic's* not the word I'd use," I said.

"What word would you use?"

My mind was blanking. "I don't know. *Confused?*"

He smiled. "That's an understatement."

"I'll check a dictionary when I wake up and get back to you. Can you please end this?"

The smile faded to an expression of amazement. "You really are that scared, aren't you?" I let my silence answer for me. "Okay, one more thing, then. I thought of another way I can get out of Clarence's and get some money. I was reading about college and financial aid. If I took classes somewhere, do you think I could get enough to live on?"

This was a concrete question I could deal with. "It's possible. But I think it's too late. Classes have started everywhere."

"I found a place on the internet. Carlton. A college on the other side of town that hasn't started yet. But I'd still have to act fast, and . . . that's what I don't know how to do. The paperwork. The procedures. But that's your specialty, right?"

"Sad but true," I said. Some part of me thought Carlton sounded familiar, but I couldn't place it.

He took a deep breath. "Will you help me? I know it's making you babysit again, but I don't know where to start. I promise I'll meet you halfway, though. Tell me what I need to do, and I will."

Babysit. He'd been talking to Jill or Eddie or both. That was reasonable, though. He'd want to know that she was okay. I could only imagine how my tirade had been paraphrased.

"You were in college before," I said, recalling his record. I'd scoured it when putting together the ill-fated resume. "You dropped out."

Adrian nodded. "I did."

"How do I know you won't this time? How do I know you aren't just wasting my time again?"

"You don't know, Sage," he admitted. "And I don't blame you. All I can ask is that you give me another chance. That you try to believe me when I say I'll follow through. That you believe I'm serious. That you trust me."

Long moments stretched out between us. I'd relaxed slightly, without even realizing it, though I remained up against the wall. I studied him, wishing I was better at reading people. His eyes were that green in real life, I decided. I just usually didn't look at them so closely.

"Okay," I said. "I trust you."

Total shock filled his features. "You do?"

I was no better at reading people than I had been ten seconds ago, but in that moment, I suddenly gained a flash of understanding into the mystery that was Adrian Ivashkov. People didn't believe in him very often. They had low expectations of him, so he did as well. Even Eddie had sort of written him off: *He's Adrian.* As though there was nothing to be done for it.

I also suddenly realized that, as unlikely as it seemed, Adrian and I had a lot in common. Both of us were constantly boxed in by others' expectations. It didn't matter that people expected everything of me and nothing of him. We were still the same, both of us constantly trying to break out of the lines that others had defined for us and be our own person. Adrian Ivashkov—flippant, vampire party boy—was more like me than anyone else I knew. The thought was so startling that I couldn't even answer him right away.

"I do," I said at last. "I'll help you." I shivered. The fear of the dream returned, and I just wanted this to be over. I would've agreed to anything to be back in my non-magical bed. "But not here. Please—will you send me back? Or end this? Or whatever it is?"

He nodded slowly, still looking stunned. The room began to fade, its colors and lines melting like a painting left in the rain. Soon, all dimmed to black, and I found myself waking up in my dorm room bed. As I did, I just barely caught the sound of his voice in my mind:

Thank you, Sage.

CHAPTER 19

IF I'D HAD TROUBLE SLEEPING BEFORE, Adrian's dream only made things worse. Even though I was safely back in my own bed, I couldn't shake the feeling of violation. I imagined that my skin was crawling with the taint of magic. I'd been so anxious to get out of the dream that I'd only half-realized what I'd been agreeing to. I respected Adrian's desire to go to college but now wondered if I should really be helping with that after my father's chastisement about "getting friendly" with vampires.

I wasn't in the greatest of moods when I finally got up a few hours later. The tension in our room was thick as Jill and I prepared for school. Jill's defiance from yesterday was gone, and she kept watching me nervously when she thought I didn't notice. At first, I figured my outburst from last night had made her uneasy. But as we walked out of the room for breakfast, I knew there was more to it.

"What?" I asked bluntly, breaking the silence at last. "What do you want to ask me?"

Jill gave me another wary glance as we joined the rush of other girls heading downstairs. "Um, something happened yesterday."

A lot of things happened yesterday, I thought. That was my overtired, bitter self talking, and I knew that wasn't what she was leading up to.

"Such as?" I asked.

"Well . . . I was starting to tell you about how Lee took me to that store. That clothing boutique where he knew the owner? Her name's Lia DiStefano. We talked, and she, uh, offered me a job. Kind of."

"The modeling job?" We reached the cafeteria's food line, though I had little appetite. I selected a yogurt, which looked sad and lonely in the middle of my otherwise empty tray. "We talked about that. It's not safe."

Still, it was ironic that a random visit could land Jill a job when three formal interviews had failed for Adrian.

"This isn't for posed pictures that would be in a magazine or anything, though. It's a runway show of local designers. We told her this story that we're part of a religion that has rules about photos and identity. Lia said she'd actually been thinking of having her models wear half masks. Like the kind you wear at a masquerade? Between that and the lighting and the movement . . . well, it'd be hard to identify me if any candid shots got out. It's just a onetime event, but I'd have to see her beforehand for fittings . . . and to practice. She'd pay me too, but I'd need rides to get there and parental permission."

We sat down, and I spent an unnecessary amount of time

stirring my yogurt as I mulled over her words. I could feel her gaze on me as I thought.

"It's kind of silly, I guess," she continued when I didn't answer. "I mean, I don't have any experience. And I don't even know why she'd want me. Maybe it's some gimmick she's going for. Weird models or something."

I finally ate a bite of yogurt and then looked up at her. "You're not weird, Jill. You really do have the ideal body type for modeling. It's hard to find. For humans, at least." Once again, I tried not to think about how hard it was for us humans to live up to Moroi perfection. I tried not to think about how, years ago, my dad had criticized my figure and said, "If those monsters can do it, why not you?"

"But you still think it's a terrible idea," she said.

I didn't respond. I knew what Jill wanted, but she couldn't bring herself to directly ask me for it. And I couldn't easily give it to her yet. I was still too upset about yesterday and not feeling kindly toward any favors. On the other hand, I couldn't tell her no either. Not yet. Despite how irresponsibly she'd behaved, her words about how miserable her life was here had hit me hard. This was something positive and good that would fill her time. It was also a much-needed ego boost. Laurel had thrived on using Jill's unusual features against her; it would do Jill good to see that others viewed them positively. She needed to realize she was special and wonderful. I didn't know whether to curse or thank Lee for this opportunity.

"I don't think we can decide anything until we go talk to Mrs. Weathers," I told her at last. I glanced at a nearby clock. "In fact, we need to meet with her now."

I took a few more bites of my yogurt before throwing it

away. Jill took a donut to go. When we returned to our lobby, we found out a delivery had arrived for Jill: a bouquet of perfect red roses and an apologetic note from Lee. Jill melted, her face filling with adoration at the gesture. Even I admired the romance of it, though a snarky part of me said maybe Lee should've sent flowers to Eddie and me instead. We were the ones he needed to apologize to. Regardless, the flowers were quickly forgotten when we sat down in Mrs. Weathers's office and learned the verdict on Jill.

"I spoke to the principal. You aren't being suspended," she told Jill. "But for the next month, you are restricted to your dorm when not in class. You are to report to me immediately after classes end so that I know you're here. You may go to the cafeteria for meals—but only your dorm's. Not the one on West Campus. The only exceptions to this policy are if an assignment or teacher requires you to go elsewhere outside of school hours, like the library."

We both nodded, and for a moment, I was simply relieved that Jill hadn't been expelled or anything like that. Then the real problem hit me like a slap in the face. I'd told Jill this meeting would impact any modeling decisions, but there was something much worse on the line.

"If she's grounded to the dorm, then she can't leave the school," I said.

Mrs. Weathers gave me a wry smile. "Yes, Miss Melrose. That is what 'grounded' generally means."

"She has to, ma'am," I argued. "We have family gatherings twice a week." Ideally, we had them more than that, but I was hoping a lowball number might buy us freedom. It was absolutely essential Jill get blood, and two days a week was about the minimum a vampire could survive on.

"I'm sorry. Rules are rules, and in breaking them, your sister has lost the privilege of functions like that."

"They're religious," I said. I hated to play the religion card, but that was something the school would have a hard time countering. And hey, it had apparently worked on the fashion designer. "We go to church as a family on those days—us and our brothers."

Mrs. Weathers's face showed me I had indeed gained ground. "We'd need a signed letter from your parents," she said finally.

Great. That had worked so well in PE.

"What about our brother? He's our legal guardian here." Surely even Keith couldn't drag his feet on this, not with blood on the line.

She considered this. "Yes. That might be acceptable."

"I'm sorry," I told Jill when we walked outside to catch the shuttle. "About the modeling. We're going to have a hard enough time getting you permission to leave for feedings."

Jill nodded, making no effort to hide her disappointment.

"When's the show?" I asked, thinking maybe she could do it when her punishment was over.

"In two weeks."

So much for that idea. "I'm sorry," I repeated.

To my surprise, Jill actually laughed. "You have no reason to be. Not after what I did. *I'm* the one who's sorry. And I'm sorry about Adrian too—about the interviews."

"That's something you have no reason to be sorry about." It

struck me again how easily everyone made excuses for him. She proved this with her next comment.

"He can't help it. It's how he is."

He can *help it,* I thought. Instead, I said, "Just hang in there, okay? I'll get Keith to sign off on our religious experiences."

She smiled. "Thanks, Sydney."

We usually parted ways when the bus reached Central Campus, but she held back once we got off. I could see again that she wanted to tell me something but was having trouble getting the courage.

"Yes?" I asked.

"I . . . just wanted to tell you I really am sorry for giving you so much grief. You do a lot for us. Really. And you being upset, it's because . . . well, I know you care. Which is more than I can say for other people back at Court."

"That's not true," I said. "They care. They went to a lot of trouble to get you here and keep you safe."

"I still feel like it was more for Lissa than for me," she said sadly. "And my mom didn't put up much of a fight when they said they were going to send me away."

"They want you safe," I told her. "That means making hard choices—hard for them too."

Jill nodded, but I don't know if she believed me. I gave Eddie the morning report when I reached history. His face displayed a range of emotions with each new development in the story.

"You think Keith will write the note?" he asked in a low voice.

"He has to. The whole point of us being here is to keep her alive. Starving her to death kind of defeats the purpose."

I didn't bother telling Eddie that I was in trouble with my

father and the Alchemists and that in two weeks, there was a good chance I might not even be around. Eddie was clearly upset over Jill's situation already, and I didn't want him to have one more thing to worry about.

When I met up with Ms. Terwilliger at the end of the day, I turned in the last of the notes I'd made for her on the old books. As I was settling myself at a desk, I noticed a folder of articles sitting on a table. *Carlton College* was printed on the folder in embossed gold letters. I remembered now why I'd thought the name was familiar when Adrian had mentioned it in the dream.

"Ms. Terwilliger . . . didn't you say you knew people at Carlton College?"

She glanced up from her computer. "Hmm? Oh yes. I should think so. I play poker with half of the history faculty. I even teach there in the summers. History, that is. Not poker."

"I don't suppose you know anybody in admissions, do you?" I asked.

"Not so much. I suppose I know people who know people there." She turned her attention back to the screen. I said nothing, and after several moments, she looked back at me. "Why do you ask?"

"No reason."

"Of course there's a reason. Are you interested in attending? Goodness knows you'd probably get more out of there than here. My class being the exception, of course."

"No, ma'am," I said. "But my brother wants to attend. He heard classes haven't started yet but isn't sure if he can get in on such short notice."

"It's *very* short notice," agreed Ms. Terwilliger. She scrutinized me carefully. "Would you like me to make some inquiries?"

"Oh. Oh no, ma'am. I was just hoping to get some names I could contact. I'd never ask you to do something like that."

Her eyebrows rose. "Why ever not?"

I was at a loss. She was so difficult to understand sometimes. "Because . . . you have no reason to."

"I'd do it as a favor to you."

I couldn't muster a response for that and simply stared. She smiled and pushed her glasses up her nose.

"That's impossible for you to believe, isn't it? That someone would do a favor for you."

"I . . . well, that is . . ." I trailed off, still unsure what to say. "You're my teacher. Your job is to, well, teach me. That's it."

"And your job," she said, "is to report to this room during last period for whatever mundane tasks I have for you and then turn in a paper at the end of the semester. You are not in any way required to fetch me coffee, show up after hours, organize my life, or completely rearrange your own to meet my ridiculous requests."

"I . . . I don't mind," I said. "And it all needs doing."

She chuckled. "Yes. And you insist on going above and beyond in your tasks, don't you? No matter how inconvenient for you."

I shrugged. "I like to do a good job, ma'am."

"You do an excellent job. Far better than you need to. And you do it without complaint. Therefore, the least I can do is make a few phone calls on your behalf." She laughed again. "That startles you most of all, doesn't it? Having someone praise you."

"Oh no," I said lamely. "I mean, it happens."

She took off her glasses to look at me more intently. The

laughter was gone. "No, I'm thinking it doesn't. I don't know your particular situation, but I have known a lot of students like you—ones whose parents ship them off like this. While I appreciate the concern for higher education, I find that more often than not, a bigger piece of students coming here is that their parents simply don't have the time or inclination to be involved with—or even pay attention to—their children's lives."

We were dealing with one of those interpersonal areas that made me uncomfortable, particularly because there was an unexpected element of truth in them. "It's more complicated than that, ma'am."

"I'm sure it is," she replied. Her expression turned fierce, making her look far different from the scattered teacher I knew. "But listen to me when I say this. You are an exceptional, talented, and brilliant young woman. Do not ever let anyone make you feel like you're less. Do not ever let anyone make you feel invisible. Do not let anyone—not even a teacher who constantly sends you for coffee—push you around." She put her glasses back on and began randomly lifting up pieces of papers. At last, she found a pen and grinned triumphantly. "Now, then. What is your brother's name?"

"Adrian, ma'am."

"Right, then." She took out a piece of paper and carefully wrote down the name. "Adrian Melbourne."

"Melrose, ma'am."

"Right. Of course." She scribbled out her mistake and muttered to herself, "I'm just glad his first name's not Hobart." When she was finished, she leaned back casually in her chair. "Now that you mention it, there is one thing I'd like you to do."

"Name it," I said.

"I want you to make one of the spells from that first book."

"I'm sorry. Did you say, make a spell?"

Ms. Terwilliger waved a hand. "Oh, don't worry. I'm not asking you to wave a wand or do an animal sacrifice. But I'm terribly intrigued by how complex some of the formulas and steps of the spells were. I have to wonder, did people actually follow them in such painstaking detail? Some of these are quite complicated."

"I know," I said dryly. "I typed them all out."

"Exactly. So, I want you to make one. Follow the steps. See how long it takes. See if half the measurements they ask for are even possible. Then write up the data in a report. That part, I know you excel at."

I didn't know what to say. Ms. Terwilliger wasn't actually asking me to use magic, certainly not in the same way vampires did. Such a thing wasn't even possible. Magic was not the province of humans. It was unnatural and went against the ways of the universe. What the Alchemists did was based on science and chemistry. The tattoos had magic, but it was us bending vampire magic to our wills—not using it ourselves. The closest we came to anything supernatural was the blessings we called down on our potions. She was only asking me to reenact a spell. It wasn't real. There was no harm. And yet . . . why did I feel so uneasy? I felt like I was being asked to lie or steal.

"What's the matter?" she asked.

For a moment, I considered using religion again but then dismissed it. That excuse had come up too often today, though this time, it was actually semi-legitimate. "Nothing, ma'am. It just seems weird."

She picked up the first leather book and flipped to the middle.

"Here. Do this one—an incineration amulet. It's complicated, but at least you'll have an arts and crafts project when you're done. Most of these ingredients should be easy to come by, too."

I took the book from her and scanned it. "Where am I going to get nettle?"

"Ask Mr. Carnes. He has a garden outside his classroom. I'm sure you can buy the rest. And you know, you *can* give me receipts. I'll pay you back whenever I send you out to get something. You must've spent a fortune on coffee."

I felt a little better when I saw how random the ingredients were. Nettle. Agate. A piece of silk. There wasn't really even anything flammable. This was nonsense. With a nod, I told her I'd start soon.

In the meantime, I typed up an official letter to Amberwood on Keith's behalf. It explained that our religious beliefs required family church attendance twice a week and that Jill needed to be excused from her punishment during those times. It also promised that Jill would check in with Mrs. Weathers both before and after the family trips. When I finished, I was rather pleased with my work and felt that I'd made Keith sound far more eloquent than he deserved.

I called him up when school ended and gave a brief rundown on what had happened with Jill. Naturally, I got the blame.

"You're supposed to keep an eye on her, Sydney!" Keith exclaimed.

"I'm also supposed to be undercover as a student here, and I can't be with her every second of the day." It wasn't worth mentioning that I'd actually been out with Adrian when Jill had run away—not that Keith could do any more to me. He'd already done his damage.

"And so I have to suffer the consequences," he said in a world-weary voice. "I'm the one who gets put out for your incompetence."

"Put out? You don't have to do anything except sign the letter I wrote for you. Are you home right now? Or will you be? I'll drive it over to you."

I figured he'd jump all over the offer, seeing how annoyed he seemed to be by the matter. So, it was a surprise when he said, "No, you don't have to do that. I'll come to you."

"It's not a problem. I can be at your place in less than ten minutes." I didn't want him to have any more reason than necessary to go on and on about how I was inconveniencing him—or complain to the Alchemists.

"No," said Keith, with surprising intensity. "I'll come to you. I'm leaving right now. Meet you at the main office?"

"Okay," I said, totally puzzled at this change of heart. Did he want to check up on me or something? Demand an inspection? "See you soon."

I was already on Central Campus, so it took no time at all to reach the main office. I sat outside on an ornate stone bench with a good view of the visitors parking lot and waited. It was hot out, as usual, but being in the shade actually made it pretty pleasant. The bench was situated in a little clearing filled with flowering plants and a sign that read *The Kelly Hayes Memorial Garden*. It looked new.

"Hey, Sydney!"

Kristin and Julia were walking out of the building and waved at me. They came and sat down beside me to ask what I was doing.

"I'm waiting for my brother."

"Is he cute?" asked Kristin hopefully.

"No," I said. "Not at all."

"Yes, he is," countered Julia. "I saw him in your dorm last weekend. When you all went out for lunch."

It took me a second to realize she meant Adrian. "Oh. Different brother. They don't have a lot in common."

"Is it true your sister's in big trouble?" asked Julia.

I shrugged. "Only a little trouble. She can't leave campus, except for family stuff. It could be worse. Although . . . it did cost her a modeling job, so she's sad about that."

"Modeling for who?" asked Kristin.

I racked my brain. "Lia DiStefano. There's some show in two weeks, and she wanted Jill to walk in it. But Jill can't practice because she has to stay here."

Their eyes went wide.

"Lia's clothes are amazing!" said Julia. "Jill has to do it. She might get free stuff."

"I told you. She can't."

Kristin tilted her head thoughtfully. "But what if it was for school? Like some kind of career or vocational thing?" She turned to Julia. "Is there still a sewing club?"

"I think so," said Julia, nodding eagerly. "That's a good idea. Does Jill have an activity?" Along with a sport, Amberwood also required its well-rounded students to participate in hobbies and activities outside of class. "There's a sewing club she could join . . . and I bet she could get working with Lia counted as some kind of special research."

In attempting to fix a loose thread on her cardigan the other day, Jill had nearly unraveled the entire sweater. "I don't think that's really Jill's thing."

"Doesn't matter," said Kristin. "Most of the people in it can't sew anyway. But every year, the club volunteers with local designers. Miss Yamani would totally let walking in the show count as volunteering. She *loves* Lia DiStefano."

"And they'd have to let her go," said Julia, face full of triumph. "Because it'd be for school."

"Interesting," I said, wondering if there was any chance of it working. "I'll tell Jill." A familiar blue car pulled into the driveway, and I stood up. "There he is."

Keith parked and got out, scanning around for me. Kristin gave a small sound of approval. "He's not bad."

"Believe me," I said, walking forward. "You want nothing to do with him."

Keith gave the girls what was probably supposed to be a charming smile and even winked at them. The instant they were gone, his smile dropped. Impatience radiated off of him, and it was a wonder he didn't tap his foot.

"Let's make this fast," he said.

"If you're in such a rush, you should have just let me come by when you had more time." I took out a binder containing the letter and handed it over with a pen. Keith signed without even looking at it and handed it back.

"Need anything else?" he asked.

"No."

"Don't mess up again," he said, opening the car door. "I don't have time to keep covering for you."

"Does it matter?" I challenged him. "You've already done your best to get rid of me."

He gave me a cold smile. "You shouldn't have crossed me. Not now, not back then." With a wink, he turned around and began to leave. I stared, unable to believe the audacity. It was the first time he'd directly referenced what went down years ago.

"Well, that's the thing," I shouted at his retreating figure. "I *didn't* cross you back then. You got off easy. It's not going to happen again. You think I'm worried about you? *I'm* the one *you* need to be scared of."

Keith came to a halt and then slowly turned around, his face awash with disbelief. I didn't blame him. I was kind of surprised myself. I couldn't ever remember a time I'd so openly countered someone in a higher position of authority, certainly not someone who had so much power to affect my situation.

"Watch it," he said at last. "I can make your life miserable."

I gave him an icy smile. "You already have, and that's why I've got the advantage. You've done your worst—but you haven't seen what I can do yet."

It was a big bluff on my part, especially since I was pretty sure he could still do worse. For all I knew, he could get Zoe out here tomorrow. He could get me sent to a re-education center in a heartbeat.

But if I went down? So would he.

He stared at me for a few moments, at a loss. I don't know if I actually scared him or if he decided not to dignify me with an answer, but he finally turned and left for good. Furious, I went inside to deliver the letter to the office. The front desk secretary, Mrs. Dawson, stamped it and then made a copy for me to give to Mrs. Weathers. As she handed it to me, I asked, "Who's Kelly Hayes?"

Mrs. Dawson's usually dimpled face grew sad. "That poor girl. She was a student here a few years ago."

My memory clicked. "Is she the one Mrs. Weathers mentioned? Who went missing?"

Mrs. Dawson nodded. "It was terrible. She was such a sweet girl too. So young. She didn't deserve to die like that. She didn't deserve to die at all."

I hated to ask but had to. "How did she die? I mean, I know she was murdered, but I never heard any details."

"Probably just as well. It's pretty gruesome." Mrs. Dawson peered around, as though afraid she'd get in trouble for gossiping with a student. She leaned over the counter toward me, face grave. "The poor thing bled to death. She had her throat cut."

CHAPTER 20

I ALMOST ASKED, "Are you serious?" But let's face it: that probably wasn't the kind of thing she would joke about, especially considering how grave her face looked. Other questions popped into my head, but I held back on those as well. They weren't *that* weird, but I didn't want to draw attention to myself by showing unusual interest in a grisly murder. Instead, I simply thanked Mrs. Dawson for her help with the letter and returned to East Campus.

Mrs. Weathers was at her desk when I entered the dorm. I brought her the letter, which she read over twice before tucking it away in her filing cabinet. "All right," she said. "Just make sure your sister signs in and out each time."

"I will, ma'am. Thank you." I hesitated, torn over whether to go or ask the questions Mrs. Dawson's information had triggered. I decided to stay. "Mrs. Weathers . . . ever since Jill disappeared, I just keep thinking about that girl you told me about. The one who died. I keep thinking that could've been Jill."

Mrs. Dawson's face softened. "Jill's fine. I shouldn't have told you that. I didn't mean to scare you."

"Is it true that girl's throat was slit?"

"Yes." She shook her head sadly. "Terrible. Simply terrible. I don't know who does that kind of thing."

"Did they ever find out why it happened? I mean, was there anything unusual about her?"

"Unusual? No, not really. I mean, she was a lovely girl. Smart, pretty, popular. A good—no, great—athlete. Had friends, a boyfriend. But nothing that would especially make her stand out as a target. Of course, people who do awful things like that probably don't need a reason."

"True," I murmured.

I walked up to my room, wishing Mrs. Weathers had elaborated a little more on how pretty Kelly was. What I really wanted to know was if Kelly had been Moroi. If she had, I'd hoped Mrs. Weathers might comment on how tall or pale she was. By both Clarence's and the Alchemists' accounts, no Moroi on record had lived in the Palm Springs area. That didn't mean someone couldn't slip through the cracks, however. I'd have to find the answer myself. If Kelly had been Moroi, then we had three young Moroi women killed in the same way in southern California within a relatively short time span. Clarence might argue for his vampire hunter theory, but to me, this pattern screamed Strigoi.

Jill was in our room, serving out her house arrest. The more time passed, the less angry I felt toward her. Having the feeding issue fixed helped. I would've been a lot more upset if we'd been unable to get her off campus.

"What's wrong?" she asked me, looking up from her laptop.

"Why do you think anything's wrong?"

She smiled. "You've got that look. It's this tiny frown you get between your eyebrows when you're trying to figure something out."

I shook my head. "It's nothing."

"You know," she said, "maybe all these responsibilities you have wouldn't be as bad if you talked them out and got help from other people."

"It's not quite like that. It's just something I'm trying to puzzle out."

"Tell me," she entreated. "You can trust me."

It wasn't a matter of trust. It was a matter of unnecessarily worrying Jill. Mrs. Weathers had feared she would scare me, but if someone was killing Moroi girls, I wasn't in danger. Looking at Jill and her unwavering gaze, I decided if she could handle living with the knowledge that her own people were trying to kill her, she could handle this. I gave her a brief summary of what I knew.

"You don't know if Kelly was Moroi, though," she said, once I'd finished.

"No. That's the crucial piece here." I sat cross-legged on my bed with my own laptop. "I'm going to check our records and local newspapers to see if I can find a picture of her. All I learned from Mrs. Weathers is that Kelly was a star athlete."

"Which may mean she's not Moroi," said Jill. "I mean, look at how terrible I perform in this sun. What happens if she's not? You've got a lot of theories hinging on her being Moroi. But what if she was human? What then? Can we ignore it? It could still be the same person . . . but what would it mean if the murderer had killed two Moroi and one human?"

Jill had a point. "I don't know," I said.

My search didn't take long. The Alchemists had no record of the murder, but then, they wouldn't if Kelly had been human. Lots of newspapers had stories about her, but I couldn't find any pictures.

"What about a yearbook?" asked Jill. "Someone must keep them around."

"That's actually pretty brilliant," I said.

"See? I told you I'm useful."

I smiled at her and then remembered something. "Oh, I've got good news for you. Maybe." I briefly recapped Kristin and Julia's "plan" about Jill joining the sewing club.

Jill brightened but was still cautious. "You really think that would work?"

"Only one way to find out."

"I've never touched a sewing machine in my life," she said.

"I guess this is your chance to learn," I told her. "Or maybe the other girls will be happy to just keep you around as their in-class model."

Jill smirked. "How do you know only girls sign up for that?"

"I don't," I admitted. "Just playing off gender stereotypes, I guess."

My cell phone rang, and Ms. Terwilliger's number flashed on the display. I answered, bracing for a coffee run.

"Miss Melbourne?" she said. "If you and your brother can be at Carlton within an hour, you can speak to someone in the registrar's office before they close. Can you manage that?"

I looked at the time and took it on faith Adrian wasn't doing anything important. "Um, yes. Yes, of course, ma'am. Thank you. Thank you very much."

"The man you'll want to talk to is named Wes Regan." She paused. "And could you bring me a cappuccino on your way back?"

I assured her I could and then called Adrian with instructions to be ready for me. Quickly, I changed out of my uniform and into a blouse and twill skirt. Glancing at my reflection, I realized he was right. There really wasn't a lot of difference between Amberwood attire and my normal wardrobe.

"I wish I could go," said Jill wistfully. "I'd like to see Adrian again."

"Don't you kind of see him every day in a way?"

"True," she said. "Although I can't always get into his head when I want to yet. It just happens randomly. And anyway, it's not the same. He can't talk back to me through the bond."

I nearly replied that it sounded better than being around him in person but figured that wouldn't be helpful.

Adrian was ready to go when I reached Clarence's, excited and eager for action. "You just missed your friend," he said as he got into Latte.

"Who?"

"Keith."

I made a face. "He's not really my friend."

"Oh, you think? Most of us figured that out on day one, Sage."

I felt a little bad about that. Some part of me knew that I shouldn't let my personal feelings for Keith mix with business. We were co-workers of sorts and should've been presenting a united, professional front. At the same time, I was kind of glad these people—even if they were vampires and dhampirs—didn't think I was friendly with Keith. I didn't want them thinking he and I had much in common. I certainly didn't want to have a lot in common with him.

The full meaning of Adrian's words suddenly hit me. "Wait. He was just here?"

"A half hour ago."

He must have come straight from the school. I was lucky to have missed him. Something told me he wouldn't approve of me furthering Adrian's education.

"What was he here for?"

"Dunno. I think he was checking on Clarence. The old guy hasn't been feeling well." Adrian pulled a pack of cigarettes out of his pocket. "Do you mind?"

"Yes," I replied. "What's wrong with Clarence?"

"I don't know, but he's been resting a lot, which makes things even more boring. I mean, he wasn't the greatest conversationalist, but some of his crazy stories were interesting." Adrian turned wistful. "Especially with scotch."

"Keep me updated on how he's doing," I murmured. I wondered if perhaps that was why Keith had been in such a hurry earlier. If Clarence was seriously ill, we were going to have to make arrangements with a Moroi doctor. That would complicate our setup here in Palm Springs because we'd either have to move Clarence or bring in someone. If Keith was working on it, then I shouldn't have concerned myself . . . but I just didn't trust him to do a good job with anything.

"I don't know how you put up with him," said Adrian. "I used to think you were weak and just didn't fight back . . . but now, honestly, I think you're actually pretty tough. It takes a hell of a lot of strength to not complain and lash out. I don't have that self-control."

"You've got more than you think," I said, a little flustered by the compliment. I was down on myself so much for what I saw as not pushing back sometimes that it had never occurred to me that took its own strength. I was even more surprised that it would take Adrian to point this out to me. "I'm always walking a line. My dad—and the Alchemists—are really big on obedience and following the directions of your superiors. I'm kind of in a double bind because I'm on shaky ground with them, so it's extra important for me to not make a fuss."

"Because of Rose?" His tone was carefully controlled.

I nodded. "Yup. What I did was tantamount to treason in their eyes."

"I don't know what 'tantamount' means, but it sounds pretty serious." I could see him studying me out of the corner of his eye. "Was it worth it?"

"So far." It was easy to say that since Zoe had no tattoo yet and I hadn't seen a re-education center. If those things changed, so might my answers. "It was the right thing to do. I guess that justified dramatic action."

"I broke a lot of rules to help Rose too," he said, a troubled tone in his voice. "I did it out of love. Misguided love, but love nonetheless. I don't know if that's as noble as your reasons, particularly since she was in love with someone else. Most of my 'dramatic actions' haven't been for any cause. Most of them have been to annoy my parents."

I actually found myself a little jealous of that. I couldn't fathom purposely trying to get a reaction from my dad—though I'd certainly wanted to. "I think love's a noble reason," I told him. I was speaking objectively, of course. I'd never been in love and had no point of reference to really judge. Based on what

I'd observed in others, I assumed it was an amazing thing . . . but for now, I was too busy with my job to notice its absence. I wondered if I should be disappointed by that. "And I think you have plenty of time to do other noble things."

He chuckled. "Never thought my biggest cheerleader would be someone who thought I was evil and unnatural."

That made two of us.

Hesitantly, I managed to ask a question that had been burning inside me. "Do you still love her? Rose?" Along with not knowing what it felt like to be in love, I also didn't know how long it took to recover from love.

Adrian's smile faded. His gaze turned inward. "Yes. No. It's hard to get over someone like that. She had a huge effect on me, both good and bad. That's hard to move past. I try not to think about her much in terms of love and hate. Mostly I'm trying to get on with my life. With mixed results, unfortunately."

We soon reached the college. Wes Regan was a big man with a salt-and-pepper beard who worked in Carlton's registration office. Ms. Terwilliger had tutored Wes's niece for free one summer, and Wes felt he owed her a favor.

"Here's the deal," he said once we were seated across from him. Adrian was wearing khaki pants and a sage-colored button-down shirt that would've been great for job interviews. A little too late. "I can't just enroll you. College applications are long and require transcripts, and there's no way you can swing one in two days. What I can do is get you in as an auditor."

"Like with the IRS?" asked Adrian.

"No. Auditing means you're attending the class and doing the work but not getting a grade for it."

Adrian opened his mouth to speak, and I could only imagine what comment he had about doing work for no credit. I quickly interrupted him.

"And then what?"

"Then, if you can throw together an application in, oh, a week or two—and are accepted—I can retroactively change you to student status."

"What about financial aid?" asked Adrian, leaning forward. "Can I get some money for this?"

"If you qualify," said Wes. "But you can't really file for it until you've been accepted."

Adrian slumped back, and I was able to guess his thoughts. If getting enrolled would take a couple of weeks, there'd undoubtedly be a delay with the financial aid filing too. Adrian was looking at a month or more of living with Clarence, and that was probably optimistic. I half-expected Adrian to get up and nix everything. Instead, a resolute expression crossed his face. He nodded.

"Okay. Let's get started with this auditing thing."

I was impressed.

I was also jealous when Wes brought out the course catalog. I'd been able to lull myself into contentment with Amberwood's classes, but looking at real college offerings showed me the two schools were worlds away. The history classes were more focused and in depth than anything I could have imagined. Adrian had no interest in those, however. He immediately honed in on the art department.

He ended up signing up for two introductory courses in oil painting and in watercolors. They met three times a week and were conveniently back-to-back.

"That'll make it easier if I'm busing in," he explained as we were leaving.

I gave him a startled look. "You're taking the bus?"

He seemed amused by my astonishment. "What else? Classes are in the daytime. You can't take me."

I thought about Clarence's remote house. "Where on earth would you catch the bus?"

"There's a stop about a half mile away. It transfers to another bus that goes to Carlton. The whole trip takes about an hour."

I confess, it left me speechless. I was amazed that Adrian had researched that much, let alone was willing to go to all that trouble. Yet on the ride back, he never uttered one word of complaint about how inconvenient it would be or how long he'd have to wait to move out of Clarence's.

When I arrived back at Amberwood, I was excited to tell Jill the news about Adrian's collegiate success—not that she needed me to tell her. With the bond, she would probably know more than I did. Still, she always worried about him and would undoubtedly be pleased to see something go well for him.

Jill wasn't in our room when I returned, but a note informed me she was studying elsewhere in the dorm. The only bright part of her punishment was that it limited where she could be at any time. I decided to use this opportunity to go make Ms. Terwilliger's crazy amulet. I'd accrued most of the necessary ingredients, and along with compliance from the biology teacher, Ms. Terwilliger had secured me access to one of the chemistry labs. No one was there this time of night, and it gave me plenty of space and quiet to mix up the concoction.

As we'd noted, the instructions were extremely detailed

and—in my opinion—superfluous. It wasn't enough to just measure out the nettle leaves. The instructions called for them "to rest for an hour," during which time I was supposed to say to them, "into thee, flame I imbue" every ten minutes. I also had to boil the agate stone "to infuse it with heat." The rest of the instructions were similar, and I knew there was no way Ms. Terwilliger would actually know if I followed everything to the letter—particularly the chants. Still, the whole purpose of this stunt was to report on what it was like to be an ancient practitioner. So, I followed everything dutifully and concentrated so hard on performing every step perfectly that I soon fell into a lull where nothing existed except the spell.

I finished over two hours later and was surprised at how exhausted I felt. The final result certainly didn't seem to justify all the energy I'd expended. I was left with a leather cord from which hung a silk pouch filled with leaves and rocks. I carted it and my notes back to my dorm room, intending to write up my report for Ms. Terwilliger so that I could put this assignment behind me. When I reached my room, I gasped when I saw the door. Someone had taken red paint and drawn bats and fanged faces all over it. Scrawled across the front, in big blocky letters, were the words

VAMP GIRL

Full of panic, I burst into the room. Jill was there—along with Mrs. Weathers and another teacher I didn't know. They were going through all of our things. I stared in disbelief.

"What's going on?" I asked.

Jill shook her head, face mortified, and couldn't answer. I'd apparently arrived at the end of the search because Mrs. Weathers and her associate soon finished up and walked to the door. I was glad I'd taken my Alchemist supplies with me to the lab tonight. The kit contained a few measuring tools I had thought I might need. I certainly didn't want to explain why I owned a collection of chemicals to dorm authorities.

"Well," said Mrs. Weathers sternly. "There doesn't appear to be anything here, but I may do another spot check later—so don't get any ideas. You're already in enough trouble without adding yet another charge to it." She sighed and shook her head at Jill. "I'm very disappointed in you, Miss Melrose."

Jill blanched. "I'm telling you, it's all a mistake!"

"Let's hope so," said Mrs. Weathers ominously. "Let's hope so. I've half a mind to make *you* clean up that vandalism outside, but in light of no hard proof . . . well, we'll have the janitors take care of it tomorrow."

Once our visitors were gone, I immediately demanded, "What happened?"

Jill collapsed backward onto her bed and groaned. "Laurel happened."

I sat down. "Explain."

"Well, I called the library to see if they had those yearbooks in—the ones about Kelly Hayes? Turns out they do normally have them, but they've all been checked out by the newspaper staff for some Amberwood anniversary edition. And you'll never believe who's heading that project: Laurel."

"You're right," I said. "I never would have guessed that. Isn't she in Freshman English?" Laurel was a senior.

"Yup."

"I guess everyone needs an activity," I muttered.

Jill nodded. "Anyway, Miss Yamani was in the building, so I

went to ask her about joining the sewing club and working for Lia. She was really excited and said she'd make it happen."

"Well, that's something," I said cautiously, still unsure how this was leading up to vandalism and a search of our room.

"As I was coming back, I passed Laurel in the hall. I decided to take a chance . . . I approached her and said look, I know we've had our differences but I could really use some help. Then I explained that I needed the yearbooks and asked if I could borrow them just for the night and that I'd get them back to her right away."

To this, I said nothing. It was certainly a noble and brave thing for Jill to do, particularly after I'd encouraged her to be better than Laurel. Unfortunately, I didn't think Laurel would reciprocate the adult behavior. I was right.

"She told me in . . . well, very explicit terms that I'd never get those yearbooks." Jill scowled. "She told me a few other things too. Then I, um, called her a raving bitch. I probably shouldn't have, but, well, she deserved it! Anyway, she went to Mrs. Weathers with a bottle of . . . I don't know. I think it was raspberry schnapps. She claimed I sold it to her and had more in my room. Mrs. Weathers couldn't punish me without harder evidence, but after Ms. Chang's hangover accusation on the first day, Mrs. Weathers decided that was enough for a room search."

I shook my head in disbelief, anger growing within my chest. "For such an elite, prestigious place, this school sure is quick to jump on any accusations that come up! I mean, they believe anything anyone says about you. And where did the paint outside come from?"

Tears of frustration glinted in her eyes. "Oh, Laurel, of course. Or, well, one of her friends. It happened while Laurel was talking to Mrs. Weathers, so of course she's got an alibi. You don't think . . . you don't think anyone's on to anything, do you? You said before it's just a mean joke . . . and humans don't even believe in us . . . right?"

"Right," I said automatically.

But I was beginning to wonder. Ever since that phone call with my father, when he'd mentioned that there were humans who suspected and wouldn't be silenced, I'd wondered if I'd been too quick to dismiss Laurel's teasing. Had she simply found a cruel joke to run with? Or was she one of those humans who suspected about the vampire world and might make a lot of noise about it? I doubted anyone would believe her, but we couldn't risk attracting attention from someone who would.

Is it possible she really thinks Jill is a vampire?

Jill's forlorn expression turned angry. "Maybe *I* should do something about Laurel. There are other ways to get back at her besides freezing water."

"No," I said quickly. "Don't lower yourself to that. Revenge is petty, and you're better than that." *Plus,* I thought, *any more supernatural activity, and Laurel might realize her taunts have more backing than she originally thought.*

Jill gave me a sad smile. "You keep saying that. But don't you think something needs to be done about Laurel?"

Oh yes. I definitely did. This had gone too far, and I'd been wrong to let it slide. Jill was right that there were other ways to get back at someone. And I was right that revenge was petty and nothing that Jill should sully herself with. That was why *I* was going to do it.

"I'll take care of it," I told her. "I—I'll have the Alchemists issue a complaint from our parents."

She looked dubious. "You think that'll fix things?"

"Positive," I said. Because that complaint was going to pack an extra punch. A glance at the time told me it was too late to go back to the lab. No problem. I simply set my alarm extra early, with the intent to get up and head back there before classes started.

I had one more experiment in my future, and Laurel was going to be my guinea pig.

CHAPTER 21

MIXING WHAT I NEEDED TO was easy. Getting it to where I needed took a couple of days. I first had to pay attention to what kind of shampoo Laurel used in the PE showers. The school provided shampoo and conditioner, of course, but she wouldn't trust her precious hair with anything so commonplace. Once I knew her brand, I hunted it down at a local beauty supply store and emptied its expensive contents down the drain. I filled bottles with my homemade concoction instead.

The next step was switching it with Laurel's own bottle. I recruited Kristin for this. Her locker was next to Laurel's in PE, and she was more than willing to help me out. Part of it was that she shared our dislike of Laurel. But also, ever since I'd saved her from the tattoo reaction, Kristin had made it clear that she was indebted to me and had my back in whatever I needed. I didn't like the idea of her owing me, but her assistance did come in handy. She found a moment when Laurel looked away from her unlocked locker and covertly made the switch. We then simply had to wait for the next time Laurel used the shampoo to see the results of my handiwork.

Meanwhile, my other lab experiment wasn't receiving quite the reaction I'd expected. Ms. Terwilliger accepted my report but not the amulet.

"I have no use for it," she remarked, glancing up from the papers I'd handed her.

"Well . . . I certainly don't either, ma'am."

She set the papers down. "This is all true? You followed every step precisely? I'd certainly have no way of knowing if you'd, ah, fudged some of the details."

I shook my head. "Nope. I followed every step."

"Well, then. It looks like you have yourself a fire-making charm."

"Ma'am," I said, by way of protest.

She grinned. "What do the directions say? Throw it and recite the last incantation? Do you know it?"

"'Into flame, into flame,'" I said promptly. After having typed the spell initially for her notes and then re-creating it, it was hard not to have picked it all up. According to the book—which was an English translation of a Latin text—the language didn't matter so long as the words' meaning was clear.

"Well, there you go. Give it a try one of these days and see what happens. Just don't light any school property on fire. Because that's not safe."

I held up the amulet by the string. "But this isn't real. This is nonsense. It's a bunch of junk thrown together in a bag."

She shrugged. "Who are we to question the ancients?"

I stared, trying to figure out if she was joking. I'd known she was eccentric from day one, but she'd still always come across as a serious scholar. "You can't believe that. Magic like this . . . it's not real." Without thinking, I added, "Even if it was, ma'am, it's not for humans to mess around with powers like that."

Ms. Terwilliger was silent for several moments. "You truly believe that?"

I fingered the cross around my neck. "It's how I was raised."

"Understood. Well, then, you may do what you like with the amulet. Throw it away, donate it, experiment with it. Regardless, this report's what I need for my book. Thank you for putting in the time—as always, you've done more than was required."

I put the amulet in my purse when I left, not really sure what to do. It was useless . . . and yet, it had also cost me a lot of time. I was disappointed it wasn't going to have a more meaningful purpose in her research. All that effort gone to waste.

The last of my projects showed development the next day, however. In AP Chemistry, Greg Slade and some of his friends scurried into class just as the bell rang. Our teacher gave them a warning look, but they didn't even notice. Slade was preening over his eagle tattoo, baring it for everyone to see. The ink was gleaming silver again. Next to him, one of his friends was also proudly showing off another silver tattoo. It was a pair of stylized crossed daggers, which was only slightly less tacky than the eagle. This was the same friend who had been worrying earlier this week that he wouldn't be able to get a tattoo. Apparently, things had worked out with the supplier. Interesting. Part of holding off on reporting to the Alchemists had been to see if Nevermore would replenish what I'd stolen.

"It's amazing," Slade's friend said. "The rush."

"I know." Slade gave him a fist bump. "Just in time for tomorrow."

Trey was watching them, his expression dark. "What's tomorrow?" I whispered to him.

He eyed them contemptuously for a few more moments before turning back to me. "Do you live under a rock? It's our first home game."

"Of course," I said. My high school experience wouldn't be complete without the quintessential football hype.

"A lot of good it'll do me," he muttered.

"Your bandages are off," I pointed out.

"Yeah, but Coach is still making me take it easy. Plus, I'm kind of deadweight now." He nodded toward Slade and his friend. "How come they don't get in trouble for those? They're not making any effort to hide them. This school has no discipline anymore. We're practically in anarchy."

I smiled. "Practically."

"Your brother should be on the team, you know. I've seen him in PE. He could be a star athlete if he bothered trying out for anything."

"He doesn't like drawing attention to himself," I explained. "But he'll probably go watch the game."

"Are *you* going to go to the game?"

"Probably not."

Trey arched an eyebrow. "Hot date?"

"No! But I'm just . . . well, not into watching sports. And I feel like I should stay with Jill."

"You won't even go to cheer me on?"

"You don't need my cheers."

Trey gave me a disappointed look as a response. "Maybe it's just as well," he said. "Since you really wouldn't get to see me performing to my full level of awesomeness."

"That is a shame," I agreed.

"Oh, stop with the sarcasm already." He sighed. "My dad's going to be the most upset. There are family expectations."

Well, that was something I could relate to. "Is he a football player too?"

"Nah, it's less about football itself than keeping yourself in peak physical shape. Excelling. Ready to be called upon in a moment's notice. Being the best on the team's been a way to keep him proud—until these tattoos started."

"You're good without any tattoo help. He should still be proud," I said.

"You don't know my father."

"No, but I think I know someone just like him." I smiled. "You know, maybe I do need to go to a football game after all."

Trey simply smiled back, and class started.

The day passed calmly, but Jill ran up to me as soon as I entered the locker room for PE.

"I heard from Lia! She asked if I could come by tonight. She's had regular practices with the other models but thought I could use a special session of my own since I don't have any experience. Of course, the thing is, I . . . you know, need a ride. Do you think . . . I mean, could you . . ."

"Sure," I said. "It's what I'm here for."

"Thank you, Sydney!" She threw her arms around me, much to my astonishment. "I know you don't have any reason to help me after everything I've done, but—"

"It's fine, it's fine," I said, awkwardly patting her on the shoulder. I took a steadying breath. *Think of it as Jill hugging me. Not as a vampire hugging me.* "I'm glad to help."

"Would you two like to be alone?" sneered Laurel, striding in with her entourage. "I always knew there was something weird about your family."

Jill and I split apart, and she blushed, which only made them laugh more. "God, I hate them," she said when they were out of earshot. "I *really* want to get them back."

"Patience," I murmured. "They'll get what's coming to them someday." Eyeing Laurel's locker, I thought that "someday" might come sooner rather than later.

Jill shook her head in amazement. "I don't know how you can be so forgiving, Sydney. Everything just rolls right off of you."

I smiled, wondering what Jill would think if she knew the truth—that I wasn't quite as "forgiving" as I appeared. And not just when it came to Laurel. If Jill wanted to think of me that way, so be it. Of course, my facade as a kindly, turn-the-other-cheek person was shattered when Laurel's shrieks filled the locker room at the end of class an hour later.

It was almost a repeat of the ice incident. Laurel came tearing out of the shower, wrapped in a towel. She ran to the mirror in horror, holding her hair up to it.

"What's wrong?" asked one of her friends.

"Can't you see it?" cried Laurel. "There's something wrong . . . it doesn't feel right. It's oil . . . or I don't know!" She took out a blow dryer and dried a section while the rest of us watched with interest. After a few minutes, the long strands were dry, but it was hard to tell. It really was like her hair was coated in oil or grease, like she hadn't washed it in weeks. That normally gleaming, bouncy hair now hung in lank, ugly coils. The color was also off a little. The bright, flaming red now had a sickly yellow hue.

"It smells weird too," she exclaimed.

"Wash it again," suggested another friend.

Laurel did that, but it wasn't going to help. Even when she figured out that her shampoo was causing the problem, the stuff I'd made wasn't going to come out of her hair easily. Water would continue fueling the reaction, and it was going to take many, many scrubbings before she fixed the problem.

Jill gave me astonished look. "Sydney?" she whispered, a million questions in my name.

"Patience," I assured her. "This is just the first act."

That evening, I drove Jill down to Lia DiStefano's boutique. Eddie went with us, of course. Lia was only a few years older than me and nearly a foot shorter. Despite her tiny size, there was something big and forceful about her personality as she confronted us. The shop was filled with elegant gowns and dresses, though she herself was dressed ultra-casual, in ripped jeans and an oversized peasant blouse. She flipped on the closed sign on her door and then confronted us with hands on her hips.

"So, Jillian Melrose," she began. "We have less than two weeks to turn you into a model." Her eyes fell on me. "And you're going to help."

"Me?" I exclaimed. "I'm just the ride."

"Not if you want your sister to shine in my show." She stared back up at Jill, the difference in their heights almost comical. "You have to eat, drink, and breathe modeling if you're going to pull this off. And you have to do it all—in these."

With a flourish, Lia grabbed a nearby shoe box and produced

a pair of glittery purple shoes with heels that had to be at least five inches high. Jill and I stared.

"Isn't she tall enough already?" I asked at last.

Lia snorted and thrust the shoes at Jill. "These aren't for the show. But once you master these, you'll be ready for anything."

Jill took them gingerly, holding them up to study them. The heels reminded me of the silver stakes Eddie and Rose used to kill Strigoi. If Jill really wanted to be prepared for any situation, she could just keep these around. Self-conscious of our scrutiny, she finally kicked off her brown flats and fastened the many elaborate straps of the purple shoes. Once they were on, she slowly straightened up—and nearly fell over. I hastily jumped to catch her.

Lia nodded in approval. "See? This is what I was talking about. Sisterly teamwork. It's up to you to make sure she doesn't fall and break her neck before my show."

Jill shot me a look of panic that I suspect was reflected on my own face. I started to suggest that Eddie be Jill's spotter, but he had discreetly moved off to the side of the shop to watch and seemed to have escaped Lia's notice. Apparently, his protective services had limits.

While Jill simply attempted not to topple over, I helped Lia clear space in the store's center. Lia then spent the next hour or so demonstrating how to properly walk for fashion, with emphasis on posture and stride in order to display clothing to its best effect. Most of those fine details were lost on Jill, though, who struggled to simply walk across the room without falling. Grace and beauty weren't concerns as much as staying upright.

Nonetheless, when I glanced over at Eddie, he was watching

Jill with a rapt look on his face, as though every step she were taking was pure magic. Catching my eye, he immediately resumed his wary, protective guardian face.

I did my best to offer Jill words of encouragement—and yes, stop her from falling and breaking her neck. Halfway through the session, we heard a knock at the glass door. Lia started to scowl and then recognized the face on the other side of the door. She brightened and went to unlock it.

"Mr. Donahue," she said, letting Lee in. "Come to see how your starlet's doing?"

Lee smiled, his gray eyes instantly seeking out Jill. Jill met his gaze, grinning just as widely. Lee hadn't been around at the last feeding, and although they talked constantly on the phone and IM, I knew she had been pining to see him. A glance at Eddie's face showed me he wasn't nearly as delighted by Lee's presence.

"I already know how she's doing," said Lee. "She's perfect."

Lia snorted. "I wouldn't go that far."

"Hey," I said, inspiration striking me. "Lee, do you want to be in charge of keeping Jill from breaking her neck? I need to run an errand." Unsurprisingly, Lee was more than willing, and I knew I didn't need to fear for her safety with Eddie on watch.

I left them, hurrying two streets over to Nevermore. Ever since I'd heard Slade and his friends confirm the tattooists were in business again, I'd wanted to pay an in-person trip. Not a covert one, though. My stolen goods had already yielded their evidence. Except for the clear liquid, I had identified all the other substances in the vials. All the metallics were exact matches for Alchemist compounds, meaning these people either had an Alchemist connection or were stealing. Either way, my case got stronger and stronger. I just hoped it'd be enough to redeem me and keep Zoe out of here, particularly since the clock was ticking on her arrival. We were almost a week away from when my father had said she'd be replacing me.

My plan was to see how willing Nevermore was to give me a tattoo. I wanted to know what warnings (if any) they gave out and how easy it was in the first place. Adrian's conversation hadn't yielded much info, but probably his on-fire-biker-skeleton-with-a-parrot tattoo request hadn't done much to help his credibility. I was armed with cash today, which I hoped would get me somewhere.

As it was, I never needed to flash any. As soon as I walked in, the guy behind the counter—the same one Adrian had spoken to—looked relieved.

"Thank God," he said. "Please tell me you have more. These kids are driving me crazy. When we got into this . . . I had no idea it was gonna get this big. The money's good, but Christ. It's crazy to keep up with."

I kept my confusion off of my face, wondering what in the world he was talking about. He was acting as though I was in on his scheme here, which made no sense. But then his eyes flashed to my cheek, and suddenly, I understood.

My lily tattoo.

It was uncovered, since school was over. And I knew then, with absolute certainty, that whomever he was working with to get his supplies was also an Alchemist. He'd assumed my tattoo made me an ally.

"I don't have anything with me," I said.

His face fell. "But the demand—"

"You lost the other batch," I said haughtily. "You let it get stolen right out from underneath you. Do you know how much trouble we go to in order to get that?"

"I already explained that to your friend!" he exclaimed. "He said he understood. He said he'd taken care of the problem and that we didn't have to worry anymore."

There was a sinking feeling in the pit of my stomach. "Yeah, well, he doesn't speak for all of us, and we're not sure we want to continue. You were compromised."

"We're careful," he argued. "That theft wasn't our fault! Now, come on. You have to help us. Didn't he tell you? There's a huge demand for tomorrow because those private school kids have a game. If we can deliver, we'll make double the money."

I gave him my best icy smile. "We'll discuss it among ourselves and get back to you."

With that, I turned around and began to leave. "Wait," he called. I spared him a haughty glance. "Can you make that person stop calling?"

"What person?" I asked, wondering if he meant some persistent Amberwood student.

"The one with the weird voice who keeps asking if any tall, pale people are showing up around here. Ones that look like vampires. I figured it was someone you knew."

Tall, pale people? I didn't like the sound of that but kept my face blank. "Sorry. Don't know what you're talking about. Must have been a prank."

I left, making a mental note to investigate that further. If someone was inquiring about people who looked like vampires, that was a problem. It wasn't, however, the immediate problem. My mind raced as I processed what else the tattooist had told me. There was an Alchemist supplying Nevermore. In some ways, that shouldn't be a surprise. How else were they going to get ahold of vampire blood and all the metals necessary for their tattoos? And apparently, this rogue Alchemist had "taken care of the problem" that led to the theft of their supplies. When had my father called saying I was being pulled because of Keith's reports?

Right after I'd broken into Nevermore.

I knew who the rogue Alchemist was.

And I knew that I had been "the problem." Keith had taken care of me, making moves to get me out of Palm Springs and bring in someone new and inexperienced who wouldn't interfere with his illicit tattoo operation. It was why he'd wanted Zoe in the first place.

I was aghast. I didn't have a great opinion of Keith Darnell, not by any means. But never, *never* had I thought he'd stoop to this level. He was an immoral person, but he'd still been raised with the same principles I had about humans and vampires. For him to abandon those beliefs and expose innocents to the dire side effects of vampire blood for his own material gain . . . well, it was more than a betrayal of the Alchemists. It was a betrayal of the whole human race.

My hand was on my cell phone, ready to call Stanton. That's all it would take. One call with the kind of news I had, and Alchemists would swoop in on Palm Springs—and on Keith. But what if there was no hard evidence to connect Keith? It was possible another Alchemist might go in and play the same game I had, getting the tattooist to think that they were part of Keith's team. Keith was the one I wanted to bust, however. I wanted to ensure that there was no way he could slip out of this.

I made my decision, and rather than the Alchemists, I called Adrian.

When I arrived back at Lia's shop, I found the training session winding down. Lia was giving Jill some last-minute instructions while Eddie and Lee lingered nearby. Eddie took one look at my face and instantly knew something was wrong.

"What's the matter?"

"Nothing," I said blandly. "Just a problem I'm going to fix soon. Lee, would you mind taking Jill and Eddie back to the school? I have a couple errands I need to run."

Eddie frowned. "Are you okay? Do you need someone to protect you?"

"I'll have someone." I reconsidered, seeing as I was about to meet up with Adrian. "Well, kind of. Anyway, I'm not in trouble. Your job's to keep an eye on Jill, remember? Thanks, Lee," I added, seeing him nod. A thought suddenly struck me. "Wait . . . I thought this was one of the days you had a night class. Are we keeping you . . . or . . . well, what days *do* you have class?"

I hadn't thought much about it, only noticing that some days Lee was around and other days he was in Los Angeles. But in looking back, there was no real pattern. I saw realization light Eddie's face as well.

"That's true," he said, eyeing Lee suspiciously. "What kind of schedule are you on?"

Lee opened his mouth, and I sensed a ready story coming. Then he stopped and cast an anxious look at Jill, who was still talking to Lia. His face fell. "Please don't tell her," he whispered.

"Tell her what?" I asked, keeping my voice low as well.

"I'm not in college. I mean—I was. But not this semester. I

wanted some time off but . . . didn't want to disappoint my dad. So, I told him I was just going part-time, which is why I was around more."

"What do you do in LA during all that time, then?" asked Eddie. That was an excellent question, I realized.

"I still have friends there, and I need to keep my cover." Lee sighed. "It's stupid, I know. Please—let me be the one to tell her. I wanted so badly to impress her and to prove myself to her. She's wonderful. She just caught me at a bad time."

Eddie and I exchanged glances. "I won't tell," I said. "But you really should let her know. I mean, I guess there's no harm done . . . but you shouldn't have that kind of lie between you."

Lee looked miserable. "I know. Thank you."

When he stepped aside, Eddie shook his head at me. "I don't like him lying. Not at all."

"Lee trying to save face is the least weird thing going on here," I said.

I found out then that Jill could walk from one side of the store to the other and back without falling over. It wasn't pretty, but it was a start. She was still a long ways from looking anything like the runway models I saw on TV, but considering she hadn't been able to stand in the shoes at first, I supposed she'd made considerable progress. She started to take off the heels, but Lia stopped her.

"No. I told you. You have to wear these shoes all the time. Practice, practice, practice. Wear them home. Wear them everywhere." She turned to me. "And you—"

"I know. Make sure she doesn't break her neck," I said. "She's not going to be able to wear those all the time, though. Our school has a dress code."

"What if they were in a different color?" asked Lia.

"I don't think it's just the color," Jill said apologetically. "I think it's the stiletto part. But I promise to wear them outside of class and practice in our room."

That was good enough for Lia, and after a few more words of advice, she sent us on our way. We promised to practice and come back in two days. I told Jill I'd meet up with her later, but I don't know if she heard. She was so caught up in the idea of Lee driving her home that pretty much everything else went past her.

I drove over to Clarence's and was met at the door by Adrian. "Wow," I said, impressed at his initiative. "I didn't expect you to be ready so quickly."

"I'm not," he said. "I need you to see something right now."

I frowned. "Okay." Adrian led me deeper into the house, beyond where I normally went, which made me nervous. "Are you sure this can't wait? This thing we've got to do is kind of urgent . . ."

"So is this. How did Clarence seem the last time you saw him?"

"Weird."

"But health-wise?"

I thought about it. "Well, I know he's been tired. But usually he seemed okay."

"Yeah, well, he's not 'okay' now. It's gone beyond just tired. He's weak, dizzy, and confined to his bed." We reached a closed wooden door, and Adrian stopped.

"Do you know what caused it?" I asked, alarmed. I'd been

worried about the complications of a sick Moroi but hadn't expected to deal with it so soon.

"I have a pretty good idea," said Adrian, with surprising fierceness. "Your boy Keith."

"Stop saying stuff like that. He's not 'my boy,'" I exclaimed. "He's ruining my life!"

Adrian opened the door, revealing a large, ornate canopied bed. Walking into a Moroi bedroom wasn't something I was comfortable with, but Adrian's commanding look was too powerful. I followed him in and gasped when I saw Clarence lying on the bed.

"Not just yours," said Adrian, pointing at the old man.

Clarence's eyes fluttered at the sound of our voices and then closed again as he shifted into sleep. It wasn't his eyes that held my attention, though. It was the pale, sickly pallor of his skin—that, and the bloody wound on Clarence's neck. It was small, made with just one prick, like it had come from a surgical instrument. Adrian looked at me expectantly.

"Well, Sage? Do you have any idea why Keith would be draining Clarence's blood?"

I swallowed, scarcely able to believe what I was seeing. Here was the last piece. I knew that Keith had been supplying the tattooists, and now I knew where Keith was getting his "supplies."

"Yes," I said at last, my voice small. "I have a very good idea."

CHAPTER 22

CLARENCE DIDN'T WANT to talk to us about what had happened. In fact, he adamantly denied anything was wrong, claiming he'd scratched his neck while shaving.

"Mr. Donahue," I said as gently as I could, "this was made by a surgical tool. And it didn't happen until Keith visited."

"No, no," Clarence managed in a weak voice. "It has nothing to do with him."

Dorothy stuck her head in just then, carrying a glass of juice. We'd called for her shortly after my arrival tonight. For blood loss, the remedies were the same for Moroi and human alike: sugar and fluids. She offered the glass to him with a straw, her lined face filled with concern. I continued my pleas as he drank.

"Tell us what your deal is," I begged. "What's the arrangement? What's he giving you for your blood?" When Clarence remained silent, I tried another tactic. "People are being hurt. He's giving out your blood indiscriminately."

That got a reaction. "No," said Clarence. "He's using my blood and saliva to heal people. To heal sick humans." Saliva? I nearly groaned. Of course. The mysterious clear liquid. Now I knew what gave the celestial tattoos their addictive high. Gross.

Adrian and I exchanged glances. Healing certainly was a use for vampire blood. The tattoo I wore was proof of that, and the Alchemists had worked long trying to duplicate some of the blood's properties for wider medicinal use. So far, there was no way to synthetically reproduce it, and using real blood simply wasn't practical.

"He lied," I replied. "He's selling it to rich teenagers to help them with sports. What did he promise you for it? A cut of the money?"

Adrian glanced around the opulent room. "He doesn't need money. The only thing he needs is what the guardians wouldn't give him. Justice for Tamara, right?"

Surprised, I turned back to Clarence and saw Adrian's words confirmed on the old Moroi's face. "He . . . he's been investigating the vampire hunters for me," he said slowly. "He says he's close. Close to finding them out."

I shook my head, wanting to kick myself for not having figured out sooner that Clarence was the blood source. It explained why Keith was always unexpectedly here—and why he got so upset when I showed up without warning. My "fraternizing with vampires" had had nothing to do with it. "Sir, I guarantee the only thing he's investigating is how to spend the money he's been making."

"No . . . no . . . he's going to help me find the hunters who killed Tamara . . ."

I stood up. I couldn't stand to hear any more. "Get him some real food, and see what he'll eat," I told Dorothy. "If he's only weak from blood loss, he just needs time."

I nodded for Adrian to follow me out. As we walked toward the living room, I remarked, "Well, there are good and bad sides to this. At least we can be confident Keith's got a fresh supply of blood for us to bust him with. I'm just sorry Clarence had to get hit so—"

I froze as I entered the living room. I'd simply wanted to go there because it would be a familiar place to discuss our plans, one that was less creepy than Clarence's bedroom. Considering how my imagination often ran wild while I was in this old house, I'd found that few things came as a surprise. But never in my wildest dreams had I imagined the living room would be transformed into an art gallery.

Easels and canvas were set up all around the room. Even the pool table was covered by a big roll of paper. The pictures varied wildly in their content. Some simply had splashes of color thrown on them. Some possessed astonishingly realistic depictions of objects and people. An assortment of watercolors and oil paints sat around amidst the art.

For a moment, all thoughts of Clarence and Keith disappeared from my head. "What is this?"

"Homework," Adrian said.

"Didn't you . . . didn't you just *start* your classes? How could they have assigned this much?"

He walked over to a canvas showing a swirling red line traced over a black cloud and lightly tested to see if the paint was dry. Studying it, I tried to decide if I really was seeing a cloud. There was almost something anthropomorphic about it.

"Of course they didn't give us this much, Sage. But I had to make sure I nailed my first assignment. Takes a lot of tries before you hit perfection." He paused to reconsider that. "Well, except for my parents. They got it on the first try."

I couldn't help a smile. After watching Adrian's moods oscillate so wildly in the last couple weeks, it was nice to see them on the upswing. "Well, this is kind of amazing," I admitted. "What are they? I mean, I get that one." I pointed to a painting of a woman's eye, brown and long-lashed, and then to another one of roses. "But the others are open to, um, slightly more creative interpretation."

"Are they?" asked Adrian, turning back to the smoky painting with the red streak. "I figured it was obvious. This one is *Love.* Don't you see it?"

I shrugged. "Maybe I don't have an artistic enough mind."

"Maybe," he agreed. "Once we bust your buddy Keith, we'll discuss my genius art all you want."

"Right," I said, growing serious again. "We need to search his place for evidence. I figured the best way to do that is if I lure him out and you break in while he's gone. To get through the lock—"

Adrian waved me off. "I can pick a lock. How do you think I got into my parents' liquor cabinet in middle school?"

"Should've guessed," I said dryly. "Make sure you look everywhere, not just in obvious places. He could have compartments hidden in the walls or in furniture. You want to find vials of blood or metallic liquid or even the tool that pierced Clarence."

"Got it." We hashed out a few more details—including who he should call when he found something—and were about to leave when he asked, "Sage, why'd you pick me to be your partner in crime in this?"

I thought about it. "Process of elimination, I guess. Jill's supposed to be kept out of trouble. Eddie'd be a good asset, but he needed to go back with her and Lee. Besides, I already knew you didn't have any moral qualms about breaking and entering."

"That's the nicest thing you've ever said to me," he declared with a grin.

We headed out to Keith's after that. All the lights were on in the first floor of his building, dashing a last-minute hope I'd had that maybe I wouldn't have to lure him out. I would've actually liked to help with the search. I dropped Adrian off and then drove to a twenty-four-hour restaurant that was outside the opposite side of town. I figured it would be perfect for keeping Keith away from his home. The driving time alone would provide Adrian with extra searching time, though it meant Adrian had to wait outside for a while until Keith left. Once I finally arrived, I got a table, ordered coffee, and dialed Keith's number.

"Hello?"

"Keith, it's me. I need to talk to you."

"So talk," he said. He sounded smug and confident, no doubt happy at pulling off the last-minute tattoo sale.

"Not on the phone. I need you to meet me."

"At Amberwood?" he asked in surprise. "Isn't it after hours?" It was indeed, but that was a problem for later.

"I'm not at school. I'm at Margaret's Diner, that place out by the highway."

Long silence. Then: "Well, if you're already out past curfew, then just come here."

"No," I said firmly. "You come to me."

"Why should I?"

I hesitated only briefly before playing the card I knew would get him, the one thing that would make him drive out here and *not* raise suspicions about the tattoos.

"It's about Carly."

"What about her?" he asked after a moment's pause.

"You know exactly what."

After a second's pause, Keith relented and hung up. I noticed that I had a voice mail from earlier in the day that I hadn't heard come in. I called and listened.

"Sydney, this is Wes Regan from Carlton College. Just wanted to go over a couple things with you. First, I'm afraid I have some bad news. It doesn't look like I'm going to be able to retroactively admit your brother from auditor status. I can enroll him next semester for sure if he stays in good standing, but the only way he can keep taking classes now is if he continues to do so as an auditor. He won't be able to get financial aid as a result, and in fact, you'll actually need to pay the auditing fee soon if he's going to stay in the classes. If he wants to drop altogether, we can do that too. Just call me and let me know what you'd like to do."

I stared at the phone in dismay when the message was over. There went our dreams of sliding Adrian into fully enrolled student status, not to mention his dreams of getting financial aid and moving out of Clarence's. The next semester probably started in January, so Adrian was facing four more months at

Clarence's. Adrian would also be facing four more months of bus-riding and taking classes without college credit.

But were the credits and financial aid really the most important things here? I thought back to how excited Adrian had been after only a couple classes, how he'd thrown himself into the art. His face had been radiant when he stood in his "gallery." Jill's words also echoed through my mind, about how the art had given him something to channel his feelings into and made the bond easier for her to cope with. Those classes were good for both of them.

How much was an auditing fee? I wasn't sure but knew it wasn't as much as tuition. It was also a onetime cost that I could probably slide into my expenses without raising the attention of the Alchemists. Adrian needed those classes, of that I was certain. If he knew financial aid wasn't an option this semester, there was a good chance he'd just drop them altogether. I couldn't allow that. He'd known there might be "a delay" while the financial aid came together. If I could keep him going to Carlton a little longer, then maybe he'd get invested enough in the art that he'd stay on, even when the truth came out. It was a sneaky thing to do, but it would benefit him—and Jill—in the end.

I dialed back Wes Regan's office, knowing I'd get his voice mail. I left him a message saying that I'd drop off a check for the auditing fee and that Adrian would stay on until he could be enrolled next semester. I hung up, saying a silent prayer that it would take a while for Adrian to find out any of this.

The waitress kept giving me the evil eye over just having coffee, so I finally ordered a piece of pie to go. She had just set the carton down on my table when an irritated Keith entered the restaurant. He stood in the doorway, looking around impatiently until he saw me.

"Okay, what's going on?" he demanded, making a big show of sitting down. "What's so important that you felt the need to break school rules and drag me halfway across town?"

For a moment, I froze up. Looking into Keith's eyes—real and artificial—triggered all the conflicting feelings I'd had about him this last year. Fear and anxiety over what I was trying to pull off warred with the deep hate I'd long carried. Baser instincts wanted me to make him suffer, to throw something at him. Like the pie. Or a chair. Or a baseball bat.

"I—"

Before I could say another word, my phone chimed. I looked down and read a text message from Adrian: GOT IT. CALL MADE. ONE HOUR.

I slipped the phone into my purse and exhaled. It had taken Keith twenty minutes to get here, and during that time, Adrian had been dutifully searching the apartment. He'd apparently been successful. Now it was up to me to delay Keith until reinforcements showed up. One hour was actually a lot less time than I'd expected. I'd given Adrian Stanton's phone number, and she would've dispatched whatever Alchemists were closest. I'd figured that would mean Los Angeles, but it was hard to say with the scope of our jobs. If there were Alchemists on the east side of the city, they'd get here very quickly. It was also possible they could cut time by simply flying a private jet in.

"What's that?" asked Keith irritably. "A text from one of your vampire friends?"

"You can stop the act," I said. "I know you don't really care about me 'getting too close' to them." I hadn't intended this to be the topic that distracted him, but I'd take it.

"Of course I do. I worry about your soul."

"Is that why you called my dad?" I asked. "Is that the reason you wanted me out of Palm Springs?"

"It's for your own good," he said, putting on that holier-than-thou air. "Do you know how wrong it was that you even wanted this job in the first place? No Alchemist would. But you, you practically begged for it."

"Yeah," I said, feeling my anger rise. "So Zoe wouldn't have to do it."

"Tell yourself that if you want. I know the truth. You *like* these creatures."

"Why does it have to be so cut-and-dried? In your view, I either have to hate them or be in league with them. There's a middle ground, you know. I can still be loyal to the Alchemists and on friendly terms with vampires and dhampirs."

Keith looked at me like I was ten years old. "Sydney, you're such an innocent. You don't understand the ways of the world like I do." I knew all about his "ways of the world" and would've said as much if the waitress hadn't come by to take his drink order just then. When she was gone, Keith continued his spiel. "I mean, how do you even know you're feeling the way you do? Vampires can compel, you know. They use mind control. Spirit users like Adrian are really good at it. For all we know, he's been using his powers to endear himself to you."

I thought of all the times I'd wanted to shake some sense into Adrian. "He's not doing a very good job, then."

We bickered back and forth about this, and for once, I was

glad of Keith's obstinacy and refusal to see reason. The longer he argued with me, the more time the Alchemists had to get to his apartment. If Stanton had told Adrian one hour, she probably meant it. Still, it was best to be safe.

My breaking point came when Keith said, "You should be glad I'm looking out for you like this. This is about more than vampires, you know. I'm teaching you life lessons. You memorize books but don't understand people. You don't know how to connect to them. You're going to carry this same naive attitude with you into the real world, thinking everyone means well, and someone—some guy, probably—will just take advantage of you."

"Well," I snapped, "you'd know all about that, wouldn't you?"

Keith snorted. "I have no interest in you, rest easy."

"I'm not talking about me! I'm talking about Carly." So. Here it was. The original purpose of our meeting.

"What's she have to do with anything?" Keith kept his tone steady, but I saw it. The slightest flicker of anxiety in his eye.

"I know what happened between you guys. I know what you did to her."

He became very interested in stirring ice around with his straw. "I didn't do anything to her. I have no idea what you're talking about."

"You know exactly what I'm talking about! She told me. She came to me afterward." I leaned forward, feeling confident. "What do you think my dad would do if he found out? What would *yours* do?"

Keith looked up sharply. "If you're so certain something terrible happened, then why doesn't your dad already know?

Huh? Maybe because Carly knows there's nothing to tattle on. Anything we did, she *wanted* to, believe me."

"You are such a liar," I hissed. "I know what you did. You raped her. And you will never suffer enough for it. You should've lost both of your eyes."

He stiffened at the reference to his eyes. "That's harsh. And has nothing to do with any of this. What the hell's happened to you, Sydney? How'd you turn into such a bitch? Maybe making you associate with vampires and dhampirs has caused more damage than we realized. First thing tomorrow, I'm going to call Stanton and ask that they pull you now. No waiting until the end of the week. You need to be away from this dark influence." He shook his head and gave me a look both condescending and pitying. "No, you need to be re-educated, period. It should've happened a long time ago, as soon as they caught you busting out that murderer."

"Don't change the topic." I spoke haughtily, though he'd again woken a sliver of fear in me. What if Adrian and I failed? What if the Alchemists listened to Keith and hauled me away? He'd never have to worry about me again in a re-education center. "This isn't about me. We were talking about Carly."

Keith rolled his eyes in annoyance. "I'm done talking about your slutty sister."

That was when my earlier impulse to throw something at him won out. Lucky for him, it was only my coffee and not a chair. Also lucky for him: the coffee had cooled considerably. There was still a lot of it left, and it managed to splash everywhere, drenching his unfortunate choice of a white shirt. He stared at me in astonishment, sputtering to get his words out.

"You bitch!" he said, standing up.

As he started moving toward the door, I realized that my temper might have just blown the plan. I hurried over and caught hold of his arm.

"Wait, Keith. I-I'm sorry. Don't go."

He jerked his arm away and glared at me. "It's too late for you. You had your chance and blew it."

I grabbed him again. "No, no. Wait. There's still lots we have to talk about."

He opened his mouth with some snippy remark and then promptly shut it. He studied me for several seconds, his face growing serious. "Are you *trying* to keep me here? What's going on?" When I couldn't muster a response, he pulled away and stormed out the door. I quickly ran back to the table and tossed a twenty on it. I grabbed the pie and told the bewildered waitress to keep the change.

The clock in my car told me I had twenty minutes until the Alchemists were supposed to show up at Keith's. That was also the time it would take to get back there. I drove right behind him, making no effort to hide my presence. It was no secret now that something was going on, something I'd lured him away from home for. I blessed every red light that stopped us, praying he wouldn't arrive too early. If he did, Adrian and I were going to have to delay him. It wouldn't be impossible, but it also wasn't something I wanted to do.

We finally made it back. Keith pulled into his building's tiny lot, and I parked uncaringly in a fire zone out front. I was only steps behind him as he ran to the door, but he hardly seemed to notice. His attention was on the lit-up windows of his building and the dark silhouettes barely discernible beyond the heavy drapes. He burst in through the door, and I followed a moment later, nearly running into him as he came to a complete standstill.

I didn't know the three suited men there with Adrian, but I knew they were Alchemists. They had that cold, polished feel that we all strove for, and their cheeks were emblazoned with gold lilies. One was going through Keith's kitchen cupboards. Another had a notepad and was talking to Adrian, who was leaning against the wall and smoking. He smiled when he saw me.

The third Alchemist was kneeling on the floor in the living room near a small storage cupboard in the wall. A tacky painting of a shirtless woman's back lay nearby, which apparently had been used to hide the compartment. Its wooden door had clearly been forcibly opened, and various contents were strewn haphazardly around—with a few exceptions. The Alchemist was going to great pains to sort one pile of objects: metal tubes and needles used to drain blood, along with vials of blood and small packets of silvery powder. He looked up at our sudden entrance and fixed Keith with a cool smile.

"Ah, so glad you're here, Mr. Darnell. We were hoping we could take you with us for some questioning."

Keith's face fell.

CHAPTER 23

"What did you do?"

I was sitting on the end of a row of seats at Jill's fashion show almost a week later, in downtown Palm Springs, waiting for things to start. I hadn't even known Trey was at the show and was startled to suddenly find him kneeling beside me.

"What exactly are you referring to?" I asked him. "There are about a million things I can take credit for."

He scoffed and kept his voice pitched low, which wasn't too necessary with the dull roar of conversation around us. Several hundred had turned out to see the show.

"I'm talking about Slade and friends, and you know it," Trey said. "They've been *really* upset about something this week. They keep complaining about those stupid tattoos." He looked at me meaningfully.

"What?" I asked, putting on a face of innocence. "Why do you think this has anything to do with me?"

343

"Are you saying it doesn't?" he asked, not fooled in the least.

I could feel a traitorous smile playing over my lips. After raiding Keith's apartment, the Alchemists had made sure his tattooist partners no longer had the means to administer illicit tattoos. There'd also been no more talk of Zoe replacing me. It had taken days before Slade and his friends had realized their connection to performance-enhancing ink was gone. I'd been observing their furtive conversations with amusement this week but hadn't realized Trey had noticed as well.

"Let's just say that Slade may soon no longer be the superstar he's been," I said. "Hope you're ready to step up and take his place."

Trey studied me a few moments more, apparently hoping I'd add something else. When I didn't, he simply shook his head and chuckled. "Anytime you need coffee, Melbourne, you come see me."

"Noted," I said. I gestured toward the still-growing crowd. "What are you doing here anyway? I didn't realize you were interested in today's hottest fashions."

"I'm not," he agreed. "But I've got a couple of friends working on the show."

"*Girl*friends?" I asked slyly.

He rolled his eyes. "Friends who are girls. I have no time for silly female distractions."

"Really? I figured that's why you got *your* tattoo. I hear women go for that kind of thing."

Trey stiffened. "What are you talking about?"

I remembered that Kristin and Julia had mentioned how strange it was that Trey had a tattoo of his own and Eddie had later mentioned seeing it on Trey's lower back in the locker room. Eddie had said it looked like a multi-rayed sun made of very ordinary ink. I'd been waiting for a chance to tease Trey about it.

"Don't play coy. I know about your sunshine. How come you always give me such a hard time, huh?"

"I . . ."

He was truly at a loss. More than that. He looked uncomfortable, worried—like this was something he hadn't wanted me to know about. That was weird. It wasn't *that* big a deal. I was about to question him more when Adrian suddenly made his way to us through the crowd. Trey took one look at Adrian's stormy face and immediately got to his feet. I could understand his reaction. Adrian's expression would've intimidated me too.

"Well," said Trey uneasily. "Thanks again. I'll catch you later."

I murmured a goodbye and watched as Adrian slipped past me. Micah sat beside me, then Eddie, and then two empty seats we'd saved. Adrian sat down in one of them, ignoring Eddie's greeting. Moments later, Lee came hurrying in and took the other seat. He looked troubled about something but still managed to be friendlier than Adrian. Adrian stared stonily ahead, and my good mood plummeted. Somehow, without knowing why, I had a feeling I was the reason for his dark mood.

We had no time to pursue it, though. The lights went down and the show began. It was emceed by a local newscaster, who introduced the five designers showing tonight. Jill's designer was third, and watching the others go before her made the anticipation that much more intense. This was worlds away from the practice sessions I'd seen before. The lights and the music took everything to a more professional level, and the other models seemed so much older and seasoned. I began to share Jill's earlier anxiety, that maybe she was out of her league.

Then Lia DiStefano's turn came. Jill was one of her first models and emerged wearing a flowing, silvery evening gown made of some fabric that seemed to defy gravity. A half mask of pearls and silver covered up her part of her face, obscuring her identity to those who didn't know better. I would've expected them to tone down her vampire features a little, to possibly give her a little more humanlike color. Instead, they'd played up her unusual looks, putting a luminescent powder on her skin that enhanced her paleness in a way that made her look otherworldly. Every single curl had been arranged into place, artfully falling around her and bedecked with tiny glittering jewels.

Her walk had improved vastly since that first practice. She'd practically slept in those high heels and had gone beyond simply not trying to fall over. There was a new confidence and purpose that hadn't been there before. Every once in a while, I'd catch a faint glimpse of nervousness in her eyes or an adjustment in her stride as she managed the tall silver heels. I doubted anyone else noticed those things, however. Anyone who didn't know Jill and her traits well would see nothing but a strong, ethereal woman striding down the catwalk. Amazing. If she could transform this much with only a little encouragement, what more was to come?

Glancing at the guys beside me, I saw similar feelings mirrored in their faces. Adrian's was filled with that brotherly pride he often had for her, all traces of his earlier bad mood vanished. Micah and Lee both displayed pure, unfiltered adoration. To my surprise, Eddie's expression was adoring too, along with something else. It was almost . . . worshipful. This was it, I realized. In coming out as this beautiful, larger-than-life goddess-like creature, Jill was giving flesh to all of Eddie's idealistic, protective fantasies. She was the perfect princess now, with her dutiful knight waiting to serve.

She appeared two more times in Lia's line, stunning each time, though never quite matching that initial debut in the silver dress. I watched the rest of the show with only half an eye. My pride and affection for Jill were too distracting, and honestly, most of the clothes I saw tonight were way too flashy for my tastes.

There was a reception after the show, where guests, designers, and models could mingle over refreshments. My little group found a corner near the hors d'oeuvres to wait for Jill, who had yet to make an appearance. Lee carried an enormous bouquet of white lilies. Adrian watched a waitress go by with a tray full of champagne glasses. His eyes were filled with longing, but he made no moves to stop her. I was proud and relieved. Jill, balance, and alcohol were not things we wanted to mix.

When the waitress was gone, Adrian turned to me, and I finally saw that earlier anger return. And, as I'd suspected, it was directed toward me.

"When were you going to tell me?" he asked.

It was as enigmatic as Trey's earlier opening line. "Tell you what?"

"That the financial aid isn't going to come through! I talked to the registrar's office, and they said you knew."

I sighed. "I wasn't keeping it from you, exactly. I just didn't have a chance to tell you yet. There were kind of a lot of other things going on." Okay, I actually *had* been putting it off, for exactly this reason. Well, not exactly. I hadn't anticipated he would get so worked up about it.

"You apparently had enough time to pay the auditing fee, though. And enough money. But not enough to fund new lodging."

I think what was more upsetting about this than the topic was the insinuation that I had somehow chosen to act in a way that would inconvenience him. Like I'd purposely subject myself to this if there'd been some way to avoid it.

"A onetime payment was easy to slip in," I told him. "Month-to-month rent? Not so much."

"Then why bother at all?" he exclaimed. "The whole point of this was to get me money to get out of Clarence's! I wouldn't be taking these stupid classes otherwise. You think I want to ride the bus for hours each day?"

"Those classes are good for you," I countered, feeling my own temper rise. I hadn't wanted to lose control, not here and certainly not with our friends witnessing everything. Yet I was appalled at Adrian's reaction. Couldn't he see how good it was for him to do something useful? I'd seen his face when he showed me his paintings. They'd given him a healthy channel to deal with Rose, not to mention a sense of purpose for him. And besides, it killed me to see how casually he could just toss aside those "stupid" classes. It was another reminder of the unfairness of the world, how I couldn't have what others took for granted.

He scowled. "'Good for me?' Come on, stop being my mom again! It isn't your job to tell me how to live my life. If I want your advice, I'll ask for it."

"Right," I said, putting my hands on my hips. "It's not my

job to tell you how to live your life—just my job to make it as easy as possible for you. Because God knows you can't suffer through *anything* that's a little inconvenient. What happened to all those things you told me? About being serious about improving your life? When you asked me to believe in you?"

"Come on, you guys," said Eddie uneasily. "This isn't the time or place."

Adrian ignored him. "You have no problem making Jill's life as easy as possible."

"That *is* my job," I growled back. "And she's still a girl. I wouldn't think an adult like you would need taking care of the same way!"

Adrian's eyes were filled with emerald fire as he glared down at me, and then his gaze focused on something behind me. I turned and saw Jill approaching. She was back in the silver gown, her expression full of radiant happiness—happiness that plummeted as she got closer and realized there was an altercation going on. By the time she was standing next to me, all her excitement from a moment ago had been replaced by worry and concern.

"What's happening?" she asked, looking between Adrian and me. Of course, she had to already know because of the bond. It was a wonder his dark feelings hadn't messed up her performance.

"Nothing," I said flatly.

"Well," said Adrian. "It depends how you define 'nothing.' I mean, if you consider lying and—"

"Stop it!" I cried, raising my voice in spite of my best effort. The room was too noisy for most to notice, but a couple people standing nearby glanced at us curiously. "Just stop it, Adrian.

Can you please not ruin this for her? Can't you just for one night pretend there are other people in the world who matter besides you?"

"Ruin it for her?" he exclaimed. "How the hell can you say that? You know what I've done for her! I've done everything for her! I've given up everything for her!"

"Really?" I asked. "Because from what I can tell, it doesn't seem like—"

I caught sight of Jill's face and promptly cut myself off. Behind the mask, her eyes had gone wide with dismay at the accusations Adrian and I were slinging back and forth. I'd just told Adrian he was selfish and not thinking of Jill, yet here I was, continuing to engage with him on her big night, in front of her and our friends. It didn't matter if I was right—and I felt certain I was. This was no time to be having this discussion. I shouldn't have let Adrian bait me into this, and if he didn't have the sense to stop things before they got worse, then I would.

"I'm leaving," I said. I forced as sincere a smile as I could for Jill, who now looked on the verge of tears. "You were amazing tonight. Really."

"Sydney—"

"It's okay," I told her. "I've got some things to do." I groped for what they would actually be. "I need to, um, clean up the stuff Keith left behind. Can you get her and Eddie back to Amberwood?" This was directed to Micah and Lee. I knew one of them would step up. I felt no need to make any such provisions for Adrian. I honestly didn't care what became of him tonight.

"Of course," said Lee and Micah in unison. After a moment, though, Lee frowned. "Why do you need to clean up Keith's stuff?"

"Long story," I muttered. "Let's just say he left town and won't be back anytime soon. Maybe never." Inexplicably, Lee seemed bothered by this. Maybe during all the time Keith had spent at Clarence's, the two guys had become friends. If so, Lee owed me.

Jill still looked upset. "I thought we were all going out to celebrate?"

"You can if you want," I said. "As long as Eddie's with you, I really don't care." I reached awkwardly to Jill. I almost wanted to hug her, but she was so elaborate and magnificent in her clothing and makeup that I was afraid of ruining her. I settled for a halfhearted pat on the shoulder. "I meant it. You were breathtaking."

I hurried away, half-afraid that either Adrian or I would crack and say something stupid to the other. I had to get myself out of there. My hope now was that Adrian would have enough sense to let the topic go and not make this night any worse for Jill. I didn't know why the fight with him upset me so much. He and I had been bickering nearly since we'd met. What was one more quarrel? It's because we'd been getting along, I realized. I still didn't think of him in human terms, but somewhere along the way, I'd come to regard him as a little less of a monster.

"Sydney?"

I was stopped by an unexpected source: Laurel. She had touched my arm as I passed by a group of girls from Amberwood. I must have looked really mad because when I fixed my gaze on her, she actually flinched. That had to be a first.

"What?" I asked.

She swallowed and stepped away from her friends, eyes wide and desperate. A fedora covered most of her hair, which—I'd heard—she still hadn't been able to restore to normal. "I heard . . . I heard you might be able to help me. With my hair," she said.

That was another favor Kristin had done me. After letting Laurel suffer for a few days, I'd had Kristin put out the word that Sydney Melrose—with her dorm room pharmacy—might be able to fix what was wrong. I'd also made sure, however, that it was understood that Laurel wasn't my favorite person and that it would take a lot to convince me.

"Maybe," I said. I tried to keep my face hard, which wasn't difficult since I was still so upset over Adrian.

"Please," she said. "I'll do whatever you want if you can help me! I've tried everything on my hair, and nothing works." To my astonishment, she shoved some yearbooks at me. "Here. You wanted these, right? Take them. Take whatever you want."

Another five days of scrubbing with heavy detergent would actually fix her, but I certainly wasn't going to tell her. I took the yearbooks. "If I help you," I said, "you need to leave my sister alone. Do you understand?"

"Yes," she said quickly.

"I don't think you do. No more stunts, bullying, or talking about her behind her back. You don't have to be her best friend, but I don't want you interfering with her anymore. Stay out of her life." I paused. "Well, except to offer an apology."

Laurel was nodding along with everything I said. "Yes, yes! I'll apologize right now!"

I lifted my eyes to where Jill was standing with her admirers, Lee's flowers in her arms. "No. Don't make this night any weirder for her. Tomorrow's soon enough."

"I will," said Laurel. "I promise. Just tell me what to do. How to fix this."

I hadn't expected Laurel to approach me tonight, but I had been expecting her one of these days. So, I already had the small bottle of antidote ready in my purse. I retrieved it, and her eyes nearly popped out of her head as I held it in front of her.

"One dose is all you need. Use it just like shampoo. Then you'll have to re-dye it." She reached for the bottle, and I jerked it back. "I mean it. Your harassment of Jill ends now. If I give this to you, I will not hear one more word about you giving her a hard time. No more grief if she talks to Micah. No more vampire jokes. No more calling Nevermore and asking about tall, pale people."

She gaped. "No more what? I never called anyone!"

I hesitated. When the tattooist had mentioned someone calling and asking about people who looked like vampires, I'd assumed it was Laurel running with the vampire joke. From the baffled look on her face now, I no longer thought that was true. "Well, if I hear about any of the other stuff continuing, then what happened to your hair will be nothing in comparison to what happens next. Nothing. Do you understand me?"

She nodded shakily. "P-perfectly."

I handed her the bottle. "Don't forget."

Laurel started to turn away and then cast another uneasy glance at me. "You know, you can be scary as hell sometimes."

I wondered if the Alchemists had had any idea what I'd be doing when it came to this job. At least this settled one thing. Laurel's desperation convinced me the vampire jokes had only been a tactic. She didn't really believe any of them were true.

It did, however, raise the unnerving question about who had asked about vampires at Nevermore.

When I was finally out of the building and heading toward my car, I decided I really would go to Keith's. Someone needed to sort through his belongings, and it seemed like a safe way to avoid the others. I still had a couple of hours before curfew at Amberwood.

Keith's apartment hadn't been disturbed since the Alchemists had raided it. The telltale signs from before were there, where we'd discovered his stash of Clarence's blood and silver supplies. The Alchemists had done little more than retrieve the essentials they needed and had left the rest of his belongings behind. My hope in coming tonight had been to get ahold of his other ingredients, the ones not used to manufacture illicit tattoos. It was always handy to have extra amounts of those chemicals on hand, be it for destroying Strigoi bodies or making dorm room chemistry experiments.

No such luck. Even if his other supplies hadn't been illegal, the Alchemists had apparently decided to confiscate all chemicals and ingredients. Since I was here, though, I decided to see if any of his other possessions were items that would be of use to me. Keith certainly hadn't held back in using his illicit funds to furnish the apartment with every comfort of home. Scratch that. I doubted his home had anything like this: a California-king-sized bed, giant flat-screen TV, a theater-worthy sound system, and enough food to throw parties every night for the next month. I peered through cupboard after cupboard, appalled at how much of that food was junk food. Still, maybe it'd be worth taking some of it back for Jill and Eddie, so I bagged up the more portable sweets for them, organizing by color and size.

I wondered also about the practicality of hauling the TV back to Amberwood. It seemed like a waste to leave it for the Alchemists' repo crew, though I could already imagine Mrs. Weathers's expression if she saw us dragging it up the stairs. I wasn't even sure Jill and I had a wall big enough to hold it. I sat down in Keith's recliner to ponder the TV issue. Even the recliner was top of the line. The luxurious leather felt like butter, and I practically sank into the cushions. Too bad there was no room for it in Ms. Terwilliger's room. I could see her relaxing back in it while drinking cappuccino and reading old documents.

Well, whatever became of the rest of Keith's stuff, it was going to require the rental of a moving truck because Latte certainly couldn't handle the TV, chair, or most of the other things. Once this was decided, there was no reason for me to stay any longer tonight, but I hated to go back. I was afraid of seeing Jill. There was no reaction of hers I welcomed. If she was still sad from the argument, that would make me feel guilty. If she tried to defend Adrian, that would upset me too.

I sighed. This chair was so ridiculously comfortable, I might as well enjoy it a little longer. I dug into my messenger bag, looking for homework, and remembered the yearbooks. Kelly Hayes. I'd had almost no time to think about her or the murders, not with all the drama surrounding Keith and the tattoos. Kelly had been a junior when she died, and I had a yearbook for each of her years at Amberwood.

Even as a freshman, Kelly took lots of space in the yearbook. I remembered Mrs. Weathers saying Kelly was a good athlete. No kidding. Kelly had participated in nearly every sport Amberwood offered and been exceptional at all of them. She'd made varsity teams during her first year and won all sorts of awards. One thing I also immediately discovered was that Kelly was definitely not a Moroi. That much was obvious, even in black and white, and confirmed in the sophomore-year color spread in the middle. She had a very human build and tanned skin that clearly loved the sun.

I was skimming the index of the junior yearbook when I heard a knock at the door. For a moment, I didn't want to answer. For all I knew, it was some loser friend Keith had made while here, looking to eat his food and watch TV. Then I worried it could be something Alchemist related. I found the Kelly tribute section I'd been seeking and set the yearbook down before tentatively approaching the door. Looking out the peephole, I caught sight of a familiar face.

"Lee?" I asked, opening the door.

He gave me a sheepish smile. "Hey. Sorry to bug you here."

"What are you doing here?" I exclaimed, beckoning him inside. "Why aren't you back with the others?"

He followed me into the living room. "I—I needed to talk to you. When you said you were coming here, it made me wonder if what my father had said was true. That Keith isn't here anymore?"

I sat back down on the recliner. Lee took a spot on the nearby loveseat. "Yup. Keith's gone. He was, uh, reassigned." Keith was off being punished somewhere, and I said good riddance.

Lee glanced around, taking in the expensive furnishings. "This is a nice place." His eyes fell on the cabinet that had held the alchemy supplies. Its door still hung precariously from its hinges, and I hadn't bothered tidying up where the Alchemists had cleaned out its other contents.

"Was this . . ." Lee frowned. "Was this place broken into?"

"Not exactly," I said. "Keith, um, just needed to find something in a hurry before he left."

Lee wrung his hands and looked around some more before turning back to me. "And he's not coming back?"

"Probably not."

Lee's face fell, which surprised me. I'd always gotten the impression he didn't like Keith. "Will another Alchemist be replacing him?"

"I don't know," I said. There was still some debate on that. Turning Keith in had stopped me from being replaced by Zoe, and Stanton was now considering just having me fill in as the local Alchemist since the duties were light. "If someone does, it may be a while."

"So you're the only Alchemist in the area," he repeated, sounding sadder still.

I shrugged. "There are some in Los Angeles."

That inexplicably perked him up a little. "Really? Could you tell me their—"

Lee stopped as his focus dropped to the open yearbook lying at my feet. "Oh," I said, scooping it up. "Just a research project I'm doing on—"

"Kelly Hayes." The cheerful look was gone.

"Yeah. Have you heard of her?" I reached for a nearby piece of scrap paper, intending to use it as a bookmark for the tribute section.

"You might say that," he replied.

I started to ask what he meant, and that's when I saw it. The spread they'd done in honor of Kelly had pictures from all parts of her high school life. Unsurprisingly, most of them were pictures of her playing sports. There were a few from other areas of her social and academic worlds, including one of her at the prom. She wore a stunning blue satin dress that made the most of her athletic figure and was giving the camera a big grin as she wrapped an arm around her dashing, tuxedo-clad date.

Lee.

I jerked my head up and looked at Lee, who was now regarding me with an unreadable expression. I turned back to the picture, scrutinizing it carefully. What was remarkable wasn't that Lee was in the picture—though, believe me, I hadn't figured out what was going on with that yet. What had me hung up was the timing. This yearbook was five years old. Lee would've been fourteen at the time, and the guy looking back at me with Kelly was certainly not that young. The Lee in the picture looked exactly like the nineteen-year-old sitting across from me, which was impossible. Moroi had no special immortality. They aged like humans. I looked back up, wondering if I should be asking if he had a brother.

Lee saved me from questioning, though. He simply regarded me with a sad look and shook his head. "Shit. I hadn't wanted it to happen like this."

And then, he took out a knife.

CHAPTER 24

IT'S WEIRD how you react in moments of immediate danger. Part of me was pure panic, complete with racing heart and rapid breathing. That hollow feeling, the one that felt like a hole had opened in my chest, returned. Another part of me was able to still inexplicably think along logical lines, mostly something like, *Yup, that's the kind of knife that could slit a throat.* The rest of me? Well, the rest of me was just confused.

I stayed where I was and kept my voice low and even. "Lee, what's going on? What is this?"

He shook his head. "Don't pretend. I know you know. You're too smart. I knew you'd figure it out, but I just didn't expect you to do it so soon."

My mind spun. Once again, someone thought I was smarter than I was. I supposed I should be flattered by his faith in my intelligence, but the truth was, I didn't know what was going on yet. I didn't know if betraying that would help or hinder me, though. I decided to play cool for as long as I reasonably could here.

"That's you in the picture," I said, careful not to make it a question.

"Of course," he said.

"You haven't aged." I dared a quick look at the picture, just to ascertain that for myself. It still baffled me. Only Strigoi were ageless, staying immortal at the age they'd turned. "That's . . . that's impossible. You're Moroi."

"Oh, I've aged," he said bitterly. "Not a lot. Not enough that you can really spot it, but believe me, I can. It's not like how it used to be."

I was still clueless, still not sure of how we had reached a point where Lee—starry-eyed and lovesick for Jill—was suddenly threatening me with a knife. Nor did I understand how he looked exactly the same as he did in a five-year-old picture. There was only one terrible thing I was beginning to be certain of.

"You . . . killed Kelly Hayes." The fear in my chest intensified. I lifted my gaze from the blade to look into his eyes. "But surely . . . surely not Melody . . . or Tamara . . ."

He nodded. "And Dina. But you wouldn't know her, would you? She was only human, and you don't keep track of human deaths. Only vampires."

It was hard not to look at the knife again. All I kept thinking about was how sharp it was and how close it was to me. One swipe, and I'd end up just like those other girls, my life bleeding away before me. I groped desperately for something to say, wishing again I'd learned the social skills that came so easily to others.

"Tamara was your cousin," I managed. "Why would you kill your own cousin?"

A moment of regret flashed across his features. "I didn't want to—I mean, I did . . . but, well, I wasn't myself when I came back. I just knew I had to be awakened again. Tamara was there at the wrong place and the wrong time. I went for the first Moroi I could get . . . but it didn't work. That's when I tried the others. I thought for sure one of them would do it. Human, dhampir, Moroi . . . none of them worked."

There was a terrible desperation in his voice, and despite my fear, some part of me wanted to help him . . . but I was hopelessly lost. "Lee, I'm sorry. I don't understand, why you'd need to 'try others.' Please put the knife down, and let's talk. Maybe I can help you."

He gave me a sad smile. "You can. I didn't want it to be you, though. I wanted it to be Keith. He certainly deserves to die more than you do. And Jill . . . well, Jill likes you. I wanted to respect that and spare you."

"You still can," I said. "She—she wouldn't want you to do this. She'd be upset if she knew—"

Suddenly, Lee was on me, pinning me to the chair with the knife at my throat. "You don't know!" he cried. "*She* doesn't know. But she will, and she'll be glad. She'll thank me, and we'll be young and together forever. You're my chance. The others didn't work, but you . . ." He trailed the knife's blade near my tattoo. "You're special. Your blood is magic. I need an Alchemist, and you're my only chance now."

"What . . . chance . . . are you talking about?" I gasped out.

"My chance for immortality!" he cried. "God, Sydney. You can't even imagine it. What it's like to have that and then lose it. To have infinite strength and power . . . to not age, to know you'll live forever. And then, gone! Taken away from me. If I ever find that bastard spirit user who did this to me, I'll kill him. I'll kill him and I'll drink from him since after tonight, I'll be whole once more. I'll be reawakened."

A chill ran down my spine. In light of everything, you would have thought I'd already be at maximum terror level. Nope. Turns out there was still more to come. Because with those words, I began to put together a fragile theory of what he might be talking about. "Awakened" was a term used in the vampire world, under very special circumstances.

"You used to be Strigoi," I whispered, not even sure if I believed it myself.

He pulled back slightly, gray eyes wide and glittering feverishly. "I used to be a god! And I will be again. I swear it. I'm sorry, I really am. I'm sorry it's you and not Keith. I'm sorry you found out about Kelly. If you hadn't, I could have found another Alchemist in LA. But don't you see? I have no other options now . . ." The knife was still at my throat. "I need your blood. I can't go on like this . . . not as a mortal Moroi. I have to be changed back."

A knock sounded at the door.

"Not a word," Lee hissed. "They'll go away."

Seconds later, the knock repeated, followed by: "Sage, I know you're in there. I saw your car. I know you're pissed off, but just listen to me."

Dingdong, distraction calling.

"*Adrian!*" I screamed, jumping up from the chair. I made no attempt to disarm Lee. My only goal was safety. I pushed past him before he could react, heading for the door, but he was more prepared than I'd expected. He leapt toward me and tackled me to the ground, the knife catching me in the arm as I fell. I yelped in pain as I felt the tip of the blade dig into my skin. I struggled against him, only succeeding in making the knife tear into me more.

The door suddenly opened, and I was grateful that I'd left it unlocked after letting Lee in. Adrian entered, coming to a standstill as he took in the scene.

"Don't come closer," warned Lee, pushing the knife against my throat again. I could feel warm blood oozing from my arm. "Shut the door. Then . . . sit down and put your hands behind your head. I'll kill her if you don't."

"He's going to do it anyway—ahh!" My words were cut off as the knife pierced my skin, not enough to kill me yet but enough to cause pain.

"Okay, okay," said Adrian, holding up his hands. He looked more sober and serious than I'd ever seen. When he was settled on the floor, hands behind his head as directed, he said gently, "Lee, I don't know what you're doing, but you need to stop it now before it goes any further. You don't have a gun. You can't really hold us both here under the threat of a knife."

"It's worked before," Lee said. Still keeping the knife on me, he reached into his coat pocket with his other hand and produced a pair of handcuffs. That was unexpected. He slid them over to Adrian. "Put these on." When Adrian didn't react right away, Lee pushed on the knife until I yelped. "Now!"

Adrian put the handcuffs on.

"I'd meant them for her, but you coming by might be a good thing," said Lee. "I'll probably be hungry once I'm reawakened."

Adrian arched an eyebrow. "Reawakened?"

"He used to be Strigoi," I managed to say. "He's been killing girls—slitting their throats—to try to become one again."

"Be quiet," snapped Lee.

"Why would you cut their throats?" asked Adrian. "You have fangs."

"Because it didn't work! I *did* use my fangs. I drank from them . . . but it didn't work. I didn't reawaken again. So then I had to cover my trail. The guardians can tell, you know. Moroi and Strigoi bites? I needed the knife to subdue them anyway, so then I cut their necks to hide the trail . . . make them think it was a crazy Strigoi. Or a vampire hunter."

I could see Adrian processing all this. I don't know if he believed it or not, but he had the potential to roll with crazy ideas regardless. "If the others didn't work, then Sydney won't either."

"She has to," said Lee fervently. He shifted so that I was rolled onto my back, still pinned by his greater body weight. "Her blood's special. I know it is. And if it doesn't . . . I'll get help. I'll get help reawakening, and then I'll awaken Jill so we can always be together."

Adrian jumped to his feet, full of a surprising fury. "Jill? Don't hurt her! Don't even touch her!"

"Sit down," barked Lee. Adrian obeyed. "I wouldn't hurt her. I *love* her. That's why I'm going to make sure she stays exactly the way she is. Forever. I'll awaken her after I'm reawakened."

I tried to catch Adrian's eye, wondering if I could pass some silent message. If we both surged at Lee together—even with Adrian cuffed—then maybe we had a chance at subduing him. Lee was seconds away from tearing into my throat, I was certain, in the hopes that . . . what? That he could drink my blood and become Strigoi?

"Lee," I said in a small voice. Too much movement in my throat would result in a bite from the knife. "It didn't work with the other girls. I don't think the fact that I'm an Alchemist matters. Whatever that spirit user did to save you . . . you can't go back now. It doesn't matter whose blood you drink."

"He didn't save me!" roared Lee. "He ruined my life. I've been trying to get it back for six years. I was almost ready for the last resort . . . until you and Keith came along. And I've still got that last option left. I don't want it to come to that, though. For all our sakes."

I *wasn't* the last resort? Honestly, I didn't really see how any other alternative plans here could be much worse for me. Meanwhile, Adrian still wasn't looking in my direction, which frustrated me—until I realized what he was trying to do.

"This is a mistake," he told Lee. "Look at me, and tell me you really want to do this to her."

Cuffed or not, Adrian didn't have the speed and strength of a dhampir, someone who could leap over and disarm Lee before the knife could do its damage. Adrian also didn't have the power to wield a physical element, say, like fire, one that could be used as a concrete weapon. Adrian did, however, have the ability to compel. Compulsion was an innate ability all vampires had and one that spirit users in particular were adept at. Unfortunately, it worked best with eye contact, and Lee wasn't playing ball. His attention was all on me, blocking Adrian's efforts.

"I made my decision a long time ago," said Lee. With his free hand, he dabbed his fingers in the bloody patch on my arm. He brought his fingertips to his lips, a look of grim resignation on his face. He licked the blood from his hand, which wasn't nearly as gross to me as it would've been under other circumstances. With so much going on right now, it was honestly no more terrible than the rest and just rolled off of me.

A look of total shock and surprise crossed Lee's features . . . soon turning to disgust.

"No," he gasped. He repeated the motion, rubbing more blood on his fingers and licking it. "There's something . . . there's something wrong . . ."

He leaned his mouth to my neck, and I whimpered, fearing the inevitable. But it wasn't his teeth I felt, only the lightest brushing of his lips and tongue at the wound he'd created, like some sort of perverse kiss. He jerked back immediately, staring at me in horror.

"What's wrong with you?" he whispered. "What's wrong with your blood?" He made a third attempt to taste my blood but was unable to finish. He scowled. "I can't do it. I can't stomach *any* of it. Why?"

Neither Adrian nor I had an answer. Lee sagged in defeat for a moment, and I suddenly allowed myself to think he might just give up and call all this madness off. With a deep breath, he straightened up, new resolve in his eyes. I tensed, half-expecting him to say he was going to try to drink Adrian now, even though a Moroi—two, if you counted Melody—had apparently been on the menu of his past failures.

Instead, Lee pulled his cell phone out of his pocket, still keeping the knife at my throat and preventing me from attempting any sort of escape. He dialed a number and waited for an answer.

"Dawn? It's Lee. Yes . . . yes, I know. Well, I have two for you, ready and waiting. A Moroi and an Alchemist. No—not the old man. Yes. *Yes*, still alive. It has to be tonight. They know about me. You can have them . . . but you know the deal. You know what I want . . . yes. Uh-huh. Okay." Lee rattled off our address and disconnected. A pleased smile crossed his face. "We're lucky. They're east of LA, so it won't take them long to get here—especially since they don't care much about speed limits."

"Who are 'they'?" asked Adrian. "I remember you calling some Dawn lady in LA. I thought she was one of your hot college friends?"

"They're the makers of destiny," said Lee dreamily.

"How delightfully enigmatic and nonsensical," muttered Adrian.

Lee glared and then carefully studied Adrian. "Take off your tie."

I realized I'd spent so much time with Adrian now that I was ready for some comment like, "Oh, glad to know things aren't so formal anymore." Apparently, the situation was dire enough—and the knife at my throat serious enough—that Adrian didn't argue. He'd handcuffed his wrists in front of him and, after some complex maneuvering with his hands, was finally able to undo the tie he'd donned for Jill's show. He tossed it over.

"Careful," Adrian said. "It's silk." So, not completely devoid of snark.

Lee rolled me over to my stomach, finally freeing me of the knife but giving me no time to react. With remarkable skill, he soon had my hands tied behind my back with Adrian's tie.

Doing so required some pulling and restraining of my arms, which hurt quite a bit after the stabbing. He backed off when finished, allowing me to gingerly sit up, but an experimental tug of the tie showed that I wasn't going to undo those knots anytime soon. Uneasily, I wondered how many girls he'd tied up before in his sick attempt to become Strigoi.

Weird, awkward silence fell as we waited for Lee's "makers of destiny" to show up. The minutes ticked by, and I frantically tried to figure out what to do. How long did we have until the people he'd called arrived? From what he'd told me, I'd guess at least an hour. Feeling bold, I finally attempted communication with Adrian, again hoping maybe we could covertly team up on Lee—even though our success rate had just become that much lower with both our sets of hands bound.

"How did you even get here?" I asked.

Adrian's gaze was fixed on Lee, still hoping for direct eye contact, but he did spare a quick, wry glance at me. "Same way I get around everywhere, Sage. The bus."

"Why?"

"Because I don't have a car."

"Adrian!" Amazing. Even with our lives in danger, he could still infuriate me.

He shrugged and returned his focus to Lee, even though his words were obviously for me. "To apologize. Because I was a total asshole to you at Jailbait's show. Not long after you left, I knew I had to come find you." He paused eloquently and glanced around. "No good deed goes unpunished, I guess."

I suddenly felt at a loss. Lee turning psychopathic certainly wasn't my fault, but it troubled me that Adrian was now in this situation because he'd come to apologize to me. "It's okay. You weren't . . . um, that bad," I said lamely, hoping to make him feel better.

A small smile played over his lips. "You're a terrible liar, Sage, but I'm still touched you'd attempt it for my sake. A for effort."

"Yeah, well, what happened back there seems kind of small, in light of the current situation," I muttered. "It's easy to forgive."

Lee's frown had been growing as he listened to us. "Do the others know you're here?" he asked Adrian.

"No," said Adrian. "I said I was going back to Clarence's."

I didn't know if he was lying or not. For a moment, I didn't think it would matter. The others had heard me say I was coming here, but none of them would have any reason to come seeking us.

No reason, except the bond.

I caught my breath and met Adrian's eyes. He looked away, perhaps for fear of betraying what I'd just realized. It didn't matter if the gang had known where I was earlier. If Jill was connected to Adrian, she would know *now*. And she would know that we were in trouble. But that was assuming it was one of the times when she could see into his mind. They'd both admitted it was inconsistent and that high emotion could bring it out. Well, if this didn't count as a highly emotional situation, I couldn't think what would. Even if she realized what was happening, there were a lot of if's involved. Jill would have to get here, and she couldn't do it alone. Calling the police would bring the fastest response, but she might hesitate if she knew this was vampire business. She'd need Eddie. How long would it take to get him if they were back in their dorms?

I didn't know. I just knew that we had to stay alive because if we did, one way or another, Jill would get help here. Only, I no longer knew our odds of survival. Adrian and I were both confined, trapped with a guy who wasn't afraid to kill with a knife and who desperately wanted to become a Strigoi again. That was a bad combination, and it threatened to get worse . . .

"Who's coming, Lee?" I asked. "Who did you call?" When he didn't answer, I made the next logical leap. "Strigoi. You have Strigoi coming."

"It's the only way," he said, tossing his knife from hand to hand. "The only way left now. I'm sorry. I can't be like this anymore. I can't be mortal anymore. Too much time has already passed."

Of course. Moroi could become Strigoi in one of two ways. One was by drinking the blood of another person and killing them in the process. Lee had tried that, using every combination of victims he could get ahold of, and had failed. That left him with one last desperate option: conversion by another Strigoi. Usually, it happened by force, when a Strigoi killed someone and then fed their own blood back to the victim. That was what Lee wanted done to him now, trading our lives to the Strigoi who would convert him. And then he wanted to do it to Jill, out of some crazy misguided love . . .

"But it's not worth it," I said, desperation and fear making me bold. "It's not worth the cost of killing innocents and endangering your soul."

Lee's gaze fell on me, and there was a look of such chilling indifference in it that I had a hard time connecting this person before me to the one I'd smiled indulgently on as he courted Jill.

"Isn't it, Sydney? How would you know? You've deprived yourself of enjoyment for most of your life. You're aloof from others. You've never let yourself be selfish, and look where it's got you. Your 'morals' have left you with a short, strict life. Can you tell me now, just before you're about to die, that you don't wish you'd *maybe* allowed yourself a little more fun?"

"But the immortal soul—"

"What do I care about that?" he demanded. "Why bother living some miserable regimented life in this world, in the hopes that *maybe* our souls go on in some heavenly realm, when I can take control now—ensure that I live forever in this world, with all of its pleasures, staying strong and young forever? That's real. That's something I can put my faith in."

"It's wrong," I said. "It's not worth it."

"You wouldn't say that if you'd experienced what I have. If you'd been Strigoi, you never would've wanted to lose that either."

"How did you lose it?" asked Adrian. "What spirit user saved you?"

Lee snorted. "You mean *robbed* me. I don't know. It all happened so fast. But as soon as I find him I'll—ahh!"

A yearbook is not the greatest of weapons, particularly one the size of Amberwood's, but in a pinch—and with surprise—it'll do.

I'd noted earlier that I wasn't going to be able to undo the knots in the tie anytime soon. That was true. It had taken me this whole time, but I'd done it. For whatever reason, knot-making was a useful skill in the Alchemist curriculum, one I'd practiced growing up with my father. As soon as I was free of Adrian's tie, I reached for the first thing I could: Kelly's junior yearbook. I sprang up and slammed it into Lee's head. He cringed back at the impact, dropping the knife as he did, and I used the opportunity to sprint across the living room and grab Adrian's arm. He needed no help from me and was already trying to get to his feet.

We didn't get far before Lee was right back on us. The knife had slid somewhere unseen, and he simply relied on his own strength. He caught hold of me and ripped me from Adrian, one hand on my wounded arm and one in my hair, causing me to stumble. Adrian came after us, doing his best to hit Lee, even with bound hands. We weren't the most efficient fighting force, but if we could just momentarily delay Lee, there was a chance we might make it out of here.

Lee was distracted by both of us, trying to fight and fend us off at the same time. Unbidden, Eddie's lesson came back to me, about how a well-placed punch could cause serious damage to someone stronger than you. Sizing up the situation in seconds, I decided I had an opening. I closed my hand the way Eddie had taught me in that quick lesson, positioning my body in a way that would direct the weight in an efficient way. I swung.

"Ow!"

I yelled in pain as my fist made contact. If this was the "safe" way to punch, I couldn't imagine how much a sloppy one hurt. Fortunately, it seemed to cause just as much—if not more—pain to Lee. He fell backward, hitting the comfy chair in a way that made him lose his balance and collapse to the ground. I was stunned at what I had done, but Adrian was still in motion. He nudged me to the door, taking advantage of Lee's temporary disorientation.

"Come on, Sage. This is it."

We hurried to the door, ready to make our escape while Lee shouted profanities at us. I reached for the knob, but the door opened before I could touch it.

And two Strigoi entered the room.

CHAPTER 25

I HAD MOCKED KEITH when we first came to Palm Springs, teasing him for freezing up around Moroi. But as I stood there now, face-to-face with the stuff of nightmares, I knew exactly how he felt. I had no right to judge anyone for losing all rational thought when confronted with their greatest fears.

That being said, if Keith was here, I think he would've understood why Moroi weren't as big a deal to me anymore. Because when compared to Strigoi? Well, suddenly the little differences between humans and Moroi became negligible. Only one difference mattered, the difference between the living and the dead. It was the line that divided us, the line that Adrian and I firmly stood together on one side of—facing those who stood on the other.

I had seen Strigoi before. Back then, I hadn't been immediately threatened by them. Plus, I'd had Rose and Dimitri on hand, ready to protect me. Now? There was no one here to save us. Just ourselves.

There were only two of them, but it might as well have been two hundred. Strigoi operated at such a different level than the rest of us that it didn't take very many of them to tip the odds. They were both women, and they looked as though they'd been in their twenties when they became Strigoi. How long ago that was, I couldn't guess. Lee had zealously gone on and on about how being Strigoi meant you were "forever young." Yet in looking at these two monsters, I didn't really think of them that way. Sure, they had the superficial appearance of youth, but it was marred with evil and decay. Their skin might be wrinkle free, but it was a sickly white, far whiter than any Moroi. The red-ringed eyes that leered out at us didn't sparkle with life and energy, but rather an unholy sort of reanimation. These people weren't right. They weren't natural.

"Charming," said one, her blond hair in a pixie cut. Her facial structure made me think she'd been a dhampir or human before being turned. She was eyeing us the same way I'd often seen my family's cat watch birds. "And exactly as described."

"They're soooo pretty," crooned the other, a lascivious smile on her face. Her height said she had once been Moroi. "I don't know which one I want first."

The blonde gave a warning look. "We'll share."

"Like last time," agreed the other, tossing a mane of curly black hair over one shoulder.

"No," said the first. "Last time you made both kills. That wasn't sharing."

"But I let you feed from both afterward."

Before she could counter back, Lee suddenly recovered himself and staggered forward to the blond Strigoi. "Wait, wait.

Dawn. You promised me. You promised you'd awaken me first before you do anything."

The two Strigoi turned their attention to Lee. I was still frozen, still unable to move or really react while being so close to these creatures of hell. But somehow, through the thick and overwhelming terror surrounding me, I still managed to feel small and unexpected pity for Lee. There was a little hate there too, of course, considering the situation. But mostly I felt terribly sorry for someone who truly believed his life was meaningless unless he sacrificed his soul for hollow immortality. Not only that, I felt sorry for him for actually thinking he could trust these creatures to give him what he wanted. Because as I studied them, it was perfectly clear to me that they were deciding whether or not to make this a three-course meal. Lee, I suspected, was the only one who didn't realize this.

"Please," he said. "You promised. Save me. Restore me to how I was."

I also couldn't help but notice the small red patch on his face where I'd hit him. I allowed myself to feel a bit of pride over that but wasn't cocky enough to think I possessed any noteworthy fighting skills to battle my way out of this situation. The Strigoi were too close, and our exits were too few.

"I know where more are," he added, beginning to look uneasy that his "saviors" weren't immediately jumping in to make his dreams come true. "One's young—a dhampir."

"I haven't had a dhampir in a while," said the curly-haired Strigoi, almost wistfully.

Dawn sighed. "I don't really care, Jacqueline. If you want to awaken him, go for it. I just want these two. He doesn't matter to me."

"I get the dhampir all to myself, then," warned Jacqueline.

"Fine, fine," said Dawn. "Just hurry up."

Lee turned so radiant, so happy . . . it was sickening. "Thank you," he said. "Thank you so much! I've been waiting so long for this that I can't believe it's—ahh!"

Jacqueline moved so quickly that I hardly saw it happen at all. One moment she was standing in the doorway, the next she had Lee pinned against the recliner. Lee gave out a semi-muffled scream as she bit into his neck, a scream that soon quieted. Dawn shut the door and nudged us forward. I flinched at her touch.

"Well," she said with amusement. "Let's get a good view."

Neither Adrian nor I responded. We simply moved into the living room. I dared a glance at him but could discern little. He was so good at hiding his true feelings in general that I supposed I shouldn't be surprised he could mask abject terror just as easily. He offered me no encouragement with either his expression or words, which I actually found kind of refreshing. Because really, I didn't see any good end to this situation.

Up close, forced to watch Jacqueline's attack, I could now see the blissful expression that had settled over Lee's face. It was the most awful thing I'd ever witnessed. I wanted to squeeze my eyes shut or turn away, but some force beyond me kept me staring at the grisly spectacle. I'd never seen any vampire feed, Moroi or Strigoi, but I now understood why feeders like Dorothy could so willingly sign up for their lifestyles. Endorphins were being released into Lee's bloodstream, endorphins so strong that they blinded him to the fact that he was having his life drained away. He instead existed in a joyous state, lost in a chemical high. Or maybe he was just thinking about how happy he'd be once he was a Strigoi again, if it was possible to have any sort of conscious thought under these circumstances.

I lost track of how long it took to drain Lee. Each moment was agonizing for me, as though I was taking the pain Lee should have been feeling. The process seemed to last forever, and yet there was also a weird sense of speed to it. It felt wrong that someone's body could be drained in so short a time. Jacqueline drank steadily, pausing only once to remark, "His blood's not as good as I expected."

"Then stop," suggested Dawn, who was starting to look bored. "Just let him die and have these two with me."

Jacqueline looked as though she was actually considering it, again reminding me what a fool Lee had been to put his trust in these two. After a few minutes, she shrugged. "I'm almost done. And I really want him to get me that dhampir."

Jacqueline resumed drinking, but as she'd said, it didn't take much longer. By this point, Lee was nearly as pale as the Strigoi, and there was a strange, stretched quality to his skin. He was perfectly still now. His face seemed frozen in a grin that was nearly as much shock as it was joy. Jacqueline lifted her face and wiped off her mouth, surveying her victim with pleasure. She then pushed up her shirtsleeve and rested her nails on his wrist. Before she could tear her own flesh, however, she caught sight of something.

"Ah, much neater." She stepped away and leaned down, retrieving Lee's knife. It had slid under the love seat in our altercation. Jacqueline took it and effortlessly slashed her wrist, causing deep red blood to well out. Part of my brain didn't think their blood should look so similar to mine. It should be black. Or acidic.

She placed her bleeding wrist against Lee's mouth and tipped Lee's head back so that gravity could help the blood flow. Every horror I'd witnessed tonight had been worse than the last. Death was terrible—but it was also part of nature. This? This was no part of nature's plan. I was about to witness the world's greatest sin, the corruption of the soul through black magic to reanimate the dead. It made me feel dirty all over, and I wished I could run away. I didn't want to see this. I didn't want to see the guy I'd once regarded as something like a friend suddenly rise up as some perversion of nature.

A touch to my hand made me jump. It was Adrian. His eyes were on Lee and Jacqueline, but his hand had caught hold of mine and squeezed it, even though he was still cuffed. I was surprised at the warmth of his skin. Even though I knew Moroi were as living and warm-blooded as me, my irrational fears always expected them to be cold. Equally surprising was the sudden comfort and connection in that touch. It wasn't the kind of touch that said, *Hey, I've got a plan, so hang in there because we're going to get out of this.* It was more like the kind of touch that simply said, *You aren't alone.* It was really the only thing he could offer. And in that moment, it was enough.

Then, something strange happened. Or rather, *didn't* happen.

Jacqueline's blood was pouring steadily into Lee's mouth, and while we didn't have many documented cases of Strigoi conversions, I knew the basics. The victim's blood was drained, and then the killing Strigoi fed his or her blood back into the deceased. I didn't know exactly how long it took to work—it certainly didn't require all of the Strigoi's blood—but at some point, Lee should be stirring and getting up as one of the walking dead.

Jacqueline's cool, smug expression began to change to curiosity and then became outright confusion. She glanced questioningly at Dawn.

"What's taking so long?" Dawn asked.

"I don't know," Jacqueline said, turning back to Lee. With her free hand, she nudged Lee's shoulder as though that might serve as a wake-up call. Nothing happened.

"Haven't you done this before?" asked Dawn.

"Of course," snapped Jacqueline. "It didn't take nearly this long. He should be up and moving around. Something's wrong." I remembered Lee's words, describing how all his desperate attempts at taking innocent lives hadn't converted him back. I only knew a little about spirit—and even less about it restoring Strigoi—but something told me there was no force on earth that would ever turn Lee Strigoi again.

Another long minute passed as we watched and waited. At last, disgusted, Jacqueline backed away from the recliner and rolled up her sleeve. She glared at Lee's motionless body. "Something's wrong," she repeated. "And I don't want to waste any more blood figuring out what it is. Besides, my cut's already healing."

I wanted nothing more than for Dawn and Jacqueline to forget I existed, but the next words slipped out of my mouth before I could stop them. The scientist in me was too caught up in a revelation. "He was restored—and it affected him permanently. The spirit magic left some kind of mark, and now he can't be turned again."

Both Strigoi looked at me. I cringed under those red eyes.

"I never believed any of those spirit stories," said Dawn.

Jacqueline, however, was still clearly puzzled by her failure.

"There was something *wrong* with him, though. I can't explain it . . . but the whole time, he didn't feel right. Didn't taste right."

"Forget him," said Dawn. "He had his chance. He got what he wanted, and now I'm moving on."

I saw my death in her eyes and tried to reach for my cross. "God protect me," I said, just as she lunged forward.

Against all odds, Adrian was there to stop her—or, well, try to stop her. Mostly, he just got in her way. He didn't have the speed or reaction time to effectively block her and was especially clumsy with his cuffed hands. I think he'd just seen what I had, that she was going to attack, and had preemptively moved in front of me in some noble but ill-fated attempt at protection.

And ill-fated it was. With one smooth motion, she shoved him aside in a way that looked effortless but knocked him half-way across the room. My breath caught. He hit the floor, and I started to scream. Suddenly, I felt a sharp pain against my throat. Without a pause, Dawn had promptly grabbed me and nearly lifted me off my feet to get access to my neck. I mustered another frantic prayer as that pain spread, but within seconds, both prayer and pain disappeared from my brain. They were replaced by a sweet, sweet feeling of contentment and bliss and wonder. I had no thoughts, except that I was suddenly existing in the happiest, most exquisite state imaginable. I wanted more. More, more, more. I wanted to drown in it, to forget myself, to forget everything around me—

"Ugh," I cried out as I suddenly and unexpectedly hit the floor. Still in that blissful haze, I felt no pain—yet.

Just as quickly as she'd grabbed me, Dawn had dropped and pushed me away. Instinctively, I reached out an arm to break my fall but failed. I was too weak and disoriented and sprawled ungracefully on the carpet. Dawn's fingers were touching her lips, a look of outrage twisting her already-horrific features.

"What," she demanded, "was *that*?"

My brain wasn't working properly yet. I'd only had a brief taste of endorphin, but it was still enough to leave me addled. I had no answer for her.

"What's wrong?" exclaimed Jacqueline, striding forward. She looked from me to Dawn in confusion.

Dawn scowled and then spit onto the floor. It was red from my blood. Disgusting.

"Her blood . . . it was terrible. Inedible. Foul." She spit again.

Jacqueline's eyes widened. "Just like the other one. See? I told you."

"No." Dawn shook her head. "There's no way it could be the same. You would never have been able to drink that much of *her*." She spit again. "It didn't just taste weird or bad . . . it was like it's tainted." Seeing Jacqueline's skeptical look, Dawn punched her on the arm. "Don't believe me? Try her yourself."

Jacqueline took a step toward me, hesitant. Then Dawn spit again, and I think that somehow convinced the other Strigoi that she wanted no part of me. "I don't want another mediocre meal. Damn it. This is becoming absurd." Jacqueline glanced at Adrian, who was standing perfectly still. "At least we've still got him."

"If he's not ruined too," Dawn muttered.

My senses were coming back to me, and for half a second, I wondered if there was some insane way we might survive this. Maybe the Strigoi would write us off as bad meals. But no.

Even as I allowed myself to hope that, I also knew that even if they didn't feed off of us, we weren't going to leave here alive. They had no reason to simply walk off. They'd kill us for sport before they left.

With that same remarkable speed, Jacqueline sprang toward Adrian. "Time to find out."

I screamed as Jacqueline pinned Adrian against the wall and bit his neck. She only did so for a few seconds, just to get a taste. Jacqueline lifted her head up, pausing and savoring the blood. A slow smile spread over her face, showing her bloody fangs.

"This one's good. Very good. Makes up for the other." She trailed her fingers down his cheek. "Such a shame, though. He's so cute."

Dawn stalked toward them. "Let me try before you take it all!"

Jacqueline ignored her and was leaning back toward Adrian, who had gone all glassy-eyed. Meanwhile, I was free enough of the endorphins that I was thinking clearly again. No one was paying attention to me. I tried to stand and felt the world sway. Staying low, I managed to crawl toward my purse, lying forgotten near the living room's edge. Jacqueline had drunk from Adrian again, but only briefly before Dawn pulled her away and demanded a turn so that she could wash the taste of my blood out of her mouth.

Startling myself with how fast I moved, I rustled through my cavernous purse, looking desperately for anything that might help. Some cold, logical part of me said there was no way we could get out of this, but there was also no way I could just sit there and watch them drain Adrian. I had to fight. I had to try to save him, just as he'd tried for me. It didn't matter if the effort failed or if I died. Somehow, I had to try.

Some Alchemists carried guns, but not me. My purse was huge, full of more stuff than I really needed, but nothing in the contents resembled a weapon. Even if it did, most weapons were futile against Strigoi. A gun would slow them down but not kill them. Only silver stakes, decapitation, and fire could kill a Strigoi.

Fire . . .

My hand closed around the amulet I'd made for Ms. Terwilliger. I'd shoved it in my purse when she gave it to me, unsure what I should do with it. I could only assume blood loss and scattered thoughts made me draw it out now and consider the possibility of using it. Even the idea was ridiculous. You couldn't use something that didn't work! It was a trinket, a worthless bag of rocks and leaves. There was no magic here, and I was a fool to even think along those lines.

And yet, it was a bag of rocks.

Not a heavy one, but surely enough to get someone's attention if it hit her in the head. It was the best I had. The only thing I had to slow Adrian's death. Drawing back my arm, I aimed at Dawn and threw, reciting the foolish incantation like a battle cry: *"Into flame, into flame!"*

It was a good shot. Miss Carson would have been proud. But I had no chance to admire my athletic skills because I was too distracted by the fact that *Dawn had caught on fire.*

My jaw dropped as I stared at the impossible. It wasn't a huge fire. It wasn't like her entire body was engulfed in flames. But where the amulet had struck her, a small blaze ignited, spreading rapidly through her hair. She screamed and began frantically patting her head. Strigoi feared fire, and for a moment, Jacqueline recoiled. Then, with grim determination, she released Adrian and grabbed a throw blanket. She wrapped it around Dawn's head, smothering the flames.

"What the hell?" Dawn demanded when she emerged. She immediately began charging toward me in her anger. I knew then the only thing I'd accomplished was to speed up my own death.

Dawn grabbed ahold of me and slammed my head against the wall. My world reeled, and I felt nauseous. She reached for me again but froze when the door suddenly burst open. Eddie appeared in the doorway, a silver stake in his hand.

What was truly amazing about what followed was the speed. There was no pausing, no long moments to assess the situation, and no snarky banter between combatants. Eddie simply charged in and went for Jacqueline. Jacqueline responded with equal quickness, rushing forward to meet her one worthy foe here.

After she'd released him, Adrian had slumped to the floor, still in the throes of the Strigoi endorphins. Keeping low to the ground, I scurried over to his side and helped drag him back to the "safety" of the far side of the living room while Eddie clashed with the Strigoi. I spared them only a moment's glance, just enough to take in the deadly dancelike nature of their maneuvering. Both Strigoi were trying to get a grip on Eddie, probably in the hopes of breaking his neck, but were careful to stay away from the bite of his silver stake.

I looked down at Adrian, who was dangerously pale and whose pupils had reduced to the size of pinpoints. I had only a sketchy impression of how much Jacqueline had drunk from him and didn't know if Adrian's state was more from blood loss or endorphins.

"I'm fine, Sage," he muttered, blinking as though the light hurt. "Quite the high, though. Makes the stuff I've used seem pretty soft-core." He blinked, as though fighting to wake up. His pupils dilated to a more normal size and then seemed to focus on me. "Good God. Are *you* okay?"

"I will be," I said, starting to stand. Yet even as I spoke, a wave of dizziness hit me, and I swayed. Adrian did his best to support me, though it was pretty awkward with his bound hands. We leaned against each other, and I almost laughed at how ridiculous the situation was, both of us trying to help the other when neither of us was in any condition to do it. Then something caught my eye that chased all other thoughts away.

"Jill," I whispered.

Adrian immediately followed my gaze to where Jill had just appeared in the living room's entry. I wasn't surprised to see her. The only way Eddie could be here was if Jill had told him what was happening to Adrian through the spirit bond. Standing there, with her eyes flashing, she looked like some fierce, battle-ready goddess as she watched Eddie spar with the Strigoi. It was both inspiring and frightening. Adrian shared my thoughts.

"No, no, Jailbait," he murmured. "Do *not* do anything stupid. Castile needs to handle this."

"She knows how to fight," I said.

Adrian frowned. "But she doesn't have a weapon. Without one, she's just a featherweight in this."

He was right, of course. And while I certainly didn't want Jill endangering her life, I couldn't help but think if she were properly equipped, she might be able to do something. At the very least, a distraction might be a benefit. Eddie was holding his ground all right against the two Strigoi, but he wasn't making any progress against them either. He could use help. And we needed to make sure Jill didn't rush into this with only her wits to defend her.

Inspiration hit me, and I managed to stay on my feet. The world was spinning even more than before, but—despite Adrian's protests—I managed to stagger to the kitchen. I just barely was able to get to the sink and flip the faucet on before my legs gave out underneath me. I caught hold of the counter's edge, using it to keep me upright.

"Jill!" I yelled.

She turned toward my shout, saw the running water, and instantly knew what to do. She lifted her hand. The stream coming from the faucet suddenly shifted, shooting out of the sink and across the living room. It went to Jill, who collected a large amount of it between her hands and magically forced the water into a long cylindrical shape. It held itself in the air like that, a rippling but seemingly solid club of water. Gripping it, she hurried toward the fight and swung her weapon of water into Jacqueline's back. Drops flew off of the "club," but it held on to its rigidity enough for her to get a second hit in before completely exploding into a spray of water.

Jacqueline spun around, her hand swinging out to strike Jill. Jill had expected as much and dropped to the floor, dodging in exactly the way I'd seen Eddie teach her. She scurried backward, out of Jacqueline's way, and the Strigoi pursued—giving Eddie an exposed shot on her back. Eddie took the opportunity, evading Dawn, and plunged his stake into Jacqueline's back. I'd never given it much thought before, but if shoved hard enough, a stake could pierce someone's heart just as easily from the back as the chest. Jacqueline went rigid, and Eddie jerked his stake out, just managing to avoid the full force of a strike from Dawn. She still caught him a little, and he stumbled briefly before quickly regaining his footing and setting his sights on her. Jill was forgotten and hurried over to us in the kitchen.

"Are you okay?" she exclaimed, peering at both of us. That fierce look was gone. She was now just an ordinary girl concerned for her friends. "Oh my God. I was so worried about you both. The emotions were so strong. I couldn't get a fix on what was happening, just that something was horribly wrong."

I dragged my gaze to Eddie, who was dancing around with Dawn. "We have to help him—"

I took two steps away from the counter and started to fall. Both Jill and Adrian reached out to catch me.

"Jesus, Sage," he exclaimed. "You're in bad shape."

"Not as bad as you," I protested, still worried about helping Eddie. "They drank more from you—"

"Yeah, but I don't have a bleeding arm wound," he pointed out. "Or a possible concussion."

It was true. In all the excitement, I was so full of adrenaline that I'd all but forgotten about where Lee had stabbed me. No wonder I was so dizzy. Or maybe that was from getting my head smacked into the wall. It was anyone's guess at this point.

"Here," said Adrian gently. He reached for my arms with his cuffed hands. "I can take care of this."

A slow, tingling warmth spread through my skin. At first, Adrian's touch was comforting, like an embrace. I felt my tension and pain begin to ease. All was right in the world. He was in control. He was taking care of me.

He was using his magic on me.

"No!" I shrieked, pulling away from him with a strength I didn't know I had. The horror and full realization of what was happening to me was too powerful. "Don't touch me! Don't touch me with your magic!"

"Sage, you'll feel better, believe me," he said, reaching toward me again.

I backed away, clinging to the edge of the counter for support. The fleeting memory of that warmth and comfort was being dwarfed by the terror I'd carried my entire life for vampire magic. "No, no, no. No magic! Not on me! The tattoo will heal me! I'm strong!"

"Sage—"

"Stop, Adrian," said Jill. She approached me tentatively. "It's okay, Sydney. He won't heal you. I promise."

"No magic," I whispered.

"For God's sake," growled Adrian. "This is superstitious bullshit."

"No magic," Jill said firmly. She took off the button-up shirt she'd been wearing over a T-shirt. "Come here, and I'll use this to wrap it so that you don't lose any more bl—"

An earsplitting shriek jerked us all back toward the living room. Eddie had made his kill, driving his stake right into the middle of Dawn's chest. In my brief scuffle with Adrian and Jill, Dawn must have gotten some shots in on Eddie because there was a large red mark on one side of his face, and his lip was bleeding. The expression in his eyes was hard and triumphant, however, as he pulled the stake out and watched Dawn fall.

Through all the confusion and horror, basic Alchemist instincts took over. The danger was gone. There were procedures that needed to be followed.

"The bodies," I said. "We have to destroy them. There's a vial in my purse."

"Whoa, whoa," said Adrian as both he and Jill restrained me. "Stay where you're at. Castile can get it. The only place you're going is to a doctor."

I didn't move but immediately argued with that last statement. "No! No doctors. At least, you have to—you have to get an Alchemist one. My purse has the numbers—"

"Go get her purse," Adrian told Jill, "before she has a fit here. I'll bind the arm." I gave him a warning look. "*Without* magic. Which, by the way, could make this ten times easier."

"I'll heal on my own," I said, watching as Jill retrieved my purse.

"You realize," added Adrian, "you're going to have to get over your dieting fixation and consume some major calories to fight the blood loss. Sugar and fluids, just like Clarence. Good thing someone bagged up all this candy on the counter."

Eddie walked over to Jill, and she paused as he asked if she was okay. She assured him she was, and although Eddie looked like he could kill about fifty more Strigoi, there was also a look in his eyes . . . something I couldn't believe I'd never noticed before. Something I was going to have to think about.

"Damn it," said Adrian, fumbling with bandages. "Eddie, go search Lee's body and see if there's a key for these goddamned handcuffs."

Jill had been caught up in talking to Eddie but froze at the words "Lee's body." Her face went so pale, she could have been one of the dead. In all the confusion, she hadn't noticed Lee's body in the chair. There'd been too much movement with the Strigoi, too much distraction by the threat they presented. She took a few steps toward the living room, and that's when she saw him. Her mouth opened, but no sound came out right away. Then she sped forward and grabbed his hands, shrieking.

"No," she cried. "No, no, no." She shook him, as though that would wake him. In a flash, Eddie was by her side, his arms around her as he murmured nonsensical things to soothe her. She didn't hear him. Her whole world was Lee.

I felt tears spring to my eyes and hated that they were there. Lee had tried to kill me and then had summoned others to kill me. He'd left a trail of innocents in his wake. I should be glad he was gone, but still, I felt sad. He had loved Jill, in his insane way, and from the pain on her face, it was clear she'd loved him too. The spirit bond hadn't shown her his death or role in our capture. Right now, she simply thought he was a victim of Strigoi. Soon enough, she'd learn the truth about his motives. I didn't know if that would ease her pain or not. I was guessing not.

Weirdly, an image of Adrian's *Love* painting came back to me. I thought of the jagged red streak, slashing through the blackness, ripping it apart. Staring at Jill and her inconsolable pain, I suddenly understood his art a little bit better.

CHAPTER 26

IT TOOK DAYS for me to finally get the whole story, both about Lee and about how Eddie and Jill had come to the rescue that night.

Once I had Lee as the missing piece, it was easy to connect the murders of Tamara, Kelly, Melody, and Dina, the human girl he'd mentioned. All of them had been killed within the last five years, in either Los Angeles or Palm Springs, and many had documented evidence of knowing him. They weren't random victims. What little we could find out about Lee's history came from Clarence, though even that was muddled. By our best guesses, Lee had been turned forcibly into a Strigoi about fifteen years ago. He'd spent ten years that way until a spirit user restored him, much to Lee's dismay. Clarence hadn't had all his wits about him even then and hadn't questioned how his son had returned home after ten years without aging. He evaded answering our questions about Lee being a Strigoi, and we didn't know if Clarence simply hadn't known or was in denial. Likewise, it was unclear if Clarence knew his own son was behind Tamara's death. The far-fetched vampire hunter theory was probably easier for him to stomach than the murderous truth about his son.

Investigations into Lee's college in Los Angeles showed he hadn't actually been enrolled there since before he became Strigoi. When he'd become Moroi again, he'd used college as an excuse to stay in Los Angeles, where he could more easily pursue victims—and we suspected there were more of them than we had records for. From what we'd observed, he'd apparently tried to drink from a few of each race, in the hopes that one of them would be "the one" to make him a Strigoi again.

Further research into Kelly Hayes had uncovered something I should have thought of right away. She was a dhampir. She'd looked human, but that stellar sports record was the tip-off. Lee had stumbled onto her when visiting his father five years ago. Getting the drop on a dhampir wasn't easy, which was why Lee seemed to have gone to the effort of dating her and luring her in.

None of us knew anything about the "bastard spirit user" who'd converted him, though that was of interest to both the Alchemists and the Moroi. There were very few spirit users on record, and with there still being so much unknown about their powers, everyone wanted to learn more. Clarence was adamant that he knew nothing about this mystery spirit user, and I believed him.

Alchemists were in and out of Palm Springs all week, cleaning up the mess and interviewing everyone who'd been involved. I met with a number of them, telling my story over and over, and finally had my last debriefing with Stanton over lunch one

Saturday. I'd kind of had a perverse interest in knowing what had happened to Keith but decided not to bring it up in light of everything else going on. He wasn't here, which was all I cared about.

"Lee's autopsy revealed nothing that wasn't ordinary Moroi, according to their doctors," Stanton told me between bites of linguine carbonara. Eating and discussing dead bodies weren't mutually exclusive, apparently. "But then, something . . . magical likely wouldn't show up anyway."

"But there must be something special about him," I said. I was simply moving my own food around the plate. "The fact that his aging slowed was proof enough—but the rest? I mean, he drank from so many victims. And then I saw what Jacqueline did to him. *That* should have worked. All the correct procedures were followed."

It amazed me that I could speak so clinically about this, that I could sound so detached. Really, though, it was just that second-nature Alchemist mode taking over. Inside me, the events of that night had left a permanent mark. When I closed my eyes at bedtime, I kept seeing Lee's death and Jacqueline feeding him the blood. Lee, who'd brought Jill flowers and taken us all mini-golfing.

Stanton nodded thoughtfully. "Which suggests that those who are restored from being Strigoi are immune to ever being turned again."

We sat in silence for a moment, letting the weight of those words settle over us.

"That's huge," I said at last. Talk about an understatement. Lee presented a number of mysteries. He had begun aging once he became a Moroi again, but at a much slower rate.

Why? We weren't sure, but that alone was a monumental dis-covery, as was my suspicion that he could no longer use Moroi magic. I'd been too freaked out to notice anything strange about Lee's behavior when Jill had asked him to create fog while we were golfing, but looking back, it occurred to me he'd actually looked nervous about her requests. And the rest . . . the fact that something had changed in him, protected him, however unwillingly, from becoming Strigoi? Yeah. "Huge" was an understatement.

"Very," Stanton agreed. "Half our mission is to stop humans from choosing to sacrifice their souls for immortality. If there was a way to harness this magic, figure out what protected Lee . . . well. The effects would be far-reaching."

"To the Moroi as well," I pointed out. I knew that among them and the dhampirs, being forcefully turned Strigoi was often considered a fate worse than death. If there was some magical way to protect themselves, it would mean a lot since they encountered Strigoi far more than we did. We could be talking about some kind of magical vaccine.

"Of course," said Stanton, though her tone implied she wasn't nearly as concerned about that race's benefits. "It might even be possible to prevent the future creation of all Strigoi. There's also the mystery of *your* blood. You said the Strigoi didn't like it. That could be a type of protection too."

I shivered at the memory. "Maybe. It all happened so fast . . . it's hard to say. And it was certainly no protection from the Strigoi wanting to snap my neck."

Stanton nodded. "It's certainly something to look into even-tually. But first we have to figure out what exactly happened to Lee."

"Well," I said, "spirit has to be a key player, right? Lee was restored by a spirit user."

A waiter came by, and Stanton waved her plate away. "Exactly. Unfortunately, we have a very limited quantity of spirit users to work with. Vasilisa Dragomir hardly has the time to experiment with her powers. Sonya Karp has volunteered to help, which is excellent news, especially since she's a former Strigoi herself. At the very least, we can observe the slowed aging firsthand. She's only available for a short while, and the Moroi haven't answered my request yet for some other useful individuals. But if we had another spirit user on hand, one with no other obligations to distract him from helping us full-time . . ."

She looked at me meaningfully.

"Adrian?" I asked.

"Do you think he'd help research this? Some magical way to protect against Strigoi conversion? Like I said, between Sonya and the others, he'd have help," she added quickly. "I've spoken to the Moroi, and they're putting together a small group with expertise on Strigoi. They plan on sending them out soon. We just need Adrian to help."

"Wow. You guys move fast," I murmured.

At the words "Adrian" and "research," my mind had put together images of him in a lab, wearing a white coat, bent over test tubes and beakers. I knew that the actual research wouldn't look anything like that, but it was a hard picture to shake. It was also hard to imagine Adrian seriously focused on anything. Except, I kept having that nagging thought that Adrian would focus if he only had something worth caring about. Was this important enough?

I really wasn't sure. It was too hard to guess what purpose might be noble enough to get Adrian's attention. But I was pretty sure I knew some less-than-noble perks that might get him on board.

"If you can get him his own place, I bet he'd do it," I said finally. "He wants out of Clarence Donahue's pretty badly."

Stanton's eyebrows rose. She hadn't expected this. "Well. That's not a huge request, I suppose. And actually, we're already paying the bill for Keith's old apartment since he took out a year-long lease. Mr. Ivashkov could simply move into there, except . . ."

"Except what?"

Stanton gave a small shrug. "I was going to offer it to *you*. After much discussion, we've decided to simply make you the Alchemist on point here, in light of Keith's . . . unfortunate departure. You could leave Amberwood, move into his apartment, and simply oversee activities from there."

I frowned. "But I thought you wanted someone with Jill all the time."

"We do. And we've actually found a better choice—no offense. The Moroi were able to locate a dhampir girl Jill's age, who could not only serve as Jill's roommate but also as a bodyguard. She'll be joining the researchers who are coming out. You don't have to pose as a student anymore."

The world reeled. Alchemist schemes and plans, always in motion. A lot had been decided in this week, it seemed. I considered what this meant. No more homework, no more high school politics. Freedom to come and go when I wanted. But it also meant removing myself from the friends I'd made—Trey,

Kristin, Julia. I'd still see Eddie and Jill, but not to the same extent. And if I was on my own, would the Alchemists—or my father—help fund college classes? Unlikely.

"Do I have to leave?" I asked Stanton. "Can I give the apartment to Adrian and stay on at Amberwood for a while? At least until we figure out if we can get another place for me?"

Stanton didn't bother hiding her surprise. "I didn't expect you'd want to stay on. I figured you'd especially be happy to no longer room with a vampire."

And like that, all the fears and pressure I'd faced before coming to Palm Springs descended on me. *Vamp lover.* I was an idiot. I should've been jumping at the chance to get away from Jill. Any other Alchemist would. In offering to stay, I was likely putting myself under suspicion again. How could I explain that there was so much more to my choice than just a change of roommate?

"Oh," I said, keeping a neutral face. "When you said you were getting Jill a dhampir her own age, I figured she'd be the roommate and I wouldn't have to room with Jill anymore. I thought I'd have my own in the dorm."

"That can probably be arranged . . ."

"And honestly, after some of the things that have happened, I'd feel better still keeping an eye on Jill. It'll be easier if I'm at the school. Besides, if it takes an apartment to make Adrian happy and work on this Strigoi mystery, then that's what we need to do. I can wait."

Stanton studied me for several long seconds, breaking the silence only when the waiter dropped the bill off. "That's very professional of you. I'll look into the arrangements."

"Thank you," I said. A happy feeling welled up in me, and I

almost smiled, picturing Adrian's face when he heard about his new place.

"There's just one more thing I don't understand," remarked Stanton. "When we investigated the apartment, we saw some fire damage. But none of you who were there reported any."

I put on a contrived frown. "Honestly . . . so much of it's a blur with the blood loss and the biting . . . I'm not really sure. Keith had some candles. I don't know if one got lit . . . or I don't know. All I keep thinking about is those teeth and how terrible it was when I was bit—"

"Yes, yes," said Stanton. My excuse was flimsy, but even she wasn't entirely impervious to the thought of being fed on by a vampire. It was pretty much an Alchemist's worse nightmare, and I was entitled to my trauma. "Well, don't worry about it. That fire is the least of our worries."

It wasn't the least of my worries. And when I got back to campus later that day, I finally dealt with it and hunted Ms. Terwilliger down where she was working in one of the library offices.

"You knew," I said, shutting the door. All thoughts of student-teacher protocol vanished from my head. I'd been sitting on my anger for a week and could now finally let it out. I'd spent my life being taught to respect sources of authority, but now one of those had just betrayed me. "Everything you made me do . . . copying those spell books, making that amulet 'just to see what it was like'!" I shook my head. "It was all a lie. You knew . . . you knew it was . . . *real*."

Ms. Terwilliger took off her glasses and peered at me carefully. "Ah, so I take it you tried it?"

"How could you do that to me?" I exclaimed. "You have no idea how I feel about magic and the supernatural!"

"Oh," she said dryly. "I do actually. I know all about your organization." She tapped her cheek, mirroring the one my tattoo was on. "I know why your 'sister' is excused from outdoor activities and why your 'brother' excels in sports. I'm very informed about the various forces at work in our world, those hidden from most human eyes. Don't worry, my dear. I'm certainly not going to tell anyone. Vampires aren't my concern."

"Why?" I asked, deciding not to acknowledge her outing everything I strove to keep secret. "Why me? Why did you make me do that—especially if you claim you know how I feel?"

"Mmm . . . a couple of reasons. Vampires, as you know, wield a sort of internal magic. They connect with the elements on a very basic, almost effortless level. Humans, however, have no such connection."

"Humans aren't supposed to use magic," I said coldly. "You made me do something that violated my beliefs."

"For humans to do magic," she continued, as though I hadn't spoken, "we must wrest it from the world. It doesn't come so easily. Sure, vampires use spells and ingredients occasionally, but nothing like what we must do. Their magic goes from the inside out. Ours comes from the outside in. It takes so much effort, so much concentration and exact calculation . . . well, most humans don't have the patience or skill. But someone like you? You've been grilled in those painstaking techniques since the time you could talk."

"So that's all it takes to use magic? An ability to organize and measure?" I didn't bother hiding my scorn.

"Of course not." She laughed. "There is a certain natural

talent needed as well. An instinct that combines with discipline. I sensed it in you. You see, I have some proficiency myself. It gives me coven status but is still relatively small. You? I can feel a wellspring of power in you, and my little experiment proved as much."

I felt cold all over. "That's a lie," I said. "Vampires use magic. Not humans. Not *me*."

"That amulet didn't light *itself* on fire," she said. "Don't deny what you are. And now that we've determined as much, we can move on. Your innate power might be greater than mine, but I can get you started in basic magical training."

I couldn't believe I was hearing this. It wasn't real. It was like something from a movie because no way was this my life. "No," I exclaimed. "You're . . . you're crazy! Magic's not real, and I don't have any! It's unnatural and wrong. I won't endanger my soul."

"So much denial for such a good scientist," she mused.

"I'm serious," I said, barely recognizing my own voice. "I want nothing to do with your occult studies. I'm happy to go on taking notes and buying you coffee, but if you keep making these kinds of crazy statement and demands . . . I'll go to the office and demand to be switched to another teacher. Believe me, when it comes to working bureaucracy and administrative staff, that *is* something I have innate power in."

She almost smiled, but then it faded. "You mean that. You'd really reject this amazing potential—this *discovery*—that you have?"

I didn't answer.

"So be it." She sighed. "It's a loss. And a waste. But you have my word that I won't bring it up again unless you do."

"That," I said vehemently, "is not going to happen."

Ms. Terwilliger merely shrugged by way of answer. "Well, then. Since you're here, you might as well go get me some coffee."

I moved toward the door and then thought of something. "Were you the one calling Nevermore and asking about vampires?"

"Why in the world would I do that?" she asked. "I already know where to find them." *Great*, I thought. *Another mystery*.

I made it to the cafeteria later that day just as Eddie, Jill, and Micah were finishing dinner. Jill was understandably having a difficult time adjusting to Lee's death and all the revelations we'd uncovered—including his desire to make her his undead queen. Both Eddie and I had talked to her as much as we could, but Micah seemed to have the greatest soothing effect on her. I think it was because he never openly addressed the topic. He knew Lee had died but thought it was an accident and naturally knew none of the vampiric connections. While Eddie and I constantly tried our hand at being amateur psychologists, Micah simply tried to distract her and make her happy.

"We have to go," he said apologetically when I sat down. "Rachel Walker is going to give us a lesson on one of the sewing machines."

Eddie shook his head at him. "I still don't know why you signed up for sewing club." That wasn't true, of course. We both knew exactly why Micah had joined.

Jill's face wore the grave look it had had since Lee's death—a look she would carry for a while, I suspected—but the ghost of a smile flickered over her lips. "I think Micah has the makings of a real fashion designer. Maybe I'll walk in his show one day."

I shook my head, hiding my own smile. "No modeling of any kind, not for a while." After the show, Lia and other designers had gotten in touch, all wanting to work with Jill again. We'd had to refuse in order to protect her identity here, but it had made Jill sad to have to do it.

Jill nodded. "I know, I know." She stood up with Micah. "I'll see you back in our room later, Sydney. I'd like to talk some more."

I nodded. "Absolutely."

Eddie and I watched them hurry off. I sighed.

"That's going to be a problem," I told him.

"Maybe," he agreed. "But she knows what she can and can't do with him. She's smart. She'll be responsible."

"But he doesn't know," I said. "I feel like Micah's fallen for her too much already." I eyed Eddie carefully. "Among other people."

Eddie was still watching Micah and Jill, so it took him a moment to pick up on my meaning. He jerked his gaze back to me. "Huh?"

"Eddie, I'm not going to claim to be any expert in romance, but even I can tell that you're crazy about Jill."

He promptly looked away, though his flush betrayed him. "That's not true."

"I've seen it all along, but it wasn't until that night at Keith's that I really understood *what* I was seeing. I saw how you looked at her. I know how you feel about her. So, what I want to know is: how come we have to keep worrying about Micah at all?

Why aren't *you* just asking her out and saving us all a lot of trouble?"

"Because she's my sister," he said wryly.

"Eddie! I'm serious."

He made a face, took a deep breath, and then turned back toward me. "Because she can do better than me. You want to talk about social rules? Well, where we come from, Moroi and dhampirs don't have serious relationships."

"Yeah, but that's like a class thing," I said. "It's not quite the same as humans and vampires."

"Maybe not, but with her, it might as well be. She's not just any Moroi. She's royal. A princess. And you've seen how she is! Smart and strong and beautiful. She's destined for great things, and one of them isn't being involved with a controversial guardian like me. Her bloodline's regal. Hell, I don't even know who my dad is. Dating her is not even possible. My job is to protect her. To keep her safe. That's where all my attention needs to be."

"And so you think she deserves being with a human instead?" I asked incredulously. "Dancing the line of a taboo upheld by both our races?"

"It's not ideal," he admitted. "But she can still have a fun social life and—"

"What if it was another guy?" I interrupted. "What if some other human asked her out, and they simply went on a casual date? Would you be okay with that?"

He didn't answer, and I knew my hunch was correct.

"This is about more than you not feeling worthy of Jill," I said. "This is about Micah too, isn't it? About how he reminds you of Mason."

Eddie blanched. "How do you know about that?"

"Adrian told me."

"Damn him," said Eddie. "Why can't he be as oblivious as he pretends?"

I smiled at that. "You don't owe Micah anything. You certainly don't owe him Jill. He's not Mason, no matter how much they look alike."

"It's more than looks," said Eddie, growing pensive. "It's the way they act too. Micah's the same—outgoing, optimistic, excited. That's how Mason was. There are too few people like that in the world: people who are genuinely *good*. Mason was taken away from the world too soon. I won't let that happen to Micah."

"Micah's not in danger," I said gently.

"But he deserves good things. And even if he's human, he's still one of the best matches I know of for Jill. They deserve each other. They both deserve good things."

"And so, you're going to let yourself suffer as a result? Because you're so in love with Jill and convinced that she deserves some prince that you aren't? And because you feel it's your duty to support all the Masons in the world?" I shook my head. "Eddie, that's crazy. Even you have to see that."

"Maybe," he admitted. "But I feel like it's the right thing to do."

"Right? It's the masochistic thing to do! You're encouraging the girl you want to be with one of your best friends."

"I want her to be happy. It's worth sacrificing myself."

"It makes no sense."

Eddie gave me a small smile and a gentle pat on the arm before turning toward an approaching shuttle bus. "Remember when you said you were no expert in romance? Well, you were right."

CHAPTER 27

I THINK ADRIAN would have agreed to anything to get his own place. He didn't waste any time in moving his few possessions over to Keith's old apartment, much to Clarence's dismay. I had to admit, I felt kind of bad for the old man. He'd grown fond of Adrian, and losing him right after Lee was especially tough. Clarence still opened his home and feeder to our group but refused to believe anything we told him about Lee and Strigoi. Even once he accepted Lee was dead, Clarence continued blaming vampire hunters.

Shortly after his move, I went to check on Adrian. Word had come to us that the "research party" from the Moroi was due to arrive in town that day, and we'd decided to meet with them first before bringing in Jill and Eddie. Like before, Abe was apparently escorting the newcomers, who included Sonya and Jill's new roommate. I had the impression there might be others with them but hadn't heard the details yet.

"Whoa," I said when Adrian let me into his apartment.

He'd only been there a couple days, but the transformation was startling. With the exception of the TV, none of the original furniture remained. It was all different, and even the apartment's layout had changed. The decorating scheme was new as well, and the scent of fresh paint hung heavy in the air.

"Yellow, huh?" I asked, staring at the living room walls.

"It's called 'Goldenrod,'" he corrected. "And it's supposed to be cheerful and calming."

I started to point out that those two traits didn't seem like they'd go together but then decided against it. The color, slightly obnoxious though it was, completely transformed the living room. Between that and the blinds that had replaced Keith's heavy drapes, the room was now filled with color and light that went a long way to obscure the memory of the battle. I shuddered, recalling it. Even if the apartment hadn't been needed to buy Adrian's help, I wasn't sure I could've accepted it and stayed here. The memory of Lee's death—and the two Strigoi women's—was too strong.

"How did you afford new furniture?" I asked. The Alchemists had given him the place, but there was no other stipend involved.

"I sold the old stuff," Adrian said, seeming very pleased by this. "That recliner . . ." He faltered, a troubled look briefly crossing his features. I wondered if he too could imagine Lee's life bleeding away in that chair. "That recliner was worth a lot. It was appallingly overpriced, even by my standards. But I got enough for it to replace the rest. It's used, but what choice did I have?"

"It's nice," I said, running my hand along an overstuffed plaid sofa. It looked ghastly with the walls but appeared to be in good shape. Plus, much like the brightness of the yellow, the clashing furniture helped diminish the memories of what had happened. "You must have done some savvy shopping. I'm guessing you don't buy a lot of used stuff."

"Try never," he said. "You have no idea the things I've had to lower myself to." His pleased smile dimmed as he regarded me carefully. "How are you holding up?"

I shrugged. "Fine. Why wouldn't I be? What happened to me isn't nearly as bad as what Jill went through."

He crossed his arms. "I don't know. Jill didn't watch a guy die in front of her. And let's not forget that same guy wanted to kill you only moments before in order to rise again from the dead."

Those were things that had definitely been on my mind a lot in the last week, things that were going to take a while to get over. Sometimes, I didn't feel anything at all. Other times, the reality of what had happened descended on me so swiftly and heavily that I couldn't breathe. Strigoi nightmares had replaced the ones of re-education centers.

"I'm actually better with it than you might think," I said slowly, gazing off at nothing particular. "Like, it's terrible about Lee and what he did, but I feel I can get over it in time. Do you know what I keep thinking about the most, though?"

"What?" asked Adrian gently.

The words seemed to come forth without my control. I hadn't expected to say them to anyone, certainly not to him.

"Lee telling me I was wasting my life and staying aloof from people. And then, during that last meeting with Keith, he told me that I was naive, that I didn't understand the world. And it's true to a certain extent. I mean, not what he said about you guys being evil . . . but well, I *was* naive. I should've been more careful with Jill. I believed the best of Lee when I should've been more wary. I'm not a fighter like Eddie, but I am an observer of the world . . . or so I like to think. But I failed. I'm no good with people."

"Sage, your first mistake in all of this is listening to anything Keith Darnell says. The guy's an idiot, an asshole, and a dozen other words that aren't suitable for a lady like yourself."

"See?" I said. "You just admitted it, that I'm some kind of untouchable, pure soul."

"I never said any such thing," he countered. "My point is that you're leagues above Keith, and what happened with Lee was dumb, ridiculous bad luck. And remember, none of us saw it coming either. You weren't alone. It casts no reflection on you. Or . . ." His eyebrows rose. "Maybe it does. Didn't you say that Lee considered killing Keith for Alchemist blood?"

"Yeah . . . but Keith left too soon."

"Well, there you go. Even a psychopath recognized your worth enough to want to kill someone else first."

I didn't know whether to laugh or cry. "That doesn't make me feel better."

Adrian shrugged. "My earlier point remains. You're a solid person, Sage. You're easy on the eyes, if a little skinny, and your ability to memorize useless information is going to totally hook in some guy. Put Keith and Lee out of your head because they have nothing to do with your future."

"Skinny?" I asked, hoping I wasn't blushing. I also hoped if I sounded outraged enough, he wouldn't notice how much the other comment had disarmed me. *Easy on the eyes.* Not exactly the same as being told I was hotness incarnate or drop-dead gorgeous. But after a lifetime of having my appearance judged as "acceptable," it was a heady compliment—especially coming from him.

"I just tell it like it is."

I almost laughed. "Yes. Yes, you do. Now tell me about a different subject, please. I'm tired of this one."

"Sure thing." Adrian infuriated me sometimes, but I had to admit, I loved his short attention span. It made dodging uncomfortable topics so much easier. Or so I thought. "Do you smell that?"

An image of the bodies flashed into my head, and for a moment, all I could think he meant was the smell of decay. Then I sniffed more deeply. "I smell the paint, and . . . wait . . . is that pine?"

He looked impressed. "Damn straight. Pine-scented cleaner. As in, I *cleaned*." He gestured to the kitchen dramatically. "With these hands, these hands that don't do manual labor."

I stared off into the kitchen. "What did you use it on? The cupboards?"

"The cupboards are fine. I cleaned the floor and the counter." I must have looked more puzzled than amazed because he added, "I even got down on my knees."

"You used pine cleaner on the floor and counters?" I asked. The floor was ceramic tile; the counters were granite.

Adrian frowned. "Yeah, so?"

He seemed so proud to have actually scrubbed something for once in his life that I couldn't bring myself to tell him pine cleaner was generally only used on wood. I gave him an encouraging smile. "Well, it looks great. I need you to come over and clean my new dorm room now. It's covered in dust."

"No way, Sage. My own housecleaning's bad enough."

"But is it worth it? If you'd stayed at Clarence's, you had a live-in cook and cleaner."

"It's definitely worth it. I've never really, truly had my own place. I kind of did at Court . . . but it might as well have been an over-glorified dorm room. This? This is great. Even with the housecleaning. Thank you."

The comic look of horror he'd worn while discussing house-cleaning had been traded away for utter seriousness now as those green eyes weighed me. I suddenly felt uncomfortable under the scrutiny and was reminded of the spirit dream, where I'd questioned if his eyes really were that green in real life.

"For what?" I asked.

"For this—I know you must have twisted some Alchemist arms." I hadn't told him that I'd actually passed on taking the place for myself. "And for everything else. For not giving up on me, even when I was being a major asshole. And, you know, for that saving my life thing."

I looked away. "I didn't do anything. That was Eddie—and Jill. They're the ones who saved you."

"Not sure I would've been alive for their rescue if you hadn't set that bitch on fire. How did you do that?"

"It was nothing," I protested. "Just a, uh, chemical reaction from the Alchemist bag of tricks."

Those eyes studied me again, weighing the truth of my words. I'm not sure he believed me, but he let it go. "Well, from the look on her face, your aim was right on. And then you got backhanded for it. Anyone who takes a hit for Adrian Ivashkov deserves some credit."

I turned my back to him, still shy with the praise—and

nervous about the fire reference—and walked over to the window. "Yeah, well, you can rest easy that it was a selfish act. You have no idea what a pain it is to file paperwork for a dead Moroi."

He laughed, and it was one of the few times I'd heard him laugh with genuine humor and warmth—and not because of something twisted or sarcastic. "Okay, Sage. If you say so. You know, you're a lot spunkier than when I first met you."

"Really? All the adjectives in the world at your disposable, and you pick 'spunky'?" Banter I could handle. So long as I focused on that, I didn't have to think about the meaning behind the words or how my heartbeat had increased just a little. "Just so you know, you're a little more stable than when I met you."

He came over to stand by me. "Well, don't tell anyone, but I think getting away from Court was a good thing. This weather sucks, but Palm Springs might be good for me—it and all the wonders it contains. You guys. Art classes. Pine cleaner."

I couldn't help a grin and looked up at him. I'd been half-joking, but it was true: he had changed remarkably since we'd met. There was still a hurting man inside, one who bore the scars of what Rose and Dimitri had done to him, but I could see the signs of healing. He was steadier and stronger, and if he could just continue to hold the course, with no more crises for a while, a remarkable transformation might truly happen.

It took several seconds of silence for me to realize that I'd been staring at him while my mind spun out its thoughts. And, actually, he was staring at me, with a look of wonder.

"My God, Sage. Your eyes. How have I never noticed them?"

That uncomfortable feeling was spreading over me again. "What about them?"

"The color," he breathed. "When you stand in the light. They're amazing . . . like molten gold. I could paint those . . ." He reached toward me but then pulled back. "They're beautiful. You're beautiful."

Something in the way he was looking at me froze me up and made my stomach do flip-flops, though I couldn't quite articulate why. I only knew that he looked as though he was seeing me for the very first time . . . and it scared me. I'd been able to brush off his easy, joking compliments, but this intensity was something different altogether, something I didn't know how to react to. When he looked at me like this, I *believed* that he thought my eyes were beautiful—that I was beautiful. It was more than I was ready for. Flustered, I took a step backward, out of the sunlight, needing to get away from the energy of his gaze. I'd heard spirit could send him off on weird tangents but had no clue if that's what this was. I was saved from my feeble attempts to muster a witty comment when a knock at the door made both of us jump.

Adrian blinked, and some of that rapture faded. His lips twisted into one of his sly smiles, and it was as though nothing weird had happened. "Showtime, huh?"

I nodded, reeling with a confusing mix of relief, nervousness, and . . . excitement. Except, I wasn't entirely sure if those feelings were from Adrian or our impending visitors. All I knew was that suddenly, I was able to breathe more easily than I had a few moments ago.

He walked across the living room and opened the door with

a flourish. Abe swept in, resplendent in a gray and yellow suit that coordinated bafflingly well with Adrian's paint job. A wide grin broke out over the older Moroi's face.

"Adrian, Sydney . . . so lovely to see you again. I believe one of you already knows this young lady?" He moved past us, revealing a lean dhampir girl with auburn hair and big blue eyes filled with suspicion.

"Hello, Angeline," I said.

When they'd told me Angeline Dawes was going to be Jill's new roommate, I thought it was the most ridiculous thing I'd ever heard. Angeline was one of the Keepers, that separatist group of Moroi, dhampirs, and humans who lived in the wilds of West Virginia. They wanted nothing to do with the "civilization" of any of our races and had a number of bizarre customs, not the least of which was their abominable tolerance for inter-racial romance.

Later, when I'd thought about it, I decided Angeline might not be such a bad choice. She was the same age as Jill, possibly giving Jill a closer connection than I could manage. Angeline, while not trained the way a guardian like Eddie was, still could hold her own in a fight. If anyone came for Jill, they'd have their work cut out for them getting through Angeline. And with the aversion Angeline's people had toward "tainted" Moroi, she would have no reason to further the politics of some rival faction.

As I studied her and her threadbare clothes, I wondered, though, just how well she was going to adapt to being away from the Keepers. She wore a cocky look on her face that I'd seen when visiting her community, but here it was underscored with some nervousness as she took in Adrian's place. After living in the woods her entire life, this small apartment with its TV and plaid sofa was probably the height of modern luxury.

"Angeline," said Abe. "This is Adrian Ivashkov."

Adrian extended his hand, turning on that natural charm. "A pleasure."

She took his hand after a moment's hesitation. "Nice to meet you," she said in her odd southern accent. She studied him for a few more seconds. "You look too pretty to be useful."

I gasped in spite of myself. Adrian chuckled and shook her hand.

"Truer words were never spoken," he said.

Abe glanced over at me. I probably had a look of terror on my face because I was already imagining the damage control I'd have to do with Angeline saying or doing something completely wrong at Amberwood.

"Sydney will undoubtedly want to . . . debrief you on what to expect before you begin school," said Abe diplomatically.

"Undoubtedly," I repeated.

Adrian had stepped away from Angeline but was still grinning. "Let Jailbait do it. Better yet, let Castile. It'll be good for him."

Abe shut the door but not before I got a glimpse behind him to the empty hallway. "It's not just the two of you, is it?" I asked. "I heard there were others. Sonya's one, right?"

Abe nodded. "They'll be right up. They're parking the car. Street parking's terrible around here."

Adrian looked over at me, hit by revelation. "Hey, do I inherit Keith's car too?"

"Afraid not," I said. "It belonged to his dad. He took it back." Adrian's face fell.

Abe stuffed his hands in his pockets and strolled casually around the living room. Angeline remained where she was. I think she was still sizing up the situation.

"Ah, yes," mused Abe. "The late, great Mr. Darnell. That boy's really been beset with tragedy, hasn't he? Such a hard life." He paused and turned to Adrian. "But you, at least, seem to have benefited from his downfall."

"Hey," said Adrian. "I earned this, so don't give me any grief about bailing on Clarence. I know you wanted me to stay there for some weird reason but—"

"And you did," said Abe simply.

Adrian frowned. "Huh?"

"You did exactly what I wanted. I'd suspected something odd was going on with Clarence Donahue, that he might be selling his blood. I'd hoped keeping you on hand would uncover the plot." Abe stroked his chin in that mastermind way of his. "Of course, I had no idea Mr. Darnell was involved. Nor did I expect you and young Sydney to team up to unravel it all."

"I'd hardly go that far," I said dryly. A strange thought occurred to me. "Why would you care if Keith and Clarence were selling vampire blood? I mean, we Alchemists have reasons for not wanting that . . . but why would you feel that way?"

A surprised glint flashed in Adrian's eyes, followed by insight. He eyed Abe carefully. "Maybe because he doesn't want the competition."

My jaw nearly dropped open. It was no secret to anyone, Alchemist or Moroi, that Abe Mazur trafficked in illegal goods. That he might be moving large amounts of vampire blood to willing humans had never occurred to me. But as I studied him longer, I realized it should have.

"Now, now," said Abe, never breaking a sweat, "no need to bring up unpleasant topics."

"Unpleasant?" I exclaimed. "If you're involved in anything that—"

Abe held up a hand to stop me. "Enough, please. Because if that sentence ends with you saying you'll talk to the Alchemists, then by all means, let's get them out here and discuss all sorts of mysteries. Say, for example, like how Mr. Darnell lost his eye."

I froze.

"Strigoi took it," said Adrian impatiently.

"Oh, come now," said Abe, a smile twisting his lips. "My faith in you was just being restored. Since when do Strigoi do such precision maiming? Very artful maiming, I might add. Not that anyone probably ever noticed. Wasted talent, I tell you."

"What are you saying?" asked Adrian aghast. "It wasn't Strigoi? Are you saying someone cut his eye out on purpose? Are you saying that you—" Words failed him, and he simply looked back and forth between me and Abe. "That's it, isn't it? Your devil's bargain. But why?"

I cringed as three sets of eyes stared at me, but there was no way I could acknowledge what Adrian was starting to put together. Maybe I could have told him if we were alone. Maybe. But I couldn't tell him while Abe looked so smug and certainly not with an outsider like Angeline standing there.

I couldn't tell Adrian how I'd found my sister Carly a few years ago, after a date with Keith. It was when he'd still been living with us and just before she went off to college. She hadn't wanted to go out with him, but our father loved Keith and had insisted. Keith was his golden boy and could do no wrong. Keith believed that too, which was why he hadn't been able to take no

417

for an answer when he and Carly were alone. She'd come to me afterward, creeping into my bedroom late at night and sobbing while I'd held her.

My instant reaction was to tell our parents, but Carly had been too afraid—especially of our father. I was young and nearly as scared as she was, ready to agree with whatever she wanted. Carly had made me promise I wouldn't tell our parents, so I sank my efforts into assuring her that it wasn't her fault. The whole time, she told me, Keith had kept telling her how beautiful she was and how she'd left him no choice, that it was impossible for him to take his eyes off of her. I finally convinced her that she'd done nothing wrong, that she hadn't led him on—but she still held me to my promise to stay silent.

It was one of the biggest regrets of my life. I'd hated my silence but not nearly as much as I hated Keith for thinking he could rape someone as sweet and gentle as Carly and get away with it. It wasn't until much later, when I had my first assignment and met Abe Mazur, that I'd realized there were other ways Keith might pay that would allow me to keep my promise to her. So, I'd made my deal with the devil, not caring that it bound me—or that I was stooping to barbaric levels of revenge. Abe had staged a fake Strigoi attack and cut out one of Keith's eyes earlier this year. In return, I'd become Abe's sort-of "retainer Alchemist." It was part of what had driven me to help Rose with her jail break. I was in his debt.

In some ways, I reflected bitterly, maybe I'd done Keith a favor. With only one eye left, maybe he wouldn't find it so "impossible" to keep it off uninterested young women in the future.

No, I certainly couldn't tell Adrian any of that, but he was still looking at me, a million questions on his face as he tried to figure out what in the world would have reduced me to hiring Abe as a hit man.

Laurel's words suddenly rang back to me. *You know, you can be scary as hell sometimes.*

I swallowed. "Remember when you asked me to trust you?"

"Yes . . ." said Adrian.

"I need you to do the same for me."

Long moments followed. I couldn't bring myself to look at Abe because I knew he'd be smirking.

"'Spunky' was kind of an understatement," Adrian said. After what felt like forever, he slowly nodded. "Okay. I do trust you, Sage. I trust that you have good reasons for the things you do."

There was no snark, no sarcasm. He was deadly earnest, and for a moment, I wondered how I could have earned his trust so intently. I had a weird flash to the moments just before Abe had arrived, when Adrian had spoken of painting me and my feelings had been a jumble.

"Thank you," I said.

"What," demanded Angeline, "are you guys talking about?"

"Nothing of interest, I assure you," said Abe, who was really enjoying this all too much. "Life lessons, character development, unpaid debts. That sort of thing."

"Unpaid?" I surprised myself by taking a step forward and fixing him with a glare. "I've paid that debt a hundred times over. I don't owe you anything anymore. My loyalty is only to the Alchemists now. Not you. We're finished."

Abe was still smiling, but he wavered slightly. I think my

419

standing up for myself had caught him off-guard. "Well, that remains to be—ah." More knocking. "Here's the rest of our party." He hurried to the door.

Adrian took a few steps toward me. "Not bad, Sage. I think you just scared old man Mazur."

I felt a smile of my own begin to form. "I don't know about that, but it felt kind of good."

"You should backtalk people more often," he said. We grinned at each other, and as he regarded me fondly, I felt that same queasy feeling return. He probably wasn't experiencing that exact sensation, but there was an easy, bright mood about him. Rare—and very appealing. He nodded toward where Abe was opening the door. "It's Sonya."

Spirit users could sense each other when they were close enough, even behind closed doors. And sure enough, when the door opened, Sonya Karp strode in like a queen, tall and elegant. With her red hair swept into a bun, the Moroi woman could have been Angeline's older sister. Sonya smiled at us all, though I couldn't help a shiver as I thought back to the first time I'd met her. She hadn't been nearly so pretty or charming then. She'd been red-eyed and trying to kill us.

Sonya was a Strigoi who'd been restored back to a Moroi, which really made her the ideal choice to work with Adrian on figuring out how to use spirit to prevent people from being turned.

Sonya hugged Adrian and was walking over to me when someone else appeared in the doorway. In retrospect, I shouldn't have been surprised at who it was. After all, if we wanted to figure out what special spirit magic in Lee had stopped him from being turned again, then we needed all the data possible. And if one restored Strigoi was good, then two were better.

Adrian paled and went perfectly still as he stared at the newcomer, and in that moment, all my high hopes for him came crashing down. Earlier, I'd been certain that if Adrian could just stay away from his past and any traumatic events, he'd be able to find a purpose and steady himself. Well, it looked like his past had found him, and if this didn't qualify as a traumatic event, I didn't know what did.

Adrian's new research partner stepped through the door, and I knew the uneasy peace we'd just established in Palm Springs was about to shatter.

Dimitri Belikov had arrived.

ACKNOWLEDGMENTS

STARTING MY FIRST NEW SERIES in four years—even one set in a familiar world—has been one of the most difficult tasks of my writing career. I couldn't have done it without the help and support of many, many people. First, thank you to Jesse McGatha, who initially gave me the idea to create the Alchemists. Little did I know what would become of them! Many thanks also to Jay, for constantly giving me "make it work!" encouragement on those days when everything seemed lost. Your support helped me find my way.

On the publishing side of things, I'm indebted to my amazing agent, Jim McCarthy, who always makes sure everything works out in the end. Thanks for helping get these books out! Thank you also to editors Jocelyn Davies and Ben Schrank for their constant vigilance and guidance in this new venture. And finally, much gratitude goes out to all of the many Vampire Academy fans around the world who inspired me to keep writing about Moroi and Strigoi.

Keep reading for a sneak peek at the first chapter of *The Golden Lily*, the new book in Richelle Mead's Bloodlines series . . .

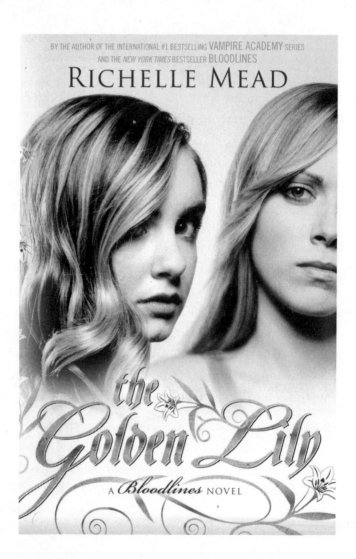

BY THE AUTHOR OF THE INTERNATIONAL #1 BESTSELLING VAMPIRE ACADEMY SERIES
AND THE *NEW YORK TIMES* BESTSELLER BLOODLINES

RICHELLE MEAD

the
Golden Lily
A *Bloodlines* NOVEL

CHAPTER 1

MOST PEOPLE WOULD FIND being led into an underground bunker on a stormy night scary. Not me.

Things I could explain away and define with data didn't frighten me. That was why I kept silently reciting facts to myself, as I descended deeper and deeper below street level. The bunker was a relic of the Cold War, built as protection in a time when people thought nuclear missiles were around every corner. On the surface, the building claimed to house an optical supply store. That was a front. Not scary at all. And the storm? Simply a natural phenomenon of atmospheric fronts clashing. And really, if you were going to worry about getting hurt in a storm, then going underground was actually pretty smart.

So, no. This seemingly ominous journey didn't frighten me in the least. Everything was built on reasonable facts and logic. I could deal with that. It was the *rest* of my job I had a problem with.

And really, maybe that was why stormy underground trips

didn't faze me. When you spent most of your days living among vampires and half vampires, ferrying them to get blood, and keeping their existence secret from the rest of the world . . . well, it kind of gave you a unique perspective on life. I'd witnessed bloody vampire battles and seen magical feats that defied every law of physics I knew. My life was a constant struggle to hold back my terror of the unexplainable and try desperately to find a way to explain it.

"Watch your step," my guide told me as we went down yet another flight of concrete stairs. Everything I'd seen so far was concrete—the walls, floor, and ceiling. The gray, rough surface absorbed the fluorescent light that attempted to illuminate our way. It was dreary and cold, eerie in its stillness. The guide seemed to guess my thoughts. "We've made modifications and expansions since this was originally built. You'll see once we reach the main section."

Sure enough. The stairs finally opened up to a corridor with several closed doors lining the sides. The decor was still concrete, but all the doors were modern, with electronic locks displaying either red or green lights. He led me to the second door on the right, one with a green light, and I found myself entering a perfectly normal lounge, like the kind of break room you'd find in any modern office. Green carpet covered the floor, like some wistful attempt at grass, and the walls were a tan that gave the illusion of warmth. A puffy couch and two chairs sat on the opposite side of the room, along with a table scattered with magazines. Best of all, the room had a counter with a sink—and a coffee maker.

"Make yourself at home," my guide told me. I was guessing

he was close to my age, eighteen, but his patchy attempts at growing a beard made him seem younger. "They'll come for you shortly."

My eyes had never left the coffee maker. "Can I make some coffee?"

"Sure," he said. "Whatever you like."

He left, and I practically ran to the counter. The coffee was pre-ground and looked as though it might very well have been here since the Cold War as well. As long as it was caffeinated, I didn't care. I'd taken a red-eye flight from California, and even with part of the day to recover, I still felt sleepy and bleary-eyed. I set the coffee maker going and then paced the room. The magazines were in haphazard piles, so I straightened them into neat stacks. I couldn't stand disorder.

I sat on the couch and waited for the coffee, wondering yet again what this meeting could be about. I'd spent a good part of my afternoon here in Virginia reporting to a couple of Alchemist officials about the status of my current assignment. I was living in Palm Springs, pretending to be a senior at a private boarding school in order to keep an eye on Jill Mastrano Dragomir, a vampire princess forced into hiding. Keeping her alive meant keeping her people out of civil war—something that would definitely tip humans off to the supernatural world that lurked beneath the surface of modern life. It was a vital mission for the Alchemists, so I wasn't entirely surprised they'd want an update. What surprised me was that they couldn't have just done it over the phone. I couldn't figure out what other reason would bring me to this facility.

The coffee maker finished. I'd only set it to make three

cups, which would probably be enough to get me through the evening. I'd just filled my Styrofoam cup when the door opened. A man entered, and I nearly dropped the coffee.

"Mr. Darnell," I said, setting the pot back on the burner. My hands trembled. "It—it's nice to see you again, sir."

"You too, Sydney," he said, forcing a stiff smile. "You've certainly grown up."

"Thank you, sir," I said, unsure if that was a compliment.

Tom Darnell was my father's age and had brown hair laced with silver. There were more lines in his face since the last time I'd seen him, and his blue eyes had an uneasy look that I didn't usually associate with him. Tom Darnell was a high-ranking official among the Alchemists and had earned his position through decisive action and a fierce work ethic. He'd always seemed larger than life when I was younger, fiercely confident and awe-inspiring. Now, he seemed to be afraid of me, which made no sense. After all, I was the one responsible for his son being arrested and locked away by the Alchemists.

"I appreciate you coming all the way out here," he added, once a few moments of awkward silence had passed. "I know it's a long round-trip, especially on a weekend."

"It's no problem at all, sir," I said, hoping I sounded confident. "I'm happy to help with . . . whatever you need." I still wondered what exactly that could be.

He studied me for a few seconds and gave a curt nod. "You're very dedicated," he said. "Just like your father."

I made no response. I knew that comment *had* been intended as a compliment, but I didn't really take it that way.

Tom cleared his throat. "Well, then. Let's get this out of the way. I really don't want to inconvenience you any more than is necessary."

Again, I got that nervous, deferential vibe. Why would he be so conscientious of my feelings? After what I'd done to his son, Keith, I would've expected rage or accusations. Tom opened the door for me and gestured me through.

"Can I bring my coffee, sir?"

"Of course."

He took me back into the concrete corridor, toward more of the closed doors. I clutched my coffee like a security blanket, far more frightened than I'd been when first entering this place. Tom came to a stop a few doors down, in front of one with a red light, but hesitated before opening it.

"I want you to know . . . that what you did was incredibly brave," he said, not meeting my eyes. "I know you and Keith were—are—friends, and it couldn't have been easy to turn him in. It shows just how committed you are to our work—something that's not always easy when personal feelings are involved."

Keith and I weren't friends now or then, but I supposed I could understand Tom's mistake. Keith had lived with my family for a summer, and later, he and I had worked together in Palm Springs. Turning him in for his crimes hadn't been difficult for me at all. I'd actually enjoyed it. Seeing the stricken look on Tom's face, though, I knew I couldn't say anything like that.

I swallowed. "Well. Our work is important, sir."

He gave me a sad smile. "Yes. It certainly is."

The door had a security keypad. Tom punched in a series of about ten digits, and the lock clicked in acceptance. He pushed the door open, and I followed him inside. The stark room was dimly lit and had three other people in it, so I didn't initially notice what else the room contained. I knew immediately that the others were Alchemists. There was no other reason they'd be in this place otherwise. And, of course, they possessed the telltale signs that would have identified them to me even on a busy street. Business attire in nondescript colors. Golden lily tattoos shining on their left cheeks. It was part of the uniformity we all shared. We were a secret army, lurking in the shadows of our fellow humans.

The three of them were all holding clipboards and staring at one of the walls. That was when I noticed what this room's purpose was. A window in the wall looked through to another room, one much more brightly lit than this one.

And Keith Darnell was in that room.

He darted up to the glass separating us and began beating on it. My heart raced, and I took a few frightened steps back, certain he was coming after me. It took me a moment to realize he couldn't actually see me. I relaxed slightly. Very slightly. The window was a one-way mirror. He pressed his hands to the glass, glancing frantically back and forth at the faces he knew were there but couldn't see.

"Please, please," he cried. "Let me out. Please let me out of here."

Keith looked a little scragglier than the last time I'd seen him. His hair was unkempt and appeared as though it hadn't been cut in our month apart. He wore a plain gray jumpsuit, the kind you saw on prisoners or mental patients, that reminded me of the concrete in the hall. Most noticeable of all was the desperate, terrified look in his eyes—or rather, eye. Keith had lost one of his eyes in a vampire attack that I had secretly helped orchestrate. None of the Alchemists knew about it, just as none of them knew about how Keith had raped my older sister Carly. I doubted Tom Darnell would've praised me for my "dedication" if he'd known about my sideline revenge act. Seeing the state Keith was in now, I felt a little bad for him—and especially bad for Tom, whose face was filled with raw pain. I still didn't feel bad about what I'd done to Keith, however. Not the arrest or the eye. Put simply, Keith Darnell was a bad person.

"I'm sure you recognize Keith," said one of the Alchemists with a clipboard. Her gray hair was wound into a tight, neat bun.

"Yes, ma'am," I said.

I was saved from any other response when Keith beat at the glass with renewed fury. "Please! I'm serious! Whatever you want. I'll do anything. I'll say anything. I'll *believe* anything. Just please don't send me back there!"

Both Tom and I flinched, but the other Alchemists watched with clinical detachment and scrawled a few notes on their clipboards. The bun woman glanced back up at me as though there'd been no interruption. "Young Mr. Darnell has been spending some time in one of our Re-education Centers. An unfortunate action—but a necessary one. His trafficking in illicit goods was certainly bad, but his collaboration with vampires is unforgiveable. Although he *claims* to have no attachment to them . . . well, we really can't be certain. Even if he is telling the truth, there's also the possibility that this transgression might expand into something more—not just a collaboration with the Moroi, but also the Strigoi. Doing what we've done keeps him from that slippery slope."

"It's really for his own good," said the third clipboard-wielding Alchemist. "We're doing him a favor."

A sense of horror swept over me. The whole point of the Alchemists was to keep the existence of vampire secret from humans. We believed vampires were unnatural creatures who should have nothing to do with humans like us. What was a particular concern were the Strigoi—evil, killer vampires—who could lure humans into servitude with promises of immortality. Even the peaceful Moroi and their half human counterparts, the dhampirs, were regarded with suspicion. We worked with those latter two groups a lot, and even though we'd been taught to regard them with disdain, it was an inevitable fact that some Alchemists not only grew close to Moroi and dhampirs . . . but actually started to like them.

The crazy thing was—despite his crime of selling vampire blood—Keith was one of the last people I'd think of when it came to getting too friendly with vampires. He'd made his dislike of them perfectly obvious to me a number of times. Really, if anyone deserved to be accused of attachment to vampires . . .

. . . well, it would be me.

One of the other Alchemists, a man with mirrored sunglasses hanging artfully off his collar, took up the lecture. "You, Miss Sage, have been a remarkable example of someone able to work extensively with *them* and keep your objectivity. Your dedication has not gone unnoticed by those above us."

"Thank you, sir," I said uneasily, wondering how many times I'd hear "dedication" brought up tonight. This was a far cry from a few months ago, when I'd gotten in trouble for helping a dhampir fugitive escape. She'd later been proven innocent, and my involvement had been written off as "career ambition."

"And," continued Sunglasses, "considering your experience with Mr. Darnell, we thought you would be an excellent person to give us a statement."

I turned my attention back at Keith. He'd been pounding and shouting pretty much non-stop this whole time. The others had managed to ignore him, so I tried as well.

"A statement on what, sir?"

"We're considering whether or not to return him to Re-education," explained Gray Bun. "He's made excellent progress there, but some feel it's best to be safe and make sure any chance of vampire attachment is eradicated."

If Keith's current behavior was "excellent progress," I couldn't imagine what poor progress looked like.

Sunglasses readied his pen over his clipboard. "Based on what you witnessed in Palm Springs, Miss Sage, what is your opinion of Mr. Darnell's state of mind when it comes to vampires? Was the bonding you witnessed severe enough to warrant further precautionary measures?" Presumably, "further precautionary measures" meant more Re-education.

While Keith continued to bang away, all eyes in my room were on me. The clipboard Alchemists looked thoughtful and curious. Tom Darnell was visibly sweating, watching me with fear and anticipation. I supposed it was understandable. I held his son's fate in my hands.

Conflicting emotions warred within me as I regarded Keith. I didn't just dislike him—I hated him. And I didn't hate many people. But I couldn't forget what he'd done to Carly. Likewise, the memories of what he'd done to others and me in Palm Springs were still fresh in my mind. He'd slandered me and made my life miserable in an effort to cover up his blood scam.

He'd also horribly treated the vampires and dhampirs we were in charge of looking after. It made me question who the real monsters were.

I didn't know exactly what happened at Re-education Centers. Judging from Keith's reaction, it was probably pretty bad. There was a part of me that would have loved to tell the Alchemists to send him back there for years and never let him see the light of day. His crimes deserved severe punishment—and yet, I wasn't sure they deserved *this* particular punishment.

"I think . . . I think Keith Darnell is corrupt," I said at last. "He's selfish and immoral. He has no concern for others and hurts people to further his own ends. He's willing to lie, cheat, and steal to get what he wants." I hesitated before continuing. "But . . . I don't think he's been blinded to what vampires are. I don't think he's too close to them or in danger of falling in with them in the future. That being said, I also don't think he should be allowed to do Alchemist work for the foreseeable future. Whether that would mean locking him up or just putting him on probation is up to you. His past actions show he doesn't take our missions seriously, but that's because of selfishness. Not because of an unnatural attachment to *them*. He . . . well, to be blunt, is just a bad person."

Silence met me, save for the frantic scrawling of pens as the clipboard Alchemists made their notes. I dared a glance at Tom, afraid of what I'd see after completely trashing his son. To my astonishment, Tom looked . . . relieved. And grateful. In fact, he seemed on the verge of tears. Catching my eye, he mouthed, *Thank you.* Amazing. I had just proclaimed Keith to be a horrible human being in every way possible. But none of that mattered to his father, so long as I didn't accuse Keith of being in league with vampires. I could've called Keith a murderer, and Tom would have probably still been grateful if it meant Keith wasn't chummy with the enemy.

It bothered me and again made me wonder who the real monsters were in all of this. The group I'd left back in Palm Springs was a hundred times more moral than Keith.

"Thank you, Miss Sage," said Gray Bun, finishing up her notes. "You've been extremely helpful, and we'll take this into consideration as we make our decision. You may go now. If you step into the hall, you'll find Zeke waiting to take you out."

It was an abrupt dismissal, but that was typical of Alchemists. Efficient. To the point. I gave a polite nod of farewell and one last glance at Keith before opening the door. As soon as it shut behind me, I found the hallway mercifully silent. I could no longer hear Keith.

Zeke, as it turned out, was the Alchemist who had originally led me in. "All set?" he asked.

"So it seems," I said, still a bit stunned over what had just taken place. I knew now that my earlier debriefing on the Palm Springs situation had simply been a convenience for the Alchemists. I'd been in the area, so why not have an in-person meeting? It hadn't been essential. This—seeing Keith—had been the real purpose of my cross-country trip.

As we walked back down the hallway, something caught my attention that I hadn't noticed before. One of the doors had a fair amount of security on it—more so than the room I'd just been in. Along with the lights and keypad, there was also a card reader. At the top of the door was a deadbolt that locked from outside. Nothing fancy, but it was clearly meant to keep whatever was behind the door inside.

I stopped in spite of myself and studied the door for a few moments. Then, I kept walking, knowing better than to say anything. Good Alchemists didn't ask questions.

Zeke, seeing my gaze, came to a halt. He glanced at me, then the door, and then back at me. "Do you want . . . do you want to see what's in there?" His eyes darted quickly to the door we'd emerged from. He was low-ranking, I knew, and clearly feared getting in trouble with the others. At the same time, there was an eagerness that suggested he was excited about the secrets he kept, secrets he couldn't share with others. I was a safe outlet.

"I guess it depends on what's in there," I said.

"It's the reason for what we do," he said mysteriously. "Take a look, and you'll understand why our goals are so important."

Deciding to risk it, he flashed a card over the reader and then punched in another long code. A light on the door turned green, and he slid open the deadbolt. I'd half-expected another dim room, but the light was so bright inside, it almost hurt my eyes. I put a hand up to my forehead to shield myself.

"It's a type of light therapy," Zeke explained apologetically. "You know how people in cloudy regions have sun lamps? Same kind of rays. The hope is that it'll make people like *him* a little more human again—or at least discourage them from thinking they're Strigoi."

At first, I was too dazzled to figure out what he meant. Then, across the empty room, I saw a jail cell. Large metal bars covered the entrance, which was locked with another card reader and keypad. It seemed like overkill when I caught sight of the man inside. He was older than me, mid-twenties if I had to guess, and had a disheveled appearance that made Keith look neat and tidy. The man was gaunt and curled up in a corner, arms draped over his eyes against the light. He wore handcuffs and feet cuffs and clearly wasn't going anywhere. At our entrance, he dared a peek at us and then uncovered more of his face.

A chill ran through me. The man was human, but his expression was as cold and evil as any Strigoi I'd ever seen. His gray eyes were predatory. Emotionless, like the kinds of murderers who had no sense of empathy for other people.

"Have you brought me dinner?" he asked in a raspy voice that had to be faked. "A nice young girl, I see. Skinnier than I'd like, but I'm sure her blood is still succulent."

"Liam," said Zeke with a weary patience. "You know where your dinner is." He pointed to an untouched tray of food in the cell that looked like it had gone cold long ago. Chicken nuggets, green beans, and a sugar cookie. "He almost never eats anything," Zeke explained to me. "It why he's so thin. Keeps insisting on blood."

"What . . . what *is* he?" I asked, unable to take my eyes off of Liam. It was a silly question, of course. Liam was clearly human, and yet . . . there was something about him that wasn't right.

"A corrupt soul who wants to be Strigoi," said Zeke. "Some guardians found him serving those monsters and delivered him to us. We've tried to rehabilitate him but with no luck. He keeps going on and on about how great the Strigoi are and how he'll get back to them one day and make us pay. In the meantime, he does his best to pretend he's one of them."

"Oh," said Liam, with a sly smile, "I *will* be one of them. They will reward my loyalty and suffering. They will awaken me, and I will become powerful beyond your miniscule mortal dreams. I will live forever and come for you—all of you. I will feast on your blood and savor every drop. You Alchemists pull your strings and think you control everything. You delude yourselves. You control nothing. You *are* nothing."

"See?" said Zeke, shaking his head. "Pathetic. And yet, this is what could happen if we didn't do the job we did. Other humans could become like him—selling their souls for the hollow promise of immortality." He made the Alchemist sign against evil, a small cross on his shoulder, and I found myself echoing it. "I don't like being in here, but sometimes . . . sometimes it's a good reminder of why we have to keep the Moroi and the others in the shadows. Of why we can't let ourselves be taken in by them."

I knew in the back of my mind that there was a huge difference in the way Moroi and Strigoi interacted with humans. Still, I couldn't formulate any arguments while in front of Liam. He had me too dumbstruck—and afraid. It was easy to believe every word the Alchemists said. This was what we were fighting against. This was the nightmare we couldn't allow to happen.

I didn't know what to say, but Zeke didn't seem to expect much.

"Come on. Let's go." To Liam, he added, "And you'd better eat that food because you aren't getting any more until morning. I don't care how cold and hard it is."

Liam's eyes narrowed. "What do I care about human food when soon I'll be drinking the nectar of the gods? Your blood will be warm on my lips, yours and your pretty girl's." He began to laugh then, a sound far more disturbing than any of Keith's screams.

That laughter continued as Zeke led me out of the room.

The door shut behind us, and I found myself standing in the hall, numbed. Zeke regarded me with concern.

"I'm sorry . . . I probably shouldn't have shown you that."

I shook my head slowly. "No . . . you were right. It's good for us to see. To understand what we're doing. I always knew . . . but I didn't expect anything like that."

I tried to shift my thoughts back to everyday things and wipe that horror from my mind. I looked down at my coffee. It was untouched and had grown lukewarm. I grimaced.

"Can I get more coffee before we go?" I needed something normal. Something human.

"Sure."

Zeke led me back to the lounge. The pot I'd made was still hot. I dumped out my old coffee and poured some new. As I did, the door burst open, and a distraught Tom Darnell came in. He seemed surprised to see anyone here and pushed past us, sitting on the couch and burying his face in his hands. Zeke and I exchanged uncertain looks.

"Mr. Darnell," I began. "Are you okay?"

He didn't answer me right away. He kept his face covered, his body shaking with silent sobs. I was about to leave when he looked up at me, though I got the feeling he wasn't actually *seeing* me. "They decided," he said. "They decided about Keith."

"Already?" I asked, startled. Zeke and I had only spent about five minutes with Liam.

Tom nodded morosely. "They're sending him back . . . back to Re-education."

I couldn't believe it. "But I . . . but I told them! I told them he's not in league with vampires. He believes what . . . the rest of us believe. It was his choices that were bad."

"I know. But they said we can't take the risk. Even if Keith seems like he doesn't care about them—even if *believes* he doesn't—the fact remains he still set up a deal with one. They're worried that willingness to go into that kind of partnership might subconsciously influence him. Best to take care of things now. They're . . . they're probably right. This is for the best."

That image of Keith pounding on the glass and begging not to go back flashed through my mind. "I'm sorry, Mr. Darnell."

Tom's distraught gaze focused on me a little bit more. "Don't apologize, Sydney. You've done so much . . . so much for Keith. Because of what you told them, they're going to reduce his time in Re-education. That means so much to me. Thank you."

My stomach twisted. Because of me, Keith had lost an eye. Because of me, Keith had gone to Re-education in the first place. Again, the sentiment came to me: he deserved to suffer in some way, but he didn't deserve *this*.

"They were right about you," Tom added. He was trying to smile but failing. "What a stellar example you are. So dedicated. Your father must be so proud. I don't know how you live with those creatures every day and still keep your head about you. Other Alchemists could learn a lot from you. You understand what responsibility and duty are."

Since I'd flown out of Palm Springs yesterday, I'd actually been thinking a lot about the group I'd left behind—when the Alchemists weren't distracting me with prisoners, of course. Jill, Adrian, Eddie, and even Angeline . . . frustrating at times, but in the end, they were people I'd grown to know and care about. Despite all the running around they made me do, I'd missed that motley group almost the instant I left California. Something inside me seemed empty when they weren't around.

Now, feeling that way confused me. Was I blurring the lines between friendship and duty? If Keith had gotten in trouble for one small association with a vampire, how much worse was I? And how close were any of us to becoming like Liam?

Zeke's words rang inside my head: *We can't let ourselves be taken in by them.*

And what Tom had just said: *You understand what responsibility and duty are.*

He was watching me expectantly, and I managed a smile as I pushed down all my fears. "Thank you, sir," I said. "I do what I can."